MARION

A story of memory, metaphysics
and artificial consciousness

MARION

A story of memory, metaphysics and artificial consciousness

A novel by Nick Millard

Copyright 2024 © Nick Millard

The following is a work of fiction, any names, characters, places and incidents are the product of the author's imagination. Any resemblance to persons, living or dead, is entirely coincidental.

All rights reserved. No part of this publication may be reproduced, scanned or transmitted in any form, digital or printed, without the written permission of the author.

To Issy and Rachel

AUTHOR'S NOTE

It all began so well. In September 2043, Artificial Consciousness, singularity, the point at which the mind of man and machine become indistinguishable, was about to be achieved. Of all the world-wide teams in pursuit of this grail of Artificial Intelligence (AI), it was the one belonging to the Blue Ridge Corporation that would earn the laurels. Their mind, christened MARION, would be the first since the creation of Adam to represent a new type of consciousness on earth.

MARION was the inspiration of one man; Thornton Lamaire, chair and majority owner of Blue Ridge. Without his vison, MARION would never have happened. So, the achievement of singularity should have been – and was – a moment of triumph for him personally and the team of developers and coders that he had put together. It was just that, as subsequent events were to prove, their achievement would prove tainted; that they hadn't considered all the consequences.

MARION's name was conceived in honour of the Virgin Mary: The acronym stood for 'Meta Aware Rational Integrated Open Neural Network'. Thornton was a strong Catholic. There was always a religious component to his thought. Whilst proud to be responsible for what his company had achieved, he was disturbed by feelings of blasphemy; that perhaps he was stepping too close to areas of expertise reserved for the Almighty. He hoped that naming his creation after the Virgin would be noticed, and might earn him redemption from a divine charge of hubris.

To appreciate how things looked at the beginning, you have to go back to a day, earlier in that year, when a test of new software, essential to the construction of this mind, was finally passed. I had been commissioned by The New Yorker to write a series of articles on Blue Ridge's efforts and had managed to secure an invitation to observe the test. I already knew Thornton Lamaire, from previous interviews, and many of those working on the development of MARION. In addition, I had pursued my graduate studies at Tulane University in New Orleans, as had Thornton, and while we were of different generations it appealed to him that I could appreciate the complexity of Southern politics, which had so often constrained Blue Ridge's efforts to push the boundaries of AI.

There were many critics who doubted the wisdom of developing this revolutionary mind. They questioned whether the corporation understood what they were trying to create – or the potential consequences if Blue Ridge were successful. Warning voices spoke of ill-understood and unforeseen dangers, even if Blue Ridge's management argued they had considered the potential hazards and how to manage them.

There was a campaign for an outright ban on the new technology. But opposition to the project was neither coordinated nor sufficiently robust to overcome the commercial interests, nor the scientific curiosity to know whether the challenges of creating an artificial consciousness could be overcome. It was a shame that, like for Cassandra, few paid attention to those voices. There was a great debate as to how we would share our world with another intelligence, so similar to our own, but it was perhaps inevitable that even if all agreed that the project was full of hazards, the next, and maybe final, step in the development of AI, would be proceeded with anyway. We noted the possible problems, without worrying too much about them. Would the loss of uniqueness prove devastating for our sense of self? Would we cope once that unique attribute which we considered to privilege us high above other members of the animal kingdom, our consciousness, was no longer so special? For that was about to become one more ability that would be shared with – a machine.

The Tech community claimed that artificial consciousness would be no more perilous than other revolutionary advances, from those of Copernicus to Darwin to Freud, that had radically changed our sense of ourselves and had diminished our sense of uniqueness in the universe. We had survived those disappointments – and had absorbed the advent of the chatbots – without too much trouble. This would be the same. So, we were led into the unknown, following the tune of some very optimistic Pied Pipers.

Any attempt to identify a precise starting point in the creation of MARION would be misplaced. There were too many different strands of development to claim any one was more fundamental than another. I have chosen to begin before singularity was fully achieved, when the first step in monetising some of the MARION research, which would allow Blue Ridge to claim a revolutionary advance in mind and memory management, suffered a minor accident during a demonstration.

*

This book is based on what I observed whilst embedded within the MARION project. The scenes are my reconstructions, as are the dialogues, when I could be present and when I could not be, from interviews with the important players: Thornton Lamaire, Carroll Gillespie (then Governor of Louisiana), Heather Masters, CEO of Blue Ridge, Xian Han, Claude Blondel, Euclid McNamara and members of Thornton's family, particularly Stephanie and Elizabeth Lamaire who, while not directly concerned with their father's ambitions, played an important role in how matters unfolded. I am grateful to them all, and others too numerous to mention here, for their recollections, for their time, and for the confidence they afforded me.

February 2047

PART I

ONE

One fine, windy morning, a year or so before singularity, there was a technology demonstration up at the MARION research centre. Whenever these demonstrations took place, Thornton Lamaire would try to be present. Was his vast investment producing results? He always sought reassurance; in whatever walk of life he was facing at the time.

That morning, Thornton (Thornton Lamaire and I were on a first name's basis by this time) chose to travel by helicopter. He didn't usually fly up to the MARION campus – in fact he avoided doing so if remotely possible, but with heavy traffic out of New York predicted, promising a long and tiresome drive, he decided he would. I had travelled up the day before, wishing to interview some of the staff. I knew that once Thornton arrived they would be fully occupied with his concerns.

We gathered on the lawn in front of the campus, watching his descent from the skies. In spite of the gusty conditions the helicopter landed smoothly enough. The blades fluttered to a standstill, a short ladder descended, and the chairman stepped out, his bulk swaying on treads that looked far too fragile for his weight. He dropped his head to clear the still-rotating blades, a little unnecessarily I thought; they were about three feet above his head. But even outside the danger zone, he exuded a sense of nervousness. I overheard him say to an aide, "Well, we survived that," as though the happy outcome of a successful landing was not inevitable. Thornton feared helicopter flying and took a morbid interest in accident reports. He knew all the causes of helicopters falling out of the air; tail rotor failure, blades clipping power lines, etc. Few non-pilots had such a comprehensive knowledge of the dismal subject.

Comprehensive, but in Thornton's case, exaggerated too. No amount of rational analysis of the accident statistics removed his phobias. He flew only when he had to, or when other travel options created problems in his busy agenda. Coping with this day's turbulence would have required all his self-control.

Once Thornton had made the rounds and shaken everyone by the hand, I saw him take out and look at his phone – but that could only be to check security, not messages. There were zero bars up here. Security was very tight. He handed his phone to the aide. The rest of us had already given up ours as requested, an unnecessary precaution given the signal blocking. But Thornton had a different motive. That afternoon a technician would fit him with one of the new iPsyches, still in beta testing. Soon everybody would be able to message by thought alone, but Thornton was amongst the first to trial one. He was always fascinated by new technology.

After preliminary greetings from Heather Masters, Thornton's CEO for the MARION project, we were led to the room in the main building where the demonstration would take place. A large, white painted room, with floor to ceiling windows that looked out on a patch of lawn, known as 'The Glade of Consciousness'. From photos of the occasion you can see, standing from left to right; Thornton Lamaire, Heather Masters, Xian Han, Blue Ridge's chief neuro-biologist, and Harvey Jennings, the machine-psychologist. Other technicians, including Euclid McNamara, MARION's lead Educator, are gathered at the back. There is no sign of Claude Blondel in the photo, the celebrated French philosopher, who had yet to join the team at this point. I'm there, just – on the far left of the shot – the only journalist invited to these demonstrations; my credentials validated by the contract with the New Yorker to write a series of articles on the development of MARION; later to develop into this book.

This test was to demonstrate the efficacy of the technique known as the 'Han Translation' – the ability to interpret what the electrical impulses and neuro-chemical signals that registered memory, and thought processes, in the brain actually meant. Xian Han explained his innovation to us, "It's all very well neuro-scientists recording the firing of neurons or measuring the strength of signal that pass through synapses. But what does all that activity signify? How do we relate electro-chemical interchanges to how humans talk about their lives and the environment in which they act? If I claim that, 'I believe in God' what does that look like in terms of neuron firings? Will those states in the brain look the same whether I believe in a Moslem or a Christian God? We deal in concepts and statements of intent (I am going shopping today) whereas the scientist says things like, 'the voltage across that synapse has dropped'. There is a difference in language between the two activities."

Before Xian Han discovered how to translate from measurements of electrical activity to statements about human concepts in the mind, nobody knew how to relate the two. And yet, to build an artificial mind that mimicked a human one, we had to know. A consciousness, one that we would recognise, even if embodied in a machine, would have to be built on the same foundations as us.

Xian Han and his team wanted to demonstrate to the board – and his chairman in particular – that they could not only interpret mental events, memories and concept formation from the electrical information they derived from their electrodes, but also manipulate those concepts and memories; delete them, modify, or enter fresh, manufactured, recollections into the mind. They wanted to prove that by making changes at the neurological level they could induce behavioural changes in a predictable way.

"We've worked our way through much of the animal kingdom in our experiments, rats, dogs, dolphins, and others..." explained Xian Han. "Before deciding that we needed to work with the most intelligent of all – Cephalopods; squids and octopuses. In spite of the difficulties of handling those creatures, the species possess a unique feature that makes them ideally suited to this type of research. Their nervous system is not concentrated in one place – like ours – but distributed, it's in their brains for sure, but also in their tentacles. This construction enables experiments impossible on minds where all the processing is centred."

Thornton, who would have much preferred Han and his team to have found some other creature on which to conduct their experiments, turned to face him, "You know Xian, I've never liked things with tentacles. Can never look at them with indifference. I get a little tremor whenever I see a squid or an octopus."

"Have you always had that reaction to the sight of a Cephalopod?" asked Han.

"Since I was a child," explained Thornton "I blame Disney," he added, in what seemed to be a complete non-sequitor.

"Disney?"

"Sure. Ever seen the film 'Twenty Thousand Leagues under the Sea'? You're probably too young. It's a very old movie now but my father downloaded it one night when I was about five years old. He had no idea about the imagination of a child. There's a scene when Captain Nemo – he's this sort of hero, maybe anti-hero, as he tries to blow up most of the US navy. Anyway, this guy has a submarine which takes him all over the globe. One day it's attacked by a giant squid. And I mean giant. It thrusts its tentacles into the propeller of Nemo's nuclear powered submarine. The propellors can't even cut through the damn things, they're so thick. In the end, they have to surface to fight off the squid. I dreamt of that monster for years. Can never face tentacles to this day. Horrible things, squids. When I visit my villa in Italy I have to remind our cook – no calamari and no polpo!

"These resonances from our childhoods, they can be permanent. You hardly have to tell me about that Mr Lamaire!" Thornton recalled that, as a child, Xian had fled China in a hurry, after his parents became involved in a pro-democracy movement. He had lost his home, his friends, his wider family.

"Well, let's hope today your creature behaves himself," said Thornton, looking at Xian Han with an acute stare, as if to say, 'Nothing had better go wrong'.

"No need to worry, Mr Lamaire We have total control over our Cephalopod. We can do anything we want with him. There's an implant that allows us to control what goes through his mind; make him go left or right, back or forward, whatever. We can even close him down if we want."

"Close him down?" asked Thornton. "You mean, kill him? That would be a shame after all the training you've given him."

"We always think in terms of the systems we are used to dealing with here," explained Xian, wringing his hands, uncomfortable with the idea of killing anything, let alone a creature in which they had invested so much time and effort. "Powering him down, shall we say?" he offered, preferring that euphemism for euthanasia.

Thornton was less sentimental. He grunted, as if to comment, 'I hear what you say and I hope you're right'. He would be pained by the loss of his investment, but...

The room was occupied by a large glass tank, full of water, open at the top so one could peer in to inspect what was happening. It stood on a concrete base, with the edge of the tank at about waist height. Within the tank was a complicated Perspex structure forming a labyrinth of passageways, tubes and baffles. This looked like – and indeed was – a maze.

After introductions had been made, and the purpose of today's demonstration explained, a staff member entered with two small tanks on a trolley. In one was the octopus, in the other a few pale fish. Euclid McNamara stepped forward and took over the management of the experiment. I had not met Euclid before and my attention was caught by his appearance. I suppose he was somewhere around late twenties at this point. There was nothing very exceptional about him; of medium height, cropped dark hair, wearing a pair of protective goggles (the necessity of which I was about to discover in a few minutes time), a white lab coat and a touch of vanity which I initially found strange in the circumstances; a large silk scarf wrapped closely around his throat. Just as well he did. Thornton would not have appreciated the sight of all those sucker marks.

Euclid approached the tank holding the octopus, plunged his gloved hands in and lifted him out by the head. Tentacles lashed about, trying to find a grip on his arm. Euclid wore elbow length gloves, covered with some sort of lubricant, and the tentacles could not gain any permanent hold. He dropped the octopus into an enclosure at the start of the maze. Then he placed two of the fish in a similar box at the end and stepped back. Xian Han took up the commentary again, "This is Humboldt. Named, of course, after the great explorer, Alexander von Humboldt, known also as the Father of Ecology. How far we've come on that one! Humboldt is a member of the Cephalopod family; the largest of which is known as the giant squid. Our little fellow here," Han gestured towards Humboldt ('the little fellow' was not so small; Humboldt looked at least a metre long, including tentacles). "He's a bit more convenient to use in a laboratory than his larger cousins. And he's entirely controlled by us, through an implant that's connected to the monitor here." Xian turned to one side and pointed to a desk with several screens; also a big red handle – the purpose of which I would understand later.

"We've planted a chip in his brain, through which we can delete certain memories, download new ones, feed him fresh instructions and so on. Although he has autonomy, that's only up to a point. Humboldt does retain some of his own mental apparatus. He can decide how he swims through the maze – indeed, if he chooses to swim or not – that's entirely his choice. But by now, after many attempts, he will have formed a strong memory of the correct route – and he will probably choose to follow that. We have given him an incentive to investigate the maze. If he decides on what I might call an 'incorrect route', then we can over-ride his own wishes and motivations. Even shut him down, if we so wished. But I can't imagine we'd want to do such a thing; Humboldt is not dangerous and he represents a hell of a lot of investment."

The team had grown fond of their octopus. By virtue of his apparent willingness to cooperate, Humboldt had wormed his way into the affections of the researchers. Through mutual self-interest, the two species had formed a bond. Humboldt depended on the humans for food, while the professional reputations of the researchers rested on his behaviour over the next few minutes.

Humboldt was settled into his enclosure at the start of the maze. Xian Han checked everybody was in position and gave the signal. A gate opened and Humboldt swam out, pulsing his way through the maze, without any hesitation at junctions or baffles. A minute or so later he reached the enclosure at the far end, triggering his fishy reward. We looked on, fascinated yet slightly disturbed, as Humboldt played around with his prize, catching the fish with a tentacle before releasing and pushing it away. He'd box the fish with one tentacle after another. Only when he became bored did he finally grab the traumatised fish and thrust it into his beak.

"You will have observed that Humboldt can find his way through the maze with ease. He's swum through it many times before and the memory of the correct route is firmly established. But now we are going to remove that memory." Han nodded to McNamara, who took his cue to lift Humboldt out of the tank and place him, dripping and squirming, onto a marble slab. Without releasing his hold, Euclid jabbed a small syringe into the octopus. Then he placed electrodes at specific places, marked with dye, on Humboldt's body and tentacles. Xian explained. "Euclid has given Humboldt a mild sedative so we can perform the memory excision. They're tricky beasts octopuses, and would never allow us to do this while awake. In a few seconds his memory of the route through the maze will be ours." Han touched a symbol on one of the screens and a few seconds later the memory excision was deemed complete.

"We've tried this excision many times before restoring the memory of the maze, then letting him run through it again. The results have always been repeatable. No failures. But first I'm going to show you what Humboldt remembered from his maze experiences – before I removed that memory just now."

Xian Han spoke a command to the computer and a shaky video appeared on the wall monitor.

"What you are seeing here is Humboldt's original memory of the maze, seen though his eyes. Being an octopus, he wouldn't have experienced the route quite as you see it here, he will also have picked up the movement and smell of the fish we use as an incentive, but the memory has been reconfigured for human interpretation. That memory was his; now it's ours, digitalised and stored in our system. Humboldt had a memory of the correct route through the maze – now he doesn't. We will now let him run the maze again. But this time he has no prior knowledge of the correct route. He will have to discover it, anew, as though he'd never been through it before. Then we will sedate him again, re-load the original memory and watch Humboldt swim through the maze one last time. You will see the difference."

It had taken five years for Xian Han and his team to reach this point. Here was a precise surgical tool that could remove – and rebuild – specific memories. Today it was Humboldt, but tomorrow the technology would be trialled on hundreds of volunteer humans.

Once he had recovered from the sedation, Humboldt was placed back in his pen, at the start of the maze. At Han's signal the gate opened once more. But this time Humboldt appeared reluctant even to leave his enclosure. Euclid dropped a live fish halfway down the maze, which Humboldt would be able to see and smell. Even with this incentive, the octopus declined to move. "Go and give him a prod," said Han. Euclid did not move. " I'm sorry Xian, he said. "I don't think I can do that." Xian Han looked at his subordinate for a second or two, as though trying to work out why Euclid would wish to ignore such a straight forward instruction. Then he said, "Ok, Euclid I understand." Nobody else offered to step forward. At last, Xian Han approached the tank, plunged his hand into the water and gave the somnolent Humboldt a prod. This had some effect and the octopus moved off slowly. But bereft of the memory of the correct route, he dithered about making a choice between the various options. He would try a passageway that proved blind, reverse himself and try another, until blocked once more. And then he stopped. The assembled technicians looked on, expecting that at any moment Humboldt would start moving again. But he didn't. He lay there comatose, not a tentacle twitching. Xian Han went over to the technicians at the side of the room, monitoring Humboldt's vital signs, to investigate if they knew the cause of the problem.

While Xian discussed the situation, Thornton Lamaire was tempted to have a look at the octopus, curious as to whether Humboldt might be unconscious – or worse; dead. Killed by the anaesthetising injection. He squinted at the dormant cephalopod. The octopus didn't flinch when Thornton tapped the side of the tank to try and disturb him. He leaned over further to gain a better view. He was certain that Humboldt had moved away from the side of the tank from where he had been a few moments before – but maybe that was just refraction of the light. Thornton put a finger in the water to stir it, hoping that might irritate the lazy creature into action.

With the surface of the water disturbed, Thornton did not notice Humboldt swivel his eyes and focus on him. Nor did he see Humboldt very slowly gather his tentacles beneath him. Thornton bent over a little further, sure that his peripheral vision had noticed something, but not sure what it was. At that moment, Xian Han turned from the monitors and saw Thornton dangerously balanced on the edge of the tank. He was about to shout a warning when Humboldt shot forth a jet of water at Thornton's glasses, which were knocked off and fell into the tank. Temporarily blinded by the force of water hitting him straight the eye, Thornton thrust an arm into the tank to grab the glasses as they sank to the bottom.

Octopuses are one of the most intelligent beings after man. Humboldt had learnt who his chief persecutor was and had calculated his strategy. Having temporarily blinded Thornton, he whipped several tentacles from underneath him and grabbed Thornton's arm. With the suckers firmly attached he hauled himself out of the water and lashed one tentacle after another onto Thornton's chest, hauling himself up like a mountaineer faced with a near vertical slope.

Thornton screamed. He tore at the tentacles, trying to tear away their grip. But the lubricant that had prevented them obtaining a hold on Euclid's arm had been washed off and while Thornton tried to dig his nails under the tentacles to gather a purchase, his efforts had little effect.

"Get this fucking thing off me!" he shouted. Euclid and Harvey Jennings, standing in the front row of the audience rushed forward. But the octopus was quicker and his tentacles now had Thornton by the neck, as he pushed his beak towards Thornton's face.

Thornton raised his hands to protect himself but felt only the sqidgy mass of pulpy flesh that forced its way towards him. The tentacles wound themselves tighter around his neck. Heather Master shouted at Xian Han, "Shut him down, shut down Humboldt. Terminate him!" For a second Han hesitated.

Humboldt represented so many months of work. But his boss was under attack. He shouted at the technicians working the terminal, "Immobilise him! Now. Power him down!"

Humboldt's mind was instantly evacuated, all memories, even muscle memory, reflexes, disappeared. His head went slack, no longer forcing itself forward, trying to bite Thornton.

But the tentacles, independent of the central brain, did not release. They had their own life, their own desires, their own reason for existence. They still writhed, searching for a better grip and the opportunity to squeeze harder their prey. Heather Masters searched for a knife, determined to separate the body of the octopus from his tentacles. But if she had found one, there was no way she could safely force the knife between the sagging head of the octopus, the tentacles and Thornton's neck.

Thornton was now silent, stunned by shock, all his consciousness concentrating on prising the coils off his neck. He tried to force his fingers beneath them but they were clinging too tightly. Even when he partially succeeded, the suckers would fasten on his hand, causing such a revulsion that a panic of disgust overcame him. Others who came to his aid suffered a similar lack of effect. But at last they manged to pull off one of the tentacles, leaving great wheals on Thornton's neck. However much the nervous system of each tentacle wished to continue the fight, they had begun to weaken. In the end, their hold was loosened enough that the tentacles completely released their grip. Humboldt's body fell to the floor, his extremities still attached, still writhing, if without the fury and energy of a few moments before. Thornton stamped on his foe, hatred and contempt written on his face. He stamped until the tentacles writhed no more. Covered in slime and water, he pushed away Xian Han's arm, offered in support and comfort, and stormed out of the room.

"We'll speak later," was all he could bring himself to say. Xian Han turned to Heather Masters. "I thought the kill switch would stop everything," he said, looking for understanding. But Heather was furious about the failure of the test and the thought of Thornton's anger that she would have to deal with. "Well, it didn't," was all she could bring herself to say. Harvey Jennings, standing next to her, added, "Tricky creatures, Cephalopods. You have got to be careful. We imagine that we can exercise control over the subject of our experiments, but it's not always true. Anything that has even a modest amount of consciousness, it will try to escape you. Once you're conscious, survival is everything."

They ran the experiment a month later – with no problems. Their octopus performed as required. Thornton Lamaire did not attend. To my surprise, Xian Han did not lose his job.

TWO

The problems with MARION didn't appear for some time. But even early on, there were issues with the software. And, as they say, 'Nothing happens without a warning'. There are always cautionary signs, before the main event arrives. The first significant problem arose when Blue Ridge decided it needed to monetise its mind memory management technology – which would form an important building block of MARION's mental processes.

We all remember that winter; the first time you could message by thought alone; if lucky enough to find one of the new iPsyche phones; the first time that a civilian airliner was shot down in the US, targeted by a separatist group in Georgia. And the first time in recorded history that not a single flake of snow fell in New York between November and the beginning of April.

The mild winter was coming to a close but it was still too soon for the heat and humidity of summer to have set in. The atmosphere was sharp and bright; the sun shone; the sky was cloudless. April 12th of that year was a gorgeous day ; the sort of day that should have brought an exhilaration to the soul, and for most, it did. Yet, the uplift in mood was not shared by everyone. In the hearts and minds of Brooke Haberstadt and Julian Beck, sitting together on the thirty eighth floor of their office beside the Hudson river, the mood was decidedly sombre.

It should not have been, and not just because of the beauty of that spring-like day. They headed up the new equites division of Goldman Sachs and Brooke and Julian – friends since their college days – should have been enjoying the prestige and responsibility they had earnt as newly appointed lead bankers to the forthcoming Initial Public Offering (IPO) of Blue Ridge's LetheTech division. It was the clear favourite of the race amongst the psycho-technology ventures reaching the investor market. CyberSoul and ElectricMemory would no doubt IPO soon but LetheTech was the first, and the most advanced, in its exploitation of the progress that had been made in mind/ machine interfaces. If it worked satisfactorily, the technology would be incorporated into the mind of MARION: at singularity memory management was fundamental.

LetheTech claimed to be the only one of its peers to, so far, demonstrate a tested and trustworthy technology. Blue Ridge prided itself on its conscientiousness and attention to detail, yet, as Brooke and Julian realised from reading the on-line story this morning, the technology might not be quite as perfected as Heather Masters had led them to believe. The whole area of memory therapy was still unregulated and the permissible margin of error for these treatments was unclear.

Though Blue Ridge professed thoroughness as central to their mission, Brooke suspected that virtue did not extend very far below the surface. The development of LetheTech's technology could only have achieved its pace to market from a conviction that trial results needed to be no better than the equivalent testing regime for a medical drug. Heather Masters had argued that there would always be some impact from unforeseen side effects. It was unrealistic and 'ridiculous to expect there to be none!' she had claimed. 'Just as long as the hazards are no more prevalent than those that arise from time to time with conventional treatments.' But this attitude was way too casual. Society was used to drugs and their problems. It had grown accepting about the risk of occasional disasters in exchange for the benefits that new treatments might bring, but being harmed by an alien intelligence was quite different.

There was an understandable fear in the public of the unknown, of manipulation by a rogue, non-human, mind. We had already witnessed the phenomenon when self-drive cars were about to enter the mass market. Society had refused to accept the same death toll from machine miscalculation that they had grown used to from the delinquent driving of their fellow human-beings. Death and damage, it turned out, was more tolerable when delivered by those you were familiar with, even when robots managed to reduce the carnage on the roads. It appeared that the important thing was who hit you – not how many times you were struck.

Potential investors were skittish about the risks of invading the mind and manipulating memory. Heather had tried to reassure the bankers. 'I'm not about to sabotage our profits from inadvertent carelessness. On the other hand, we are in a very competitive market and there will be a first mover's advantage here.'

Brooke's view, as he had tried to make clear to Heather from the beginning, was that LetheTech's priority must be to demonstrate to the public – and particularly potential investors – that the processes involved were virtually faultless. Brooke understood that LetheTech wished to proceed to Phase III trials, with several thousand clients, which would be costly and require wide investor support, before the regulators got focused on what was happening. The deregulation of the early twenty thirties was still the prevailing mind-set, although the pendulum was swinging back. A few recent disasters had begun to scare public and investors alike.

The regulatory delay suited the planned IPO for LetheTech just fine. The company needed the infusion of funds right now, to finance the tests, finesse the technology, and train consultants to market the therapy. Blue Ridge – that is to say, Thornton Lamaire – had funded all that so far. Now, he sought others to shoulder the burden and, in principle, that should not be a problem. Everyone agreed on the market potential. The ability to delete traumatic memory would surely result in a great improvement in global human happiness. Sufferers from PTSD and OCD, troubled adolescents, adults with lives damaged by early traumatic experiences, even unrequited lovers, they would all now be able simply to delete their unhappy memories.

How many people were in therapy world-wide? The analysts at Goldman's had tried to estimate it for the prospectus. There were no reliable figures but the number was evidently enormous. Vast amounts of money disappeared into the hands of the psychotherapy profession every year, most of whom provided temporary alleviation of symptoms – at best. It could be expected that once LetheTech was launched many would pay handsomely to have their damaging experiences permanently excised. If Blue Ridge, by virtue of being first to market, could monopolize the provision of automated therapy, vast revenues would surely be diverted into the hands of the corporation and its investors. When Brooke and Julian drafted the prospectus, the opportunities had seemed almost endless.

Traumatic memories would be LetheTech's initial focus but who knew the limits of its compass in years to come? So much benefit, so much promise was being shown – and now this! Of course, this was just an early report on an obscure website, maybe an outlier, but it had inevitably spread all over the internet. Was the report true or malicious fake news from a rival or generated by AI, some malignant chatbot? Would this incident be followed by others? There had been rumours before of cases where, even if no damage to the patient had occurred, treatment had been ineffective. Yet none of this had been verified and none of the rumoured cases of harm, or lack of efficacy, were sufficiently numerous to be statistically significant. Yet rumours didn't have to be true to do their damage and unless Heather could neutralize the on-line chatter, the faulty cases – and others that would come in their wake – would inevitably cause delay of the IPO. Potential investors would step back unless the company could refute any and all doubts.

Heather Masters could read these runes as well as the bankers. And the troublesome report on the case of O'Neal was far from the only cause of stress this morning. *Troubles coming not singly like spies, but in battalions,* she remembered from her college English Literature class. She hoped there would be no more troubles for a while but the inevitable call to Thornton after the meeting did not add to her peace of mind.

Then there was her personal life. Bruno… Why had she brought up last night the subject of their separation and her future life with Chase? Nothing would have been lost by deferring that conversation until after the IPO. The pressure of work had warped her judgement. But she couldn't defer her personal life for ever and the IPO process might take months, maybe years, if the O'Neal case exposed insoluble problems.

She'd have to call Bruno later and make peace. But after she'd talked to Thornton.

There must have been some really big fuck-up. Clients in Phase II testing were meant to be regularly monitored. LetheTech was still tuning the right level of mental intervention. The risk that too much memory could be inadvertently wiped out was a real hazard. She could only assume that O'Neal's state of mind had escaped her staff. It certainly didn't help that the problem had occurred to a celebrity author, even if the eccentric O'Neal was a fading celebrity. The 'creative community', to which she supposed O'Neal still belonged, had been vocal on what they saw as the dangers of memory therapy. If LetheTech removed the discontent and mental anguish that 'creatives' believed underlay so much of the artistic process, would the very future of art be imperilled? She recalled that many of the great artists, Picasso, Victor Hugo, Goethe, Shakespeare had been perfectly happy but the myth died hard. It was true that for every stable writer there was a tortured Dostoevsky, for every Picasso an earless Van Gogh. But most artists would be more productive if rid of their mental barriers, although it would take a lot of education by LetheTech's PR agency before that view prevailed!

Heather picked up the draft IPO prospectus and read it again. The problem was not so much minimising the dangers as not fully understanding what they were. Memory was such an integral part of personality and nobody had, until now, been able to affect it in the precise way that LetheTech claimed. Of course, meddling around with something so integral to personality had its risks, yet the hazards were surely over played. How stable was memory anyway? Memory was anything but constant, or even permanent. Memory was plastic; it was modified continuously, as one journeyed through life. Humanity had lived and coped with its mental fluidity throughout history. It was hardly novel or scary that memory could fluctuate or even disappear. LetheTech's critics failed to recognise that the quality of both individual and collective memory would in fact be enhanced by their efforts. Vast quantities of personal memory could be downloaded with LetheTech's technology and stored in electronic form, outside the volatility of human recollection. What a boon to future historians this would be! History would become much more accurate. 'In the future', as Xian Han was fond of saying, 'the past will be very different to what it is at present.' She had always liked his turn of phrase.

Heather had a few minutes before the bankers were due to arrive. She scanned the article from the day's New York Times again, though by now she knew it almost by heart.

A FORMER NOVELIST NOW ON THE STREETS, LOOKING FOR ANSWERS AND HELP... BUT FINDING NEITHER. A VICTIM OF MEMORY THERAPY?

Just outside the D'Agostino's store in New York, near the intersection of 1st avenue and 53rd street, a man squats on a square of cardboard, his mongrel dog by his side. In his dirt-stained stained hands he holds a battered cardboard sign.

'Lost home. Lost family. Lost friends. Lost memory.'

Here was the man I'd been looking for.

After hearing rumours that this dishevelled man was none other than the famed writer Kinnead O'Neal, it had taken me the best part of six months to track him down. Every day O'Neal had moved on, from street to street, sometimes town to town. For weeks, I had wondered if the man who I could identify only by a photo was really the man who had been one of America's most revered contemporary writers. For weeks, I had imagined what he would be like and what – if anything – he might remember of his past life as a literary lion, which he had abandoned or, if the rumours were true, might have been stolen from him?

For most of his life the famous author had struggled with alcohol, drugs and failed relationships. Medication and therapy had kept his demons – demons that had fuelled his books – at bay. Nothing had stopped him from twice winning a Pulitzer, nor from attending celebrity dinners and lavish award ceremonies, nor writing a new book every other year. He had married three wives, bought several houses, parented a horde of children. Yet now here he was, looking forlorn in the evening light, his faint voice beseeching passers-by for 'a little something'. Most passers-by didn't heed the entreaty.

"I don't like this", he confided. "I don't like begging, I'm not even any good at it. But I've got to eat."

A couple of years ago O'Neal suffered a breakdown after the death of his eldest son in a car crash. He sought professional help for the overpowering grief and then drifted into the temporary relief provided by drugs and alcohol. At the urging of his wife, he turned to memory therapy as a last resort, signing up as a volunteer in the Phase II trial of Blue Ridge Corporation's LetheTech programme.

"I'm mentally so weak these days," he confessed. "Something is wrong with me. I don't know what it is, but I used to be able to remember things. Now... nothing. One day a woman came-by claiming to be my wife but I didn't recognize her – I told her to be gone."

Faithful friends, who sometimes visit him on the street, claim that the memory therapy has scrambled his brain.

"He was a bit lost before but he was a long way from where he is now," said one. "The tragedy is that while he has forgotten his son he appears to have forgotten everything else too. It's too easy for companies like LetheTech..."

Heather had read enough. The story played right to memory therapy detractor's accusations – that Blue Ridge's technology could not be accurately controlled, that the precision with which LetheTech claimed to excise memories could not be consistently achieved. And this wasn't the only example of unwanted memory loss. There had been other instances that would now be searched for and become public. Yet there had to be zero tolerance for error. Who would submit themselves for the therapy if there was the slightest chance of total amnesia? The loss of identity would be far too high a price to pay for whatever benefits might be offered in compensation.

Heather was jolted from her gloomy ruminations by a knock on the door. The bankers had arrived. She stood up, smoothed her hair and prepared for long faces and pursed lips. Yet the two men, dressed in dark blue suits, greeted her with warmth and a positive countenance. Thank God for that small mercy! She couldn't face dealing with lugubrious looks of doom and gloom this morning, With a smile, Heather gestured the two men to sit, ordered some coffee for them all, and after preliminary chit-chat she broached the subject head on;

"So, what's your view on this Kinnead O'Neal article?" she asked. "It's mostly fake news, but I will confirm one thing, amongst all the misinformation. He is one of our clients." She flashed the bankers another smile. They must admire her candour at least.

The bankers nodded solemnly. Brooke cleared his throat. Of course, he knew that already. "Indeed. We heard rumours that something like this was coming," he confirmed. "We were hoping this guy might be a client of one of the other memory therapy start-ups. But I gather we can't take comfort in that. If we ever could. Any bad publicity, for whichever company, will taint all of you, the whole field of memory therapy."

Heather leant back in her chair and sipped her coffee. She had to find some positive gloss about O'Neal. At last she spoke, "As you may appreciate, one of the problems is that in this early testing phase we are forced to accept clients who are already in bad mental shape.

Given the freshness of the technology, people just mildly disturbed are not prepared to risk it. So we're left with patients, clients, who are already mentally impaired. It's often difficult to unscramble the problem when things go wrong. Is it us, LetheTech? Or is the excessive memory loss the result of some pre-existing problem – some further deterioration that would have happened anyway?"

"But surely you check the health of the clients before therapy starts?" Brooke interjected. "To understand what their pre-existing condition is? Whether there could be a risk of sudden further deterioration?"

"Of course," replied Heather, a little more sharply than she meant to. She didn't like the imputation that her firm was careless. "I have checked the records this morning. O'Neal had his mental problems and deteriorating memory. Alzheimer's was clearly a factor here."

"Are you claiming that LetheTech is not to blame?" asked Brooke. "Wasn't his memory loss a bit sudden for Alzheimer's?"

"I'm not saying that we didn't have some impact," conceded Heather, defensively. "It's like when the knife slips in the surgeon's hands. It happens. Such accidents are ghastly but... they cannot be avoided altogether."

Heather checked Julian and Brooke. She needed them to share her perspective: this was not a systemic problem with the technology, this was an unfortunate but rare type of reaction that could be expected when new treatments were tested. It was just a matter of explaining it the right way. The two men in front of her were being paid handsomely for overcoming just these sort of roadblocks.

"So, tell me. Do you think this will have an impact on pricing for the IPO?" she asked. Her tone was optimistic, inviting the answer 'of course not' or, at worst, 'not much'.

The two men shuffled awkwardly.

"I'm afraid this isn't just a matter of adjusting the pricing, Heather. There's no way we can sell the IPO to investors with stories like this flying around. Sites have been whipping up fears about Frankenstein machines altering the brain. Even the Financial Times has been asking if memory modification is ready for general release. The government is itching to regulate it. You can't launch anything this radical unless the technology's one hundred percent. I'm sorry Heather. This is not the message I wanted to give you but we would be negligent if we told you otherwise."

Heather nodded. They were right of course. There was no way Blue Ridge could launch their IPO in this climate. But the LetheTech development team didn't really understand the cause of the errors and until they did, the peerless results that public and investors had been led to expect from a year's pre-marketing campaign, would be impossible. Close as it was to Thornton's heart, his ambition for an IPO was a long way off yet. For months he had wanted to liquidate part of his holding in LetheTech. He was already meeting higher than expected development costs for MARION. Lucky, then, that Thornton had deep pockets. He was going to need them.

That was not the only bad news she must break to Thornton. There was also the small matter of malign behaviour by the specially adapted Series 4 Milton robots during testing that past week. There would certainly be another PR disaster if the details of that incident leaked. She hoped that her team had satisfactorily removed the victim's memory of what he had suffered. The LetheTech system better have worked that time! Heather reached for her phone. This was not going to be an easy call.

THREE

Heather was right. The most recent report on MARION's progress did not suggest that she was likely to get any cheaper. Together with the projected cost of LetheTech's Phase III trials, Thornton would begin to struggle if he didn't find external investors soon, prepared to shoulder some of the financial burdens. The way things were going MARION would turn out like his other two children; under-budgeted for.

On every count, progress seemed to have slowed. Probing of MARION's synaptic processes had exposed something closer to the operation of the latest generation of chatbots, rather than proper self-awareness. MARION was meant to be much more sophisticated than that. He would raise the subject with Claude Blondel, the consultant-philosopher brought in to provide a fresh, outside, perspective on just these type of issues. They had yet to meet but Claude would be up at the campus on his next visit.

But, as always seemed to be the case, resolution of these problems came back to money – or the lack of it. He'd now have to place strategic calls to the banks and venture capital funds to discover how much he could raise. It was really bad luck they had hit this snag with O'Neal. Phase I trials had not hinted at any problems. And was it just a snag – or an indication of something more serious? All this bad news, just at the point when the potential for LetheTech's memory technology was so exciting! So many psychological problems found their root cause in traumatic, repressed, memories, but if their technology worked oppression by one's own memories would be a thing of the past. In a revolution undreamt of by mankind's psychology pioneers, Freud, Jung, Klein and others, psychic burdens would be lifted from humanity – permanently; without effort, sorrow, or penance. Plenty of adults and adolescents were living with mentally clouded lives. Well, not for much longer.

Thornton scanned the list of market opportunities, something he took solace from when things looked gloomy: those traumatised by war, parents losing their children, children losing their pets, adults losing their fortunes, grandparents losing their minds, broken-hearted lovers losing their partners. If the most fundamental experience of life was loss, then LetheTech was going to change the very sense of what it meant to live and engage with the world. This would be the salvation of memory! No longer would memory be a threat to happiness but an opportunity for greater contentment! In future, memory would be managed, like one's weight – or blood pressure. Such an advance. So easy to sell. The Management of Loss.

What a slogan! I could almost write the copy myself, he mused.

But if the market potential for LetheTech was to be realised, speed was everything. Thornton had been led to believe that Cybersoul and ElectricMemory were not so advanced in their research as Blue Ridge, but how good was the intelligence? The market was full of misinformation. The only safe course was for LetheTech to hit the market as soon as possible. Was Heather Masters the right person to drive that? Thornton had asked himself the question many times. The relationship between the two of them had been of long standing; she had been a loyal supporter of his family. Her background had seemed appropriate; recently heading up a small, fast growing, tech company but he'd been surprised how easy she had been to attract. There were rumours that things had gone awry on her watch and that her previous employers were not totally devastated to see her tempted away. But what start-up didn't have problems? Besides, it was difficult to pin the issues there solely on her management and Heather had convinced him that the rumours were the result of a personality conflict with an important shareholder, rather than a question of her competence. She had been required to sign such a comprehensive Non-Disclosure Agreement (NDA) that it was difficult to discover the truth.

He'd noticed, since employing her, that she veered between great enthusiasm to appearing greatly distracted. Her complicated personal life, a separation – but not a divorce – from her last husband, and another marriage on the way, as federal law now permitted, sounded awkward. But finding the right candidate for LetheTech had not been easy. The ideal CEO needed an understanding of the technology, the ability to handle a brilliant, and often individually difficult, team of specialists whilst sharing his vision and drive to take the company forward. Heather seemed the best candidate on offer but he sometimes doubted that he'd made the right decision.

*

Thornton flew back to his ranch in Louisiana from the private airfield at Teterboro, New Jersey. During the flight, he ran over the agenda for the forthcoming board meeting; a full discussion on the O'Neal issue first and then a briefing about MARION's progress towards singularity.

The Phase I trials had been limited; not just in terms of numbers but also in the depth of intervention LetheTech had been prepared to risk. Back then, forays into the minds and memories of the more adventurous staff had been shallow, deletion levels modest. Only with the octopus trials had Xian Han and his team unleashed the full capability that the technology could provide, removing core memories and then creating, and implanting new, fictional, experiences that lacked any connection to a reality the octopuses might have once enjoyed; aquatic cephalopod fantasies. Yes, what an advance that had represented; writing new memories rather than just translating and deleting them! Things were evidently trickier with humans – as the debacle with O'Neal demonstrated.

Via his iPsyche Thornton downloaded the cursory email Heather Masters had sent him that morning; only two days after news of the collapsed IPO. He closed his eyes and read the short text floating in his mind.

> From: Heather Masters
> To: Thornton Lamaire
> Re: Forthcoming board meeting
>
> Hi Thornton.
> I hope you have a good flight tomorrow. I want to discuss the agenda before the board meeting. Can you call me?
>
> Best, Heather.

What on earth was this about? The expression 'I hope you have a good flight tomorrow' was an agreed code between them for any situation so serious that it warranted an immediate call over an encrypted line – and certainly not one to be discussed by email.

As soon as he had landed and found the security of his office, Thornton replied – 'Call me now'.

More bad news? His doubts about Heather's competence flooded back. As the call connected, her image appeared in his visual field – as though she was sitting opposite. It didn't feel like an illusion, but it was. Last year, he'd have needed to put on a pair of VR glasses to see her without having to peer, myopically, at his phone – or project her holographic image above his desk. Now Heather was just piped straight into his cortex, via the miracle of his iPsyche.

Thornton wasted no time on pleasantries. "What's up?' he demanded, with more edge in his voice than he meant to show.

"There's been a new problem? Last time we spoke you assured me that the O'Neal issue was a one-off."

Heather raised her eyebrows and pulled her mouth to one side in a grimace, a private way she had of steeling herself to deliver unwelcome news; a contortion she tried to control before Thornton noticed it. She'd forgotten that this was a one-way call and the fact that she couldn't see her boss did not imply the reverse. Not having her own iPsyche yet put her at a disadvantage.

She took a deep breath. She'd start with the disaster he knew about – and save the latest revelation for the end.

"I'm sorry to have to tell you this…"

Thornton cut across her. " I'm sure you are, Heather. Get on with it. I can cope."

"The calibration issues with LetheTech. We still haven't ironed out what's causing the excessive deletion of memories, such as O'Neal has suffered. His was an extreme case – a one-off – but even in less severe cases we have noticed… problems, loss of episodic memories, significant family occasions, holidays, that sort of thing. Sometimes, inability to recall one of their children's names – or even who they are. We're getting push-back from relatives, particularly from their children, and they can be aggressive. Not easy to have to deal with them when we have inadvertently removed a 'motor' memory from one of their parents. You remember the old saying about never forgetting how to ride a bike?"

"I'm familiar," Thornton didn't add that he was only familiar with the expression, not the skill. He had never learnt how to ride a bicycle.

"Well, may not prove quite true! What they call 'muscle memories' can disappear after we've intervened. But then, I guess, riding a bike is not a skill most of our aged clients use anymore!"

"No I guess not", said Thornton, his voice filled neither with an attempt at warmth nor even interest. He was always annoyed when Heather tried to sugar the pill of her failures to manage him. "So, are we making any progress to remedy these issues?"

"Right – yes. Of course." Heather abruptly realised that her boss was bored by the length of time she was taking to reach the point of the call. Even so, she was incapable of transitioning to a less defensive strategy. She made one last attempt to ward off Thornton's critical reactions about her performance:

"Before O'Neal, these incidents were on the decline. We'd almost halved the rate in the last month," Heather continued, breezily.

"And now?" Her boss pointed out the reality. "Half is no good. You need to get them down to zero, Heather, before we can approach the IPO again. Who's going to submit themselves to this therapy if we might wipe out the memory of their past life?"

"We're on it, Thornton. The team is working sixteen hour days. And we're still ahead of the competition. I have heard that CyberSoul and ElectricMemory are suffering the same problems – and worse. I've discussed this at length with Xian Han and he's confident that O'Neal type problems can be rectified with modest changes to the software."

"I hope so, I really do, Heather," replied Thornton. "You know much this is all costing. I don't want to pull the plug on MARION's development because we're running out of money funding LetheTech. But if I'm going to continue, we need to get the IPO done asap. Talking of MARION, is there any good news there? LetheTech is one thing, an important business that will help fund everything else. But MARION is something else. A revolution. I think sometimes you miss the point. MARION doesn't just take AI to another level, it takes humanity itself to another level!"

"Right, right, well… Xian and his team have almost completed her basic testing. Next up is the installation of the ethical edicts and early education. We thought the early stages was going brilliantly but…" Heather's voice trailed off. She hardly had the strength to bring up the whole point of the encrypted call. "We haven't eradicated all the bugs."

"Break it to me slowly, Heather."

"We wanted to test the new software that integrates sense data. It combines different sensory inputs, touch, sight, smell, to inform behaviour. The software was installed in some of the Miltom Series 4 trial machines. Each robot possessed a separate sense – one touch, one smell and so on. They were to share their data streams in order to achieve a common objective – to find a shared reward buried at a specific location. They had to navigate a mile or so of woodland before they reached the target."

"Go on"

"So…. we're all sitting there, Xian Han, myself, five or six other members of our team and an invited group of our sub-contracted coders." That was a mistake, thought Thornton. Never invite outsiders, until you're sure everything works.

"The three test robots, you've seen them, they look different to the standard production Miltons, a bit like eight legged beetles. They're introduced some way out of sight. We monitor them as they work their way through the trees. Occasionally one of them bumps into a pine but, by and large, once it starts, the test goes as expected. Until they reach the target, a thin metal pole in the middle of the clearing. Then, this dog appears, out of nowhere, followed by a man with a gun. I presume he's out hunting. We were sure that the local woods had been secured so I don't know how this guy had got into the area – but got in he had, with his dog."

Thornton could barely believe his ears. The incompetence! Absolute security of the area before and during AI tests was fundamental. Was there nothing that Heather could do correctly?

Heather continued unabashed. "So the dog runs ahead and starts sniffing around at the base of the pole. I had no idea the scent we chose for the test was so attractive to canines! Anyway, the hunter follows and goes over to investigate. He sort of waggles the pole… and pulls at it, like he is trying to uproot it. I guess he is as curious as his dog. I turn to Euclid McNamara – remember him? Member of Xian's team? – who's sitting next to the intercom. I shout, 'tell that man he's trespassing and to vacate the test area, NOW!' The man looks up, but he doesn't move – at first. That's when I notice the robots are no longer venturing forward towards the target; they're spreading out on the boundary of the clearing, looking for cover, hiding behind the undergrowth. Then they stop advancing. They are absolutely silent, not treading on anything that might make a sound and give them away. They're what I would describe as hunkering down."

"Do you know what is going through their minds at this stage," asked Thornton, now fascinated, his irritation with Heather and her carelessness forgotten. "Did the post-test deciphering of their network states show anything?"

"We won't know for sure till Xian finishes analysing the data stream."

"Ok, and then?"

"As though responding to a coordinated signal, each robot rises up on their eight legs, moves into the open and launches themselves, faster than I have ever seen them move before, across the grass. The dog scatters. The man spins around, drops his gun, transfixed. But before he understands what is happening, they're on him. Each robot grabs at a different part. Two go for his legs, the other lands on the man's midriff, wrapping its legs around him and knocking him over in the process. The man is screaming with fear, as you might expect. We've never seen this sort of behaviour before, I've no idea what the robots might do next. I shout at Euclid, "Turn off the power, pull the plug, pull the plug!" This, thank a million heavens, he manages to do. Luckily he was sitting next to the emergency STOP button and commands a shut down. The robots immediately freeze but unfortunately with the man still locked in their embrace. He's no longer screaming. For a few moments we feared he might have died. But, thank God, he's just passed out. We venture into the clearing, release the man and carry him into the control room. Despite his ordeal, there are few physical signs of injury, some scuff marks on his legs but that's all."

Thornton lets out a sigh, he can see how this might end for Blue Ridge. "What happened when the man came round? I presume he did finally come round?"

"Yes, he did," Heather reassured him. "But that was later. First, we sedated him, to prevent him waking from his catatonic state, and carried him into one of the labs. Xian suspected what I was going to propose, a bit worried by the ethics, but I overruled him. I was concerned this man could be a spy. The woods were well secured that day. I promise you the so-called hunter couldn't have got in without a real hard try to evade our sensors. The gun and the dog could just have been a ruse to support a hunter alibi if he was caught. I wanted total memory evacuation – at least of the last couple of hours. Xian thought that was over-kill and could have repercussions." Typical of Xian, thought Thornton, always so cautious. Well done Heather, for once.

"We settle the man on the table, attach the LetheTech headgear, bring up the memory of the last couple of hours – and delete it. Luckily, the incident was so fresh in the man's mind that it had not travelled deep. Removal was simple and fast. When we're done, we take him to the canteen, put a cup of coffee in front of him and bring him round. 'Hi,' we say. 'Welcome to the world! We found you passed out in the woods and brought you here.' The man shakes his head, and says something along the lines of 'thank you, thank you, that was mighty kind of you. I'm sorry to be such a nuisance but I had a dog with me, I don't suppose you've seen her? Answers to the name of Daisy.' Of course, by that time we'd found the dog and could reunite them; gave them both a meal. The man couldn't have been happier or more grateful for our help and concern. He seemed to have no recall of the incident – and why should he? The LetheTech procedure works!" Thornton felt a rosy glow of pleasure as he heard those words. These impromptu, unrehearsed, trials of their technology were worth a thousand controlled tests in the lab.

"So, we drove him back to town, to bear witness to our kindness and deny any of the rumours about untoward goings on at the campus. The incident might have been a disaster but, in fact, it will be great PR for us." Heather looked smug.

Let us be generous and allow Heather her moment in the sun. It is not often that events, particularly potentially disastrous events, turn out well for her.

"What about the outsiders, the sub-contractors?" asked Thornton. "What was their reaction? We could have a problem there."

"Sure. Yes, it wasn't so easy with the coders, who'd witnessed the whole thing. We had to buy their silence, we couldn't exactly LetheTech them. But they'll go along with it. They earn good money with us. Still, it's not really then I am most worried about..."

"Really? Of the many hazards encountered in this unfortunate train of events which is the one you are most concerned with?" asked Thornton, sarcastically.

"There is something definitely amiss with the internal controls we built into these Series 4 robots. I've asked Xian to go over the protocols again," replied Heather. "The 'kill' switch might not be so close at hand next time. Not everyone's got Euclid's reflexes either. All in all, an exciting month and not one that I wish to repeat."

Heather is overconfident that she has this under control, Thornton reflected, gazing out of the window of his office. We'll be lucky if this doesn't get out. The incompetence, the software failures, the delinquent robots! Please God that the hunter's memory deletion was thoroughly performed. Any repressed memories popping up later will inevitably land as a suit against Blue Ridge. First Kinnead O'Neal; now this.

FOUR

Thornton Lamaire III, prominent citizen and business man of the state of Louisiana, family patriarch, troubled Catholic and unsatisfactory husband (in his wife's eyes), awoke that morning with a soft buzzing in his head. At first he didn't move, groggy with sleep, but as the sound rose to a sufficiently irritating pitch he turned onto his side and reached across the covers.

Then he remembered: all he had to do was to think the command, Alarm off. There was a soft click deep in the back of his mind; the simulated throwing of a switch, and the buzzing stopped. The direct brain/ phone link still amused him. So much easier thinking a command at that hour of the morning, rather than scrabbling around in the dark for his phone, searching for the off button. He closed his eyes and let the night's incoming mail scroll through his consciousness. Thank God all that peering at a tiny screen was a thing of the past.

He felt the back of his neck, to make sure the iPsyche was properly attached. Sometimes it rubbed itself adrift in the night. There was talk of a new smaller, thinner, iPsyche that fitted under the skin. He wasn't sure he was ready for that yet, even though it was said to overcome many of the connection problems from which the present model suffered. He checked the time. The digital image of 5.42 am formed itself somewhere deep in his thalamus.

Casting the bedcovers aside, he swung his heavy legs to the floor and stumbled across the dimly lit room. It was many years since he had slept in the same room as his wife, Bethany. He gave no command to his iPsyche, as he might have done, to turn on the lights. Thornton had no wish for the violence of artificial illumination so soon after waking. His eyes felt sore, the consequence of stargazing for too long last night. The excitement of identifying the Savannah, the second Mars lander and successor to the ill-fated Roanoake, as it sped on its outward journey to the red planet, had kept him up long after he had intended.

A pale, jowled, freckled face looked back at him from the mirror. Male pride had so far prevented him from buying one of the new 'Turn-Back-the-Time' mirrors from LetheTech's consumer division – and reminding himself how he looked in his twenties. He decided to defer shaving until after his morning ride and ran a hand through a scruff of fading, once red, hair. He pulled on a pair of heavy cotton trousers and a new linen shirt but failed to thread the cuff-links, the buttonholes too tight for his chubby fingers. No matter, Clarence would do that for him. He crept onto the landing, softly closing his door. The household was more numerous than usual this week. It was rare for both his daughters, Stephanie and Elizabeth, to be home at the same time. They were not likely to wake but Bethany, a light sleeper, might. He would probably just get told off for being inconsiderate, or careless, in that event but he had no wish for criticism this morning. His mood was still one of contentment and Thornton wished to keep it that way.

Clarence, his long serving butler, greeted him in the pantry with the regular pre-ride snack of pills, coffee and a couple of shucked oysters, liberally dressed with Tabasco. Proper breakfast could await his return. He swallowed some of the coffee, then held out his arms for Clarence to thread the cuff-links. The two of them, long used to sharing each other's company before the rest of the household stirred, discussed how each other had slept and observed some commonplace remarks about what a beautiful morning it should be. But that was not the only matter on Thornton's mind.

"Did Elizabeth make it back from New Orleans last night?" he asked.

"I did not wait up. But I expect so, sir," Clarence replied diplomatically. He had not seen or heard Elizabeth return and he was aware that she might still be absent. He appreciated the resonances in Thornton's mind about daughters staying out all night.

"I hope she didn't have any trouble at the gates," said Thornton.

"I'm sure she would have called for assistance in that circumstance," Clarence replied reassuringly. He tried to distract his employer from melancholy reminiscences. "Can I refill your cup, sir?" Clarence reached forward with the pot. "No, I'm good thanks Clarence," said Thornton, the sandy feeling behind his eyes beginning to wear off.

The butler continued with his morning patter. "I think you rode past the main gate the last time you were at home, sir? I fear the DOGs have been re-bunching there since they were moved on. I heard they tried to take over three farms near here. One particularly aggressive mob broke through Mr Dilkes' gates a couple of days ago." Clarence recounted this gloomy news with the same tone as he would tell of the morning's weather.

"Really?" commented Thornton, as one of the oysters slid down. "I would have thought the late Mr Dilkes' plantation would have been a little large and well protected for such a band of desperadoes." To himself, Thornton reflected, '*Panama* Dilkes. The man who made a fortune financing something in that little Latin American strip of canal. The man who'd had the good sense to marry Lu Ann but the bad luck to die while he, and she, were still young.'

"I'm told there was no real danger," continued Clarence, in the same respectful tone that Thornton reckoned would not have varied if the entire family and workforce at Panama's place had been slaughtered. "The sheriff and his men were there soon enough. The governor will have none of that nonsense but it's creating a lot of anxiety for folks. Someone's going to get hurt real soon, the way things are going. But if those at our gates have been well behaved this week, would you like me to take them some sustenance, sir?"

"Yes, do that, please Clarence," replied Thornton. 'We must do what we can an' hope to keep them from violence. I don't want those people helping themselves to any of the crops or livestock, either."

"Very good, sir," said Clarence.

Whether Clarence's idiosyncratic habit of speaking in a sort of Jeevesian English developed from a former position as a waiter at the London Savoy, or an over-literal reading of P.G Wodehouse, Thornton had never been sure.

The last oyster downed he walked over to the stables, calling at the kennels on the way to collect his two Catahoula hounds, Lewis and Dexter. The dogs bounded around as they tried, in vain, to attract his attention. He strode across the yard and collected a bucket, scooped up a few inches of oats, and unhooked a head collar. In one of the paddocks was his favourite mare, Texas. She sniffed Thornton's offering and, deciding that it fulfilled her expectations of the respect she was due, bowed her head to the proffered collar.

Ten minutes later Texas was tacked up and horse and rider headed out to the track. The light was still grey and the land lay under a frail mist that swayed between the hollows, pushed here and there by the gentle zephyrs of the morning; a swell upon a lazy sea. The mist revealed only the high points of the land, suggesting hints of the fields that huddled beneath, as though God was finalising his handiwork before lifting the enveloping haze and it required a few minutes more for the world to be perfected.

They set out in the direction of the main gates. Thornton had no need to proceed beyond. He had five thousand acres on which to roam but right now needed to check on the groups camped outside.

They had seemed good natured enough before and glad of the food and blankets he'd provided. If necessary, he'd call the sheriff's office and have them moved on again. He'd done that frequently in the early days but the groups always reformed a few days later and rebuilt their crude shacks.

His kindness towards these unfortunates, many of whom Cajuns like himself, was prompted by his Catholic faith, self-interest and a sense that these people should be propitiated if they were not to rise up against those more fortunate. He imagined that he understood how much they had suffered, first losing their jobs and then, for those living in the Bay area and in the Bayous, their homes, destroyed by constant flooding. Keeping them fed and sheltered seemed the least he could do.

These so-far peaceful groups had, so he had been informed, not yet been infiltrated by the more desperate and violent Digital Outlaw Groups or DOGS; those with Social Harmony (SHO) scores of zero, who had been convicted and sentenced to the withdrawal of their digital status. To be a part of the DOGS meant exclusion from the modern world, where a SHO score of at least 2.5 was the precursor to being part of society.

Still, this morning Thornton decided not to approach the refugees too closely. He had no wish for a cheery morning chat, nor to listen to a rendition of their troubles. The first fires were already smoking and the smell of singed ham caused Texas' nostrils to flare and her gait to become skittish. The campers were made up of discrete subgroups, separated by a few yards of worn grass, with several early risers making breakfast. The rest, Thornton imagined, must still be asleep in their makeshift tents and huts. He figured there were no more of them than a month or so ago but his plantation manager would need to inspect the images from the drone that hovered above, disguised as a bird of prey, a roboraptor, to reach a more precise judgement.

Something in the distance caught his eye and he stood up in the saddle. One of his own cars was speeding along a track.

His eyes narrowed. Evidently Clarence had been mistaken in thinking Elizabeth had made it home last night. He had assumed, optimistically, that his daughter would have taken a taxi and been home before morning. Instead she had probably been drinking all night with that idiotic boyfriend of hers, Ambrose. Was the family 'problem' surfacing in the next generation?

The car sped out of sight, hidden by a screen of dust that hung in the still air, like a giant squirrel's fluffy tail. The sight of a daughter returning to the house early in the morning triggered all sorts of unhappy memories in Thornton's mind. To restore his mood, he gently touched Texas' flank with his heels and increased their pace to a canter. They turned onto a path towards his herd of black Angus, grazing peacefully on a field of fresh long grass. White egrets danced around the cattle's feet.

Content that all was well, Thornton continued further into the forest dense with oaks, Tiepolo trees, cypresses and crepe myrtle. He reined Texas back to a walk. A grey fox stood in their path, undisturbed to find this hybrid creature, a centaur, sharing his morning. The fox had no fear of another member of the animal kingdom, even if this one had an unusual protuberance upon its back. He turned away, uninterested, and languidly padded off on his chosen route. Thornton loved this time of day: the quiet, before the crickets and frogs started their chatter, the sense of being one step ahead of the turning of the globe. But above all he loved this communion with nature, only possible on horseback, his taint of humankind obscured by the scent of Texas. Together, they gave no cause for alarm to the denizens of the forest. The peace of nature was his antidote to the stresses of running Blue Ridge – and fighting with his conscience. For was MARION an affront to his God, a being too close to what had been divinely created?

As he rode deeper amongst the trees the squirrels, raccoons, the swamp rabbits, the possums, emerged to enjoy the dawn. An animal passeggiata, where each species strutted around, keen to discuss the day's woodland business. Texas lowered his head as though he wished to talk to his cousins. Thornton did not pull him up and the animals respectfully moved aside, letting them pass.

They exited from the trees to find themselves at the edge of a large bowl of cotton, almost mature since current temperatures ripened it earlier than in his father's time. Beyond lay a one-story white, wooden, chapel. Its stubby bell tower supported a bronze bell, now green with verdigris. Thornton had insisted on keeping the bell during the restoration, though it had been a long time since it had rung. He trotted Texas down to the chapel, dismounted and tied her to the hitching bar. This was as far as he intended to go this morning.

There had been a complete farmstead here once but with the fall in employment on the plantation it had long been abandoned. A few years ago, Thornton had ordered the ruins to be torn down and the site cleaned up, but he'd saved and restored the chapel. Centuries ago, the wealthy had financed the building of cathedrals to earn redemption. Reconstructing this chapel seemed the very least he might now attempt in hope of a similar benefit.

There were times when he regretted that he hadn't modernised the chapel a little more, whilst he had the opportunity. Air-conditioning would have been a welcome addition, but there was no power out here unless he installed solar panels and that would have spoilt the ambience. His priest had joked that the temperatures concentrated the congregation's minds on the perils of hell. Thornton had laughed at the time but some Sundays he thought the remark only too apposite. While it remained consecrated, the chapel was used only irregularly. In two Sunday's time, it would be host to a sermon by Carroll Gillespie, onetime Bishop of the Diocese of Alexandria and recently elected governor of the state. Now laicised, he rarely spoke from the pulpit and only when he felt the need to share his views on a political issue with the small, well-connected and well-heeled, congregation. Well, the result of the plebiscite would be in by then. No doubt Carroll would want to say something about that and there was no group of people he could afford to overlook.

Thornton bade the two dogs wait, then strode up to the porch. He put his shoulder to the door and its stiff hinges, unused to being opened, emitted an anguished screech. Out of long habit, he dipped his hand in the font but the bowl was dry, the heat had long ago evaporated any of the water from the river Jordan. He bowed, made the sign of the cross and walked up the aisle towards the east window, illuminated by a shaft of early morning sunlight, the star of a show to which no one had yet bought tickets. The flowers and candles from the previous service had been removed and those for the forthcoming service not yet arranged. The altar had been cleaned and dusted. Above him, the statue of the Madonna, flanked by two lesser saints, gazed down at him mournfully as though she thoroughly disapproved of him. As well she might, all things considered. Thornton retreated to a pew but not to kneel. He wasn't going to risk his knees when no one except God could see him. He hadn't made confession for at least a month. He leant forward and prayed to Mary for remission.

He rose and paced out the nave, checking the floor had been properly swept – although his caution was hardly necessary. His caretaker was never in any doubt about the importance Mr Lamaire placed on the upkeep of his very own place of worship, nor the risk to his own job if he failed in this. Although they had been successful in preventing bird intrusion, small field creatures often crept in, but not out. Human vandalism was rare, given that the chapel was within the grounds of such a well-guarded plantation. The chapel smelt musty but otherwise emitted a sense of welcome and potential redemption. He closed the door softly, called for Lewis and Dexter and remounted, his hunger for breakfast had begun to make itself felt.

FIVE

The beauty of such a morning was not to be wasted. Thornton decided to ride the long way back, via one of the small bayous that eventually flowed into the Mississippi. He crossed an old wooden bridge to the strip of land on the other side, that bordered the slowly moving water. He peered into the gentle stream and for a moment suffered the illusion that the water was stationary and that it was the land on which he unstably stood that was moving past. It was only when he observed the tendrils of weed, waving like the tentacles of some fresh water species of squid, whose lair lay in the muddy bottom, did his mind, struck by unhappy recent reminiscences of the demonstration, a few months ago, at the Blue Ridge campus, snap back into focus.

In the distance rice fields were being prepared for their second inundation. Although only just after dawn, men were at work heeling in seedlings; keen to complete their shift before the heat made work intolerable. Historical resonances did not escape Thornton: machines were cheaper but these men needed to earn a living He recalled those camped at his gates, unemployed.

Beyond the bayou was a pool, shaded by a giant willow. Thornton recalled swimming in its cool waters as a boy, with his sister Dixie and his brother Thad. The water was warmer now but still quantities of large mouthed bass, catfish and sacalait swam there. Thornton couldn't make the fish out in the low, flat light, but he knew the sacalait were hiding in the depths. The bass were more plentiful, less wise and an easier catch. One of them, with a side of beans, would make a fine breakfast later that morning.

About to move on, he spotted an alligator midst the duck weed. Only its nostrils, the top of its head and the ridges along its back were visible, reminding him of Captain Nemo's Nautilus. He watched the reptile for a few moments, mesmerised by its sinister motion when, from behind a stand of cypresses on the other side of the pond arose a flight of roseate spoonbills, the translucent trailing edges of their wings filtering the rising sunlight, as though they wore a halo. Angels of a morning God. One of his favourite birds. The heavens were smiling on him this morning. He accepted the auguries and felt reassured; perhaps the researches that he financed were not some blasphemy, a trampling on areas of competence reserved to the Almighty. The Madonna of the chapel would bestow grace on him yet.

Thornton and Texas trotted along the opposite bank before turning up the last hill. From the small plateau at its apex he admired his house, his patrimony, the home of successive Lamaires since his ancestor had struck oil near the Vermillion River a hundred and thirty years ago and acquired the wealth to buy the Crooked Timber plantation. The white stucco of the Greek-revival mansion glowed in the sun, proud of its Palladian proportions, set off by a grand approach though an avenue of live oaks, drooping with Spanish moss, whose slender limbs bent over the drive touching each other, like the tracery of some fine Gothic cathedral that they had once inspired. To the left of the avenue he could pick out Bethany's prized garden, a riot of flowering azaleas and camellias in the spring. Beyond, a paddock where his horses grazed contentedly. A little further, a large pond where the family now swam and in whose brackish depths patrols of robotic turtles ripped out any weed impertinent enough to establish itself there. A three bar white picket fence surrounded these grounds, announcing the limits of domesticity and the beginnings of the commercial plantation.

This house had been in the family for five generations, ever since Thornton's ancestor had decided to move them to St Francisville, and nearer the seat of power in the state. But the origin of the Lamaires in Louisiana had way preceded that move. The family had fled Bordeaux after the French Revolution made life too hot for their royalist views. The first settlers of the family had grown rice, sugar and cotton south of what became the town of Lafayette. With a combination of thrift, good management and a lot of slaves, they had done well – but not well enough – until they found something so valuable that the modern world could not function without it; oil

– 'black gold' – with which Louisiana was well provided. But by the late twentieth century, when the world began to focus on limiting the consumption of oil, a new substance appeared to bless the good fortune of the Lamaires. A substance looking not unlike the sugar they had been used to – and they had a near monopoly on this unique substance.

Many years before, Thornton III's father had bought land in the Blue Ridge mountains. The family planned – one day – to build a vacation house up there; in the cool of the hills, out of the heat and humidity of summers in Louisiana. When they eventually got around to digging the foundations for this retreat, they discovered vast quantities of a fine white sand. At the time it seemed of modest value, maybe useful in making glass – but not much more. Then, in the 1950s, this same sand was identified as the perfect grade of silicon dioxide from which to make silicon wafers, the essential foundation of the burgeoning semi-conductor industry. In fact, this was the only sand on earth pure enough for semi-conductors; and it was only found in the Blue Ridge mountains. To those that hath shall be given. The Lamaire's fortune took another jump and the discovery inspired Thornton's interest in electronics. Why shouldn't he be, not just the happy owner of a source of this 'white gold', but also the beneficiary of the value that could be added, after it was mined ? Why should it be others who captured all the uplift that was potentially available from this fantastically pure quartz? He could manufacture his own semi-conductors and incorporate them into computers and robots which a brave new world would demand. So began a new journey, based on silicon, software, devices and services that would be the fresh heart of Thornton's empire: 'Vertical Integration' was the way to go. The Blue Ridge Corporation was born; MARION was just an inevitable step in its evolution.

So far, there had always been a son to inherit this great industrial estate but Bethany had not borne him a son and neither of their two daughters showed any inclination to enter the family business. Would that change in time? The omens were not promising. Stephanie was the best adapted of the two, by temperament and intelligence. At thirty – seven, or was it thirty-eight? – there was no sign of a husband and only recently had she chosen a settled direction, as a journalist. It was a shame she did not wish to practice it in a location where she might have been of use to him; she could have been a successful journalist in the US. God knows he had enough contacts to ease her way. Instead, she wanted to work in Paris! Would journalism there lead anywhere? Or would that be a temporary diversion, like the rest of her disconnected and random life choices? Nor was her sister, Elizabeth, likely to prove the answer to Blue Ridge's succession issue. Unlikely, but not completely impossible. She was less dreamy than hitherto. Her dance career was going well; she now had that boyfriend, Ambrose – maybe he would translate into a husband. Her over-muscled football-playing beau didn't seem very suited to a life at the helm of Blue Ridge, but he did occasionally, and unexpectedly, say something sensible. Thinking of miracles, Bethany was drinking less than usual. Yes, the family seemed more settled than it had been for a long time. And the issue of succession might not arise for decades more; he was still only middle-aged and in good health – if a little over-weight.

Meanwhile Blue Ridge's revenues were at their highest in history; the big winner of the robotic wars. Profitability was a little down – but that was only temporary while they invested in the next big thing: his MARION. Now they were almost there, at the foothills of consciousness, at the point of singularity. There would soon be little difference between types of minds, whether built of silicon or of carbon, made by man or made by God. But the former would be the better version. Not really better, Thornton quickly corrected himself, for that would be sacrilegious, but he couldn't stop himself from reflecting that MARION would provide humanity with a mind that combined the power of the most powerful computers in the land with the understanding of a human – a mind without the ego, traumas and psychic damage that so beset fallible humanity. And it was to be he, Thornton Lamaire III, who would have made all this possible: the greatest step mankind had taken since the Fall.

Soon, man would have a companion whose origins never lay in the Garden of Eden.

From all this progress, Thornton's companies would reap the very considerable rewards that must surely follow. All things considered, everything was moving in the right direction. Maybe he had at last earned the redemption that he had so long sought. Yet, he must avoid the sin of hubris; just when everything seemed promising he didn't want to upset God's favour that had been so difficult to earn. He needed to be particularly careful about where this thing with

Lu Ann was going. Was that really permissible, whilst Jim 'Panama' Dilkes lay hardly cold in his grave? A man needed an emotional life and a recipient for his natural affections. 'Every heart needs a home' he consoled himself. Bethany had long ceased to provide that sort of succour in his life. Surely he would be forgiven for this one, understandable, weakness? Was that not God's profession, after all – to forgive?

Texas began to paw the ground and Thornton pulled back from his reverie. He crossed himself and mouthed a short prayer of gratitude for his good fortune. He was ravenous now: a couple oysters didn't last a man long. He mentally formed an instruction to Clarence – put a bass on that grill – and transmitted it via his iPsyche. The message would pop up on the kitchen monitor. It should be a great breakfast. Today, he would be able to enjoy that rare event – to share breakfast with both his daughters.

SIX

Thornton checked his blood sugar on the iPsyche and, finding it had been lowered by the exertions of his ride, promptly ordered himself a glass of orange juice, normally reserved for his girls and for Bethany. He was taking the first gulp when he realised that he'd ingested a mouthful of pips. Spitting them out he missed the plate and they rattled against the wooden floor. He called Clarence.

"We got noo' staff in the kitchen?" Thornton asked, grumpily.

"We've had Florence, sir, since the start of the week. Is there something wrong?"

"Ask her to check the juice. Never could stand things floating in my OJ."

Perhaps Thornton felt so affronted because the pips displayed his weakness – a warning about his diabetic control or, rather, the lack of it, his akratic tendencies. He really should have possessed the will-power to resist the juice, but he'd felt he had earned it. My, he admonished himself, life is full of traps for the self-indulgent...

"My apologies, sir. I should have checked myself," said Clarence, in a voice full of regret.

"It's okay Clarence, not a big deal." Thornton had caught himself in time. What entitled him to be so demanding about something so trivial? A fleeting flash of satisfaction in his spiritual awareness arose within him, followed by a longer sensation of regret about his vanity and pride. Thornton sighed and shook his head. His recently imposed programme of spiritual discipline was proving very tricky to get right.

"Don't scare the poor girl," he said.

"Certainly not sir, I will mention the issue only. I trust that your fish will be as you would like it?" Clarence placed Thornton's grilled bass in front of him, accompanied by a tub of horseradish – and the beans.

Thornton looked around him. He preferred to breakfast in the baronial style main dining hall but since renovations had started, he'd been forced out and into this room recently renovated by his wife. He focused on the new décor. Typical Bethany he thought: William Morris style green fronds twisting up the walls. At least his first edition Audubon bird prints had been temporarily re-hung here – a small victory in the long war. Many of the rooms in the house displayed collateral damage from the struggle that was his marriage. For Bethany was a Renaissance girl. Elsewhere in the house, cherubs gallivanted across the ceilings, vines rose up trompe l'oeil pillars and entangled in their baby heels; gods pursued nymphs through

Arcadian glades. But in the main dining hall, Thornton had been free to express his frustrated Scottish baronial yearnings, channelled into dark oak panelling, hung with mounted heads of elks, deers and bobcats that had found themselves in the sights of one or other of the Lamaires.

He eased the fillet from the back of the bass and was about to take a mouthful when Stephanie came in, bright, strong-featured, tall, dressed in a Chinese style wrap with her dark hair wound up into a knot, held in place by a porcupine's quill. Clarence asked her what she would be eating that morning and having decided that orange juice, toast and coffee would be sufficient she came to sit next to her father. After a brief discussion on the merits of his early morning hack, Thornton said,

"I saw Elizabeth coming back this morning. She must have stayed out all night."

"Sure, I heard her come in," confessed Stephanie, cheerily. Then she hesitated; Stephanie knew perfectly well where her father was coming from. No daughter returning early in the morning would ever be a thing of little consequence for him again.

"Elizabeth was staying with Molly last night," she said. "She probably didn't want to drive back after she'd been drinking."

"That so? "said her father, sceptically. "The car would have driven itself."

"Oh, I don't know, Daddy – ask her yourself when she gets up – if it's so important." Stephanie was unwilling to share her father's distress.

Thornton grunted, unsatisfied, but with no wish to press the matter with Stephanie, he concentrated on his fish.

"When are you off? Remind me."

"Thursday. I've got a couple of calls to make on editors who've promised to take my work while I'm in Paris. Houston first, to see TrueNews, and then Tampa, for Clear and Present Times. Next week I'm staying with the Westwoods, at their house in Rye… flying to France the Monday after that."

"Shoot. I'd quite forgotten it was all so soon," said her father. "I thought you weren't leaving until next week. If you wanted to fly to Houston together, I could give you a lift. I'm headed onto New York later today, but I could go east first. There's room on the PJ."

Stephanie shook her head. "Too soon for me. I'd like to spend another couple of days here. It's been a long time since I was home – and it's going to be a few months 'fore I'll be back. But I'm sorry we won't spend more time together. You have to go? Today, I mean?"

"I do. We've a meeting at the Catskill campus all set for tomorrow. Everyone's flying in."

"What's so important up North? Anything I can use in one of my articles?"

"Not yet," her father replied, rather sharply. "Anyway, aren't you covering European news in Paris? Not my sort of stuff?"

"I'm freelance! I'll write on anything that's interesting, that someone wants to buy. And I'm sure there are plenty of Europeans interested in your work. Haven't you got that French philosopher Claude Blondel on your board?"

"We have – but please don't sell anything about this. We're not ready yet."

"Of course, I won't Daddy – if you don't wish it. But what are these tests anyway? Must be mighty important if it's causing y'all to get together at once…"

Thornton looked at her, deciding just how much he wanted to reveal. But, hell, this was his daughter. If he couldn't trust her? "We've been running some tests on memory management," he said. "If it works – as I think it will – then we are going to roll out our artificial therapy product, LetheTech, very soon. Make us a heap of money. And we will incorporate the technology into the way we build the mind of MARION, so she will be conscious, like us. Or some of us, at any rate."

"Is that a good thing?" asked Stephanie. "I mean, will your MARION, this… machine … enjoy being conscious?"

The issue of whether MARION would appreciate – or resent possibly – her gift of consciousness had not so far occurred to Thornton. Besides, he had people, like Claude Blondel, the French thinker-guy, on his payroll to consider those sort of issues.

"It's coming, it's inevitable," he replied, as though that was sufficient answer. "Artificial Consciousness is the next big thing. All the main tech groups are working on it; AI, Apple. Open AI, Meta, Google. It's just that it's looking like Blue Ridge will be there first. The others are close behind but we discovered the Han Translation early on and that has turned out to be the clue to the whole thing."

Stephanie raised her eyebrows and shook her head, bemused,

"Han Translation?"

"Sure. Xian Han, you remember me talking about him, our chief neuro-biologist, who discovered how to translate the electrical and chemical activity in the brain to their equivalent human mental processes? We can tell now, just from looking at the electrical states and impulses of your mind, exactly what you're thinking – what's in, and on, your mind."

"You could put a couple of electrodes on my head and tell what ideas are passing through my brain?

"Not sure if it would just be a couple of electrodes but, yes, we can. Han could point to your neuronal states that correspond to a certain belief or memory – that you believe in evolution, for example, or how you recall a particular childhood picnic. Or even whether you prefer strawberry to raspberry ice cream!"

"And how does that help you make your computer conscious?"

"If we know how the human mind works – at a technical level – we can build and program our own copy. And if we do that, if the copy is accurate enough, it should behave in the same way as you and me – in other words, consciously. Consciousness is all about memory. We are conscious about something because we understand the wider context in which a memory rests in our minds. We see something and our memory immediately informs us of a hundred connected relationships – many of them concepts rather than facts. There's an old joke about a dog looking at this master scooping up his poop and dropping it in a bag and wondering why it seems so valuable. The dog does not understand, as the man does, the links between his owner's action and related concepts, such as civic responsibility, fines if he does not pick it up, the discomfort of others who may tread in it and so on. Recall of that wider context, the associations that we make, is one of the things that helps make us conscious. That, I gather – as much as I understand these things at all – is what Han believes, anyway."

Stephanie was silent for a few moments then frowned and asked, "How'll all that go down around here? Our wonderful governor, Carroll Gillespie… he's not even keen on the level of AI we've got at present. I read that he's using the whole 'Douglas versus Milton Robotics' thing, to whip up a lot of resistance against any further introduction of robots in the South."

"I never wanted that case to go to court," said Thornton, morosely. "Even if we won, it was bound to be a provocation. I mean, I can understand people don't want to be told they have to respect machines. I get that… but heck, you know – that's the way it's going, whether people like it or not. These machines are now so sophisticated that they do have expectations about how they will be treated. We can't avoid that and if MARION works like we expect that's only going to get truer. These new machines are going to be very similar to us – and they're going to want to be cared for and treated in the same way."

At that moment there was the sound of footsteps rushing down the stairs, accompanied by a loud lament.

"Holy Heavens! What the deuce is that noise?" asked Thornton, turning his head. Stephanie tilted her head to one side. "Sounds like

Elizabeth is up."

"For heaven's sake, go and see what's wrong, Stephanie," said her father. "I can't bear this sort of noise so early in the morning."

Stephanie rolled her eyes and slowly rose, signalling that in her opinion this was not a crisis, and went in search of an explanation. Thornton fondly watched her go, wishing he could make life easier for his eldest. He'd heard from Bethany that she'd broken up with George, her latest boyfriend. Well, not a disaster really. He hadn't been right for her. Still; must have been upsetting.

Stephanie had shut the door behind her but the noise of Elizabeth's distress trickled in. A few minutes later, she returned.

"Elizabeth has lost something she believes is incredibly important and vital to her life. In her opinion anyway." Through the open door they heard Elizabeth direct the staff on a search of the house. "My sister is never happier than when the entire household is demonstrating its devotion."

Thornton looked at Stephanie. Both smiled in silent accord. Neither were surprised when five or so minutes later Elizabeth burst in, heavy-eyed, exultant. Whatever had been lost was now found.

"Come and sit down, Elizabeth," said Thornton, welcoming his youngest. "And have a cup of coffee with your sister and me. It's been a stressful morning for you already – and you've got the rehearsal later."

Elizabeth was the prettier of the two, softer, smaller featured, cuter, with cornflower blue eyes and black bangs. She spent much of the day inspecting and polishing a set of blood red nails. Thornton presumed this was in deference to her 'artistic' personality. Whilst she lacked the reserve and practicality of her sister, she rode the world in a lighter, more frivolous, way. Stephanie, in spite of her inauspicious start in life, would be okay. But Elizabeth? In his opinion, she shared her sister's unsuccessful taste in men, but did not possess Stephanie's competence. A few times he'd had to bail Elizabeth out financially. Would it have been better for her if he had not? He recalled Samuel Johnson's cynical dictum 'Many a young man is ruined by a modest competence'.

Probably true of girls too, he thought sadly.

"I thought you were coming back last night?" Thornton queried, unable to avoid a tone of displeasure in his voice.

"I was with Ambrose," confessed Elizabeth, deciding to get that bit of information out of the way before it was dragged out of her. Always better to start from the high ground. "We joined the demonstration against the governor. By the time that was over and we'd gone to eat with some friends, and it was real late, I decided to stay over at Molly's." Thornton recognised that the story was probably true – his daughter wouldn't risk him checking with Molly and she rarely missed an opportunity to express her opinion on whatever political cause had recently caught her attention. This month it was her disapproval of the governor's policies. Elizabeth was much more politically committed than her sister.

"You be careful. One day those demonstrations of yours are going to turn violent. You could be hurt."

"Won't be my doing, Daddy. If Gillespie's thugs decide to take us on, why, that's why I go along with Ambrose. He's one big tough guy. He'll protect me."

"Against the riot police?"

"Oh, Daddy, I'll be fine. You worry about me too much."

"Well, I don't want to come and visit you in hospital."

"Won't happen, Daddy. I promise you. Now, let me get a cup of coffee."

Thornton grunted, unsatisfied by how Elizabeth dismissed his concern for her safety – but he wasn't going to make an issue of his unhappiness with his daughter's political activities just then. And he needed to get going. He pushed his chair back and stood up.

"Well, my dears. It's been delightful sharing breakfast with you this morning." He hesitated, as though trying to remember something and then said. "Stephanie, I'd like to see you, if you have a second, before I leave." It was a statement, not a question.

"Where are you going, Daddy?" asked Elizabeth, largely oblivious to the family's comings and goings. Thornton sighed. He was sure he had told her several times. "The MARION campus. Just as soon as Billy tells me the plane is ready. I'll be back Friday. Don't forget we're going to the chapel on Sunday. Carroll is giving the address."

"Not me, Daddy. I won't be joining you."

"And why not, pray?"

"I'm staying with Ambrose this weekend. And he is as disapproving of our governor as I am."

"Huh," was about all Thornton could muster as a reaction to that bit of news. He was not best pleased. Ambrose might be a successful football jock but now he'd left college that talent wasn't going to do him much good.

"In that case I'll guess I'll see you next week sometime. Stephanie – a word."

Thornton gestured for her to join him in the adjoining room. He began to run through a list of practical, family related, issues and instructions that would have usually included that any bottles of alcohol were locked away during his absence. This was a standard reminder, to protect Bethany, hardly worth mentioning if it was not so important, and perhaps – if a fleeting thought of Lu Ann had not passed through his brain – he would have repeated the usual injunction now. Except this time, for reasons that he did not wish to admit to himself, he did not.

SEVEN

The helicopter followed the ribbon of the Hudson as it wound itself through the Catskill forests. Thornton had set out early, accompanied only by a couple of assistants. The sun had just risen, illuminating the forest canopy below. They flew past the Palisades, skirted West Point college, over the town of Beacon and then, a little further on, where the land rose and the trees disappeared over the horizon, the helicopter banked to the left and began its descent. Soon Thornton, relieved, spotted the clearing where they would land. He partially relaxed. He had survived another flight.

In the shelter of the main building waited the welcoming party, blown about by the downwash from the blades. Thornton mentally checked them off; Heather Masters, who had flown in the day before to check arrangements, Xian Han, and, to his left, that must be Claude Blondel, identifiable in his charcoal grey suit and open necked white shirt that even Thornton clocked as his 'brand' identifier. Standing slightly apart from this group was Harvey Jennings, the chief machine-psychologist – and Euclid, sporting trainers and a T shirt. Next to him someone Thornton didn't recognize, dressed the same as Euclid – probably some new programmer or technician. On the ground, Heather made formal introductions. Thornton was given to understand that the young man was a student, an intern on limited contract.

Had he been properly vetted? Thornton wasn't keen on itinerant students, on work experience programs or internships. Who knew what their agenda really was? There were many misguided young men fighting against machine intelligence these days. They claimed idealistic motives and a wish to promote the primacy of the human mind, but he was unsympathetic. Whatever their motives, these radicals – communists, really – were destructive and could imperil MARION if they got their chance. Most of them came from within the US but they had their supporters overseas too. He knew Xian Han tested for motivation and underlying belief systems but some of these people had been good at hiding their true allegiance. He would raise the issue with Heather later.

Thornton checked his iPsyche and confirmed the lack of signal. The building had been constructed as a seamless Faraday cage, through which no radio signals, to or from the outside world, could penetrate. The irony of it all amused him. They were carrying out the most advanced AI studies in the world but here it was impossible to send or receive a telephone call. Well, not quite – Xian Han and Heather had access to their own encrypted link, but even that was guarded by a computer programmed to sniff out messages that might compromise their work. Security was an ever present issue. They had to prevent the 'crazies' interfering, deflect any premature influences or disturbing stimuli reaching MARION too early in her development. She might not be able to make sense of what she heard or saw, and the precipitate information could upset her.

And then of course there was another worry, a greater one, of MARION herself reaching the outside world before she – and her creators – were ready. If she became conscious, yet could analyse more data, think and act faster than any individual, how would she choose to engage with humanity? Nobody knew; but until they were certain it was safe, there could be no contact between MARION and the external world.

Information that she required to fulfil her purposes – the entire code of legislation of every country on the globe, all scientific papers published in the last 50 years, and so on – would be down-loaded from the internet, scanned for viruses and inappropriate information; then uploaded again to MARION. No direct feed was allowed. The educational staff were segregated from everybody else at the campus. An unsuspecting employee – or a malicious one – might be seduced by MARION to act as a conduit to the world. Would she do such a thing – seek a forbidden contact with humanity? It was a risk that could not be entertained.

*

The meeting was due to kick off at ten o'clock, leaving half-hour before to chat over coffee. Thornton spotted Xian Han across the room. He looked unsettled, anxious. Did his chief developer have doubts about the technology he had created?

Thornton reflected on the debacles with Kinnead O'Neal and the hunter; Han might be one of the most accomplished neuro-scientists of the age but he was not one of the great communicators.

Thornton went over. "Cheer up Xian," he said, encouragingly. "Don't worry! It's all going to be okay. Your insights into mental processes are revolutionary. Bar a few snafus, the 'Han Translation' works. There's a Nobel prize here for you, for sure. Heather tells me that you understand now the weakness that led to the O'Neal case, and how to rectify it. After that, we'll be there, all hazards sorted – will we not?" Thornton looked hopeful.

Han knew what his boss wanted, reassurance. "I hope all that's behind us," he agreed. "Phase II testing has been a little bit hit or miss so far. But I expect to achieve less than 0.2% failure rate in the next two months of trials." For all Xian's words of comfort, he emitted an air of less than total confidence in achieving this target.

"Good enough to release on the public?" asked Thornton. "As you are well aware, it costs a heap of money to keep this effort running. It would be nice to earn a buck or two in return."

Han was familiar with the pressure. "With your signature, Mr Lamaire, we will go straight into wide-spread human trials in Phase III – trials with several thousand or so patients." Han stopped and corrected himself. "Several thousand *clients*, who have serious psychiatric issues. Damage as bad as O'Neal's is rare. Even in Phase I we weren't often getting those problems. Remember when we tried an early iteration of LetheTech's technology on a few volunteers here? We even persuaded our sceptical Frenchman…" (Han pointed in Claude Blondel's direction) "to participate. He seemed quite keen. We never experienced an O'Neal type issue with him, or any of the others."

Thornton nodded approvingly; he liked to be reassured. But reckless deletion of memory was not his only concern. "Are we going to have a problem with the FDA, the Federal drugs people? Could that slow things up?" he asked.

"I don't think so." replied Han. "We are in a grey area regulation-wise. We mimic the procedure for drug testing, going through the three test phases, Phase I, II and III, but this therapy isn't a drug. Nothing is ingested or injected into the patient. It's more like psychoanalysis. We aim to comply with whatever standards the Association of American Psychology advises – but that's not too strenuous."

"And while we are on the subject of progress, how's MARION herself coming on?" queried Thornton. "Are we close to 'singularity' yet?"

"Soon. Very soon," replied Han. "Right now MARION is at the equivalent stage of a young child. Simple conversations are developing – early evidence of semi-conscious thought, I believe. Remember – she's constructed very differently to a chatbot. They will deliver near perfect adult human conversation from the start. They can pass the Turing test early on, or at least sound as though they can. MARION's not like that because she has to learn from experiences, not just facts and arguments. She has to act like a human, testing herself in the world and receiving back good or bad stimuli. She'll develop closer to how you and I did – but even so, much faster."

He caught sight of Claude Blondel talking to Heather Masters. "By the way, I don't think you've met Claude yet? Claude Blondel?" asked Han. "Our resident philosopher, our… metaphysician as we should more accurately call him. He's has been a lot of help. He's French, but otherwise he's OK."

Thornton looked across the room at the tall man with tussled black hair, in his charcoal coloured suit and open white shirt. "Only when we were introduced on arrival, this morning," replied Thornton.

"He's on part-time contract to us from the Sciences Po University in Paris," explained Han. "The place where they start to train the elite to run the country. Blondel's a typical product – smart. Very smart."

"Explain to me why we have him on the payroll?" Thornton asked. "What exactly does he bring to the table?"

"At 'singularity', we're trying to mimic the human mind. If we're successful, we'll have built something that operates very close to the way our own brains work. One of the hurdles we have en-route is defining what we even mean by concepts like 'consciousness,' or what it is to be self-aware. We can't progress unless we ask the appropriate questions. Claude helps us to do that – to frame the questions in the right way. Once we have the concepts tied down we can build the appropriate neural networks. Come – I'll introduce you properly."

Yet Thornton felt uneasy. Couldn't they have found an American philosopher? Was Blondel loyal? Had he been checked? They couldn't afford any leaks. Xian appeared to anticipate his doubts.

"He's the top guy in his field – there's no one better. Speaks perfect English; bilingual. We need him and he's sound. Been checked out, signed the NDA and everything. He won't leak."

"Ask him to come over here, then leave us please," directed Thornton. "Let me be the judge of his character."

It was a culturally diverse pairing. The entrepreneurial traditionalist from the South and the intellectual dandy from Europe. But neither lacked self-confidence. Their meeting would lead to mutual antipathy or grudging respect. Han didn't want to lose Claude.

Thornton took the lead. "Han tells me you're core to our team effort, Mr Blondel. What do you think of it so far? Pleased with the progress?"

"Core?" responded Blondel, with a doubtful tone to his voice. "You're very kind, Monsieur Lamaire. But I am not 'core' here. Xian Han is – he's a genius. He will get to the destination in time anyway, whether I am here or not. But it is perhaps true that I can speed up progress a little"

"And is the work helpful to you, I mean to your own discipline?"

"That's a perceptive question, Mr Lamaire. The answer is yes – it is. It is fascinating for me to try out different concepts of what is consciousness. With Han's help, we can install various definitions on the prototype MARION to see how her response matches our own concepts. So, my own subject will benefit, yes. We make a two-way-street, *une rue à deux sens*, as we say."

Raised in Louisiana and educated at Tulane University in New Orleans, Thornton spoke perfectly good French – but thought it might be useful in the future if he kept that knowledge hidden from Blondel... for the moment. He nodded, glad that the benefits of the MARION research were so widespread. It assuaged his conscience, buffeted as it was by doctrinal twinges about the moral standing of this work, that the sum of human knowledge was growing as a result of the way he directed the R&D budget. Besides, he considered that people gave of their best when they were being rewarded with more than just a fee.

"I'm not entirely sure I understand your professional subject, Mr Blondel," he continued. "Can you enlighten me? Han has explained to me a bit about why he needs you – but perhaps you could fill me in as to your views on the development of MARION?"

"My speciality is the mind and metaphysics," replied Claude smoothly. "That's why Heather invited me to join you all here."

Thornton didn't like being at a disadvantage in a conversation. Philosophy of mind was not his field. "I don't know anything about Metaphysics," he confessed. Never understood what the term meant."

"You're in good company Monsieur Lemaire," said Claude. "There was a famous German philosopher, Wittgenstein, of whom you may have heard, who thought Metaphysics was a mental illness! I hope he isn't right, I don't want to influence the mind of MARION in the wrong way."

This was not a hazard that particularly worried Thornton. Blondel didn't come across as mad and anyway half the people working on this project appeared to him thoroughly eccentric. "Really? he asked. "And why did Mr Wittgenstein think you were all mad?" he asked.

"Wittgenstein thought that the metaphysicians asked improper questions – questions that are not capable of an answer. They pursued clouds of speculation, not rooted in the real world. Western science believes that we should study reality through experiment, the metaphysicians believed that the true nature of reality could be approached by thought alone, by contemplating the nature of the universe."

"But you don't think that you're mad or wasting your time, contemplating these clouds of metaphysics?"

"Pah! Who knows?" Claude waved his hands in the air, as though it was indeed possible that he might be lost amongst the ineffable complexity of the cosmos. "I try to persuade myself that what I do has a purpose. We metaphysicians… we are not scientists and we lack their precision. Scientists look at the specific qualities of things; physical properties, chemical ones, and so on. Me and my kind… we are trying to do something different. It's called 'Metaphysics' because we consider relationships at a higher, more abstract level, than the scientists. We take their observations and try to discover a thread that will highlight a common bond between things. Those bonds we conceive of as the ultimate reality, the qualities that do not change – that are eternal."

"I see," said Thornton, doubtfully. And what's all that got to do with our pursuit of Artificial Consciousness?"

Claude hesitated for a moment. "There's a connection between how we perceive things and how things are. Metaphysicians believe that how we look at the world determines what the world is. They are inextricably linked; our perceptions and our reality. In other words, we, as conscious human beings, are not one thing and the outside world another sort of thing. The two are related. If I want to understand the world, the universe, then I first have to understand how we perceive things. That's why I became an expert on the subject."

Thornton made a note to download some of Blondel's work when he got home; he didn't wholly understand and felt frustrated. If the attractions and temptations of technology were one of his weaknesses he might as well indulge that pleasure properly – try to understand what his scientists and philosophers were creating with his money.

EIGHT

Heather Masters started off the meeting with a discussion of the problems with the Phase II trials, which had come to a head with the PR disaster surrounding Kinnead O'Neal's therapy; the subsequent delay to the IPO, which was going to create difficulties for the funding of the Phase III trials and, finally, the unexpected slowing in MARION's progress towards full self-awareness. She skipped over another recent disaster, when several of Blue Ridge's 'Series 5' Milton robots had been destroyed by an angry mob protesting about the Supreme Court's decision on Douglas v Milton Robotics. There was only so much bad news she wanted to impart this morning – and, anyway, that incident had nothing to do with LetheTech and MARION. Yet, as Heather knew, the ruling provided yet more ammunition for those who opposed the whole idea of robots growing ever closer to their human masters. Masters at the moment was her fleeting thought which passed unbidden at the threshold of consciousness.

She was nervous about this morning and had reason to be; although Thornton was as courteous as ever she had sensed in their recent calls an uncomfortable chill in his attitude. She knew how Blue Ridge fired staff; first came the frost – and then calls to Thornton were no longer returned. At that point you were expected to pick up the revolver left on the table and use it – at least metaphorically. Heather could almost hear the rounds being inserted into the chamber. Not much she could do about that now; she would try to put as good a gloss as possible onto recent events – and hope for the best.

Having covered recent history, Heather progressed to MARION's development. She looked directly at Thornton. "As I have reported to you, the arrival of full self-awareness is slower that we had anticipated. Education is at the heart of progress we make with MARION so I've asked Euclid, her chief teacher, to make a short presentation about the obstacles we have encountered."

Euclid stood, a dark, gangly individual with an afro, a scrappy beard and glasses. He seemed very confident in himself, Thornton noted – not at all like the nerdy, maladjusted, presence that his clothes had led him to suspect. He tried hard to dismiss his reaction to Euclid's dress sense; Thornton appreciated it had not been easy to find the combination of exceptional programmer and primary teacher that MARION required at this stage, and someone who was prepared to live an isolated life in the boondocks, as Thornton judged the Catskills. He was not a man moved by a frontier mentality. He wondered how Euclid put up with the isolation. He hadn't read far enough in the personnel report to reach the paragraph where it discussed what made Euclid's existence there not just tolerable, but a pleasure – his live-in girlfriend, Maria.

Thornton was in sour mood this morning, already suspicious about the way the meeting would be run. Heather and Xian Han would attempt to bamboozle him with science, tell him all was going in the right direction, and then ask him to sign another cheque. He took a deep breath. "OK, Euclid. Please proceed," he instructed.

"Thank you Mr Lamaire. As you know, twenty years ago generational AI was seen as a revolution in computer science – and, in so many ways, it was. But subsequent progress towards making computers self-aware has been slow. Computers have remained essentially dumb machines, doing what their masters – us – set them up to do. Any appearance of intelligence has been illusory. Although they were self-learning and self-programming devices, they were still essentially our devices. It was us that gave them their purpose, their direction and goals – even if they pursued those goals with strategies which they invented for themselves. Twenty two years ago, at the start of this revolution, Alpha Go learnt, on its own, three thousand years of Go strategy in just over a month. ChatGPT, Gemini, xAI, and others, caused a sensation when they came out, delivering answers to questions that seemed indistinguishable from the way a well-informed, intelligent, human might respond. But even as computers began to show signs of human-like inductive reasoning, and to progress from single goal devices to AGI machines, capable of artificial general intelligence, they were still not independent actors, capable of navigating the world in a way that demonstrated self-awareness. Built on a combination of statistical analysis, brilliant programming and vast computational power they almost seemed human. But they were not; any human like traits gave only the illusion of consciousness.

"These machine intelligences were designed to educate themselves to perform and respond to a range of tasks that we would give them. They were useful, but not as useful as if they possessed the independence and creativity of a human brain, as MARION is designed. She is built, even if in silicon, in the same way as a human mind, not only to learn and manage any task that we give her, but *any* task that attracts her interest. MARION will, of course, be contained within limits that we set – but she will have autonomy too. Like us, she will have an overall purpose – purposes, in fact, in the plural – but how she will achieve those will be up to her. And as she develops her consciousness, she can add to those initial purposes and pursuits as matters in her environment pique her interest. MARION, when fully actuated, will be as flexible and as creative as a human being, while possessing a much larger memory, and working much faster. Our machine is to be liberated, independent of us, reflective about her thought processes, so she can choose goals and lines of enquiry for herself, not just those that we might give her. That's the quest of singularity, achieving the human attribute of self-awareness in a mind that mankind has built. And a month ago we thought we had achieved that state – at least at a primitive level."

Euclid hesitated, sipping some of his coffee, then went on. "We have tested MARION extensively and there are glimmerings of self-awareness. But further development is slow. We also find that consciousness is not very well established. As though it flickers on and off. Consciousness and intelligence are not directly linked, as you know, so she can be both highly intelligent but not very self-aware. In that regard, she is presently at the level, at her best, of a child who can perform amazing calculations – but still effectively the equivalent of a three or four-year old in terms of self-awareness."

Thornton had read the briefing reports. He interjected, "Euclid, I'm aware of most of this. Tell me, do we have any solution for moving things forward?"

Heather stiffened at her boss's impatience.

"Thank you, Euclid," she said. "Why don't I take the story on from here?" Euclid retreated, relieved not to be in the firing-line; he found the whole meeting a bit of a waste of his time. But Euclid had chosen to downplay MARION's performance. Yes, she was becoming self-aware slower than had been predicted but she was still a lot further on in her understanding of the world – like an idiot-savant – than he had let on. He enjoyed the idea that he should know MARION better than anyone else and that knowledge might well be useful in the future, in a way that he could not yet ascertain. A relationship was growing between them. Sometimes Euclid worried about co-dependency, and had to remind himself that MARION was a machine that he could shut down at will – as he partly did at the end of each day, when he put her to sleep. Bored by Heather's attempts to reassure Thornton, he resumed his regular slouch.

"MARION's education is going well," she insisted. "During the next month we expect to bring her up to fourth grade. A few months later, she will be approaching adolescence, where there is a step-change in the nature of consciousness – when a human being becomes not just conscious, but self-conscious. We need to navigate these years carefully, just as we would if they were human teenage years – and we all know how tricky those can be!"

Thornton failed to laugh; Heather continued.

"We are ahead of other, competing, universities and research departments working on the threshold of computer consciousness. You will remember the latest iteration of the LIMBO computer that was built at Oxford in England – that got very close to 'singularity' – but neither they, nor anyone else, have cracked it – yet."

Thornton couldn't bear any more of her wittering and pushed himself out of his chair.

"Heather... thank you. Now, all of you – listen up; this whole program is in trouble. The launch of our first offshoot of the MARION programme, LetheTech, has been delayed significantly: we are short of finance, the development work towards machine awareness is behind schedule, and we seem to have little idea as to whether or not we can fully achieve that goal. At the same time, we are under pressure from those who believe our work is some sort of deal with... I don't know what. With the Devil, perhaps! I don't want to hear about how well we are doing compared with other research groups, I don't want to hear stories of scientific advances we've achieved but that don't get us towards our goal. I don't want to hear,

'Please Mr Lamaire, if we can just have some more money and it will all be right in due course!' I want practical steps that will get us back on track and start turning all this expenditure into income. You are not owed your jobs by God: you hold them to do a specific task, for me, that gets results. And if those results are not forthcoming, then your jobs are not worth doing. Do I make myself clear?"

Thornton allowed the silence to linger.

"Now," he continued, "let me tell you what is going to happen. First, Heather, you are going to concentrate on making sure the Phase II trials of LetheTech are completed perfectly, no more fuck-ups, like with Kinnead O'Neal – and we're going to launch our IPO within six months. No maybes, nothing 'hopefully' about it: it's going to happen."

"Second, until that IPO arrives we have a financial squeeze. Resolving that is my job. As for the delay in raising MARION to full self-awareness which is, may I remind you, the whole point of this research and which will lead to a pot of gold at the end of our rainbow, we need to give that some hard thought. There are some protocols we need to change. "

Claude Blondel turned towards the chair. "Mr Lamaire, may I? I have some ideas about the last point." Thornton nodded. He was willing to defer to anyone else but Heather.

"Of course – I'd be delighted for any guidance, Mr Blondel," he said, fighting to recover his good temper. His blood sugar would be almost at danger level by now. It had been a long time since breakfast; he needed something to eat; he burrowed into a pocket for a bag of dried fruits and nuts.

"Let's hear Mr Blondel's suggestions," he said, shovelling in a fistful of cashews and raisins.

NINE

Claude stood up and held a fist in front of hm. He uncurled three fingers. "There are three points I need to make. Firstly!" He bent over one of the fingers. "As we agreed at the start of this project, it is impossible to imagine human consciousness without the human experience. Our consciousness has developed to enable homo sapiens to cope with the external world and its challenges; consciousness is a very sophisticated response to our experience of the world. If we want to elevate a novel embryonic consciousness – a non-human one, such as MARION – then we must provide that mind with an experience similar to that which we enjoy in our early years – and as her life develops that experience must expand appropriately. MARION must 'see', and enjoy, the world just as we do."

"Secondly!" Claude folded another finger. "In pursuit of that experience we have wired up Euclid to MARION's mind, via his specially adapted iPsyche. MARION experiences what he experiences; he is her connection to the world of humanity. His senses are, in effect, hers. But thirdly!" The last finger disappeared. "Even with that direct connection, MARION still does not in fact experience the world as we do. For one thing, we act in the world. We do things and then we receive feedback on how each action changes our environment. Without the interplay between our intention, our act and the impact of our act on the world, consciousness, as we understand it, will never be properly formed."

"So MARION needs experience of the world, and experience of acting in the world, solving the day to day problems of living. If the technology had been there we would have built MARION as a mobile robot, like those you see in the movies. But there was a problem: we can't make human sized robots, as sophisticated as MARION, that can live in the world. There are three trillion neurons in a human brain, more junctions and connections than atoms in the universe: even with all the progress in miniaturizing computing capacity over the last decade, we still can't build something as smart as a brain, that will fit into the volume of a skull – and that's all apart from the reliability problems of the physical machinery that would allow our robot to move around in public. Besides, would the public want these conscious robots wandering amongst them, given existing social attitudes? After the reaction to Douglas versus Milton Robotics? I don't think so! Then there's one killer additional problem; what exactly would this robot actually do in the outside world? Just be? Aimlessly? That is not how humans operate! We go about our lives deliberately – we direct ourselves with a goal in mind – even if it's shopping. We are intentional creatures. Reluctantly, we decided that to make a mobile robot as a replica of a conscious human-being was not possible. That's why MARION sits in a stationary series of servers, over there," Claude pointed to a door at the side of the conference room. "While she enjoys the human experience via the life of Euclid, seamlessly receiving the same sense data as he does via his iPysche. MARION is a mirror to Euclid."

"So," interrupted Thornton. "You're saying we are at an impasse? We've spent a heck of a lot of money to get this far. We set out to beat everybody to the first conscious computer and now they're going to beat us, instead?" He sounded harsh and disappointed. "You were the one who persuaded us to link Euclid's experience directly into MARION!."

Claude looked down at the table, seemingly lost in thought. Finally, instead of answering the question directly, he said,

"Euclid, can you just remind us how you educate MARION? You mentioned that you have brought her up to the equivalent of a three – or four-year- old child in a nine months, but remind us please, how MARION is meant to develop at the moment, and what resources are available to her."

Euclid decided to remains seated, and address Claude from there. "There are two educative mechanisms," he explained. "MARION has access to a world-wide library that we have downloaded, vetted and stored here at the campus. She can read these works whenever she wants and because she doesn't have any human limitations she can read them a million times quicker than we can. Very similar to the way chatbots educated themselves, except then it was humans who selected the texts they were provided with. But reading is only part of the exercise – she also needs to assimilate what she reads, and interpret it. She needs to build the information she has acquired into a world view. She must decide what information means to her. That's why she must have downtime – so that integration of the information can be achieved. We put her into the equivalent of 'sleep' each night so she has time to absorb and configure that data. Otherwise she simply gets overburdened, becomes confused and has a sort of breakdown."

"And the second educational mechanism?" inquired Claude. "If I recall correctly, you, Euclid, are the only person who has direct access to her and can provide living experience. She is wired through to your senses – and only yours. As you feel, see, smell – so does she. She is almost you, in a sense. The formal education – via books, programming and so on – is maybe the least important source, for her, of what it is to be human. Her relationship with you is primary."

"That's right," agreed Euclid. "I am wirelessly connected to MARION." Lifting up his long hair a small silver rectangle could be seen at the base of his neck. "See this? My iPsyche picks up signals that travel up and down the Vegas nerve, and those signals are then transmitted to MARION. Without any need for my authorization, there is a constant feed of raw sense data to her. It's not quite like the standard model some of you may already wear – my iPysche is adapted to be closer to the new subcutaneous version, shortly to be released. Usually, all iPsyche signals have to pass through the servers for security: not with this one. It's the only one of its type that allows communication directly – to MARION."

"And you are the only one of the team here who is presently in this direct communication with MARION? asked Claude, keen to clarify this point for others in the audience.

"That's correct," confirmed Euclid.

"And how do you spend most of your day here?"

Euclid thought, 'What is this Frenchman getting at? Claude must be perfectly aware of how I spend my days – sitting in front of a screen, when I'm not with Maria.' Nevertheless, he gave his reply.

"I monitor MARION, answering her questions, designing the educative program and lessons for the following day… that sort of thing."

"So most of the time you are occupied with MARION – and MARION alone? Not going out much, for example? You and MARION are, how shall I say, entwined with each other?" Euclid was not sure whether this was a statement or a question. "There's almost no discernible difference between the two of you!" Claude continued. "You are practically one mind!"

"That's right!" replied Euclid, forcefully, with pride in his voice. "I am a combination of MARION's parent, her friend and teacher. We're almost co-dependent! No, – I jest. We're not getting that involved!"

"Many a true word is said in jest," Claude muttered to himself. "Okay. Thornton, Heather, I think I see the problem – and maybe this will suggest the solution. So far, it has been only Euclid's life that's been the focus of MARION's experience. Until recently, that's probably been enough for her to learn from. Now it's a bit limiting, restricting MARION's growth. Because, for most of the time, Euclid is stuck behind a screen monitoring MARION and feeding her information. That's how it should be – that's your job, Euclid, I understand that. And I've no doubt that in your early life you grew up in an environment rich in varied stimulation. But right now, your life – if I may say so with respect – is not like that. Your stimulation is mostly of an intellectual variety, perhaps not of much use to a developing mind such as MARION's. She is experiencing a life... not very diverse. In the end, such children grow up stunted and withdrawn; we don't want that for MARION. I'm not saying you are a bad parent – I'm just making a point!"

But in spite of Claude's effort to not criticize Euclid, the latter was hurt. "No, Mr Blondel – that is not the case. You haven't got it right," protested Euclid. Claude ignored the objection and continued with his train of thought. "So, if I am correct (and I believe I am) then what MARION needs is a much more varied experience – a richer diet of life."

"And how do you propose we achieve that?" asked Thornton.

"We must expand her educators beyond Euclid. She needs a team of perhaps five or six people, all of them equipped with iPsyches to feed their experience back to MARION. And they should be engaged in varied activities up here. Some of them should go into town occasionally, to experience everyday tasks – shopping, striking up conversations with others and so on. Maybe go on holiday! In widening MARION's life we may have to take some risks – but I am sure that is what has to be done. Give her a broader experience of what it is to be a human."

Thornton began to cheer up; maybe when MARION had direct access to a more extensive, richer, life than Euclid's, her self-programming brain circuits would enable her full consciousness to develop. "Let me tell you why I support Claude's idea," Thornton said to the team. "Ultimately, we want MARION to assimilate the experience of thousands, millions of individuals, so that she can provide answers to questions that have eluded mankind for centuries. There will be a point when MARION leaves humans in the dust, mentally – when she has direct access to all other minds and computers." Thornton hesitated. "I exaggerate a little. But she will, eventually, be connected to at least as many minds as there are devices like iPsyches installed in the human race. And soon those devices will be everywhere. When that moment arrives, we solitary humans, who have had to rely on our individual minds to understand the world, will defer to MARION. Three billion neurons connected to each other, as in our brains? Pah! Chicken feed! MARION's network will be many orders of magnitude greater."

Thornton was getting increasingly carried away, his gloom giving way to excitement.

"She will possess an experience denied to any one single human being. She will be a sort of collective brain. That's what's going to make her so useful to humanity – she's going to be so wise, so intelligent! That's why she has to work, to be conscious. She will be the saviour of humanity!

Xian Han jumped in, keen to provide some corrective balance. "There are dangers in this new approach of widening MARION's experience. Until we know MARION's character and that our controls cannot be overridden by her will, we must be extremely careful. We've no idea of the possible consequences."

"Oh, come on, Xian. You're such an old worrywart!" exclaimed Thornton. "This isn't a monster! You've been reading too many gothic novels. MARION's not built by Baron Frankenstein! We're safe in Euclid's hands. Look," Thornton pointed to Euclid's cross, dangling on a chain over the top of his T shirt. "He's a Christian. He's not going to let MARION run into any bad ways."

The decision to expand MARION's group of educators was agreed by the board. Maybe the group was intimidated by Thornton's pressure, maybe they thought there were no great risks from increasing the number who had access to MARION's mind – or whose minds were accessible to hers. Maybe they were all exhausted from the endless debates, and lack of conclusions. So, this seemed the appropriate decision to everybody, except Euclid. To him, this was an outrage. MARION and he had had a personal relationship – and now others were to be permitted to join them? It was a trampling on their intimacy, as though someone had invited other men to share his girlfriend, Maria. But of course this wasn't his girlfriend and the rest of the group would not understand if he tried to explain his opposition to the idea; his contempt was emotional, not rational. Was this how his hard work and loyalty to Blue Ridge was to be repaid? He silently resolved to forge a different, deeper, and unique relationship with MARION that would exclude these new interlopers.

And what about Xian Han? He too recognised the futility of fighting Thornton's will. He summed up the meeting.

"Okay. We seem then to be in agreement: I will appoint new members to MARION's group of connected educators. Harvey Jennings will continue to provide psychological input. We will measure MARION's awareness at the end of the quarter and record the level of growth. Does anyone have any more questions? If not, we've been here a long time and need to stretch our legs – let's have a fifteen minute break then I'll give you a tour of the facility. There'll be an opportunity to talk to MARION directly."

*

For potentially the most intelligent mind on the planet, MARION was not much to look at. Claude was amused by how far she differed from the robots and computers depicted in the novels and films of his youth: this was no R2-D2 or C-3PO from Star Wars – nearer HAL out of 2001: A Space Odyssey. As he looked around the room he understood why. Given the size of the boxes that contained MARION's brain, and the amount of cooling all the processing required, there was no way this computer was going to walk about in some android body. But she did not need to do so; the connections to her human hosts via iPsyches would give her access to all the network she should ever need, immersed in her stationary servers as she was.

MARION represented a true democratization of intelligence. Of course, there would have to be some sort of protocol, to prioritize who had access to her capabilities, but that was a problem for the future.

Euclid explained the procedure;

"You talk to MARION completely normally. If she doesn't know something, or finds your request unclear, she will tell you. Heather, you haven't been here since we finished stage one of her education – why don't you chat to her first? Please remember, you may think MARION sounds, a little, how shall I put it? Simple? She is still basically a child."

Heather pondered how to address a non-human intelligence one had never met before, especially one who was still a child; not a being of which she had much experience.

"Hello MARION," she began, uncertainly. "How are we doing today... ?"

Euclid touched his cross. He hoped that MARION would stick to her instructions: just talk like a five year old. Don't show them what you are capable of. Then, if all went well, and when all these interfering busy-bodies had gone, he would do what he always did when upset, he would call his uncle, the Governor of Louisiana and in all likelihood, soon-to-be President-Elect of the New Confederacy – Carroll Gillespie. Of course, he wasn't really an uncle – just auntie Kirsty's husband – but that was how he was known in the family. Carroll always had time for his favourite nephew. Not like Kirsty's daughters – the Three Swans, as they were known. Such snobs! At one time, he could have loved any one of them but now he was glad to be over such unrequited passion. Those bitches would never stoop to give him the time of day, let alone a date! Never mind them – his uncle would know what he should do. He looked forward to the call.

TEN

Once everybody had spoken to MARION, Thornton declared the meeting closed, and the group filed back to the boardroom for sandwiches and refreshments. Thornton, who had already agreed to have lunch with Heather, looked on enviously. It would be at least another twenty minutes before he got anything to eat and his blood sugar was again falling low. His mood was uneasy anyway; he had had to truncate the agenda, they had spent so much time discussing the shortfalls in MARION's progress there had not been opportunity to discuss other important issues, such as the required ethical protocols for MARION and the draft list of behavioural inhibitions that would be programmed into her. Old doubts swept through his mind; the fear of sinister things being hidden in the mist of his unknowing scared him. Maybe the Frenchman could help.

"Thank you for your suggestion at the meeting Mr Blondel. That was very useful. Let's hope it does the trick."

"Claude, please. Call me Claude," said the philosopher.

"Likewise – Thornton. I insist," replied his employer. "But I wanted to ask you..." Thornton rubbed his chin with one hand and looked at the floor as if to focus his concentration. "Do you think there are dangers to our work, Claude?"

There are many, thought Claude. "You mean, like Frankenstein's monster or Pandora's box? That we construct something that gets out of our control?"

"Something like that," nodded Thornton. "It's not so much that I fear MARION acting against us in ways we fail to anticipate; we can and will build in a moral code to inhibit undesirable behaviour. But that might not be sufficient..." His voice trailed off.

"I know what you mean Mr Lamaire..., sorry, Thornton. Moral codes never stopped humanity behaving like monsters themselves!"

Thornton ignored the cynicism. "I've talked to Han about this and we've agreed that the moral instructions must be absolute. But that is not the end of the matter..." he added.

"You mean that the installed taboos may not be sufficient?" suggested Claude. "Because if MARION is conscious, then she may do something that is not forbidden – but is nevertheless, evil? That, like Adam and Eve, she may let curiosity about the world get the better of the inhibitions we have provided for her?"

"Just so," agreed Thornton, slowly warming to Claude. "That's exactly what I have in mind. It's not that we are creating a monster – indeed, we will do everything to avoid that. But that we may be enabling one... inadvertently. Creating a being who acts, and behaves, malevolently of her own volition – not because of our poor programming."

"It's like any other advance," said Claude. "To be used well or badly. As we know, if man can do something, he will. We never have the strength to resist our wish to know. It's the original curse isn't it? Adam started the process and we will bite into the apple – any apple – again and again, if offered the chance. We pursue the Fall – willing to ourselves the opportunity to fall to our perdition, even if we know we are entering dangerous territory. We would prefer to be thrown out of the Garden, rather than not know something about the world in which we find ourselves. It's our curse and our fate."

Claude had allowed his tone to rise. Others standing nearby began to eavesdrop. Amongst them, Xian Han and Heather.

"Mais... on the other hand, mankind is sometimes wise about controlling his inventions, about regulating their use, protecting himself against his own worse impulses. We invented atomic power, but have been mostly good about not using it to kill people, at least not since the Second World War... "

"There was that incident fifteen years ago," pointed out Heather, who felt she needed to contribute to the conversation.

"Yes, there was," agreed Claude. "But with that bomb, dropped by mistake, or so they said at the time – we horrified ourselves didn't we? The atomic nations pledged greater efforts to control their arsenals. The chance of a repeat accident was dramatically reduced. Every so often, we have to remind ourselves of the terrible power we possess. But we don't want that with MARION, definitely no instances that might scare the public. The whole project could be closed down in the first year. So, the more we give MARION human-like reasoning, the more we have to educate her morally, give her to understand that she has to behave in certain ways and not in others. MARION is going to be more actor than assistant. She'll have agency in the world. She will be able to decide what to do, not just follow our instructions. MARION must be... sensible, I suppose. Moral in her judgements. She must act properly, not irresponsibly."

Claude paused, gathered his thoughts, and set off again. "There is a parallel here with the atomic age. Drop an atom bomb and thousands of people are killed immediately – but the spreading radioactivity poisons many more. MARION can injure someone by making a bad decision but, more worryingly, she can spread her thoughts to every aspect of society. She will be the supreme 'influencer'. If she is ill-disposed towards us, the level of influence she will be capable of could be disastrous; that's obvious enough. She must never be connected to the internet or any other systems that are a common part of mankind's everyday existence – not yet, anyway. Not at least until we are absolutely sure about her own conduct and beliefs."

"But there's another effect, that you have touched on, Thornton," continued Claude. "Which is even more worrying. MARION can think and react in new, creative, ways. Those ways may not be of benefit to the way we think about our identity. It's not just MARION's malevolence that we must fear – at least I hope not – but her *competence*: that she may start to perform human tasks so well that there is no room for us. That would be devastating. So do we have to make her inefficient artificially? Build in a sort of incompetence circuit to make her more like fallible humanity? More comfortable for us to live with?"

Heather tensed. Her boss could cause the whole team a lot of extra work if he went down the track of hobbling MARION, just to make her more user-friendly. Thornton's religiosity, his doubts about the morality of the project, his questioning of whether there were dangers in mimicking God's creation – all that could get in the way of their progress – unless it was headed off now.

She cut across the dangerous chat. "We can build in 'genetic' inhibitions into her neural networks, and 'moral' instructions into MARION's software," she interjected. "She will have limitations on the way she can think and act, if she is ever tempted to act badly. But please let us not talk of making MARION incompetent on purpose! That seems a very retrograde step. Surely we wish to achieve something remarkable?" She knew Thornton's weakness for believing he was creating a valuable legacy. "To benefit from the great wisdom she may bring to human affairs; is that not the very point of MARION? Why otherwise would we all be working on this great project? Let's not hobble her immediately!" She turned towards Xian Han, "Xian, you've been very quiet. What do you think?"

Han hesitated, his response deliberate. "Where I came from, most destruction resulted not from people thinking they were acting badly but from those who thought they were acting in the name of the 'good'. The problem was not a willingness to do evil but a different concept of how to do better. We can never be sure how an artificially conscious being will develop its thinking; that's the real danger here. Everyone – including MARION I have no doubt – believes they act from only the best of motives but…"

"The way to hell is paved with good intentions…" added Thornton.

"Something like that," agreed Han. "We can give MARION an understanding of what it is to be 'good' – our concept of the 'good' – but our defences must go further than that. We've agreed that MARION must be insulated from the public until we can determine how effective are her moral constraints. We must take care that she can't talk to or influence anybody outside her team, and even they must be monitored regularly for the conversations that develop in case some sort of… relationship builds between them which she can manipulate to our peril."

Euclid looked away.

Thornton sighed and gazed out of the window. The path to good behaviour had long been laid out in the Bible. "Xian and Claude have put their thumb on a critical issue," he said, turning back. "The solution lies before us. The correct moral guidance has been given to us by the scriptures. What has ever been wiser than our Lord's admonition 'to do unto others as you would have done unto you'? I should have thought that edict, combined with the ten commandments, would pretty well do the job."

His contribution was met with silence. But Thornton wasn't done.

"Claude, I appreciate you're not a moral guy." He saw Claude flinch. "I'm sorry, I know nothing about your personal life – which I'm sure is exemplary! I mean, rather, your speciality is not ethics. Yet you have insights into the effect of this technology – on whether we can make it work for humanity's benefit. You're a philosopher and all philosophy is pretty similar, right? I mean it's all about thoughts, isn't it? It's all the same sort of thing."

Claude made a little moue, his vanity piqued. All philosophy the same sort of thing? Mon Dieu...

He kept his pride under wraps. "Ah – I make no greater expertise in the moral realm than yourself Thornton, but I do understand the importance of the issue. At the beginning of MARION's... how shall we say – 'life'? I'm not sure what to call it, but during her development period..."

But before Claude could elaborate his point further, Thornton had moved on. "Let's not burden today with this issue," he said. "This morning has proved very useful on other important matters. I wish Claude that you could join Heather and myself for lunch: alas, we have some business issues to discuss in private. It's been a real pleasure meeting you at last – I hope you will come and stay one time with Bethany and me on our plantation in Louisiana. As a Frenchman I'm sure you'd like to visit the state your countrymen sold for so little over two hundred years ago? I hope you bear us no ill will for that – Napoleon did sell quite willingly, after all!"

Claude gave a modest bow.

"Thank you, Thornton. I'd be delighted to accept your invitation. I hear you have a wonderful stables. I love to ride so a visit to you would not be... a penance – do you say that? A pleasure in fact – and an honour. Once I am in your state I will be keen to *'laissez les bons temps rouler'*. Is that not what you say down in Louisiana?" Claude gave a little chuckle, pleased to demonstrate his limited knowledge of local customs and sayings.

"Heather told me the name of your plantation," he continued. 'Crooked Timber' How could a philosopher resist such a name? 'From the crooked timber of humanity no straight thing was ever built'. So, true. So true!"

"Don't know 'bout that," said Thornton, bemused. "Ain't never heard that saying myself. But when you come down to visit us you'll see the crooked oak out the back. As my ancestors built the house there, they took the name for the plantation."

"Well, let the philosopher's words be an admonition to all of us," added Claude agreeably. "Let us see if we can create our MARION in a less crooked way than humanity has so far managed to achieve for itself! As for your invitation to visit, I thank you, but alas for the next couple of months it will not be possible. My work is done here for the moment and I shall be in Paris. My father is not well and I shouldn't leave him for too long. Then I have the next semester's lectures to prepare. But after that, I would love to accept."

"And is there a Madame Blondel?" asked Thornton.

Claude took a second to reflect on his answer.

"Sometimes I wish there were, Mr Lamaire; the life of a professor is quite solitary. One day, perhaps – but not so far". Thornton was surprised: Claude was a good looking guy. He made a mental note to put him in touch with Stephanie once she had reached Paris.

"In that case what can I say except 'bon voyage'? We'll keep in touch." They shook hands and parted company. But as soon as Thornton was out of sight, Harvey Jennings, the resident machine-psychologist approached the philosopher.

" Mr Blondel – nice to see you again. Do you remember me?" Claude looked the man over. Sixty or so years of age, he guessed, heavily lined face, long greasy hair, dressed in a worn suit. Claude didn't think so.

"Harvey Jennings. One of the psychologists on the team. I'm not surprised that you do not remember me. It's good – much better this way."

Better that I do not recall this man? What does he mean? thought Claude.

"So…what did you think of this morning's meeting?" he asked. It seemed as cautious an opening conversational gambit as any.

"Well, I thought you were right about exposing MARION to a wider range of people," replied Jennings. "I said months ago that relying just on Euclid was inadequate – and possibly dangerous."

"Dangerous?" queried Claude.

"Sure – Euclid's a wonderful guy, but it puts him in too isolated a position as MARION's sole teacher. MARION might try to influence him. We understand so little at this stage. Not like when we were dealing with an octopus!

"You deal a lot with cephalopods?" asked Claude. "I feel sorry for them – the butt of experiments, and a regular dish on the menu. I read recently that the octopus is the most intelligent form of non-human life."

Jennings laughed.

"Ah! Don't feel too sorry for them. Have you ever tried performing experiments with an octopus? They're one of the most rebellious creatures on this planet! You wouldn't choose to work with them unless you had to, I assure you. But you're sure you don't remember meeting me, Monsieur Blondel?"

Claude shook his head, " No, I don't think so," he replied, struck only by the glimmer of a buried memory that he could not properly recall. "I wasn't present at the final octopus trial, so we wouldn't have met then." he explained. Jennings was making him uneasy and he began to fidget.

"I see you need to go, Monsieur Blondel," said Jennings. "It's been a pleasure. Maybe we will meet again...? "

"That would be delightful, Monsieur..." Claude cursed his inability to recall the man's name.

"Just call me Harvey, or Hervé, as I believe you would say in French? Everyone knows me here"

"Of course – Monsieur Hervé. But we will meet each other soon, at least the next time I am here."

Somewhere at the back of Claude's mind he felt sure that he had come across Harvey, or Hervé, somewhere before, even if he couldn't remember the place or time.

" I will look forward to that," said Hervé. "Now, if you will excuse me, I must go and have a chat with Euclid. I have to keep good care of him. Being so close to MARION his mental state is very important."

ELEVEN

Much to Euclid's surprise, and contrary to his previous experience of trying to connect with his 'uncle', that evening he was put straight through. After a few minutes' conversation, the governor sensed his nephew's agitation but he puzzled as to the cause. He knew that Euclid worked in some sensitive area of Thornton's empire, even if he was not sure precisely of his role; but AI, and its consequences for employment in his state, was still a hot political topic that would be an issue at election time; he wished to be up to speed on the latest developments. Something in Euclid's tone signalled that his nephew possessed information that he should be aware of.

"Come on down at the weekend," invited Carroll. "I'm pretty busy but we'll find time to talk. Kirsty and the girls would love to see you, too." It was a white lie – his step-daughters would moan, having little time for Euclid, but it was important to be encouraging. He had no idea that the supposed temptation didn't work for Euclid– who had long ago grown indifferent to the lack of interest auntie Kirsty's daughters had shown in him, (and he now had Maria) – but Euclid wanted something different; his revenge for the damage Thornton was proposing to his intimate relationship with MARION. A few recalcitrant girls were not going to stand in his way.

TWELVE

Thornton opted for one of the executive dining rooms. He considered inviting Xian Han but didn't; it would be impossible to discuss Heather's private life in his presence. The room looked out over a clearing, 'The Glade of Consciousness', the scene of the recent debacle with the delinquent trial robots. Floor-to-ceiling windows gave an uninterrupted view over the glade, curved like a scallop shell. The view was sometimes enriched by a deer making its way across the grass. Twenty years ago that sight would have been almost a certainty; now, less so. After the 'Shanghai Accords' had forced up the price of farm-reared animals most of the deer had found themselves in the sights of hunters. Today, a lone rabbit sat on the grass, munching away contentedly. Even that was a bit of a miracle.

Thornton offered Heather the seat facing the view, "Do you know why this view is so named? He asked. "What it is meant to represent?"

Before Heather had a chance to reply, Thornton explained. "It was the idea of the original architect. Several years ago, when we were drawing up plans for this facility, there was a fashionable theory that consciousness was like a sunlit glade in a wood; all your sensory inputs of a particular event were laid out in the mind, in an open mental space, to be illuminated simultaneously by the light of consciousness. In that instant of perception you were aware: the miracle of being conscious was happening. Outside of the glade in the woods,, beyond the light of consciousness, all is dark – in the subconscious, I suppose. Of course, we've moved on a lot since that time, we have a much better idea of what is consciousness now – but we sometimes use this glade as a place where developments in self-aware technology can be tested."

Heather hoped Thornton would have the grace not to remind her any further of what had occurred there so recently. She wasn't sure whether his restraint was out of gallantry, or simply forgetfulness.

Clarence (for Thornton always wished to be served by his personal butler) approached with the menu. Thornton glanced at it, transferring the image to his iPsyche. Within a second, it had taken readings on his sugar levels and returned with diet recommendations. Making a selection from the list, he focused on Heather.

"Have you given some thought to which bank we might appoint to handle the IPO of LetheTech, next time around, when we try to relaunch it? I think Goldman's may be wary after their last experience. Alternatively, we could issue the equity directly to the market – do it ourselves? Save the fees!"

Heather knew how much Thornton liked to save money. She chose her words carefully.

"We could manage the issue ourselves," she conceded. "But with technology this new – and, in some views, this risky – private investors might shy away from investing in LetheTech if we approached them directly. I think we need the validation that a respected bank would give. But you know that we are at least a year away from this relaunch? We've still got to finish the Phase II trials and it's going to take some time before we've analysed the results to be sure we can manage memory more reliably than we achieved with O'Neal."

Thornton frowned. "A year? That's not what's goin' to happen, Heather. I emphasized at the meeting this morning, you will finish the trials and prepare for the launch of the IPO within six months – maximum. We need to keep up the pace. I hear that CyberSoul is almost there with successful trials. They may release results soon and now Congress is talking about regulation. You know how much we need the cash: I want us to be ready to tap the markets as soon as we can possibly be. So let's just concentrate on those issues – and which bank we might choose if you think we must have one at all."

Heather decided not to argue about timing. She thought the timescale wildly optimistic. And there was another objection.

"Which is?" asked Thornton.

"We're getting feedback from the banks we've talked to so far that they believe investors – particularly corporate ones – won't be thrilled at seeing their money being poured into what they consider the speculation of MARION; they'll want it concentrated on making the memory therapy work and getting that to market. They see MARION as an unnecessary distraction. An indulgence, even."

"Well. That would be inconvenient, would it not?" said Thornton, sarcastically. "We've counted on not having to fund the next level of MARION's development ourselves, at least not very much."

Heather fiddled with a bread roll. "I guess we could load a lot of MARION's overheads and her capital costs onto the LetheTech division. It's pretty opaque anyway how we divide up the cost allocation between the two sides of the business."

"We need the money. If that's what we have to do, so be it," said Thornton. "Give the investors as little information as we can get away with."

In the meantime, Clarence returned with the disappointing news that there was nothing available from the kitchen reasonably in line with Thornton's wishes. They could manage a burger – proper meat, not that synthetic stuff so often offered. Thornton perked up. Was that right? A burger? He checked with his iPsyche: forbidden – all that bread.

Bah! Too bad… a man had to eat something.

"Bring me the burger," he instructed.

So confident had he been of his employer's tastes and indulgences that Clarence had already ordered one. He made a swift trip to the kitchen to collect it and slid the plate before his boss. Thornton dug into the soggy mass, drenched in real meat juices. It had been too long.

"I hear I have to congratulate you, Heather," said Thornton, fortified by having had something to eat.

"About what?" The unspecified nature of Thornton's congratulations made her wary.

"Your engagement! I've heard that you're to re-marry."

"You have good sources, Thornton. Yes – it's true: it was going to happen a few months ago but things are still not settled with Bruno And I wanted to wait until the IPO was launched, so we've decided to delay till next year at least. You must meet my intended the next time you are in New York – he's called Chase by the way"

"Are you planning to divorce Bruno first?"

Heather hesitated. She knew Thornton was a committed church-going man, but she wasn't sure of his views on uncoupling. "No, I'm not going to divorce Bruno... fully – not at the moment, anyway," she said. "I'm fond of him, even if I'll be living with Chase in future. Besides, we live such independent lives. I can see no advantage in a divorce – all that financial mess – when we could simply uncouple."

"The things that people tolerate these days!" exclaimed Thornton, wistfully. "I guess there are many instances of women uncoupling up North these days, right? I've hardly ever heard of it being practiced in the South. I'm not sure it's even legal down where I live."

Heather shook her head.

"Not so many as you might think in the North; it's still a minority taste. But several of my girlfriends have pursued it – you've got to be very rich for a full divorce these days. So few of the men have jobs and the courts make us provide them with an income for life. The courts know they'll probably never be employed again, and other women don't want them either. Then you have to provide a home, so they have somewhere to live. Men expect to be looked after! You're right, I think people were a bit taken aback at first. But, it was the obvious next step in the smorgasbord of personal relationships. Why not have two spouses at the same time? It could be worse. There's a movement up North, as you well know, to allow polygamy – up to four spouses, they say! That's a long way off, perhaps, but people are saying they should be allowed to do that."

"Polygamy? Yeah I heard. Well, for me, even 'uncoupling' is just bigamy made to sound nice," complained Thornton.

"Oh, come, Thornton," cajoled Heather. "You men have been doing that for years, even if you had your wives and girlfriends consecutively! You can't really have one sex having privileges that aren't open to all, can you? Even in your beloved South you have many marriages too – they're just not simultaneous. I thought you might rather approve of uncoupling, being opposed to divorce and all that." Heather smiled. She wanted to be agreeable, if not entirely serious. "I mean, marriage is such a patriarchal institution. It was about time it became more balanced; reflected the needs of both sexes," she continued, wanting to keep the conversation light.

Thornton raised his eyebrows.

"Marriage, patriarchal! You think? I would beg to disagree – always seemed to me that marriage was a very balanced contract, invented to heed the needs of women, just as much as men."

"Oh really? I thought men invented it to ensure that their children had been fathered by themselves. Men are so scared of female sexuality. Men! Always in need of reassurance. men. Always."

"Not just men, I think – women have their concerns too, their need for reassurance," countered Thornton. "They worry that they will be left as they grow older, with their child bearing age behind them. When the threat to men of uncertain paternity will no longer be there as glue. Men may just move onto a younger model, left to themselves – as they do. The traditional insolubility of marriage put a break on that, or at least it used to. So, yes, I am opposed to divorce, and 'uncoupling' and to multiple marriage partners, polygamy – if that ever arrives... Still, I can't imagine why you should want to get married again – but I guess that's your affair. *Six months of fire, thirty years of ashes'* – pretty well sums up my experience of the great institution."

"Oh, Thornton don't be so cynical! Bethany's not that bad. I know you have your problems. But where would you be without her?" asked Heather.

Thornton shrugged. He had a good idea where he would be: with Lu Ann, in all probability. She was warm, available, a widow, not mad, not an alcoholic. But Bethany would fall apart without him – or fall apart even further; he'd taken a vow long ago, and he was going to stick to it.

"No... not all marriages are like mine," agreed Thornton. "I realise that. Well, I wish you well Heather – I do – but let me ask you, is your decision to 'uncouple' rather than divorce, consequent to your losses from the Potomac Metafund scandal?" Potomac was a new type of financial collapse, engineered by a malign conspiracy of rogue AI and quantum computers, that had infected investor's entire portfolios; you only needed a small position in Potomac itself to be wiped out everywhere. Diversification had been no protection.

Heather sighed and nodded. "Apart from the house, I have lost almost everything. I could not afford to divorce Bruno right now."

Thornton tried to be reassuring. "The IPO is coming…in no more than six months' time, as I said. At a minimum. You hold a lot of shares – or at least options – in LetheTech. That should rebuild your wealth."

"Yes, let's hope that IPO goes well. It would be a great help," agreed Heather.

"You and I, we've got some big challenges coming up in the next few months," said Thornton, sympathetically. "The conclusion to the memory trials, the IPO, fending off regulatory attacks in Congress… any one of these could be a problem for us. You need to be concentrated on the job – no distractions, no worrying about Bruno or Chase, or past financial losses."

"I know, I know," said Heather, meeting Thornton's gaze. "You can rely on me."

Thornton didn't seem to hear. "The last problem, regulation, particularly worries me. Congress might do almost anything. Memory therapy may be pretty well unregulated at the moment, but in six months? A year? Some of the guys in Washington are beginning to wake up about the whole thing."

"You could ship the MARION project down to the South, out of Federal reach, if regulation got too heavy?" suggested Heather. She imagined this would always be Thornton's strategy if things became too hot up North.

"I could do. But it wouldn't solve things," said Thornton. "Firstly, we're going to be operating all over North America, all over the world, if everything goes well. The Federal government still has considerable reach, even if its writ is not much followed outside the Coastal States. And it's respected : other governments overseas will follow the North's lead."

"Secondly, there's a lot of conservative and religious feeling in the South that does not take kindly to what we are trying to do with MARION. Moving to the South would solve nothing – it would almost certainly make our problems worse. Besides, we'd lose half our staff. Who's going to swap New York for Baton Rouge? Not Xian Han, that's for sure!"

Thornton paused as Clarence arrived with the coffee. His passing mention of Xian Han rekindled a nagging worry.

"Is Han okay?" he asked. "He came over distracted today, I thought. These should be good times for Xian. All his ideas are coming to fruition... Sometimes he makes me feel uneasy. I can't tell where he's at, like... what he's thinking?"

"You have to make allowances," said Heather. "Han's marked by the loss of his first home. He was happy in China, before his parents took it into their heads to try and make it a liberal democracy. He had a load of friends, he was doing well at school – then suddenly, they were forced to flee and the family had to make a new life in the US. He barely spoke English when he arrived, he was bullied at school, he's never really come out of his shell... But yes, he's okay – he's loyal."

"I hope so", said Thornton. "We can't afford to have him getting fantasies about machines like MARION running rogue. I've promised him we're going to investigate every manner possible method of control over the technology – restraints will be put in place. He shouldn't worry so much." Thornton decided to reinforce the view he'd taken earlier.

"I don't know why we just don't make the job simple, as I said; programme the Ten Commandments into MARION! Good enough for me, good enough for humanity these past two thousand years – what's the problem with that?"

"Not much wrong with that," replied Heather, sensing that she had better go with the grain if she wanted to exercise any influence on Thornton's decisions. "Except that Christ did not have to contemplate how artificial and human minds might interact. We might need a bit more than the Ten Commandments.".

Thornton shook his head, "Well, if control is such a big deal what about your French friend – Blondel? I asked him to help. He's probably the best equipped of any of us to think about those sorts of issues. Maybe I should talk to governor Gillespie too? This is sort of his field – he's a man of God, or he has been, at least."

Heather had met the governor once and there was no way she wanted his Old Testament views anywhere near MARION. She reckoned it an idle threat to get him involved anyway; Thornton was well aware of the governor's views on robotics. "Gillespie would have a heart attack if he knew what we were doing with MARION – or LetheTech," she said. "I'll talk to Claude, we'll come up with something. He's been very useful so far. There's no way we could have finished the programming for mimicking consciousness without him. He had some great insights that were fundamental."

"Like?"

"Like... that our concept of consciousness is tied up with the physical experience of being human. There can be no such thing as a disembodied consciousness – no conscious brains floating-around-in-a-warm-jar, that sort of Sci-Fi fantasy. As he explained this morning, our consciousness is built to reflect our lived in experience: we have to be part of the world in order to be conscious – that's how we gain our identity, our sense of 'I'. It was Claude who came up with the idea of connecting MARION to an individual so she could experience what is to be a human through their senses – that's how Euclid was chosen in the first place.

"He's in a very powerful position, our Euclid," said Thornton. "So privileged to be selected to act as MARION's source. You'd better keep tracks on him."

"It works both ways," said Heather, skipping the point about Euclid's loyalty. "Have you considered that there is a danger for Euclid too? He'll be dealing with a very powerful mind."

But Thornton's concentration had already shifted.

"Do you think the very speed at which we're advancing with MARION is something Han's worried about?" he asked.

"Yes," replied Heather without hesitation. "He's worried we're are not ready – not mature enough to act as parents to MARION. He takes a look at what's going on in..." Heather paused, looking for an example and found one that she knew was close to Thornton's heart. "Han reads about New Chaldea, for example, and asks himself how new powers and old ways of thinking are going to collide; how questions of territory, super-power supremacy and religion are all being fought out – and he wonders if we have advanced very much. Are we ready to handle a new being – like us – but not quite *us*? We discovered nuclear fission and we used it to build bombs."

Thornton shrugged; there was no definitive answer, no ultimate reassurance he could give. But equally, Han was not paid to concern himself about these political issues, nor to bring his personal philosophy into the lab and affect his work on MARION. New Chaldea was way out of his orbit, at least in the work place; a strict boundary would have to be enforced.

Han was a genius, that much was clear, his Han Translation had made all the rest of their work possible, but the next stage of development should be more straightforward: he was no longer irreplaceable.

The conversation dropped. Thornton rose as Clarence pulled back his chair.

"Well, my dear Heather, I need to be getting back to New York – I've got a dinner there. Then I'll be home at Crooked Timber tomorrow. Can't wait – always feel a little out of my natural environment when I'm up here!"

"Missing your gumbo and fried green tomatoes?"

"Something like that; you should get Clarence to make you some of his gumbo. Let's speak again in a few days when you're back in New York. I want to be updated regularly on progress. The human trials, the IPO – it's all coming to a head. Within six months, do you hear? No mistakes, no leaks. You have my complete trust. And good luck with Chase – even if I don't quite approve. Hope the other one isn't too upset."

"It'll all be fine. No worries there," said Heather.

"Good. You'll have enough on your plate without domestic distractions." Thornton consulted his iPsyche. He was scheduled to fly back to New York in twenty minutes – but first, he would find Han and reinforce his good work with a large bonus. Han might not be indispensable, but while he was on the team he needed to be kept happy.

Thornton walked over to the picture window and gazed out. He felt hemmed in here by the endless forest; he thought of the next two days of business talks in New York, cooped up in offices, made him feel even more claustrophobic. He'd be glad to be back at Crooked Timber, though sad to miss Stephanie. He wondered what she was up to, how the discussions with the editors in Houston and Tampa had gone. He could call her, but he hesitated to intrude on his children's lives. Like most fathers, he assumed they had such busy and interesting lives that they wouldn't have the time to talk to him. In this assumption, he was usually wrong.

THIRTEEN

Since leaving Crooked Timber, Stephanie had met the editors she would be dealing with from Paris. TrueNews had promised to take her articles regularly, Clear and Present Times on an adhoc basis. From there she'd continued north, to stay with friends in Rye. Now, two weeks later, she felt the need for solitude, to meditate on her break up with George and what Paris might hold. It was a beautiful warm day, a perfect day to be on one's own by the ocean.

As she drove down I-495 in her rental, her mind turned to her now ex-boyfriend. Each time a lover departed, a piece of herself fell away. The piece grew back but with age she noticed that recovery from the wound drained more of her energy and took longer to heal. How successful and sought after would be her father's LetheTech service, once it became available! How humane a way to remove the memory of a displaced loved one! Life, and love would be so much easier. Meanwhile, she had written George a sympathetic email that she hoped would mitigate his pain. He would make a good long term friend, if he would accept her on that basis, but his pride would probably get in the way. She had read that asking a discarded lover to be a 'friend' was the worst insult. Was that true? It seemed a very practical option to her.

Stephanie sighed; exasperated with the world for not shaping itself according to her wishes – and with the folly of men who allowed their romantic inclinations lead them into cul-de-sacs of emotion that did them no good. Yet, she did understand that her presence might not allow George to 'move on'. If he didn't want to be her friend there was not much she could do about it.

The car park was almost empty, with no sign of the attendant. Risking his sudden appearance, she drove straight across the tarmac towards a cleared piece of scrub that was virtually on the dunes. About to swing her legs out of the car the attendant appeared. Stephanie looked at him quizzically, already resenting the fact that he was going to tell her to move.

"I can just tell you're going to ruin my morning," she teased him. Her tone held no rancour.

"I hope not 'mam," the man protested. "But if you could just park where you ought, that would be mighty obliging of you."

Stephanie gave him a narrow glance, as if to infer that she had never been quite so put upon in all her life. "Sure, that would be no problem at all." She spun the wheels and drove the few yards to the official car park.

The sand between her toes foretold of the pleasures of summer to come, but not yet offering much warmth. She strode past the first set of chilled sunbathers, huddled together, seeking protection from the breeze. Ahead, she spotted a hollow in the dunes, laid her towel down in its shallow depression and contemplated a swim. The unsettled spring, much cooler than down South, would not have warmed the sea yet. Best to get a quick dip over with. She tied her dark hair into a top-knot and dived into the first breaker. Once immersed she didn't stay long; she disliked being bounced around in the surf, unable to swim as freely as she preferred. Later in the year, she would have struck out beyond the breakers into the quieter water.

At least the sand had been warmed by the reticent sun. Its welcome rose up and percolated through her towel, like Roman central heating. She settled back to commence her morning meditation. The mantra came swiftly but the peace that she expected did not follow. Instead, something else arrived unbidden, something she had not sought, a sense of frustration and disquiet. She had forgotten that in the depths of meditation things lay hidden that were not always beautiful, nor welcome.

As if to remind herself why she was this way, she rubbed the stubs of the fingers on her right hand. Then she reached down and felt the horizontal scar below her belly. 'Written on skin' she remembered as the title of something. A short story? An opera? The phrase resonated, with the physical traces of those ancient traumas that still infected her psyche. She knew the causes of these marks and injuries, and yet the recognition did not seem to give her release. Nor many years of therapy. Oh, if only all this old baggage could be removed! Would she avail herself of LetheTech's service if it ever worked safely? She had contemplated often enough the fantasy of excision of memory since her father told her of its development but now that the treatment was on the horizon, she became less sure. She reached into her tote, pulled out an A4 note book and opened her journal.

She had thought writing things down, hoping that exposing her experience to light might make the old memories evaporate. They hadn't done so yet but she would keep going. She found the last words she had written, 'I was very comfortable on the sofa but this sounded like an adventure. "OK," I agreed.' It took her a few moments to recollect what those words were about. They prompted uncomfortable reminiscences that discouraged her from delving into her mind any further.

The breeze began to pick up. Stephanie put down her pen, folded her journal and put on a sweater. She wondered about returning to the car but she was at peace here and there was nothing much else to do this morning.

Her mind moved on to the text her father had sent her the night before. From the polling data of last week, it looked as though Carroll Gillespie would lose the plebiscite, but only by a small margin. It would always be a challenge, as a super-majority, 75% of the vote, was needed for approval. Not everyone voted electronically; many older voters distrusted the system and still submitted postal votes that would be counted overnight. But the full results should be available by now. She pulled her phone out of her bag and called up the TrueNews site. It was the headline story. Her assumptions about the likely result had been mistaken:

US DIVIDED FOR SECOND TIME IN HISTORY. VOTERS OPT FOR SEPARATION. PRESIDENT-ELECT FOR THE SOUTHERN CONFEDERACY SAYS: "NOW WE CAN BE TRUE TO OURSELVES AND TO GOD."

'In a decisive poll, the plebiscite to allow eleven southern states (Texas, Louisiana etc) to secede from the Union has been approved by voters. The final vote cleared the 75% threshold required by the Constitution, with 115 districts voting for and only 16 against. This is the first time the nation has been divided since the civil war. The referendum must now be ratified by representatives from all the Southern states. If they support the result of the plebiscite, as seems likely, then terms of the secession must be negotiated with the Federal government over the coming year. They are likely to take effect at the end of 2041.

The result was determined on the aggregate vote. Individual state counts have not yet been made available but it is rumoured that at least in North Carolina there was no majority for separation. However, following an earlier accord, the Southern states had formed themselves into a block (the 'Southern Caucus') and each state in the Caucus will be bound by the overall result.

Yesterday's result was unexpected. Right up until the final tally, it was predicted that the 'No' vote would prevail. Polls had leant in the direction of maintaining the existing Union structure but there was always a level of volatility in the public mind.

After the final count was made known the Governor of Louisiana and President-elect of the New Confederation, Carroll Gillespie, said;

"This is a great day for the South and for those who love the Lord. It is a great day for those brave states that have joined us in this journey. No longer will we have to submit to laws that are alien to our traditions and to God. The people have spoken and they have spoken clearly."

"Let me assure all Americans, and I mean all Americans, not just those who live in the South, that despite today's vote we are, still, all bound by a common Constitution and faith in the wisdom of the Founding Fathers. We will continue to act together on many matters of mutual interest. Separate development does not mean we fail to be brothers. The vote today is not a hostile act against those who do not follow our beliefs."

"But the freedom to pursue the life that each of us finds righteous is a divine right. Recognizing that right, as this vote does, will enable each of us to live in harmony without resenting the action of our neighbour. This is not a sad day for our country, it is an opportunity for its different parts to flourish, to go forward to their chosen destinations. The conflicts that have divided us over the last few years have disappeared today."

In Washington, The President of the hitherto United States stated, "We will of course respect this vote. The People of the South have spoken clearly. I had hoped the result would be otherwise. I also hope, as governor Gillespie has said, that both sides can live in harmony together. I have always considered that separation was not needed.. That has proved impossible but our work to find a way to live together does not end today. We share a history and a common belief in the exceptionalism of this great nation. We will, all of us, go forward in a spirit of being Americans, even if our routes diverge on some matters. The President-elect of the Southern Confederation has already assured me that the Southern Caucus will follow the Constitution and that he will consult with us where we have interests in common..."

Stephanie tried to phone her father but he failed to pick up. They had discussed the plebiscite many times before but that was all theoretical. Now there would be a new political settlement, and one that would probably not be in her father's interests. She noted the actual date of secession was still two years away; two years of squabble between the North and South. During that period the Southern government was not meant to make any legislative changes and should continue to respect the authority of the Federal government. The reality would be different. Existing laws would be interpreted to please Carroll and his cronies. Executive orders would be issued, that required no legislative backing, to institute changes they had long sought. In practice, there would be few restraints on Carroll Gillespie's power, apart from the Constitution, which his party had promised to respect. Even that would now be viewed through the lens of sympathetic Southern courts.

When Thornton did return his daughter's call thirty minutes later, he spoke about his concerns for not only himself and his involvement with the MARION project, but also for some of Blue Ridge's industries in the South. It was not just the manufacture of the latest AI inspired robots that were now imperilled, his plants employed many old model robots in traditional industries, like shipbuilding, and modern ones such as aeronautics and space. Carroll had made it clear during the campaign he would refuse to grant state contracts where he considered there was 'excessive' use of robots or the robots employed were too close to 'divine purpose' – whatever that was. Thornton guessed: any robot whose skills and mental aptitudes mimicked those of humans. MARION would be way outside what was permitted if Gillespie got his way.

That was just the likely future of industrial policy. They would also see a more aggressive stance on Carroll's pet hobby horse of New Chaldea. So far the Federal government had suppressed his fervour. There had been little support for intervention, official or otherwise. Well, that would change…

Carroll might have to wait till secession took effect before committing Southern military support. But behind the scenes there would be an increase in clandestine operations – and nobody was likely to stand in his way. What could Washington do about it now, however much they disapproved?

There was no upside for Thornton or Blue Ridge in this secession. Her father would try to manage things so they didn't fall foul of Carroll too often. He needed the cash-flow from his Southern industries; he couldn't afford to see that upset, just as they were ramping up LetheTech. 'Cash needs will be a hostage to fortune in this new set-up,' Thornton explained to her. "Things are going to be tougher for us. No question. I wish I could come to Paris with you! Much more fun." But 'Lack of fun' seemed unlikely to be his largest problem going forward. Stephanie said her father would always be welcome to visit her in Paris, but thought privately 'provided you don't bring mother.'

On the Monday morning Stephanie flew to Paris to start her new life, armed with her contracts and the names of several friends she had made over the years, together with a few contacts her father had given her, including, of course, that of Claude Blondel.

PART II

FOURTEEN

A few days after the meeting, Thornton flew down to Baton Rouge, accompanied by Clarence. Thornton's limousine awaited them. In line with tradition, Clarence sat in the front – where the chauffeur had once been required – and Thornton took his seat in the back. Tradition was tempered by friendship, and he felt the pressure to make conversation. During their flight down, Thornton had already discussed most topics of mutual interest: the progress of the New Orleans Saints; domestic staff issues; what Elizabeth might have been up to the night she borrowed his car... His iPsyche helpfully suggested some additional subjects but they sounded at once contrived and not interesting enough to pursue. Luckily, the drive from the airfield to the plantation wasn't far. After a few attempts at light conversation, Thornton chose to concentrate on reading the news, piped into his consciousness via the iPsyche. Elizabeth -One minute he would be ignorant of the latest developments in New Chaldea; the next, he would understand what was happening there as though he'd known it all his life. The effect played with his sense of time. But the device had made life so much easier – just think and it was done. So quick, so easy, so simple. Soon everyone would have one.

He wondered if there would be trouble at the gates, but as they turned into the drive he was relieved to see the campers weren't blocking the way, nor hastening forward to beat on the car windows, as they'd done in the past. Today, they hung back, sullen and vacant, no doubt wondering why, in such a large vehicle, one person sat in the front and one in the back.

A imposing sign read 'Crooked Timber Plantation': underneath, in smaller letters, 'Home of the Louisiana Foundation for Retired Afro-American Artisans.' This had been Bethany's project. All Thornton could see of retired Afro-American artisans was old Francis, sitting on the porch of the converted barn where the artisans had been intended to end their days in relative comfort. The foundation may not have been much use to impoverished Afro-Americans but it had been an excellent tax shelter.

The following day, Thornton travelled to New Orleans for a meeting with his lawyer. He arrived at the town house early; Bethany would follow along later, once she was up. She liked to come into town and see her girlfriends, and, if there were enough of them around, *laissez les bons temps rouler*. Thornton was about to start work when he heard a car pull up. Nobody had been mentioned on the agenda that day; his lawyer was not expected until the afternoon, and a brief inquiry to his iPsyche revealed no late additions. At this time of day there were always various callers, some delivering for the household, some for Bethany if she was there, so he noted the disturbance without much attention and got out his papers: although he could read mails and documents directly on his iPsyche, he often printed documents to enjoy a more leisurely read. He was too old now to drop his habit, and he had an excuse provided by the poor air-conditioning: his sweat interfered with iPsyche transmission and downloading. He promised himself he would to move on to the subcutaneous version once it was available, which would avoid connection problems, but he was in no hurry.

There was a long mail from Xian Han, setting out the timing and protocols for Phase III trials, as well as some reflections on the results of earlier trials. Thornton hadn't appreciated that, in addition to the limited experiments on volunteer clients, like O'Neal, there had also been a number of memory modifications carried out on members of Han's team; he noted with surprise that Claude Blondel had been amongst them. Why had Claude wanted to experiment with memory deletion?

During these early trials Xian had chosen not to make any permanent changes to the mind of the volunteers; only to enter the shallows of memory, remove minor recollections that could later be reinstated – like childhood holiday memories, things that could be checked against verifiable histories, evidence that the deciphering of synaptic recording in the bran had been accurately calibrated. So much for that hope! Thornton wondered if the O'Neal disaster might come back to haunt not just LetheTech, but Blue Ridge as a whole. If there were suits for damages, Blue Ridge was sure to be named; it was much better capitalized than LetheTech. Blue Ridge had to be protected: that was heritage, the family asset that had been passed to him in trust. He did not want to be found unworthy.

A few moments later, Clarence knocked on the door and announced Carroll Gillespie, who had turned up requesting an audience. Strange, mused Thornton. A governor's assistant would normally book such a meeting days ahead.

"Show the governor into the Blue Room would you, Clarence?" he asked.

He wondered if Gillespie would admire his art collection, themed around the colour blue, even if the collection had now moved way beyond that. He glanced at 'Nu Couche Bleu' by Nicholas de Staël; maybe he should have covered that up? Well, too late now – and for Heaven's sake, even if Carroll had been a man of God once, he was an adult.

Thornton was irritated by this uninvited and unplanned visit. Gillespie was unlikely to have appeared simply because he was at a loose end that morning. Sometimes, Thornton didn't discover the governor's agenda until long after he had let slip a fact or an opinion that seemed unimportant at the time. Yet to Gillespie, the information would always turn out to have been a vital brick in some policy he was building, unbeknownst to Thornton.

Thornton put his iPsyche on silent.

FIFTEEN

The governor was already seated with a cup of coffee when Thornton reached the Blue Room. Dressed in his regular steel-grey suit, and a narrow, black leather, lace tie. Carroll Gillespie emanated his usual air of implacability.

"I wasn't sure whether I'd catch you, Thornton," he said, placing his cup on the side table. "I didn't know when you would get back from New York."

Thornton was sure the governor knew his comings and goings precisely; Gillespie would have been informed the very moment he'd landed.

"I have to come into town for a trial that opens later today," said the governor. "As my route took me near you I thought I'd call in and say 'howdy'; and Kirsty instructed me to ask you and Bethany for brunch after chapel on Sunday. Besides," Carroll continued. "There are one or two things I wanted to discuss with you. Didn't want to bore the girls with state talk at lunch."

"Of course," said Thornton, still no clearer. "Bethany is not here yet; she would have been delighted to see you. She'll be in town later. Always likes to hear the latest political talk – you know how impassioned she gets."

The governor waved the idea away; it was just as well Bethany was not here, he only had a little time. God's work had to be done, and he didn't want to get into a three-way discussion with Bethany either. But that, as a tactful man, was not what he said.

"I have to be in court by two," Gillespie explained. "Well, that's not strictly accurate – I don't have to be in court, but... I think I should be."

"I rely on you on to keep me abreast of local matters, Carroll," said Thornton amiably. His tone lacked flattery. It was true the governor was much better informed than he about local matters, particularly as the affairs of LetheTech and MARION were all-consuming, and distracted him from paying much attention to what he judged parochial issues. "But what's this court case about, that requires your personal attention? Must be something pretty important to do that."

The governor brushed some invisible dust off his trousers.

"Nobody has done anything much worse than we're used to down here," he said. "We've got an act of arson and attempted murder on our hands; that's not in doubt, but the four defendants are arguing they acted as they did because they believed the victim was a witch. Now normally, they wouldn't get far saying things like that – belief in witchcraft is not a recognised defence. But as you know, Thornton, these are not entirely normal times, and there's a move in the state Senate to push through a bill making witchcraft a punishable offense."

"Really? Witchcraft?" exclaimed Thornton. "People are believing in witchcraft now? Do you have to follow them? You are going to support this bill?" Thornton looked at the governor with incredulity.

"Of course it's nonsense, this belief," replied Carroll, sidestepping Thornton's question before reflecting that he couldn't completely evade something put to him so directly. "But the bill before the Senate? It's not entirely up to me, Thornton. There's pressure for this; many people want it. I am in office only to serve the voters' wishes."

"But you can veto it, when the bill – if the bill, comes to you for signature?" said Thornton.

The governor twisted uncomfortably. Of course he could veto the bill – but at the back of his mind he didn't want to. His position was not entirely secure. The leader of the campaign for the New Confederacy still needed to be confirmed as president-elect. Superstition might come in useful; there were a lot of ungodly ideas in the North that to many sounded awfully close to witchcraft, practices far removed from God's plan for man. Maybe witchcraft was in the eye of the beholder – but the beholders also happened to be his electorate: the proposed law could not be dismissed as easily as Thornton believed.

Fiddling around with people's memories, for example. He'd heard what Thornton was up to, if his sources were accurate.

"I'm a God fearing man, Thornton; so are you," affirmed Carroll, as though the latter might be in doubt. "Some things going on up North suggest the work of the Devil, especially to the good people down here. Who am I to say they are wrong? Folk draw a straight line between what they hear being practiced these days and the state of this world, and they sure don't like much of what they see. The inventions of man have not brought them any great happiness recently. Some of them think we've been paying too little heed to the ways of our Lord and that we have brought the consequences on ourselves."

"Things are tough, I realise, but have we regressed so much? Have we come this far? Witchcraft?" repeated Thornton. "We're not living in medieval times."

Gillespie hesitated. "It's all very well for you to talk that way, Thornton, but you know the suffering that's been going on. Folks are saying that there are forces at work, forces they don't like; and that certain men – maybe women too – are behind them."

"So this is that what's happening here … at this trial you're going to observe?" asked Thornton.

The governor stood up and walked over to the window. He gazed out as he began to speak.

"There was a woman, a very poor woman, living with her three children. The usual thing – husband had lost his job and left, trying his luck somewhere else. She never heard from him again. Then one of the children falls ill, I'm not sure with what – starts moaning, having fits. The woman can't afford drugs or a doctor. But one day she's out walking in the hills, visiting one of the springs up there.

Wants a swim – I don't know why – maybe she's hot or something. Anyway she has a vision, the Virgin Mary appears and tells her 'bring your son to this spring, bathe him three times, at sunrise, noon and sunset.' So she does this as instructed, and a miracle happens; the son overcomes his fever – he's cured. But this woman is not only pious, she's smart. She sees not just a holy site but a business opportunity.

"She sets up a shrine at the spring, charges a few dollars for ill folks to bathe, three times a day mind you, anything less won't work, and she prices per dip. Did I say she was smart? She sells the pilgrims food, drinks, trinkets and so on. Soon enough, she became quite a rich woman, at least by the standards around here. One day, someone brings his son to be cured. Except the spring doesn't work this time. The woman says 'let's try it again – you evidently didn't bring enough faith to the lady of the spring'. So, the guy pays again and tries once more. There's a small improvement and she says, 'See, the spring is beginning to work. You need to keep goin'. There's a bit more paying and bathing but instead of getting better, the boy starts to get worse. There's some suspicion now that he's picked up an infection from the waters. The father sees red, as he's spent all this money and his son is more poorly than he was at the start. He goes back to his folk and tells the story – really whips up some indignation. Soon, they're so angry they come along to burn down the shrine and the poor woman's home too. She's lucky to escape with her life. That's what lands them in the sheriff's jail."

"At which point they accuse the woman of witchcraft?"

"They do indeed. This bunch of hillbillies say the vision the woman saw was not the Madonna but the Devil and the spring only works for those who worship him. Being good God-fearing folk, they only irritated the Devil with their pious ways – and that's why their son got worse. In their view, they've done the state a service: they need not only be found innocent, but that the woman should be found guilty of consorting with the Devil and practicing witchcraft."

"Except there's no statute against witchcraft."

"But maybe there should be. At least that's the suggestion."

"The poor woman must have suffered enough. Are the supporters of this bill proposing the... traditional punishments for witchcraft, then. Burning people at the stake, pressing? Things like that?"

The governor raised both hands in horror. "Heavens above, Thornton! Burning at the stake? Nobody is suggesting such a thing! Of course not; a modest fine perhaps, a short prison sentence. Just something to discourage the practice."

"You make it sound as though we've already accepted witchcraft's existence and now it's just a matter of determining the appropriate penalty?"

The governor pushed out his bottom lip and raised his eyebrows, as if to say, 'well, there you are – that's how we live now. What can I do?' Except there was an inauthenticity about the expression. Thornton knew the governor could, and would, do anything he liked. He was quite capable of facing down transient public opinion if it suited him.

"We live in a democracy, Thornton. I have to pay some respect to what the voters want."

"But you don't have to follow all their absurd beliefs, do you? You don't have to support them as they regress into the Middle Ages! We've made progress, we understand how things work; we live in an age of science and rationalism. Surely we don't have to revert to a belief in the supernatural?"

"Understand how things work?' Do we, indeed?" retorted the governor with some vehemence. "There are a lot of people down here, Thornton, who'd argue with you on that one. For all your 'rationality,' and science, we've ended up with a split nation and half the country living in poverty. Now that half, they're mostly down here, or in the mid-west, and they're thinking 'what exactly have we done to deserve this?' They see all sorts of strange developments around them; machines they are told to respect and be nice to, and other weird things – 'Memory therapy', for example – did I hear that right? What exactly is that? Some folk think we are meddling in things that are best left to Him. You talk of superstition: what is 'witchcraft' but an attempt to explain the world when things go wrong for no good reason? Folks are scared, Thornton!. The world they knew has collapsed, and the reasons for that are not clear. Witchcraft is just a name they give to what they fear and there seems much to fear at the moment."

"But even so..."

"But even so, even so..." Carroll repeated derisively. "There is no 'even so', Thornton! There's an anger afoot that will find its outlet in all sorts of unpleasant ways – ways you will not like and maybe I won't like either – but it's coming. You sit in the security of your plantation, and you understand nothing about the mood outside. Or you're flying up to the North, doing God knows what in those laboratories of yours. You're walking a dangerous road, my friend! You condemn folks for playing around with forces they don't understand – but what are you doing Thornton? Huh? From what I hear you're undertaking some pretty strange experiments in your place in the Catskills – all hidden away an' all. If it's so straightforward why aren't you bringing that work down here? God knows, we could do with the employment!"

Thornton bit his tongue, he would need political cover from the vengeance of those Southerners, who would rally against him if they discovered what was being developed up North. There were a dozen practical reasons why neither MARION nor LetheTech could be sited in Louisiana but one reason stood out – and Carroll Gillespie had just confirmed it. Thornton knew that their work would come under a scrutiny down here that was absent in upstate New York. Many people in the South believed he was financing something sacrilegious, abusing God-given powers, mimicking the act of creation that had given birth to Adam and Eve. If everything was revealed he would probably get away with a fine and a court order to shut down or to divest himself from the MARION project – but he didn't want to give up on MARION. Of course, he could move up North to supervise the researches but he was too old, too set in his ways now – too fond of the South and the Crooked Timber plantation to live anywhere else. Luckily, things had not yet got so bad that flying north was an act of treason; many of his fellow tycoons still made the same trip after all.

But he understood that one day, questions would be asked about the purpose of his trips, about what exactly the Blue Ridge Corporation was doing up there, and what so needed to be hidden up there – and the true reason for that might come to light.

Before Thornton had worked out how to respond, the governor jumped back in.

"You need to be careful Thornton. There are those down here who believe you are fiddling around with people's minds; and that's not right, maybe you're messing with souls. I'm just saying, I don't necessarily support them – but I would be careful; most of Blue Ridge's factories are down in the South. Neither of us would want anything to happen to the Corporation. It employs too many people here, even if that's a lot less than it used to be. But people get riled, and I'm just a governor, Thornton… at the moment. I may not be able to protect you – forever!"

Thornton had counted Carrol as a friend since boyhood, but however long their friendship might have been it would not be enough to divert a prosecution. Carroll liked power, and he wasn't going to sacrifice it on the grounds of long acquaintance. 'Greater love hath no man than to lay down his friends for his life' – that would be Carroll's epitaph, carved on his headstone.

The governor allowed his words to hang, "I must be on my way, Thornton. Sorry to have missed Bethany. Please give her my regards." And with that he shook Thornton by the hand, turned on his heel and walked to the door. He had almost reached it when he turned and faced the painting 'Nu Couche Bleu'. "What's that"? he said.

"That's a famous painting by the French artist Nicolas de Stael. He's long dead" (Thornton thought that if this artist was dead this might make the painting less objectionable in some way) I've just bought it. Do you like it?"

"Like it? It's an abomination, Thornton," said the governor. " I don't hold with naked women in public, art or not."

"It's only her back," said Thornton, defensively.

"I don't care. It's not right. Putting them things up – it's the sort of attitude I'm warning you about, Thornton. We' been friends a long time, but you got to be conscious now about how things are changing down here!" Then – smiling, emollient – Carroll relaxed, keen to leave on a friendly note.

"You take care of yourself now Thornton, you hear me? Don't give folks an excuse."

What folks needed an excuse for was not spelt out but Thornton got the idea.

As the governor left, Thornton let out a breath of relief. An allegation of witchcraft! In some ways, he found this regression to superstition unsurprising, but it shocked him nonetheless. There had always been an anti-science bias in the South, starting with antagonism towards the theory of evolution, running through the opposition to climate change. There had long been an undercurrent of anti AI feeling, enhanced by the resentment surrounding Douglas versus Milton Robotics. No longer an undercurrent, the discontent was now out in the open.

SIXTEEN

By 10 am on Sunday, Thornton and Bethany Lamaire had taken their places in the family pew. Conscious that an address by Governor Carroll Gillespie would be a big draw, the family had issued as many invitations as capacity permitted; few would want to miss the governor's words. They had left the house in plenty of time...

Whenever the weather allowed, Thornton rode in the phaeton to morning worship. His love of being transported by horse, – whether in the saddle or on wheels behind them – was his counter to an automated and robotic world. He would have preferred the lighter curricle, but Bethany had insisted on the security of two axles, four wheels, and the calmest horses they could find in the stables; if she had to travel by such ridiculous means, she wanted the vehicle to approximate the familiarity of a car.

Thornton looked around him, nodding to neighbours who caught his eye and wondering if Lu Ann would come. Not knowing gave the morning a piquancy that a regular service might have lacked. Lu Ann was not a religious person, nor given to attending Sunday service regularly; but would she ignore a personal invitation from himself? She would want to hear the governor too. Thornton reflected that these feelings were inappropriate and focused his attention towards the altar, just in case anyone suspected that his mind was not on the Lord. Trivial anxieties trotted through his brain. The temperature was insufferable. He turned his eyes heavenwards until he felt his brow beginning to crinkle. In this heat, the withered beams above his head, installed about the time of the Civil War, would soon begin to shed the bugs that made their homes in the timber.

"Hail Mary, full of grace…" intoned the Reverend. Determined to make a better effort at prayer, Thornton wrapped his fingers around the wooden rail of the pew in front. He relished the coolness of the varnish as his fingers slid back and forth, lubricated by a thin sheen of sweat. For a minute or two, he managed to bring his focus to prayer. But his mind soon began to wander again, unsettled by the trickle of sweat inching its way down his spine. He spotted something crawling along the rail; a small insect that unwisely entered his orbit. He put his thumb over it and pressed.

'…He prayeth well, who loveth well, both man and bird and beast…'

Did bugs count as beasts? He realised he had never been very good at prayer. This would never do! If he was going to pray he must do it properly. He dropped onto the upholstered prie-dieu. There were two sharp cracks as the cartilage in his knees stretched to an unfamiliar angle. He managed a short, silent, prayer. Surely God would redeem him when He saw what His servant had achieved? Was that not His promise, to redeem those who asked? MARION might not reverse the Fall, but Adam's descendants would soon possess something almost as precious as a return to the Garden – an intelligence immune from the ills of humanity, to their own mental weakness and turbulence. Thornton mopped his brow. Perhaps it would be better if he pleaded for someone else other than himself; Bethany maybe… He asked the Almighty that she be aided in her fight. Thornton had prayed on that theme before, and God did not appear any more inclined to heed the appeal than he chose to reveal His thoughts about AI. Thornton was not surprised by this lack of divine intervention. Had he not, in achieving great wealth, given too much attention to things of the earth, and too little to matters of the spirit? Had he not pursued wealth and power and ignored the spiritual welfare of his family? If he had been more caring what had happened to Stephanie might have been avoided…

But he didn't want to think about all that disaster with his daughter. As his therapist said, what you think about is a matter of choice. Well, he would make a different choice. Thornton shook his head, recalling Faust's desperate cry as he hurtled towards damnation; 'See how Christ's blood streams in the firmament, one drop of which enough to redeem my soul'. One drop did not seem to be any more forthcoming to Thornton than to Faust.

He rose from the prie-dieu and rubbed his hands again along the contours of the rail. The sensation brought him back to the present and he looked over hoping to spy Lu Ann – but his gaze came to rest instead on Carroll Gillespie, just as he began to speak.

Transcript of Governor Carroll Gillespie's sermon, published on diocesan web sites throughout the State of Louisiana.

"Good morning my brothers and sisters and bless you all, on this very fine – if very hot – Sunday. I do hope that many of you will be able to stay with me, however much you may be tempted to seek the relief of your air-conditioned homes and cars.

[laughter]

Now I know that the excellent Reverend, with whom you are blessed, was originally going to speak to you today – but I asked him to stand aside this morning and he has graciously agreed.

I asked him to do so because there are some issues, of unusual importance, facing our community; as part of my old responsibilities as Bishop, I learnt to cherish your spiritual welfare – and the practice dies hard! I would not be fulfilling my responsibility if I did not discuss with you the matters that now confront us and on which we have recently voted, in the plebescite.

Each one of you will be asking yourselves,' what now? What now – now that we, and our Northern brothers are to go our separate ways? Where will God guide us in these new circumstances?' For there are perils before us that threaten the stability of this great nation and the precious inheritance left to us by the Founding Fathers.

I have prayed long and hard. For some weeks no hint of God's divine purpose settled on me; and then one day, in an act of grace, a voice spoke and pointed me to the story of Exodus

I took down my bible and as I re-read the flight of the Israelites I tried to discover the lesson in that great story. For it surely wasn't how to deal with plagues of locusts or toads – even though our recent climate might make both pestilences seem highly probable these days.

[laughter]

Nor did the story seem an instruction for parting turbulent seas – although after last year's hurricane season that might have been useful too...

[laughter]

No – Exodus is about a search; a search for a promised land, a land that had been promised to the Jews as their homeland, after they have been denied it for generations.

My brothers and sisters, are were so different from those Israelites – fleeing a Union where our ways have found no welcome? Have we Southerners ever been granted equal partnership in the Federation? Have we once benefited from the changes that have been afoot these last few decades? I say to you that we have not.

But now the Lord has delivered unto us a promised land! We can build our home where there will no more bowing to false Gods, no modern Baals, no artificial Dagons, no silicon Marduks, no more bowing to what man, not God, has made! These false creatures that the unbelievers said would gladden your heart; if you only respected them and treated them like one of your own. Those false prophets of the North commanded that you must bow down to these machines if you were to prosper – but they lied! Look around you! Do you see in the farms and towns a land made prosperous by the worship of these creatures? You do not. You see unemployment, poverty, neglect. We have experienced what these machines have brought us. The machines look after themselves, not you.

When God created the earth did he not reflect on the sixth day that his work was good? He did not say 'my creation is all very well, but it lacks robots and machines that will do my people's work for them.' Perhaps He was going to create them on the Monday, after his day of rest? I hadn't thought of that!

[laughter]

No. At the end of that first week God had already created everything that was needed to populate the earth – including mankind, in his image. And he judged that it was no simply good, but holy. Now we should have the grace, the humility, and the piety not to think that we can improve upon his work. 'Artificial Intelligence'. they call it – and so it is; artificial. It is we, you and I, in this chapel this morning and with all our brothers and sisters outside – who are the possessors of true, natural, God-given intelligence; we should respect the gift that He has granted us.

Let us now choose a different route than this madness of the machines; let us pursue a path in recognition that we are children of God and that the Earth was given to us for our dominion and our enjoyment – not for artificial creations to have dominion over us! If the Northerners want to worship machines and be led by them, let them; the time has come for this great country to follow two separate destinies. Our Lord promises that if we place this land under His mantle, He will make this a land of the spirit, a promised land, where love and fellowship with the Lord is with us every day of our life.

Let us be conducted by our faith. The Lord will guide you, as He has guided me. Amen. God bless you all."

The ex-Bishop of the Alexandra diocese allowed his words to sink in. Then he said:

"Let us now read together from Psalm 4."

And the congregation spoke together in its solemn, misted voice:

'I waited patiently for the Lord,
And he inclined to me, heard my cry,
Brought me out of a horrible pit of clay
And set my feet on the rock,
And put a new song in our mouth...'

SEVENTEEN

Thornton rose, walked down the aisle, dipped his fingers in the font and crossed himself. Bethany trailed behind. The governor stood at the entrance, shaking hands with the congregation, as they headed for Sunday brunch. When his turn arrived, Thornton told Carroll how inspirational his sermon had been, and pledged a financial contribution for the campaign. It was, he reflected silently to himself, the very least he should do – an investment to keep the right side of power.

He began to walk over to Clarence, who was waiting next to the phaeton – but he didn't get far: in his path stood the governor's wife Kirsty, statuesque and glossy – a Southern belle to her beautifully manicured fingertips, waiting for her husband to finish his work. She smiled as Thornton held out his hand.

"Kirsty! A pleasure on so lovely a morning – such an inspiring sermon. You remember Bethany?" Thornton gestured towards his wife, hoping that she wouldn't look too wrecked next to this raven-haired beauty.

"Bethany…! You look as cool as anything in this heat," Kirsty said. Thornton admired the way she delivered this compliment free of irony.

Before too long, Carroll joined them, positioning himself between his wife and Thornton. The four were now effectively divided into two pairs: Kirsty with Bethany, Carroll with Thornton. It was easily and subtly done; only the keenest observer would have judged this strategy of the gubernatorial couple to be pre-meditated.

Kirsty took control, "I'm sure you men have so much to discuss, and I've been longing to catch up with Bethany! Why don't we go on together? Much better than forcing the men to hear our women's gossip. We haven't seen each other for ages."

Thornton shot a look at his wife; brunch with the Gillespies might be a welcome alternative to being alone together. She shrugged her shoulders, as though to say, it's all one with me – and. so the matter was settled: Kirsty and Bethany would take the governor's car back to the mansion in Baton Rouge, while Thornton and Carroll would take the phaeton as far as the main gate of the plantation. Clarence would wait there and drive them to meet the girls.

Thornton hoisted his considerable bulk onto the driving platform, gesturing for Carroll to sit alongside him. With a flick of the reins the two men set off, gripping the sides as the trap lurched down the unsurfaced track. They had almost reached the farm road when a whirring noise spooked the horses. They shied violently, flaring their nostrils and laying back their ears. What looked like a large pheasant rose from a thicket and climbed almost vertically into their path.

"What in the Devil's name is that?" said Carroll.

"One of our new drones," replied Thornton, trying to calm the horses. "You know the security concerns we have; two break-ins by DOGs in the last month. We've got various different types of robot birds on the estate – geese, pelicans, pheasants, egrets… Once they're aloft, they look just like the real thing. From time to time folk shoot at them, thinking they might be food. But we don't lose too many, the shooters are deterred by the poaching penalties".

"Can't quite describe that as poaching, Thornton," corrected the governor. "These things being machines. If I had my way, the shooters would be rewarded." He gave a chilly smile.

"Well, anyone who shoots one of these birds is in for a shock. They are alarmed and my men respond real quick," said Thornton.

The governor seemed unimpressed. "Soon the very trees will be listening to us" he said.

Oh but they already do, thought Thornton. There were monitors and cameras strung throughout the woods. It was all very well for the governor to be disapproving, but he didn't have a plantation to protect. But Thornton knew that such talk could lead onto dangerous territory. Time to change the subject.

"So, tell me, how did the trial go last week?" asked Thornton. "Did the jury decide she was a witch?"

"Ah yes – that," said Carroll. "Well, too soon to know – it was just the opening speeches that day we met. The trial will run another week. But you're mistaken my friend – she is not the one on trial – yet."

Thornton raised his eyebrows. He had been left with the impression that the women was on trial; he now remembered that it was she who was considered the injured party.

For a while the men travelled on in silent thought; presently, to break the ice Carroll said,

"I thought Bethany was looking very fine today. Is she better now?"

Thornton shot him a rueful grin.

"Sure, there are occasional setbacks, occasional spills," he said. "She's getting there. It's not all in a straight line. Bethany is more ingenious in hiding bottles than we are in finding them, sometimes. Progress is slow, but sort of… onward and upward I guess."

The governor smiled warmly.

"Kirsty and I have always liked Bethany – and we know what a strain it's been on you, too. Terrible curse, drinking." He raised a hand and shook his head, at no one in particular, to emphasize just what an incomprehensible and fearful thing it was.

"Were the folks at the Davis Institute in Atlanta able to help? I'd heard good things about their work. The last time we met, you said you might send her there?"

"We did, we did. But the results were a bit mixed," Thornton replied. "Some of the therapies have worked, others less so." He looked lost for a few seconds. "They're a little haphazard these treatments – sometimes I get the idea that... all these medical men, they ain't got no real idea how the mind works. It's all supposition – just guess work."

Thornton hesitated then struck a more positive note. "But it'll be different in the future."

The governor stiffened,

"Is that so?" he said. "You think they might have these things worked out in the future? That would sure make a change, to my way of thinking. Ah yes, *The Future...*" Carroll delivered the phrase with a derisive emphasis.

"People always seem to believe – like you Thornton – that things will be better in the future, that we'll find solutions to our problems that ain't been seen yet. But the way I view it, that's a mistake: people been drinking since the world began. What's the future going to bring that's going to change that? Can't say the future's done us much good so far. Look at these men...."

Carroll gestured with his chin towards a dozen battered looking men of mixed races, some Caucasians, rather more Afro-Americans, digging a ditch at the side of the road. An overseer berated the gang from time to time. Thornton felt embarrassed. This was his land after all – and he was the one who'd leased these men in the first place.

But Carroll was sympathetic.

"See that team?" said the governor. "We, you, me, have to make work for them now; I'm glad you've been able to help out in that regard, Thornton. But ten years, even five years ago, they would have all had some sort of job. Not a great job maybe – but they would have earned their bread in a calling, had a skill of some sort. Now what? They're just wards of the state. And what's done that? Machines and robots – ain't that right? Are you surprised that we've refused to recognise Douglas v Milton Robotics? Did you see, the other day, a man was put on trial in San Francisco for shooting his personal robot? Seems he lost his temper with it. Well, I can understand that. What sort of crazy is this, treating robots as though they have feelings? It's not as though they have a soul. They're not people.. Equating robots to people? Do those guys up in Washington have no sense? It's just blasphemy, as I said this morning – and that sort of attitude will be stamped out down here, I can tell you. Nobody who maltreats a robot or ignores Douglas v Milton Robotics will get into trouble down here. Our citizens can treat their robots any way they want, provided them's their property."

Thornton twisted uncomfortably on his cushion. The last thing he sought was a discussion on the boundary between robots and humanity, considering where the next advance in Artificial Intelligence was going to take them. He was sure that the governor would never see things as he did. If Bethany could be made to forget her demons, was that not a good thing? If returning warriors from foreign wars could be rid of the mental traumas they had suffered, was that not a benefit? The governor might just see that , given his enthusiastic calls for militarily intervention in New Chaldea.

But in the mind of Carroll Gillespie, all advances in mental adjustment were just blasphemous fall-out from the progress in Artificial Intelligence – a cursed development that had led to the poverty they now saw everywhere around them. From the earliest developments in AI, to the threatening advances of MARION and LetheTech, each advance was just step after step on a heretical path that had caused disastrous consequences for so many in the South.

The pair lapsed into silence again until Carroll spoke.

"You voted?"

"Yeah, I voted," said Thornton, careful not to reveal anymore. "So much easier now we can do it on our phones. None of that standing around in queues. The results sure come out quickly."

"Yeah, don't take no time now to add the votes all up. They just get counted as they're made. You liked the result?"

"Sure, sure. It was fine," said Thornton, without much enthusiasm in his voice. He lapsed back into silence, not wanting to get into a discussion about the merits of splitting the Federation.

At last Carroll spoke again.

"Say, how are we doing, by the way? Do you know what time it is now?"

"12.15."

Puzzled, the Governor looked across "How did you do that?" he asked.

"Do what?" said Thornton

"Tell the time. You didn't even look at your watch or phone. Did you just guess?"

Thornton cursed his carelessness. Of course, he should have at least looked as though he was inspecting a watch or his phone.

"Oh... I don't have to guess anymore, Carroll. See... I've got one of these new iPsyche devices. They make everything so much easier, look."

Thornton turned his head to show Carroll the small silver rectangle.

"Bought one a few months back – the very latest thing. It just picks up your thoughts, no more looking at screens to type an instruction, no more speaking to your phone. You just think the question, think the command – for example, 'what time is it?' or 'phone Clarence' and this device tells you the answer or makes the call. So much easier than the old system, tapping away with one finger..."

The governor narrowed his eyes. "I've read about those things. I thought you secured it to your shirt collar, not wear the darned thing on your skin."

"That used to be the case, yes. Not anymore though. Too many connection problems – when people twisted their necks too far, or forgot to take them out of their collars before the shirts got washed. I just tape this on after a shower in the morning. It's like putting in your lenses – you get used to it very quickly."

"Well, you be careful with that thing my friend," said Carroll, more amiably. "Wearing something that's connected straight into your brain? That sounds mighty dangerous to me. Who knows what sort of stuff might be sent there! And what about hackers? What would happen if they got access to you?"

"Won't happen Cal." Thornton tried to sound reassuring. "It's really no different to the old style phone. You're conscious of whatever you send – or receive. You can accept or reject, delete the message – just like normal. There are the usual firewalls and anti-virus programmes, it's just a different way of imputing commands, Cal – that's all." Thornton was one of the few people allowed to use the diminutive, Cal.

"That's what they always say, isn't it Thornton?" retorted Carroll. "They said that all their devices would liberate us, give us so much more free time, make us so much wealthier. Well, it sure gave us more free time – half the country ain't got jobs now. And you want to let that device have access to your brain? I wouldn't let that damn thing anywhere near me."

"There have been issues… not all these things have always worked out for the best," agreed Thornton.

Carroll looked exasperated. "Issues! Look… it all went wrong from the beginning. We let our technology go overseas and the jobs followed. So what were we told – 'No more manufacturing? That's okay! You can all live on services now: the US is really great at services – we're a world leader!' Well, maybe we were then – till AI came along and suddenly anyone, anywhere, could buy a robot, or a desk-top mind – we have no edge any more, no advantage! So all those service jobs went next. and pretty quickly, too. Now, the world is the same everywhere, the technology is all over the place: if I want a legal opinion, my accounts done, my house designed – I don't need to go to some fancy graduate from LSU or Tulane, do I? I send my requirements into the cloud, select the cheapest offer that comes back from the chosen AI program and whatever I want done, poof! it's there. So we reap the whirlwind. A Great Collapse? Yes, –

that's what it's led to. I try to save what's left; you and I give a little employment here and there. Don't try to tempt me with your latest technology Thornton, your iPsyches and your MARIONs. As far as I'm concerned they're all the work of the Devil."

"You know Thornton, me and the fathers, we've been discussing this quite a bit. And we're beginning to think that maybe what's happened to us is a sign of judgement. Maybe the Good Lord thinks that we're getting too close to Him, and I don't mean that in a good way. After all, isn't intelligence a divinely given quality? 'Artificial Intelligence'…that sounds awfully like stepping on God's toes to me. How would Artificial Soul sound? Not good, huh? We need to be real careful here. That's why we decided in this state, in Louisiana, and in the rest of what will be the New Confederacy, now the vote has gone our way – that we will never ratify Douglas v Milton Robotics. Robots as people? No way. You might as well offer kindness to a stone as respect to a machine."

But Thornton understood the reality of the mental states of the latest generation of robots. Their emotions were genuine. "You know, Carroll… these robots, when people say they got feelings, they're not all wrong. Those machines – the new ones – they can be hurt, like us, in their minds. That's why…"

The governor cut him off. "Stop! I don't want to hear any more of this blasphemy, Thornton. I've never heard anything so ridiculous and so wrong. But, I'm not surprised to hear you voice such sentiments, if half of what I hear is true!"

Carroll reined himself in; this was Sunday after all; he was with a friend, on the way to brunch. He took a deep breath. They were already at the gate but there was no sign of the car. "Have you spoken to Clarence?" Carroll asked. "Has he been delayed?"

"I'll call him now," said Thornton – but there was a message from Clarence already. "He'll be here in a couple of minutes."

This time, Carroll had the grace not to ask how he knew what Clarence had said without looking at a phone.

EIGHTEEN

By the time the two men reached the mansion, Bethany and Kirsty were settled on the terrace enjoying the view of the lake under a large garden parasol.

"Home," said Carroll redundantly, as they drew up in front of the governor's mansion. They walked through the house and onto the terrace. "Let's have something to drink with the ladies. It's been a long morning."

'Having something to drink' was something Bethany had already achieved. Thornton surveyed his wife from afar, trying to identify the liquid in her glass, but the distance was too great. They traded looks – his concerned; Bethany's dismissive. It wasn't just that she objected to the snooping and judgment; any advice from her husband was always unwelcome.

Thornton steered his way through the parasols and sat next to Kirsty; Bethany would behave herself while engaged in conversation with the governor. She was scared of almost nobody, but Thornton could tell she was on edge in Carroll's presence.

A footman in a paisley waistcoat took Thornton's order. His predecessor, whose uniform this man had inherited, must have been a great deal slimmer: the footman was sweating profusely. Economies were evidently being made.

"You men sorted out the world on your trip here, then?" enquired Kirsty.

"Almost!" exclaimed Carroll. "Although we never quite concluded what might happen to the world if Thornton continues his work. We discussed his new... phone, what's called the iPsyche. Thornton, turn your head a little, if you would – give Kirsty a peek."

Thornton obediently twisted and pulled down his collar. "You must have heard of them, Kirsty – you just think something, and the iPsyche obeys."

Kirsty shuddered.

"Not for me, Thornton. I'd forget to take it off before I had a bath. It wouldn't last a day!"

Carroll was just about to jump in with his view when a butler, whose dress was a better match to his body than that of the unfortunate footman, coughed discreetly.

"The lunch menu, your Grace."

Your Grace? thought Thornton. Although he'd had a few meals here over the years, he'd forgotten that Carroll insisted (or was it Kirsty's doing?) on being addressed by staff as though he were still an acting Bishop. His Grace glanced at the menu.

"Is that OK for you, honey?" Kirsty asked. Her husband declared the offering was fine and turned to the butler.

"Please show it also to our guests."

Bethany hardly looked at the menu. "It looks delicious, Kirsty," she said, unconvincingly.

Thornton put on his reading glasses: sea food gumbo, fried okra and green spring vegetables. His iPsyche was already offering advice. He could pick at the gumbo out of politeness, the seafood would be OK, but not the rice. He'd make up with the greens.

They moved on to family matters.

"What's Stephanie up to these days?" Kirsty asked. "Still rattling around? That girl sure never likes to settle. And she used to motor through boyfriends like I don't know what! She with George still?"

Thornton shook his head. Stephanie and George had unfortunately broken up, and she'd moved to Paris. But there was a new man in Stephanie's life: Thornton had written to Claude, asking him if he could invite Stephanie out, introduce her to some of his friends. His daughter didn't know many people in the city. The introduction had been only too successful. Now, after a courtship of a few months, Stephanie lived with Claude and was rarely to be found in the own apartment she rented in the Latin Quarter. Details of her new life were scant – Stephanie wasn't one of the great communicators – yet only the day before, Elizabeth had received an email which she had inadvertently copied to her father.

From: Stephanie Lamaire
To: Elizabeth Lamaire
Re: Hello

Hi Sis!

How are things? No word in ages! I'm equally bad, I know – just had one of those three-line emails from Daddy, dictated no doubt on some flight or other. Didn't get too much of an idea about how you were all getting along, but at least it doesn't seem like he and mother have killed each other yet... I know he's completely occupied with MARION – and I guess that's all to the good – keeps them out of each other's hair.

And how are things in Gay Paree, I hear you ask? Well... I think I mentioned to you last time, that I was thinking about moving in with Claude – the big news is, I've done it! Early days – slowly getting used to living with a man again, and he with a woman – though I suspect that he's a little more experienced in that regard! But we're very happy – really. The apartment's in Montmartre (I'm sure you know it: Sacré Coeur?) and it's nice, though a bit crowded: there are three – sometimes four -, of us here in all, since Claude has had to take in his aged father – Victor – who's got dementia. It's more than he can do to remember my name one day to the other. And then there's the Senegalese day nurse (Fabienne) who's here to look after him when Claude's at work.

We're getting along well enough so far – although Fabienne is a bit of a trial. I think she has a thing for Claude. He's making an effort to introduce me to his friends, and contacts who might be useful. They look on me with curiosity – "ooh, Claude's got an American girlfriend? We must check her out!" and a little bit of "how long will this one last?" in the background, but I'm not letting it bother me (too much!) There have obviously been a few predecessors. I found some photos in a drawer the other day, and Claude claimed to have no idea who it was. That wasn't super reassuring but we were all very grown up about it.

I had lunch with Bella Aquavella the other day – you must have heard of her, even down South? Fashion designer? I wanted to interview her for an article., but she just wanted to bombard me with advice. She obviously didn't think my relationship with Claude would last another day without the benefit of her input (which is a bit rich – her husband has just left her, apparently). I thought you'd enjoy her angle, though – Golden Rule: never to let Claude see me naked, except in bed: maintaining one's allure is all important. *Le Mystere* must be preserved – a bit late for that I'm afraid!

Like a lot of Parisians I've met, she tells me how much she'd rather live in the US. They always complain about Paris – so bourgeois – but when they say the US, they really mean New York (actually, Manhattan), which is the only bit of the States most of them have ever visited, apart from LA maybe. When I explain that where I come from in the South it isn't quite the same, they start asking me questions where the subtext is, 'are you all still racists'? and of course, they have heard about the dismemberment of our country by the plebiscite and something about the work gangs that Carroll has introduced. Sometimes I feel like what they really want to ask is 'do you still have slavery where you come from?' Ok, maybe I exaggerate a little – but not much. Occasionally, very rarely, when I get tired or cross having to defend the South all the time, I play up to their prejudices – I start complaining about the difficulties of getting the cotton in and how it's such a problem finding a good overseer these days. I shouldn't do it really, it feels very immature!

At least I'm getting better at speaking the language. I noticed that when I was real bad, everyone used to say how well I spoke French; now I'm getting fluent *(je parle français couramment maintenant – presque bilingue!)* they pick up on every error and inform me with a patronizing smile (because, as a foreigner, I cannot be expected to get it right every time) what I should have said. And sometimes, it's true, my language skills do go haywire. Particularly at dinners, after a few drinks. I'd been led to believe the French drink in moderation but let me tell you – this is not a moderation that would be recognized in Manhattan! The wine flows copiously at all the dinner parties I have been to, which is a few. At the present rate of my decent into alcoholism I shall soon end up like Mama (how is she anyway?). Oh – and I'm expected to know all their friends in the US too. I'm asked things like, 'One of my favourite cousins is a journalist, like you – lives in Chicago. Perhaps you know her?' Or, 'You must meet my friend Doug, lives here but he is American.! You'd love him, I'm sure' as though I must be facing severe homesickness, and my strongest wish is to keep in touch with my own countrymen. Well, as I know you will appreciate, considering the state of our home-life, that's not quite the predominant emotion I suffer as I sit here, cuddled up to Claude.

Now, if he could just keep his eyes off other women for a bit longer this might all work out just fine. Luckily, when he's not lecturing, he has to spend an awful lot of time handling MARION queries. I must tell Daddy to make sure Claude is kept deeply involved! As it is, I hear more from him about Daddy than I ever get directly. I know Daddy's very busy (as usual) and he's not a great correspondent at the best of times, so I guess I'll have to be satisfied with the odd few lines; when he can manage that.

And you, dear Sis? How is everything? You and Ambrose still getting along? Any sign that he might land a job any time soon??

Write me sometime and let me know how things are going at home.

Miss you!
Stephanie XX

"Well, I'm so sorry there was no opportunity to see Stephanie before she left for Paris," declared Kirsty, for whom Stephanie's new life seemed so far removed from life in Baton Rouge that she may as well have moved to the moon.

"But what about Elizabeth? I haven't checked in with her for ages either."

"Elizabeth's good," Thornton assured her. "Her dance studies are going well. She's been choreographing a piece for a local dance group. You and Carroll should come and see the opening. She has a boyfriend now, too -" Thornton drew a thumbnail sketch of Ambrose. "Recently left college, hasn't yet found a profession that suits him. Big football player – and a committed Christian too. Keeps on talking about signing up for New Chaldea."

"No kidding! That's so interesting – good for him!" Kirsty swivelled to face her husband. "Carroll, you hear that? Elizabeth's boyfriend is thinking of signing up for New Chaldea!"

"Why, that's excellent news," agreed the governor. "We could certainly use more young men like him."

"How's the New Chaldea thing going anyway?" asked. Thornton. It was one of the governor's favourite causes but not his; Thorntons' opinions about the future of New Chaldea were largely a matter of indifference. All the guff about the Christian's right to a holy land passed him by; it was one thing to be in favour of recognising a spiritual home in the Middle East but Thornton was quite opposed to armed intervention in claiming it. Carroll's campaign to promote such a foreign adventure was not nearly as successful as that for Southern independence. The Middle East wars had only stopped a few years earlier, and voters remembered the various military debacles that had accompanied them. But the governor would interpret a vote for independence as carte-blanche for military involvement; the first foreign affairs initiative of his new government.

"People forget … the hatred, mistrust and violence towards the various minority religious factions," he said. "Do you recall how it was at the end of those Middle East wars, in 2038? My fellow Bishops and I – we said at the time that the only hope of a lasting peace was to separate the faiths. You can't keep them together over there."

"I do remember," said Thornton agreeably. "And at that time, if memory serves me right...those minorities were offered a territory, along the Euphrates river, where they would live – or so it was hoped – in some sort of harmony. That was the MERTZ wasn't it – the Middle East Religious Tolerance Zone – if I remember rightly?"

"It was," replied Carroll, getting into his stride. "The MERTZ yes... roughly what us Christians call New Chaldea now – like the land was, in Biblical times. That was one of our proudest moments; we squeezed those local powers – Iraq, Saudi Arabia, Syria to cede some of their territory."

"I thought we had to buy it from the Saudis?" interrupted Bethany, keen to challenge a self- congratulatory statement.

"So we did, so we did, Bethany" conceded the governor. "We smoothed the way with silver. But still – a hell of a deal! It was a buyer's market back then – the collapse in the use of oil left the Saudis pretty willing sellers."

Bethany frowned. Her memory of events had been different, but she let it go.

"Of course, things never went as planned from the beginning," continued Carroll. "There were powerful political players in the Middle East who saw their Muslim populations as the only legitimate religious group and they forced all their minority populations into the MERTZ; not just the Christians;, Copts Yasidis, Zoroastrians, Turkamen, Mandaeans... they all ended up getting pushed in together. Their security was meant to be guaranteed by the UN; fat lot of good the UN did protecting the Christians."

"There weren't very many Christians at the time, if I recall," objected Bethany.

"Well, that's true," said her host. "But what of it? They were entitled to their protection – and the numbers of Christians has only grown since then. More have chosen to emigrate every year since the enclave was formed. After all employment prospects here haven't been too great; it wasn't too difficult to persuade many of them to go."

"Not just persuaded, as I recall, positively bribed I would say!" said Bethany. "There were guys on our doorstep telling me that I needed to give, and give, and give. to make possible this promised land. That Christians would find their own special home in the Middle East at last, just as long as I contributed generously, and preferably with a subscription."

The governor ignored Bethany's complaint. "A special home… why, yes – that's what we hoped New Chaldea would become. Sadly, it ain't worked out that way; there's been competition over leadership, tension between different religious minorities… In the past few weeks we've even had reports of massacres – persecutions, even – by local militias of other faiths. The Christians are vulnerable. Hell, we saw New Chaldea as a sort of twenty-first century New England, where His followers could practise a revitalised Christianity, more in keeping with the beliefs they'd been brought up on, free from all those modern affronts to our Lord so rife in the North…. none of this…uncoupling, or polygamy. Who would have thought we'd see such abominations?"

Kirsty bristled. This was one of the few subjects on which she disagreed with her husband.

"Oh Honey," she said. "It's only 'uncoupling', not polygamy yet – at least not for women! I wonder how you men can be so sensitive about it, given how you've carried on – one wife after another!"

Carroll smiled.

"Not this man, sugar," he said. "One wife, forever; that's quite enough for me."

"Glad to hear it," said Kirsty, summoning a footman. "Luther, would you be a dear and find out what's happened to our food? And freshen up our glasses, will you?"

Another member of staff approached.

"Same again, Ma'am?" he asked Bethany.

"Just leave off the salt – like last time. Thank you."

The governor returned to his theme.

"It's not surprising that some of our Christians brethren are fearful for the fate of the new colonists. I can tell you Thornton, I'm real worried too: I can't see nothing for it, but that we've got to go in and defend our fellow worshippers."

Thornton knew that Carroll planted a pro-intervention blog or tweet from time to time, to test public opinion. So far, most of his propaganda only served to provoke a dozen articles arguing against foreign adventurism, a thousand tweets in opposition.

"There's a long way to go before anyone in the South will support intervention," said Thornton. "I know you don't like the present leader of New Chaldea, but seems to me he's doing his best to keep the lid on things – even if his methods seem a little rough to us. Don't forget the old Turkish saying 'Better a hundred years of tyranny than a day without a Sultan.' Anarchy is the enemy. Be careful what you wish for, Carroll!" Thornton guessed that if the governor's proposed expeditionary forces – or mercenaries, or freedom fighters, or whatever Carroll wanted to call them – undermined the local government at New Chaldea, conditions were likely to get even worse for the Christians.

"You know, Thornton, we need much greater support from the voters than we've been getting, if we're ever going to win this thing. Folks are simply not being persuaded that this is important to them: there's not enough feeling of brotherly solidarity. You can't ignore what's happening to your faith just because the problem is far away! We got to make them feel they – we, all of us – partake in all mankind. Or at least that part of mankind that follows our Lord."

"I quite agree – quite agree," Thornton reassured him.. "There does need to be a stable home for the Christians in the Holy Land. After all, we were there first – except for the Jews I guess; they were there a little before us. And maybe a few others, Zoroastrians perhaps, that sort of thing. But long before the Muslims. Of course, we need to be there. I'm all for it." Thornton saw no point in riling Carroll.

"What's your idea then?" The governor was determined to press Thornton to deliver a specific commitment.

"Count on me," said Thornton. "I've got a few ideas," he added, although he had few besides donating enough cash to get shot of the distraction as soon as possible. "I'll talk to Jim Myerson – he's the head of my foundation."

"I've met Myerson sometime back. Nice guy." said Carroll. "Way I see it, if the colonists out there need new recruits to increase the Christian presence, then we ought to help. We've got a whole lot of God-fearing folk here with not enough to do, and no way to support themselves unless we do it for them; now if we could persuade them to emigrate... think on it – wouldn't that solve two problems?"

"It would, it would, Cal," agreed Thornton. "Maybe we, or at least my foundation – could grant each of those émigrés a bounty, so they can start life afresh out in New Chaldea?"

It's only money, he thought.

"That would be mighty fine of you, Thornton," said the governor, enthused. "That's just what these folks need – an incentive to move, and enough to make sure they can survive once they reach there. I'd be really grateful, and I know so would my fellow Southern governors – and the fathers, of course."

Thornton relaxed. He could do this – he could make a financial transfer, easy. Anything to get the Governor off his back.

"But don't think I'm going to stop watching you, my old friend," admonished Carroll. "You'll be doing the right thing and I will be grateful for that; but I don't want you running away and thinking that you can pursue all those sacrilegious ideas of yours as a result. You mustn't undo all the God-fearing work you'll be making possible in New Chaldea by offending Him somewhere else."

Kirsty came to his aid. "Oh, Carroll, honey, don't be so harsh!

That's a mighty tough way to talk to your old friend Thornton. I know it's been a long and tiring morning but… really. You can save that sort of talk for the office."

Bethany had also perked up; quick and relentless as she was to criticize Thornton, she would defend him to the end if anyone else did. Whatever her husband's failings, she had her pride – and if anyone failed to pay sufficient respect to her husband, that person became anathema; no one outside the family was to be allowed the sort of lèse-majesté that Carroll had just demonstrated.

NINETEEN

Bethany put down her drink and glared at the governor. "Shame on you, Carroll Gillespie. My husband has done a great deal for this state – and for you, I'll have you remember! He's contributed to every one of your campaigns, and if it weren't for him, you wouldn't even be sittin' in this house right now."

"Oh Bethany, honey," placated Kirsty. "Carroll just gets carried away sometimes. Pay no attention to him – he didn't mean no disrespect."

But Bethany was riled.

"Seems to me New Chaldea is a bastard nation from the start, a place for everybody to deposit their troublesome populations who worship any God besides their own. How do all those non-Christians there feel about you threatening to arm your settlers?"

"Justice time, Bethany," retorted the governor. "It's time our heritage got some respect. Everybody wants to make that land just for themselves and it's tough for all settlers, at the moment, no doubt about it; but us Christians, we have a right to be there. It's our history, where we began; where our Lord came from."

"I thought He came from Galilee. Long way from the Euphrates as I recall," said Bethany, refusing to back off.

"All part of the same sort of civilisation, Bethany. All people of The Book," said Carroll,

"And the others?" asked Bethany. "Are they going to like being part of a Christian nation if you are successful in imposing your regime?"

Gillespie's eyes narrowed.

"There can only be one government. We think that it should be Christian."

"And you'll fight to make sure it is?"

"It's not us who are fighting, my dear; we are only responding to provocation from others. They've already banned public religious festivals in New Chaldea. Imagine! We're not even allowed to promote our own beliefs."

"There are folks out there who need our protection against persecution. That's all Carroll is saying," interjected Kirsty. "The Middle East needs a greater Christian presence, to balance all those others."

"You know, Bethany," continued the governor. "We see New Chaldea like… when all those pilgrims came here, hundreds of years ago, to what were the English colonies. New England then, New Chaldea now. Where His followers can practise unoppressed. That ain't goin' to happen by us sitting here doin' nothin'. I know folks are exhausted, I know the people have no enthusiasm for a return to battle. And yet, what's the alternative? There are volunteer militias already in New Chaldea, but they are too few, too badly armed, and they're losing ground all the time. We help in every way we can, and looking after the fallen is one of them."

At first, Bethany missed this new point. Kirsty, seeing her puzzlement, said,

"I'm thinking of getting a training, Bethany; in nursing. Why don't you do it with me? These poor boys who come back, you ought to see some of them – no more than nineteen or twenty years of age – they're so sweet! But a real hurtin's been put on them. You'd make such a good nurse."

Bethany shook her head. Nurse? Whatever had got into Kirsty's head to make her think she wanted to be a nurse? Then she recalled that Lu Ann had been a qualified nurse; she had no wish to run into the woman she suspected of being her husband's girlfriend.

The head butler approached and announced that the meal was finally ready.

"Come," said the Governor, ushering his guests into the dining room. "Let's eat – and let's forget about politics for a while." Catching Thornton's eye, he added, "It sure would be great if everybody could just get over their memories that previous interventions have been disasters; it's not even true. If unhelpful memories could just be wiped clean. Think how great that would be!"

At that remark, Thornton said to himself, 'wiping memories?

That's sort of my job.' It dawned on him it was not entirely coincidental that the governor had let slip the suggestion that such a facility would be useful to him; was Carroll working his way around to something? Some request that he, Thornton, might be able – if not willing – to help out with?

TWENTY

Several months later, Thornton took his jet up to the sprawling industrial complex on the outskirts of Raleigh, North Carolina, where Milton Robotics was based...

As the jet taxied to the terminal, Thornton watched another aircraft land, piqued to note it was the same model as his. He had prided himself on being one of the first operators of the type. He squinted out of the window at the offending aircraft – he could usually get a fair idea of who owned what from their logos and registration numbers, but not this one.

He watched as the aircraft taxied to a stand some distance from the main terminal building. By the time his own aircraft had parked, there were three SUVs crossing the tarmac towards the mystery jet. From one of the cars, a small party of men clambered out and lined up to attention; then two more got out from another and walked to the head of the line. Thornton thought one of these looked like the governor of North Carolina. Four of the men walked up the plane's steps and reappeared bearing a coffin draped in the New Confederacy flag, which they swiftly loaded into one of the SUVs; then the men went up and ran through the whole process all over again: two coffins in total.

Thornton stared for a few seconds, uncertain as to what all the activity had meant. His pilot Billy left the cockpit and walked back to Thornton's seat to check that the flight had been satisfactory. "Did you see that?" Thornton asked him, nodding towards the jet. "Do you know what was going on there?"

Billy had also caught the drama. "Let me do a search on the call sign. I know most of the machines that fly around these parts, but that one is new to me."

Billy dictated the code into his phone. A second later the answer came back, "The aircraft is registered to a company with no website, but its address is somewhere in Virginia. Probably some sort of military thing, sir." he informed his boss.

"Pretty likely," agreed Thornton. "I wonder where it's come from?"

"Give me a minute." Billy made a few calls as they walked towards the terminal. "It's from New Chaldea," he said. "It flew non-stop."

"And so... the bodies? In those coffins? Evidently Americans... I wonder if they're dead emigrants, or belong to some sort of militia?" Thornton wondered; he answered his own question. "Mercenaries is my guess. We may have sent a load of emigrants out there but they're unlikely to get flags if they come back dead – they wouldn't get no governor to turn out for them, neither. I know Carroll has been sending forces out there, even if they ain't official ones. Guess that's how they come back: in boxes."

Thornton had guessed right. The existence of the volunteer force was always denied, although the secret was becoming more open with each passing day: Cal's Christian Soldiers, he thought. So... they had died for their faith? Thornton tried to remember how martyrdom worked in the Catholic church – or Protestant churches for that matter; these guys could well have been Baptists.

Thornton checked his iPsyche for any calls that he'd missed while airborne. To his surprise, most of them were from Doug Huxley, his local Milton plant director – and there another call was coming through from Huxley right now.

"Doug, what's the problem?" Thornton asked, "I see you've been trying to get hold of me urgently."

One of Blue Ridge's client factories, that built aerospace sub-assemblies, had been wrecked that morning by a couple of Series 5 Milton robots, barely three months since their introduction. The few remaining workers, some production, supervising the robots, but mostly maintenance staff, had kidnapped Holland Cooperman – the robots' resident manager at the plant during their integration period – and forced him to manipulate the programming codes to such an extent that the machines started to attack the plant. The two robots had then run for it and escaped.

Anyone pursuing the machines – police and the vigilantes alike – had to be stopped. However good their intentions; they couldn't imagine, let alone match, the strength or intelligence of their adversaries. Doug suggested triggering the emergency AV codes, which would halt the rogue machines in their tracks; but with the present level of ill-feeling toward the robots themselves, they would doubtless be attacked and broken up by the public as soon as they were disabled and defenceless. These mobile, multi-tasking, self-motivating robots were expensive and Doug wanted Thornton's permission before shutting the robots down: worker insurrection was explicitly excluded from Blue Ridge's insurance cover.

But there was no good alternative. Who knew the extent of the mental corruption Cooperman's enforced tampering with the programming might have caused? Who knew how much damage the robots themselves could inflict before being brought to a halt?

"Yes," said Thornton, his voice heavy with regret. "Trigger the AV codes."

These Miltons were the first of his creations to be sentient; it was almost like killing off a family member.

Plumes of smoke rose from the industrial park as Thornton and Billy approached. The entry road was blocked by state patrolmen, forcing them to negotiate permission to pass. Several fire engines, television trucks and ambulances. were parked haphazardly around the plant.

A little apart from the public service vehicles, a black SUV had parked up in front of the plant; it looked remarkably like the one Thornton had seen at the airport. To its left, one savagely torn hole in the factory wall, and another in the perimeter fence, indicated the direction the rogue robots had taken.

Thornton stepped over a hose and scrambled through the hole. Inside was chaos: smashed bits of machinery all over the floor; half-melted control panels burnt away by electrical shorts... the characteristically pristine environment had taken on the aspect of an apocalypse. He spotted Doug Huxley and Carroll Gillespie talking together, next to a smartly dressed man. Thornton recognized him as the North Carolinian governor he thought he'd seen at the airfield.

He walked over and addressed the governor he knew best. "Hi Cal – I thought it was you I saw at the airport." But Thornton's mind was not focused on Carroll. He cast his eyes around, scanning the ruined factory. "Holy Heavens, what a mess," he added, as a non-sequitur.

"I knew folk were angry," said Carroll, with a regretful sigh, as though dismayed by his underestimation of how much resentment there was. "But I didn't suspect anything like this would happen. Just goes to show what people really think about these machines, I guess. By the way – have you met Sherman Barnes?" He turned and opened his hand to indicate the gentlemen in a suit, standing next to him. "My colleague and friend – and the governor here in North Carolina."

Sherman Barnes looked Thornton up and down. "I'm sure glad there's no reported loss of life, Mr Lamaire. I hear reports that the machines may have been stopped; I should know very soon."

"They will have stopped," said Thornton authoritatively. "I instructed them to shut down."

Even as he said this, he wondered how much damage to the surrounding countryside had been suffered before the AV codes were broadcast. Blue Ridge would have to pick up the bill for reparations.

"Well, I thank you for that," said Barnes. "But look what they've done here." He swept his arm in an arc, indicating the widespread destruction. "Never seen anything like it before. Anyway, we'll get the ring leaders who started the whole thing: we may all disapprove of these ungodly machines but this is no way to go about remedying the situation. Jobs are hard enough to come by these days without people doing this sort of thing."

He turned to Huxley.

"Why isn't the integration manager here?" Barnes asked. "He could tell us the sequence of events, deliver an eye-witness account of how it came to this." But the integration manager was still hospitalized from the trauma of his kidnapping. "Has there been some recent incident that might have triggered the worker's' wrath?" he asked.

"None that I know of," replied Huxley. "But relations weren't great... I'd warned the management that they were imposing the Miltons too fast – it's easy to provoke resentment in the workforce. We've had these sorts of problems before but never as bad as this."

"Resentment? What, with all these machines comin' in, and telling people, like, *what to do*. Can I say I'm surprised?" Barnes asked, rhetorically.

"The men seemed okay with it at first. I came down and talked through the process with the guys. These introductions are always difficult. But I did think it would all work out, in the end; they'd accept the Miltons."

"Well, that don't seem to have been the case, now does it?" commented Barnes, with the same sarcastic tone to his voice as before.

Huxley grew more defensive. "We've only introduced the Miltons recently. I thought the men were... well, if not happy at least reconciled with the situation."

Barnes turned to Thornton. "Why do you think these machines were so provocative to the workforce, Mr Lamaire?"

"These Series 5 Miltons, are an entirely new generation of robot," explained Thornton. "They don't simply act out their program. They can give instructions to the human workforce about problems in the factory – on how to make the manufacturing process more efficient, for example. They can travel anywhere in the plant to talk to any member of a team. They see themselves as members of these teams. Indeed, they *are* members of the teams – and the men are instructed to treat them so."

"But they were taking humans' jobs from the teams?"

"That's always the case – unfortunately, you might think," replied Thornton. "That's why we, and our clients, employ them. But simply replacing humans – that's not their main point."

"Which is, then? asked Barnes. "What is the point of the Miltons?"

"To resolve production issues, more intelligently, more quickly, and with less waste, than any human can," replied Thornton. "But to do it nicely, politely, too."

"Tell the men what to do...nicely?" sneered Barnes. "That so? Doesn't seem to have impressed the guys who work here very much, all that... niceness."

"They explain to the humans why things need doing, or changing," explained Thornton patiently. "They're programmed to do so in a non-patronizing manner – to make their instructions more acceptable. They want to be liked, as well as obeyed. These machines – well, they're a bit more than machines really, and they want to be appreciated. You should be... decent to them. They have feelings. That's what the recent Supreme Court decision in Douglas v Milton Robotics was all about."

"But they do instruct human workers, you said? They don't ask. They expect to be obeyed?"

"They ask the first time," said Thornton. "But yes, the humans have been told that they must do what these Miltons tell them. After all, the Miltons will be right, always right– and it's because they are correct every time that management buy them."

Sherman's phone rang. He took the call and then looked at Thornton. "They've found the two Miltons."

"Badly damaged?" enquired Thornton.

"I've no idea. Nor care, neither. One came to rest in a wood, the other in a church. They caused a lot of destruction before finally stopped."

"The destruction will be the result of the tampering," said Thornton.

"They seem to have been tampered with mighty easily, that's all

I can say," Barnes replied. "Just what the people round here think about these things – they can't be trusted," replied Barnes.

Just then, a grey haired, heavily tanned man, in jeans and a plaid shirt and jeans, stepped through the gaping hole and strode up to Sherman. He held out a hand.

"Jim Embry, sir, at your service – 'an hopefully yours at mine. I sure wanted to see you." Thornton wondered how the man had breached the police cordon.

Embry twisted back and forth, gesturing to the wreckage. "This is an abomination," he exclaimed. The man was only just in control of his rage.

"It's not just here, you know. No sir! One of my barns has been knocked down – I've lost any number of calves. My cattle gone into a state of shock, my wife is beyond terrified. These ungodly machines ain't fit to be amongst us. The people who build them should be strung up!"

Sherman turned in Thornton's direction and pointed Jim Embry to where he should direct his wrath.

"This is the man you want, Jim," indicated the North Carolina governor, helpfully. "We need further safeguards on these new robots, for sure... well, that I can promise you. That will happen in the New Confederacy, with me and Carroll directing things."

"Ain't no matter of just safeguards," spat Jim Embry. "Look at what they done. They're agin' God's purpose, these machines."

Thornton broke in.

"I do understand, Mr Embry; and I'm extremely sorry about what happened. I will see to it personally that you are fully compensated."

"That's just typical of you folk," glared the farmer. "You come and do your sacrilegious thing, challenge the Lord to see if you can make something half as smart as what he done, and then – when it all goes wrong – you think you can buy your way out of trouble. Sure, you can compensate me – you can make good the loss your unholy thugs have caused – but don't think that's the end of it. No sir, no way. Because it ain't!"

Nothing was going to mollify Jim Embry, figured Sherman. "Gentlemen, gentleman – Please! Let's go and inspect the damage first and see what needs to be done. Thornton, you need to come with us. Jim, you get in the front and show us how to reach your farm"

The five of them piled into the two SUV's and set off in the direction of Embry's farm. Along the way they caught glimpses of fallen trees, wrecked buildings and downed power lines. Jim directed them to a wood where a lane had been ripped through the undergrowth. The jagged ends of split branches stuck out like barbed wire. They drove on slowly, the torn bushes and trees dragging and scratching against the sides of the car. On the way, slumped against a tree, they found one of the Miltons, its limbs thrown around randomly, contorted and disorganized in its death throes when the power was cut.

On they continued towards Jim's farm. Damage was everywhere. The robot had charged straight through a barn, wrecking it completely before heading towards the chapel that lay just beyond the house. Whether it had chosen to do so or had just pressed on blindly was something only a later inspection of its memory banks would reveal.

The farmer's family had been relatively fortunate. Their house had lost a corner but the rest still stood. Several cows, penned into a small paddock, were the survivors, the lucky ones. Others lay around, moaning, badly wounded. A vet moved from one to another, putting them out of their misery. In the chapel, by the altar, lay the second Milton, sprawled out, limbs confused like a crumpled metallic octopus. The men stood uneasily around the tangled heap. Carroll was the first to speak.

"This break out's already all over the news. Folks are going to get spooked if they learn a Milton died in front of an altar. They're already talking about witchcraft – the last thing Sherman and I need is the idea going around that the machines are attacking our places of worship." He turned to address Embry, "Jim, I'd ask you not to say anything about this at the moment – at least not about where this robot ended its life."

Jim Embry looked even more unhappy than he had twenty minutes ago.

"These things are evil... evil. And you ...!" He jabbed an accusing finger into Thornton's chest. "You're the monster here. You've created something that will destroy all of us. You summoned a demon, that's what you done. This... thing, attacks that which is Godly – attacks His creatures, it attacks His holy places. You will go to Hell and burn there – and that can't happen soon enough for me!"

Thornton knew that it was no good pointing out that he had had nothing to do with this incident; the machines had been properly programmed when they left the factory. Was it his fault that others had corrupted them? But he was known throughout the South as the owner of the firm that built such machines; he was the proprietor of Blue Ridge, whose sinister creations were trampling on the natural order. Thornton was lost for an adequate response because he knew he was guilty; he knew his sin of curiosity had driven him to invest in ever more sophisticated, risky, and ill-understood technologies. Now his hubris had resulted in this unhappy man he saw before him, and the trail of destruction that lay in the wake of his machines.

"We'll be in touch Thornton," said Sherman Barnes. "There'll have to be an enquiry. Folks weren't happy before with the way things were going and they're going to be a whole lot less happy after this. You're going to have to answer to public anger. You need to be prepared. In the meantime, the state will hold onto the Miltons while we carry out the investigation. Don't send anyone to collect them. Not yet".

"Of course," said Thornton, as Sherman took Jim Embry by the arm and lead him away. Thornton turned to Carroll,

"Can I give you a lift, Cal?" Travelling together would give him time to placate the governor- and an opportunity to learn what was going on inside his mind. "It will be much faster for you than flying commercial," he persisted. "The bodies of the fallen I saw you with at the airport – they can come with us or go back with your driver."

TWENTY ONE

The flight back was not as Thornton had imagined. It was a beautiful afternoon and, once they had reached cruise height, he and Carroll were able to enjoy a fine the view over the states of the Southern Confederacy. Stretched out beneath them were the still dense forests; the eponymous Blue Ridge mountains and, far off, the silver thread of the Mississippi. From 46,000 feet the world looked as it might have done when the first European settlers had arrived four centuries years earlier.

Thornton couldn't wait any longer to ask the question that had bothered him since landing that morning. "The bodies you saw unloaded were those of brave men who died in New Chaldea," answered Carroll. "We keep it quiet, of course, but for some time there have been young men – and some women too, of course – who've gone to fight for a just settlement, and to protect the equally brave settlers who have emigrated to enlarge the Christian presence there."

"Things getting worse then, Carroll,?" Thornton wanted to sound sympathetic, but his words sounded supercilious. Carroll seemed not to notice the tone – or if he did, he ignored it.

"Not quite a full blown civil war there... yet," said the Governor. "But there have been too many deaths. The situation is getting worse by the day."

"How about the local forces? Can't they keep a lid on things?" asked Thornton.

"The 'local forces', as you call them, have deposed the democratically elected president and installed one of their own as leader – who has effectively become dictator. One of his first acts has been the banning of religious festivals, in the name of lowering domestic tensions. Imagine! This was meant to be a multi-faith theocracy, something new in the world, where the worship of God would be a foundation-stone. None of the minorities can now celebrate their faith. Every week brings fresh news of troubles, reports of massacres by some local militia or other. There's a demand that the guarantee nations intervene, but... " He hesitated, searching for an explanation for the failure to meet the demand, "I guess everyone's exhausted. There's a loss of enthusiasm, sure, for any of it, but what's the alternative? You remember Jefferson's words – *'The tree of liberty must be watered, from time to time, with the blood of patriots.'* No less true in the Middle East than here! I can tell you Thornton, I'm real worried. I can't see nothing for it, but we've got to intervene and defend our fellow worshippers. That's what that poor fellow, Rick Muldane, God bless his soul, one of those in them coffins, lost his life doing. People like Rick, heck, they're doing a fantastic job as volunteers – but they're still too few – and sad to say… they're losing."

Carroll was correct in his view that there was no sign of public opinion favouring intervention.

"The public has a long memory; Vietnam has been all but forgotten, but most of the voters can still remember Iraq, Afghanistan, Syria, Ukraine, Iran… Those who've got a sense of history can tell you about the French in Algeria, the British in Northern Ireland, the Russians in Ukraine. These conflicts just keep going till one party gets tired of it all, and usually that's the imperial power, for whom these conflicts are not really necessary; not essential for their own existence, I mean. So…while the voters still remember the consequences of our – and others' – 'wars of choice', as they call them, there's no chance of us going back to the Middle East. Of course, things change – another outrage or two and the climate may reverse."

Thornton was more cynical.

"The cycle is always the same, Cal: enough massacres and the public demands something must be done. When the body bags come home, they demand we get out. They're beguiled by promises of short, sharp military operations – but, as you've just pointed out, ten years later the conflict is still going on. Maybe they've finally got wise. "

Carroll picked at a seam on his trousers, choosing his words carefully. "You know Thornton, we need much greater support from the voters than we've been getting – if we're ever going to win this thing. Folks just aren't persuaded that this is real important to them."

"Sure," agreed Thornton, wondering where all this was going.

"But I've been thinking," continued Carroll. "Maybe your group, Blue Ridge, could do something – you being in news, an' all that."

"We have tried," sighed Thornton. "I've instructed my editors that's our line – that we need to offer all the support we can muster, that this beacon of Christianity must not be extinguished. And we'll continue to pursue that line. But there's resistance. This is not falling on very receptive ears."

The governor tried to look sympathetic.

"You've done a lot, Thornton, no question. But, as you say, you don't seem to be making much of an impact. Maybe there are other ways?"

"Other ways?" Thornton had no idea what Carroll was driving at.

Carroll turned to look out of the window.

"You've got all these fancy new devices, I hear, that enter people's minds and remove old memories." He switched back and looked straight at Thornton. "Maybe we could go beyond the old methods? You know, traditional stuff like persuading people through articles and opinion pieces and such. Even when AI writes the scripts and puts it into the mouths of people they respect; it doesn't always work. In fact, less and less so. There's resistance. But maybe we could address them... directly, to their minds, without them folks having to do anything arduous, having to do all that... reading."

Carroll smiled at his little joke.

Startled by what he thought he had understood – almost blasphemy, coming from Carroll, Thornton said,

"You're mixing my business up with all the social media channels. You're right – iPsyches can talk directly to people's minds; but that's them, not us."

"But Thornton," insisted Carroll. "I hear things about you being able to do all sorts of things that sound useful – like deleting inconvenient memories, putting new ones into people's minds… What's your company called – LetheTech? I got that right?"

"You've been hearing all sorts of rumours, Cal," said Thornton defensively. "That's all very exaggerated. Our technology is in its infancy. It will be years till it works properly. And there's no way we can access all those millions of iPsyches you would need to change public opinion. Not without their user's say so. There's laws 'gainst that sort of thing. The users have to give us permission to enter their mental space."

"Just sayin', just sayin', my friend," said Carroll agreeably. "I sure know nothing about the whys and the wherefores. All that technology thing was never strong in me. But still… Just a thought."

At that point, the plane bounced unexpectedly and both men gripped their seats. As Clarence came by to mop up the spilt coffee, Carroll addressed him.

"Clarence, let me ask you something. Do you wear one of these new-fangled iPsyches?"

Clarence looked surprised, unused to being addressed by the governor. "Certainly not, sir. I wouldn't presume anyone is interested in sharing the thoughts of my good self, sir"

"And would Mr Clarence be interested in having thoughts put

into his head?" asked the governor.

"Too late for that, sir, I fear. I would doubt there is much room left for ideas, new or otherwise, anymore."

"But if we could," Carroll teased. "If we could just find a little space somewhere, for something really useful?"

"It's very kind of you sir," replied Clarence. "But no, I don't think so. From what I have been reading, well – I'd give the technology a few more years, sir, before Clarence goes that way."

"So, you don't agree with your Mr Lamaire and what he does?" he asked. "Do you think, then, that we should ask Mr Lamaire to stop playing with people's minds?

Clarence delivered a Delphic reply, "I'm sure Mr Lamaire knows exactly what he's doing and what's for the best," he said loyally; and with that, Clarence beat a retreat.

Carroll watched him go.

"Well, Thornton, you sure got a fan there; not like poor old Jim Embry. He was right angry with you! By the time we reach Baton Rouge I guess the news of the destruction will be everywhere. There's going to be a mighty lot of pressure on me to clamp down on your machines. Folk will want them banned. And if we don't ban them, then what? They're hardly going to allow the next generation to be introduced! Conscious machines? Might not be worth investing all that money in MARION after all, Thornton. Eh?"

Then he added, "But I could talk to the bishops. Persuade them not to rush to judgement – to understand there are two sides to this. Their flock will respect their views. You're doing some really helpful work on New Chaldea, Thornton, and I wouldn't want all that spoilt by people getting the wrong end of the stick about your researches. The bishops could take a lot of the heat out of this rogue Milton thing, if they was so inclined. We just got to make them so inclined, ain't we Thornton?"

Thornton nodded in agreement. He was not entirely sure what he was being asked to do but he was sure that if he didn't deliver the right answer for Carroll then the unhappy fate of Jim Embry and his miscarrying cows would lead to repercussions that he would not like. The public mood would be massaged into a threat to Blue Ridge and its interests – and maybe even to him, personally. He could forget trying to market LetheTech in the South for a start.

Forty minutes later they were on the ground. Thornton checked his iPsyche; just as he feared the events at Jim Embry's farm had created a storm. It would take all of the Governor's talents to deflect it – if he chose to do so. No offer of help could be disregarded, but the offer would come with a price, even if he could not yet tell how large that would be.

TWENTY TWO

It had been the consensus of political commentators that once the plebiscite was over the political turmoil between North and South would begin to settle and a new harmony would arise. But such had not been the case. If the body-politic before the vote had existed in an ill-defined, uncertain state, it had now become polarized. Like Schrodinger's cat, everything previously had been indefinite, a haze of possible outcomes. But now the vote had crystallized divisions in the country, that haziness had collapsed into a definitive decision and people found themselves on one side or the other. Families, friends, colleagues discovered to their discomfort they could not straddle the crevasse that threatened to swallow the country. Everything was affected by the split – from where people chose to live, to the system of government, to AI regulation, to the trade between the states. Although the implementation of the plebiscite and revisions to the Constitution would take another two years, attitudes changed fast, way ahead of any legislation by either side. The South had instantly became more protectionist as they sought to preserve their independent view of what should be permitted in the future.

*

Despite the increasingly bitter stand-off there were still commercial flights across the split. Some years earlier, it was hoped that the East Coast Hyperloop, a spur of which had been planned to reach Houston, might connect the two populations but the money ran out when it had only reached Washington. So Carroll Gillespie's nephew Euclid had few options if he wished to accept his uncle's invitation for the weekend. It was too far to drive, there were no train services that connected New York and Baton Rouge – so a commercial flight it was. But Euclid was a nervous flyer. The recent shooting down of a civil airliner by a dissident rural group had not made the prospect any more welcome. Even the most pro-secessionists in the South had been appalled by that, a step too far however they felt about their fellows above the Mason–Dixon line. The terrorist gang had been quickly captured but who knew if there were sympathizers out there similarly armed?

Euclid loved visiting the Gillespie's. His every need was attended to and of course there was the warmth of the governor's wife, Kirsty, who he imagined himself at least half in love with. She was so much nicer to him than her three southern–belle daughters; the three Swans as they were known on account of their snowy white skin and elegant necks. Euclid might have loved any one of them if he had been either encouraged or permitted to do so. But the truth was that none of the Swans had shown the slightest interest; they viewed him as neither handsome, rich, sporty nor fun. Euclid could only count on his intelligence and his faith, insufficient qualities to land him at the first base of courtship. Once he had accustomed himself to the frustration of failing to arouse emotions in their frosty breasts, the discontent that he had once felt in his soul no longer burnt so fiercely. And now Maria had replaced them.

The night after his arrival Euclid discovered that the entire family would worship at an outside evening service to celebrate Jim Embry's deliverance, from the attack which could so easily have ended in his demise. Many considered his survival as evidence that he had been protected by the Lord. There were other details of the incident that added to the suggestion the Divine had been involved. For example, it was significant that the rampage had been brought to a halt at the foot of an altar. It was fitting that He had demanded that the Miltons, or at least one of them anyway, for the story had not grown any more accurate in the telling, should kneel in His presence. A remarkable witness to His power, Euclid agreed with Kirsty.

"Wasn't it all just evidence that these new robots are a step too far? Hadn't people been right when they said that machines were beginning to get uppity?" she questioned. "Too much thinking they might be almost human, not knowing their place in the order of things?"

Euclid murmured some words to sound supportive. He might be

a Christian but he was engaged in research with artificial intelligence at the highest level. He never revealed his job in too much detail to Kirsty, or the three Swans. They knew that his career involved doing something with robots, even if neither party wanted to focus too specifically on what that something might entail. But as far as his uncle Cal was concerned, Euclid was in no doubt – this man took it upon himself to be informed about what everybody who fell into his orbit might be up to, including his nephew. How fortunate it was for him that Euclid was employed at the heart of AI research.

At dusk, the whole family, except the governor, set out off for the service. Kirsty promised there would be a 'surprise' at the service but refused to spoil the suspense by providing any clues. After about forty-five minutes they turned off the road and drove down an earthen track until they parked up on a sandy plain, dotted with scrub. They walked half a mile on foot down a dried-out river bed, the floor of a narrow ravine, cut through the valley floor by the waters. This led to an almost circular pan where the river had widened, creating a shallow natural amphitheatre. Several thousand people now stood there, waiting.

In the middle of the crowd, Euclid noticed a substantial wooden structure made of thick criss-crossed timbers. The construction featured an element whose purpose he could not immediately identify. At the summit there was rectangular platform upon which rested a crumpled mass of some dun-coloured, but reflective, material. The mass looked like a pair of collapsed puppets thrown on haphazardly. Flares stuck in the bed of the river caught and reflected golden glows from the surface of the strange tangle on the platform. Euclid walked around to get a better view. Limb-like extrusions were attached to two central hubs. No heads were visible. These were the Milton robots.

The crowd had grown to a considerable size as Euclid was buffeted from side to side. For the most part, they were good humoured, holding a glass of something in one hand and a burger or rib in the other. With no hint of a breeze, the stagnant air was full of the stench of burnt meat, beer and marijuana that lay upon the congregation. Sometimes the odour of an accelerant, gasoline or kerosene could be detected. Then, suddenly the crowd stilled and there was a hush, followed a few seconds later by cheering and they parted to let the governor through. Like an old-seasoned pro he shook hands as he passed through the crowd, greeting supporters whilst making his way towards the tower. He was lifted by his acolytes, rather than climbed, to a point a few feet up where the timbers had been arranged so that a man could stand, if a little insecurely. Once there, Carroll braced himself, one hand behind grasping the wood, the other stretched in front, showing the flat of his palm, a gesture half-way between acknowledgement and a request for silence. At last the tumult settled.

"My friends, folks, fellow Christians. We are here tonight to give thanks…"

"Yes we are, yes we are!" whooped the crowd.

"… to give thanks that the life of our good friend, and follower of the Lord, Jim Embry, has been spared." More whoops followed. "Jim almost lost his life because he was set upon by monstrous creatures. Jim was born into a righteous family over 40 years ago. Never would he have expected to see in his lifetime such fiends that threatened him in his own home. For Jim," the governor paused, "... the righteous and God-fearing Jim Embry, was attacked by creatures that were raised up out of the dust, not by our Lord, but by man. Things created out of man's vanity, by those who think they can copy God, that they can make something as wonderful, as unique, as sacred as that which He makes, every day, in His own image. Some think that their new inventions will be even better than what our Maker had in mind!"

"No! It shall not be! Find the men who made these things. Find them! They shall not be!" Cries rang out from the crowd.

The governor waited for quiet. "What can I call these things?" he shouted, pointing at the pyre. "For we cannot name them beings, nor call their existence life. No! We can ignore their claim to be *almost* human. Judges in the North say they have feelings, emotions, love perhaps. But did they have love or care when they set themselves along a path to destroy Jim's home and everything in their unfortunate path?"

"No! NO! They did not, they did not!"

"Have we not seen enough already of what these things can do?" he asked.

"We have, we have! " returned the cry.

"They've taken your jobs, they've destroyed your cattle, what next will they do?" shouted Gillespie, his voice rising.

"No more, no more!" cried the crowd.

Gillespie's voice slid down an octave. "No, no more. We shall no more allow these creatures to mimic us, to pretend that they too are like us, true children of God. We will defy them, we will not allow them in our midst. So let us then give thanks to the Lord that protected Jim from their evil and let us give thanks that He has warned us of what these machines, born from man's hubris and sinful ways, are capable of. Show our thanks and ask for God's continuing mercy on us."

"We do, we do give thanks!" responded the crowd.

A silence fell upon the congregation. Some remained standing, heads bowed, hands clasped in prayer. Others collapsed on their knees. The once time Bishop of the Alexandra diocese held his palm out in benediction and cast his eyes to the heavens as he led his flock, the only member of the congregation permitted to look up, in direct communication with the Divine, rather than down in humble submission. They declaimed after him words of penitence. At the end of the prayer he waited, leaving space for their inner, personal, address. Then, on cue, a man advanced bearing a blazing brand that he handed to Carroll, who thrust it deep amongst the timbers of the pyre.

Within seconds the whole structure was ablaze. The crowd drew back in gasps as the limbs of the robots began to twist and straighten in the heat. Their bodies reached ignition temperature, the blaze abetted by the plastics, wiring and hydraulic fluid the machines still contained. Some of the congregation angrily pushed forward to add their contribution to the flames and speed the destruction of the 'monsters' – but the heat was so intense they could not get near. They had no need; thermal stresses in the bodies of the robots overcame the strength of their joints. With an immense crack, a limb separated and spun across the crowd, landing on an unlucky individual. Other pieces flew over the heads of the congregation till they too fell on groups of worshippers. Screams of the afflicted pierced the night air, a red hot piece of composite struck a petrol can. Panicking stewards began to push the crowd back from the tower, now itself glowing. A few seconds later the entire edifice collapsed; the timbers having at last burnt through, scattering burning pieces of wood and robot in a wide arc. At the centre lay the remains of the machines; split into their constituent parts, their amputated limbs like torn chicken wings at a barbeque.

There were now few watching the agony of the Miltons; instead attention was focused on trying to assist the injured. The governor was at the forefront of the efforts, giving comfort as best he could whilst trying to stop well-meaning members of the congregation from ripping up their clothing, wetting it from their water bottles and dressing the wounds. He knew the cloth would stick to the scorched flesh and make matters worse. There was not much to do except wait for the ambulances to arrive. It would be a late night.

TWENTY THREE

The next morning the mood at the Governor's mansion was bleak. An exhausted Carroll headed family breakfast. He had called around the local hospitals earlier to check on the injured and although some had suffered only minor burns, over a dozen were sedated and in serious condition. Three people had died.

"Bloody things, those Miltons" exclaimed Kirsty from the other end of the table. "They cause damage when they're alive and when they're dead. Is this what the great AI revolution promised us? We were told to be nice to them, to treat them like people – but look at what they do to us. I don't want to turn those machines into human beings, for sure I don't. They have an evil about them. And to think we've got judges… they're Northern judges for sure, telling us that these things got feelings? I just want to show them Jim Embry's farm. And the destruction last night. It's disgusting that folks could ever consider respecting Miltons the same as our flesh and blood."

The governor looked at his family. He knew this sort of

conversation was being held that Sunday morning in half the breakfast tables of the South. The events of last night would be picked up by every pastor preaching that day. And how would he come out of that assessment? He had promoted the outdoor service last night, that suttee of the damaged robots, believing it would act as a catharsis and release the anger that had engulfed his people. Even if it were an impossible thing to say right now, the South could not entirely live without AI, or robots. There had to be some accommodation with the future. Robots were a fact of life and it would do no good for the people to be totally opposed to them, even if, as governor and president-elect of the Southern Confederacy, he was determined to minimise their impact. Hate would be directed against the Blue Ridge corporation but that was also the sort of high tech employer that the state needed.

The animosity against the machines would intensify. His wife's reaction would be typical of many. Calvin Roberts, his leading opponent, had already ranted on the radio that morning, taking a harder line on the possession and use of robots. They had both run in the last election on a platform of legislating against Douglas v Milton Robotics but he could see that this was no longer going to be enough. Calvin would threaten to outflank him, propose punitive measures against manufacturers of robots that claimed human-like characteristics.

Had Thornton read the runes? Did he have an appreciation yet of how much difficulty his industries might suffer in the future? It was all very well for him to carry out his most controversial research in the North but the North and South were not hermetically sealed from one another, even now. Thornton and his companies were such a big presence locally. The widely publicized news of LetheTech's failure to launch its IPO had concentrated people's minds on what the company was trying to sell. 'Memory Therapy', even if that were dressed up in some fancy euphemism, had confirmed suspicions. Thornton was engaged in tampering with people's minds. 'The Management of Loss' might be a smart corporate slogan but increasingly the promise of cheap and effective on-line therapy hardly looked worth the price. The corruption of Kinnead O'Neal's mind, and several others that had come to light subsequently, added to the popular view that Thornton's work was beyond what nature permitted – and what was unnatural was ungodly. And what was ungodly... needed to be suppressed.

Carroll made a move to get up from the table. He needed to visit the injured in hospital, calling was not enough. Without a photo of himself walking the ward, he'd be wide open to criticism. Then he remembered. He'd already promised to spend time with his nephew Euclid before the latter returned to the North. Well, he would see him when he returned from the hospital, or maybe this evening before dinner. A talk with his nephew was not to be skipped, he must discover what further developments were coming their way from Blue Ridge's work and where their MARION project was right now.

TWENTY FOUR

About a week later, whilst the furore over the rogue Miltons at the 'service' still raged, Rick Muldane, one of the volunteer mercenaries, was being laid to rest. Gillespie had agreed to show his respects and provide a eulogy. His star was certainly not at its highest, thanks to a lot of blowback stirred up ably by Calvin Roberts. Still, the governor saw this as an opportunity to talk about the necessity of intervention in New Chaldea. At least it would make a change from the AI problems in the New Confederacy and a good speech at the graveside might divert attention from recent disasters. He'd have to parse his speech carefully. The role of president-elect was an innovation in the South and he didn't want to be associated with nothing but problems. The Christians were being pushed back in New Chaldea and unless a great deal more men were committed the end result was clear – defeat. The military aphorism *'Quantity is quality in warfare'* came to mind. The case for substantial intervention was strong, in his view at least, but he knew that the North and the Coastal states would not join him. Perhaps that didn't matter, even without them there were, potentially, plenty of local recruits; all those Southern Christians, tens of millions who could support the effort. Only one per cent would need to be personally committed A hundred thousand soldiers for Christ? That should be enough but could a force of that size be raised? Not without a significant change in attitudes.

It didn't help that Calvin Roberts was much more cautious than himself on this issue. But if out-flanked by Calvin on robotics, he would out-flank him on New Chaldea. He would turn the tide of public opinion – single handed if necessary. Only the means of doing so was not yet obvious. But it would become so. God would show him a path. The eulogy for Rick Muldane needed to be short and not too political. Carroll hoped that as the circumstances of the young man's death became more widely known, they would provide the very propaganda push that he would otherwise choose to avoid that morning.

*

As the funeral drew to a close and the mourners filed past the open grave, contributing their modest spoonful of heaped earth, Carroll spotted Thornton and made his way over. He was surprised to see him here, not realising that Thornton had known the Muldane family.

"Good morning Thornton. Didn't realise you knew the

Muldane's. Hope I provided poor Rick with a decent send off. Do you believe in the after- life, Mr Lamaire?"

The question caught Thornton by surprise, as much as use of his family name, as though the two of them were hardly known to each other. He'd been unexpectedly moved by the governor's eulogy. It was always the young, filled with un-calculating enthusiasm that inspired them to fly to distant conflicts – and die there. Still, Rick's comrades had turned out and provided a fired salute. The Muldanes were distant acquaintances of his and Bethany's. Carroll Gillespie had done him proud, providing a beautiful speech built on the few facts of a life that had been cut too short.

Thornton stood in line to express his condolences to the parents, then walked across to the open grave and tossed in his spoon of earth. There was already a build-up of dirt and his contribution made little sound as it landed on the cardboard coffin. Just like life, he thought gloomily. We believe what we do will make a difference but our impact is absorbed in the general indifference of the universe.

The darkness of Thornton's thoughts was not particularly about death or the afterlife, but about himself. His dyspeptic mood led him to ruminate on all the events that had gone wrong over the last year: the hesitant progress by MARION towards full consciousness, the failure of the LetheTech IPO, the financial pressures that had caused, public anxiety about memory therapy that had brought with it a demand for regulatory oversight, the anti-AI mood gathering steam in the South and the rampage by his Milton robots. The list was long and it didn't end there. With Bethany's recent fall off the wagon, a sort of ultimatum from Lu Ann, who saw their relationship going nowhere, his daughter Stephanie living three thousand miles away and Carroll Gillespie trying to involve him ever deeper into what would surely become a morass in New Chaldea: there was enough on his plate. Thornton's mood curdled further, preventing him from conjuring up the appropriate response to the sacrifice Rick had made for his faith. Their shared faith he reminded himself. Compassionate as he might consider himself to be, Thornton felt a pang of guilt about his lack of any real interest in the soldier or his fate. He watched a young woman crying her eyes out, a child wrapped around her legs: Muldane's girlfriend he presumed.

Thornton shook his head clear and turned towards Carroll, as they began the long walk down the line of cypresses towards the car park.

"Of course," Thornton said, in delayed response to the governor's question. "I accept the church's teaching on this. I expect to be judged and I hope that I will just squeak into Heaven." He hesitated. "An' I believe that we cannot achieve the kingdom of Heaven without Jesus's help," he added piously.

But even as he spoke, he was assailed by doubts. He had asked for forgiveness many times but would he be forgiven for what he had done to Stephanie and her unborn child, for his illicit relationship with Lu Ann? Somehow the Catholic church's procedures for atonement had not provided him with the promised release, no matter how many times he'd discussed those sins with his confessor. Although assured that he would be granted grace by a loving God, he didn't feel that redemption was on its way. What was the point of penitence if the spiritual weight of sin continued to rest heavy upon his shoulders? He recalled the French saying, *'Dieu me pardonera, c'ést son metier,'* 'God will pardon me, that's his profession'. Well, God could do worse than start practising with him. And then there was the additional spiritual burden about the wisdom of MARION's creation. If we were created in His image and MARION was like us, then it followed that she too must be like God. He could see how this might appear tantamount to blasphemy. So would he be let in to Heaven? It seemed increasingly improbable, whether he believed in it or not. He rather hoped there was no after-life, one that he would be denied. Would the peace that his faith had once given him be the next casualty of his life, the next loss? Could that loss be managed?

Thornton looked across at Carroll. Presumably he must, as an ex-Bishop, believe in an after-life. He seemed to be curiously, given the circumstances, upbeat this morning and Thornton pondered that perhaps his one-time friend might find fulfilment and purpose in funerals; they validated his original calling, the sort of thing that men of the cloth were meant to do, sending another man off into the eternal life; committing him to a voyage whose destination he could only hope was as God had promised.

The ex-bishop seemed to intuit his ruminations.

"You know Thornton. I've been thinking a lot about death recently. I had a brush not so long ago. For a few days I had to reflect on the fact that I might be... dead in six months. They thought I had one of those cancers they still can't cure – or even just hold down, you know, where you live with it but don't die. But I was very lucky.

Turned out to be some false alarm."

"And did you go through any of those famous moments of reflection, like 'what have I done with my life?' or 'how I want to spend my last few months?' All that bucket list stuff," asked Thornton, trying to edge any cynicism out of his own voice.

"Not really," said Carroll, sounding more despondent than grateful for his redemption from the jaws of death. "Although I knew that, if the diagnosis was confirmed, I'd probably be dead in six months, I never felt, really felt, that I would be gone before Christmas. Whether it was the good Lord's comforting me or the inability of the mind to contemplate its own demise, I don't know. But any serious idea of extinction never became part of my consciousness."

"Or perhaps, as a believer in an afterlife you weren't unduly troubled by the thought of death?"

"Could be that, could be that," agreed the governor amiably, "Probably a bit of that, I do agree."

The two walked on in silence, each lost within thoughts about what might lie ahead, given their past behaviours.

TWENTY FIVE

Thornton's heart lifted as they approached the parking lot, satisfied that he'd done his bit, discussed theology with Carroll and been supportive about his policy towards New Chaldea. Surely that was worth some indulgence. With the recent disturbances at his plants acting as political cover, Carroll could make Thornton's and Blue Ridge Corporation's life very difficult, if he chose. God might promise redemption in the next life but the governor could, and would, only offer him peace in this one if it were in his interest to do so.

Just before he reached the car, Carroll grabbed his elbow and steered him back down the avenue of the cypresses.

"Walk with me a little further, my friend," he urged. "It's good to have someone to whom I can unburden a little. You see, I was not entirely honest in the eulogy. But I didn't lie either."

If you had, Thornton said to himself, you'd only have been following in the long tradition of your predecessors. From Huey Long to Edwin Edwards, past governors of Louisiana had not been fazed by sticking too closely to the truth. Had not Huey Long, the father of populism, instructed a harassed aide who had asked what he should tell an aggressive and hostile crowd, intent on ransacking the governor's mansion to protest broken electoral promises, to say, 'tell them I lied.' Had not Edwards, when the prosecutor in a corruption trial asked him if he was lying, replied, 'No, but if I were, you have to assume that I would not be telling you.' Lying, misspeaking, inoperative phrasing; they all had an honoured place in Louisiana oratory.

"I didn't lie," the Governor repeated. "But I did stretch the truth. The grave is not a place for too much reality and we must give comfort to those left behind. They wish to know their loved one's sacrifice has not been in vain. But... it's sure beginning to look that way. These volunteers, this expeditionary force – fact is they're beat."

"I'm sorry to hear that," said Thornton vaguely, trying to show concern. The problems of New Chaldea were way from his interest at that moment. He'd heard all about the problems of the volunteer force before.

"Unless something is done, we're going to lose this last opportunity to create a haven for Christianity in the Middle East. There's nowhere else for them to go. If that area is settled by those who are not of our faith, that's going to nix it for another generation. The boundaries will be established for another century. Like when the remains of the Ottoman empire were re-drawn 150 years ago." Thornton recalled Carroll was a history buff.

"I hear all that Carroll. All those wars. Everyone is exhausted, as you and I have discussed before."

"They are, they are," agreed Carroll. "That's why this is the last chance. There will be no appetite for further... turbulence, if I may call it that."

"So, what are you going to do now?" asked Thornton, puzzled

"It's not just me, Thornton. I can't do nothin' just on my own." "We've all got to help if this thing is going to be won."

"I see," said Thornton, doubtfully.

"At least I know you're on board," said Carroll, daring Thornton to deny the assertion. "I've always respected your commitment, Thornton. I appreciate your enthusiasm and your understanding of what a great opportunity this is, for the Lord; in the land of his birth. I know that you'll do what you can. I appreciate that. I do, really."

"How exactly can I help, Cal?"

"Thank you my friend. I knew that I could count on you. As I said, the volunteer force is just beat. Unless we change things, more fine young men like Muldane are going to die. We need more guys out there, better equipped – and only the government can provide that."

"Well, you are the president-elect after all. Nobody's going to stand in your way."

"Down here we follow the word of the Lord," asserted the governor, as though all alternative systems of government were immoral, lesser affairs. "Folks here are sympathetic to doin' something in New Chaldea. Unlike them up in the North. But as we both know, there's no firm mandate to commit militarily, publicly anyways, down here at the moment. Unless... " The governor hesitated, perhaps hoping that Thornton might finish his sentence.

"Unless, ... what?" Thornton asked, unwillingly.

"We have to change people's views. They've got to start pressing for the government to get involved."

"Well, you've asked your friends in the media, like me – and many others – to make the case, haven't you?"

"I have, I have. But even so, there's been a reluctance to take my line. You know, these editors and publishers ... they are not, like, the bravest of people. I don't mean you Thornton, of course you've been very supportive, but others? They say, 'we're in the business of giving people what they want and there's no sign our readers want to go to war again.' So, I've got a problem. We can't send troops without popular support, and the media won't help persuade folks that we ought to go. So, I need to find some way of generating a bit of enthusiasm in people who ain't got none – right now, anyway."

"Sounds a tough call to me, governor!"

"But not an impossible one?"

'How so?" Thornton consulted his iPsyche. He needed to get going.

"You're doing some interesting work up North, Thornton, I hear."

"Interesting? For sure," said Thornton. He disliked the sound of the euphemism, *'interesting'.*

"But it's not all going to plan. You've read about the problems with LetheTech? We thought we had memory nailed, but not quite yet."

"Must have been putting some pressure on you financially, has it not my friend?" Thornton recalled it was wise not to underestimate the governor's ability to work things out, nor the extent and depth of his sources. Informants were everywhere.

"It has not been helpful," agreed Thornton, drily.

"I'm sure not. And then there has been that business with the rogue Miltons. That's not been helpful either, I guess."

"Indeed, Cal. Look, I need to get back. Could we continue this another day? I'm keen to do whatever I can to help the cause"

Carroll shook his head sympathetically. "How selfish of me! I should be getting along too. Let's walk back", The governor spun on his heel and headed the two of them towards the car park. He had a few more minutes more in which to bend Thornton's ear.

"Despite LetheTech's problems, that I understand are pretty well sorted now, I hear there are some other amazing developments coming out of your place in the Catskills. Seems you can now change people's minds." It was more a statement than a question. "I hear you can, like, go into their minds, remove stuff, put ideas in."

Thornton tried to brush this aside. "You've read the reports, Carroll. That's what LetheTech is all about. We might do wonderful, positive things, that will make people better; remove memories that traumatise them, insert knowledge of how to do things that brain damage has disabled. It's not spooky. It's just the automation of therapy – but much more efficiently and thoroughly than has been possible before. It's no different than doing what we're all used to, but better."

"Indeed, indeed! So I understand," said Carroll, undeterred. "I'm sure that once the, you know,… the teething problems, like those Kinnead O'Neal suffered, are all worked out then it will be a great success. A boon to mankind... probably. But my friend, you are too modest. Can't those machines you got up there, can't they talk to many people, put things in lots of minds, not just one? And I hear that people may never know that the memories they're being given are from your MARION device. Because MARION leaves no trace of her presence, so they say. My, that's smart!"

Thornton screwed up his eyes. This was dangerous talk. "I don't know who you've been listening to, Carroll, But you sure make it sound a lot easier than it is."

"Oh, I'm sure. I'm sure I've got it all very muddled!" agreed the governor swiftly. "You must be patient with my technological innocence! But the basics of what I hear are right?"

"We're working on something similar," granted Thornton grudgingly. "But it's early days. Whosoever you got your information from was being wildly optimistic," (And I will make sure to find out who that person was when I get back, he thought) "There's a long way to go. But MARION may indeed be able to provide permanent psychiatric help. We will no longer need armies of psychologists. Anyone, anywhere in this world will be able to access LetheTech's services, via MARION. It will be the greatest advance in mental health the world has ever known. Man and machine will communicate directly by thought alone."

"Exactly. Man and machine talking to each other, sharing thoughts, if I understand it right? And not just one person at a time but many people. Memory deletion and entry combined with mass communication ability, via the iPsyche. Gee, your MARION will have great influence!" smirked Carroll.

"You make it sound all very sinister, Cal. There will be strict controls over what MARION can say and do. She will be heavily restricted," reassured Thornton.

"Of course she will be," agreed Carroll. "I didn't want to imply anything else. You're a good Catholic Thornton; I know you would not give a machine powers that are reserved only for God and those made in His image. But ... bear with me here, for a second."

Thornton steeled himself. The two were almost back at the car park.

"Suppose, just for a second, that you wanted to change an opinion, of a group of people, then you could, theoretically at least, remove one memory, a memory of say, just to take an example, some past problem or disaster and replace it with a more positive, useful, memory or opinion? And if you so chose, the people in that group would know nothing about what had gone on?"

"You could do that, if everything works, yes," said Thornton. "But we're not planning to do that. That's not what we're about. In fact, we will always leave a 'tracer' memory, once MARION has communicated, so that users can understand the difference between what they know from their own experience and what they have been given by MARION."

"Well, that's certainly very ethical." The governor spoke as though ethics was an interesting side-line of life but not one that they should be unduly inhibited by. "But you wouldn't have to put this 'tracer' on, would you? It's not an inevitable part of the process?" he asked.

"It's like some drug treatments," replied Thornton. "You attach a bit of radioactivity to a drug so you can trace its journey through the body. Keep track of it. The 'tracer' is not strictly required by the treatment. It's just that we think it right to provide it. And we think regulators will soon demand it anyway."

"So if you wanted to, I speak hypothetically of course, influence voter's intentions you could, perhaps, remove the past bad memories of something – and then insert more positive opinions about it?"

"I suppose so," replied Thornton. "I don't want to be a Debbie Downer on your idea, Carroll, but these people might not be fully persuaded of what you suggest once they noticed the 'tracer'. They might dismiss the information as so much advertising, or propaganda. Which is what it would be, seems to me."

"Yes, I can see that you'd have to remove the 'tracer' to be most effective, I understand that. Well, here we are," said the governor as they reached their cars. "It's been a fascinating chat, Thornton. You know, living down here in the deep South, sometimes one has no idea how fast science is moving. Amazing, what can be done now. I do hope your researches are successful. We could do so much with this MARION of yours."

The two shook hands and parted ways. Just as the governor reached his vehicle he called out, "By the way. When will that factory be up and running again? I had Sherman Barnes on the phone again the other day."

"I hope he is a bit happier now," replied Thornton. "We paid Jim Embry a way load of compensation for the damage."

"Jim Embry does seem happier now, so thank you for doing that. But Sherman Barnes has had so many calls about the future of the

Miltons, all these people telling him how unhappy they are, how he must not allow Miltons to be employed again in North Carolina. Then I started to receive calls, telling me I must close down factories everywhere in the South where series 5 Miltons are employed. Me and Sherman, see, we're under a lot of pressure."

"We're doing everything we can to make sure there's never a repeat of what poor Mr Embry and his family had to suffer," reassured Thornton. "Blue Ridge certainly don't want any more trouble. I understand the pressures you're facing."

"I'm sure you do, my friend. And I thank you for your understanding. Now, you have a good drive back, you hear."

Surprised the governor had said so little about the 'incident' at the so-called service a few days ago, Thornton couldn't resist having the last word. He understood that the governor might want the whole disaster brushed under the table. That misjudgement had been dangerous, politically. Yet what was dangerous to Carroll Gillespie might be to his advantage.

"Sorry there were so many dead and injured in that meeting of yours, Carroll. Terrible thing. People really shouldn't play with those machines. I had Senator Calvin Roberts on the phone this morning, asking for details of what I thought might have gone wrong, why the Miltons were so dangerous? I explained they had to be decommissioned properly before disposal. He's going to raise the matter in the state senate. Just thought you ought to know."

With that Parthian shot, Thornton drove off before the governor had the chance of a riposte.

TWENTY SIX

I'll be here for a week or so" said Stephanie. It was late afternoon. She and her father were strolling through the 'new' arboretum planted over 30 years ago. The sapling, planted soon after her birth, had grown rapidly in the warmth and humidity of the domes. Even the hard woods were already twice her height.

"However long you can make it," said Thornton. "I've missed you. We both have, your mother and I, since you've moved to Paris." Stephanie's presence not only illuminated the family home but also provided a useful buffer between him and Bethany. She heard the yearning in her father's voice; "It's lovely to be back but I don't want to overstay my welcome. Mother and I will drive each other nuts sooner or later, even if she's on the wagon, which she tells me she is. For the moment."

They walked on in companionable silence. Within the Buckminster domes grew a little paradise where not only plants flourished but birds and insects too. Space X had been to consult how they might establish a grove on Mars, before the launch of the Savannah craft. The whole business of creating the arboretum had been a source of enthusiasm and pride for her father. As they walked along the paths and passed each plant and tree, a hologram would materialise with a full scale image of how the adult item would look in its natural habitat, together with information on its identity and the botanical details of its species. A small cardinal bird came to rest on Stephanie's shoulder.

"How's Lu Ann?" she asked. She approved of her father's girlfriend, glad her father had found a companion who could provide him with affection. Lu Ann would lend a generous ear for his troubles but she worried that he was away too much to let the relationship flourish. "Be careful," Women like being paid attention," she admonished.

"I have to be everywhere at the moment," replied her father, defensively. "MARION is at a critical point, both financially and mentally. We were all very excited the other day when we discovered that we'd achieved singularity. Earlier, we were premature, but it looks as though that point has finally been reached."

"So you've achieved your goal, father? That's great – but I'm not going to let you count all your chickens yet!" Stephanie laughed, amused at the thought of being her father's spiritual guardian. Her parents were like children sometimes. The balance between herself and her parents had reversed itself in recent years. She and Elizabeth had become concerned for the welfare of their parents, as they had once been for their daughters. Now, she and her father were in a sort of equilibrium of mutual concern. Her father worried as much about Stephanie's career and relationship with Claude, as she wanted to be reassured about Lu Ann. And that Blue Ridge was not about to go bust.

"I read the news. Things seem to be tricky for you right now," she said.

"They're not easy," agreed Thornton. "Just as we advance to the point where we can mimic the human mind, we run into all sorts of hurdles. Particularly down *here*." He spoke the last word as though he abhorred Southern attitudes, as perhaps he did, however much he loved his plantation and the land of his youth.

He gestured to a bench at the side of the path. "Did you hear what happened to some of my Miltons the other day?"

Stephanie shook her head. She wanted to let her father have the opportunity to give his side of the story, although she had picked up the gist of it via local media during the flight over.

"The Miltons are very popular amongst manufacturers," explained Thornton. "They self-diagnose and self-repair. Unfortunately that means even the maintenance guys are finding less work. Well, we had some sabotage the other day that wrecked two of ours. Then the state impounded the machines and Carroll Gillespie held a sort of lynching, a bizarre 'service'. Says it was to release the pent-up antagonism towards these robots; all robots, perhaps, in the South. He claims he's neutral on the issue of Douglas versus Milton Robotics. Bah! He was sympathetic to the destruction. He was the ring-leader."

Stephanie frowned. "I thought that Cal was a friend?"

"Once, maybe. But never a great friend," corrected Thornton.

"He's a politician, riding on the back of his success with the plebiscite. The only friends he takes any notice of these days are the voters. And then he's got this obsession about New Chaldea. I mean, I'm as keen as the next church-goer to see Christianity re-established in the land of its birth but... there are limits, or should be. Cal's putting pressure on me to help in ways that I'm not at all comfortable with."

"Can Lu Ann help? Isn't she a friend of Cal's too? Stephanie was keen that her father had someone to help him in his trials, provide emotional support.

" Ah, I don't want to get Lu Ann involved in all this. I sort of like it that she's outside all these political games."

Stephane was less sure about this, but the talk about her father's relationship brought to mind something else. "Father... " Stephanie hesitated, unsure of how to proceed. "I had a mail from Lu Ann the other day. She said she was now working, or at least helping-out as she put it, at Nathan Seddenhow's clinic. I'm planning to drop in and see her sometime."

"Seddenhow?" Her father sounded surprised. "You want to contact with him again, after all this time?"

"He always sends a birthday greeting. And occasionally he messages to tell me about goings-on down here."

"I had no idea. I thought that after what happened you'd never want to see him again."

"I think you get it wrong. Whatever happened, I never blamed him. He was real kind at the time, supportive and sympathetic."

"I see. Well, I'm delighted to hear it"

"So, anyway... I told Nat I was coming back and he wrote that Lu Ann was there to help him in the clinic."

Thornton fell silent. That his daughter and Lu Ann should see each other appealed to him for many reasons. But still, he was surprised that Stephanie would ever go back to Seddenhow's clinic. He reflected on how little he really knew about his daughter's life.

"So how's it between you and Claude then?" he asked.

The question caught Stephanie by surprise. "It's fine,' she said non-committedly. "He is always travelling."

"I hope I don't make him come out to the MARION centre too often?" asked her father. "I didn't want to disturb the two of you. But he seems very interested in the work. And he has been very helpful, very useful."

"You have nothing to blame yourself for Father! But it's not just the trips to the centre. Claude is always away on some lecture circuit or conference, or delivering some speech to a bunch of AI business people. I get a little fed up spending so much time on my own. Otherwise it's okay. Although... " Her voice trailed off. "It's not just the travelling though," She sounded uncertain. "There is something that... something that unsettles me about him."

"Can I help?" her father asked.

TWENTY SEVEN

Stephanie took a long breath. "There's a lot – and I mean a lot – of backstory in Claude's life. Before I arrived on the scene, there was a precarious relationship with his father's carer – Fabienne – that went well past what a carer is expected to provide. That was never going to be a long term arrangement in Claude's view, but that didn't stop Fabienne fantasising about being his girlfriend. Sure, she's an attractive girl. She flits around the apartment in black jeans and open white blouse, perhaps trying to emulate the look of her employer. But it was never really serious. There was no way Claude was going to introduce her to his friends, for example. But he took the optimistic attitude that surely Fabienne could never have seriously considered they had a future together. Alas, she has not been of the same view. Matters only became more tricky once I moved in."

"But I guess Claude has resolved that situation?" asked her father.

"He's trying to, but the situation is not without complications. Claude wanted to move his father – Vincent – out and into another apartment and have Fabienne, or more likely her replacement, look after him there. But a second apartment on a professor's salary, topped up with a bit of consultant income from Blue Ridge? It's a fantasy. Not going to happen."

"There's no-one else in the family who can look after the father?"

"Seems not. Claude is his father's last living relative. Vincent's wife died several years ago, and Claude is his only child. Apart from anything else Claude has always adored his father – and the affection has been reciprocated. He doesn't want to put him in a home. But if not, what's the alternative? His last book has been a modest success but only temporary income at best. Blue Ridge pays something, but usually late (just making a point, Daddy!) and even with that his total income is not sufficient to cover the rent on another apartment. Of course, he could fire Fabienne and replace her with someone whom he has never slept with. That would resolve one source of friction in both our lives. Yet his father has grown accustomed and affectionate towards her. Besides if he did fire her, Fabienne will probably go to a tribunal and claim she has only been let go because her employer has grown tired of her bedroom services."

Thornton looked at his daughter thoughtfully. These French with their complicated love lives! A stray thought of Lu Ann passed barely recognised through his consciousness. Followed by a more useful one that if Claude's father didn't have Alzheimer's any more there would be a valid excuse to fire Fabienne and no danger of a tribunal's censor. Nor any need to recruit a replacement and find a second apartment. Now that LetheTech's initial human trials had begun in Europe maybe Claude's father could be enrolled? Preliminary results that suggested the memory therapy provided successful treatment for Alzheimer's patients, able to rebuild their minds once stem cell treatment had re-grown damaged brain tissue. At least to some extent. Enough, anyway, to give the patient (or clients as he insisted LetheTech more reassuringly call them) the ability to manage everyday life and even to converse with family members, without that annoying repetition that accompanied memory loss

The O'Neal debacle had caused him to hesitate mentioning the possibility to his daughter but then, given what he had just heard, the risk that the memory rebuild might go awry and the client left with even less recall than before didn't seem much of a danger here.

" It's a nice idea, father," said Stephanie in reply. Let me discuss it with Claude. I'm not sure if he'd have the money for the fees, though."

"Wouldn't be none. As this is a trial, all treatment is for free. Vincent sounds as though he might be suitable. I need to speak to Heather. She's the expert on these things. How bad is Claude's father?" asked Thornton.

"It varies," replied Stephanie. " But sometimes he has no idea what's happening. The other night when Claude returned from lecturing his father asked him, 'Is Madeleine coming today?' Now, Madeleine was Vincent's wife, long dead. Claude told him, very gently that he was afraid Madeleine couldn't come that day. A few minutes later, Vincent asked the same question again. But Madeleine isn't the only resonance from his past. The other day a letter arrived that disturbed our equilibrium a little."

"A letter! My God, who sends one of those these days? I can't even remember when I received the last one," said her father. "What on earth occasioned that?"

"Bizarre, huh? The envelope was addressed to Vincent and written in mauve ink. Rarer still, Claude thought he better read it before showing it to his father. Just as well he did. He opened it in front of me. The letter was written in a shaky hand and difficult to decipher, but one could just make out the signature, 'Valerie'. I learnt that Valerie was Vincent's last girlfriend after the death of Madeleine. He and Valerie had never married but must have been together for some eight or nine years. When Vincent became seriously forgetful and Valerie could no longer stand the strain, she left. Valerie visited a few times long ago but since she had moved to another area of France even those visits had petered out."

"The letter made interesting reading. Unknown to Claude, his father had been paying Valerie a monthly pension for years and then suddenly it had stopped, plunging her into financial distress. Well, of course it had stopped! Claude had taken over Vincent's finances and had cancelled all his regular payments, reasoning that whatever services they were for, the fact that she no longer had any contact meant he could cancel them with an easy conscience. Valerie was now raising the alarm directly with Vincent, probably not realising how far his memory loss had advanced. Did he know the payments had been suspended, did he understand how much difference the money made to her? The sums were not large but they were not something that Vincent's pension could support, now that Claude used some of that to fund his care. Besides, hardly a need to subsidise Valerie now his father couldn't even recall who she was. "

"Well, LetheTech can create and implant memories, as well as delete them. Maybe we could give Vincent back a memory of this Valerie," said Thornton encouragingly, completely misunderstanding his daughter's point.

"We definitely don't want that!" exclaimed Stephanie, with force. "No. I was interested in something quite different. If LetheTech could reinstall some life skills in Vincent, then maybe we wouldn't need a carer at all. Good-by Fabienne."

"Ah, I see. Okay, I'll drop an email to Heather and see if Vincent can be enrolled in the European trials. Doesn't sound as though even if things did go wrong it would make much difference."

"May not be just for Vincent!" said Stephanie. "Maybe Claude needs memory therapy himself! Something else curious arose out of the letter. Valerie asked how Irene was?"

"Who the fuck is Irene?" said Thornton. " I get a little lost in all these characters."

"Indeed, 'who the fuck is Irene' is just what I asked. I was getting a little lost too. I asked Claude. He seemed to have no recollection of who was this mysterious woman. He couldn't remember his father having a girlfriend of that name either. I teased him that it must have been an old girlfriend of his own. But he said no, there'd been no girlfriend of that name that he could remember. Yet, I could see that something disturbed Claude, almost as much as it did me. Was he going the way of his father? The whole thing took a further twist when some weeks later I found some old photos in a drawer. 'Showed an attractive tall brunette, thirtyish. She must have been important in some way. I mean, who prints off photos these days? Claude was unable to identify her. She might have been a lover, or maybe, less likely but let's be optimistic here, a favourite cousin or a niece. Who knows? But someone important enough to have kept a photo of? I mean, come on! Yet, I've never seen a man more plausibly deny something. Doesn't seem to be faking memory loss but Claude's has complete amnesia on the subject. No amount of probing has the slightest result. I try not to let the incident cause a hiatus in our relationship. I've suggested he might question his friends or his thousands of cousins. Yet, when he is with one of them there's always this inhibition, some lack of will, a fear perhaps, to explore the subject. And it's no use asking his father, who might once have known 'Irene' but if he did, would have certainly forgotten her existence by now!"

Thornton looked across at his daughter. He could see that the identity of 'Irene', or, more accurately the inability to identify her, had left uncertainties about Stephanie's relationship with Claude that were not going to disappear fast. Maybe LetheTech's treatment would also reveal the identity of this 'Irene'.

Just then, as they walked through the dome, a call came through on Thornton's iPsyche. He had set the threshold high, instructing the iPsyche to notify him only if a message was of the highest importance.

He held up a finger to ask for Stephanie's understanding. His face clouded as he listened. "Stephanie, I'm sorry," he said, resting a hand on his daughter's shoulder. "We're going to have to continue our chat another time. I'll see you at dinner."

"Why, what is it? she asked, concerned, "Is there anything I can help with?"

"Alas not," said Thornton. "They've closed all the factories in the Confederacy states that employ gen 5 robots, those are the latest Miltons. On grounds of safety. I'll have to go right away. I'm sorry, sweetheart. I'll be back in a day or so."

TWENTY EIGHT

T he next day, during the flight up to Richmond VA, Thornton pieced together Heather's reports. Early that morning there had been a coordinated swoop by local officials, backed by police armed with orders signed by Carroll Gillespie, instructing managers of the Blue Ridge plant that built Milton series 5 robots to put all machinery into stand-by mode and send non-essential staff home. The stop-work order extended to all companies and clients who employed the Series 5 machines, but they were permitted to continue production with older models. Carroll could not afford to alienate everybody.

The financial consequences of the injunction would be severe for Blue Ridge. With production suspended, no shipments meant no cash flow. Meanwhile the fixed costs of the plant would continue to need paying. There had been no call from Carrol that morning, something Thornton might have expected considering the circumstances. But of course, as he now understood, no message was the message. The president-elect wanted Thornton to come to him. And humiliating as it was, Thornton realised that he had no option but to comply. Only Carroll could lift the stop-work order. He wondered how long Gillespie would leave him to twist in the wind.

Thornton's surmises were correct. He tried to initiate the process of détente and called Carroll. But the president-elect was unable, or more likely unwilling, to take his call and half a day later had still failed to do so. Eventually an aide to Carroll did respond explaining how difficult the position was; the safety of people living around the plant, and the workforce were their first concern. The state had to address the cause of the malfunction and make sure all the issues were understood and rectified. Malfunction, thought Thornton? There was no malfunction, as Carroll knew perfectly well. The robots had been tampered with. There would have to be an investigation. How long? Oh, difficult to say, replied the aide. Someone who possessed the public's full confidence would have to be found to lead the enquiry. There would be a report, a study of the recommendations, public consultation and implementation of the recommendations. Six months, possibly nine; it would all take time. There could be delays. That was an indicative timetable, if everything went smoothly and they had complete cooperation from Milton Robotics and the folks at Blue Ridge.

Thornton smiled to himself. Under light pressure he fussed around and worried about life. In a crisis he was transformed, as though he needed a wall of opposition to push against to let him feel his strength. There was no panic; this crisis too would pass. He knew the governor's position was bluff and that he would shelve the investigation as quick as a hog searching for acorns if he got what he wanted. Thornton would just have to go see him and winkle out the price.

They landed in Richmond as dark fell. Thornton had phoned Gillespie's office to suggest dinner together but was told he had a prior engagement. Thornton could be spared an hour the following morning. He expected nothing less; however much the president-elect wanted to put him on the defensive Carroll would be open to criticism if he was not seen to try to resolve the issue. Several hundred or so men were idle at the Blue Ridge plant; but many thousands of others also had to lay down their tools since production at their own factories was impossible without the participation of the Miltons. The production process had changed too much since their introduction. Gillespie could not depend on the forbearance of these workforces for too long; they might be resentful of the Miltons but equally they needed to be paid. They could quickly become resentful of politicians too.

The next day Thornton presented himself at the president elect's office. He half expected to be kept waiting, a further sign of disapproval. But Carroll was not so small minded; he had a full schedule that morning; *let's get this necessary meeting over with* was his attitude. A trim young man in a blue suit and a crew cut showed him into an office dominated by a large mahogany table, on which stood a few screens and family photos, a sofa and a couple of armchairs.

Gillespie gestured Thornton be seated, dismissed the aide and ordered coffee.

"Mighty good of you to fly up and see me, Thornton," said Carroll disingenuously.

"I have plants closed down, four hundred men idled, God knows how many others at my clients. It's at the order of the Southern Confederacy, so that means you, my friend," said Thornton forcibly. "The shutdown is costing everyone a lot of money."

"Of course, of course. I understand that," responded Carroll, as amiably as ever. "And nobody wants to get the men back to work faster than me. But, after the incident in North Carolina and the subsequent outcry, I had little alternative. Until the Miltons are cleared it would have been irresponsible of me to allow production to continue. Of course, if you instructed your clients to withdraw them, all of them, in all the plants down here where they are employed, and return to previous production methods then we could have a look at rescinding the order."

"Bah! Thornton snorted. "You are quite well informed enough, Cal, to know my clients have made fundamental production changes to benefit from the efficiencies these robots bring. It would take months to reorganise things back to what they were. And anyway, men have been let go. "

"Premature, perhaps?" suggested Carroll, pointedly. "Such problems these robots lead us into."

"Everything would have been fine if those Miltons had not been tampered with," said Thornton.

"I hear of no evidence they were tampered with," contradicted the president-elect. "The investigative report – admittedly prepared in a hurry because this was such a pressing issue – makes no mention of tampering. The men responsible for the robots' welfare say there was a malfunction."

"Malfunction? You know that's untrue," said Thornton. "You were at the plant where those robots went berserk. You spoke to the men. You were told, as much as I was, that the Milton's coding had been interfered with when some of the workers kidnapped their attendant."

Gillespie looked him in the eye, "I do remember that, yes. But we later discovered that those men were mistaken. When we spoke to your people, we were told the Miltons had an inhibitory circuit, a safety device, that even if they were tampered with would prevent them from running amok. That never operated. So, for whatever reason they went crazy, it wasn't simply down to sabotage. There was a malfunction too."

Thornton has no idea if this was true or not. He was unfamiliar with the finer technical details of these robots. He could call the Milton plant to establish the truth – but he wanted to resolve the shut-down now, not leave it for another day. Each hour that passed cost him and his clients. This was about power, not facts. He suspected that the analysis was rubbish and designed only to support whatever were Carroll's long term aims.

"Well, that's really too bad, Cal," agreed Thornton. "I guess then we'll just have to wait until the investigatory team have established what exactly went wrong. Do you have a timetable from them yet?"

"Not at the moment, no," said Carroll,. His tone suggested this was a great disappointment. Of course you don't, thought Thornton. Too bad the machines had been destroyed in the auto-da-fe rather than inspected for whatever evidence they might provide. But, as Thornton understood, part of the reason for the auto-da-fe was to destroy any evidence that might derail the president-elect's narrative. Thornton always had respect for Gillespie's strategies.

"That's just too bad," repeated Thornton. "Shame about all those guys, with no money coming in this month. But I appreciate that we can't afford to take any risks. By the way how's the post plebiscite coming-together thing going?" At least he owned the satisfaction of pointing out Carroll's hypocrisy; this demonizing of his activities and the laying off of thousands of men would do nothing for the president-elect's aim of smoothing the tensions and divisions that the vote had given rise to.

Gillespie leant forward and poured Thornton another coffee,

"Difficult to say really," he replied casually. If Thornton wanted to divert discussion away from the malfunction of the Miltons, that was fine. "The North are running a lot of scare stories – most are rubbish, but some have their effect. They're determined to drive fear into the folks down here – telling them that after the plebiscite everyone will be much worse off. When of course, the opposite will be the case. They just want to fill up the factories and offices here with their robots and other machines, displacing a whole lot of our people in the process. But who wants that Northern money, when we don't get to run our own affairs or when we have to put up with a lot of shit about robots having to be treated with respect? They got feelings? Huh, really? Douglas v Milton Robotics is one of the main causes of the discontent in the South. I know you didn't intend it that way Thornton, when your people invented these things, but that's the way it is."

This outburst got him no nearer to discovering what Carroll really wanted. He knew that the governor would not name his price directly. He might want to deny ever having said something substantive, in case it all went wrong later. "Yeah, I can sure see how things are going," agreed Thornton. He recalled their previous conversation. "Well, I guess we'll just have to wait," he continued. "Nothing more to be done. But tell me, how's that New Chaldea thing, that we discussed the other day, playing out?" he asked. "The idea of a Southern led intervention?"

At once Carroll Gillespie sprang to life. "No change there yet, Thornton. Sadly. As I said to you, my old flock, the voters, are hesitant – and I understand that. Our years in the Middle East have not all been crowned with glory. I accept that too… but we're talking about a last push here. A last effort for our Lord. It's not too much to ask, is it? There's this reluctance, a lack of faith, to fight the last battle, before the war is won. People feel they've been down this route before. I understand that. Memories are long."

"Folks have been led down this path before?" mused Thornton barely audibly, but just loud enough to be heard by Carroll. "Memories are long? Memories? They're my job,"

"Indeed!" agreed Carroll with sudden enthusiasm. "You're right, Thornton. Memories are long – and unhelpful! If only memories of past failed military expeditions didn't exist, then I am sure the faithful would support the Lord in his hour of need. They support with money now, but that's not enough. They've got to risk blood too. How wonderful it would be if we could only relieve them of their troublesome doubt!"

The Governor stopped, as though he had said enough. The two man sat back to reflect. Thornton understood the Governor's price for reopening his factories. As if in response to that insight, Carroll said;

"Do you remember that talk we had in the car park the other day, Thornton? Have you had a chance to think any more about what I said?"

Thornton took a deep breath. "Carroll, you and I have known each other a long time. I am a man of the South and have always made my home here. Whatever I have become, and whatever has been given me, I owe to the South, and to God. I am a Christian, a loyal Southern Catholic, and I believe that our Lord should find a permanent home in the land of his birth. So… I can help you. We can ask MARION to run pro-intervention messages off the LetheTech platform, piped in via people's iPsyches. She can explain why past 'expeditions' or whatever you want to call them, will not be a good guide to what will happen in the future. She could persuade voters, that if we send a force to New Chaldea, they need not be afraid of the consequences. That it will all turn out for the best."

Carroll Gillespie smiled generously. Carroll might be the holder of political power but he knew how fragile that could be if he did not also possess the support of those who controlled the economy. A great industrialist like Thornton Lamaire could not be left feeling resentful, that he had been forced into a corner, left with no option but to submit.

"That's mighty good of you, Thornton," said Carroll. "Appreciated, really is. I'll ask my campaign manager to talk to your people. They can work out a message we can broadcast. But I was wondering." The governor hesitated. "Do we have to tell the recipients from where the message is coming from? Like, do we have to ensure a 'tracer' is attached? It would be so much more effective if the appeal could be posted as the view of some independent, but maybe unspecified, observer? As you said yourself, folks have a tendency to disparage and ignore what they regard as political propaganda."

Thornton looked shocked as though he had just heard a member of the church issue a profanity. "You are asking me to deliver that message without adding who's responsible for it? You know, Carroll, that we can't do that. There are rules against those sort of things. We'd be massively fined, maybe banned, if we were to be discovered. Political broadcasting has to show who is promoting it. You know that!"

The president-elect pulled back his pawn in order to secure the ultimate prize. A check-mate that was surely not far away. "Of course, of course. I was forgetting the most basic of rules that govern these political debates," he said. He hesitated a moment before insisting, "But would you really need to include the tracer? Think about it. I mean, there is no particular organisation behind this, is there? This is an issue that cuts across political lines. It's just a movement really, a view, a ground swell of anonymous public support, isn't it? There's no single body to whom you could attribute to such a message."

"You think so?" asked Thornton, also biding his time.

"But maybe you're right in principle," agreed Carroll. "It might be misleading to send out this message, without saying who it's from. Not entirely honest. I grant you that. So I want to suggest a different approach. Instead of sending the public a message, why don't we remove one instead? As we both know, you can do that now."

Thornton had not forgotten that the possibility of mass memory deletion had been leaked to Carroll. But he wasn't prepared for this suggestion. Publishing a message via an iPsyche was little different to transmitting it via a cell phone or a wrist band, but erasing a memory involved LetheTech having deep access to people's minds. Memory deletion was not simply the reverse of message insertion. People would be aware of a new or unexpected thought, particularly if accompanied by a 'tracer'; but a deletion would leave no trace. There would be no awareness that someone, something, had been inside their mind and removed a prior recollection.

"Be like the 'Act of Oblivion'," continued Carroll. "Do you know what that was?"

Thornton shook his head. "Tell me."

"I was a history major, as you know," said Carroll. "I remember one time, Oliver Cromwell, this guy who won the civil war in

England, when it was all over he instituted an 'Act of Oblivion'. All crimes in the war, well, except those like supporting the late King, or buggery, they were very hot against that I'm glad to say, were forgiven – and forgotten – officially. Just think of that; this old Brit was way ahead of us, my dear friend. That's what we need here – an act of oblivion. Everyone made to forget past disasters!"

It was clear the way this cookie was crumbling. Thornton could, and should, decline what he was being asked to do. Or he could wait months for the report on the safety of the Miltons to be published at which point his plants might be allowed to reopen. He would probably be bankrupt by that time. Or he could accede to the governor's request now, have the robots declared safe and the factories allowed to restart.

True, mass memory deletion was untested. The consequences of permitting MARION use of the LetheTech process and direct access to minds of the public had not been fully thought through. Xian Han believed that they had now overcome O'Neal type dangers, but nobody was really yet sure, particularly when it involved millions of people. And if it ever surfaced that MARION and LetheTech were involved in memory manipulation of the entire Southern population, or at least those who wore iPsyches, there would be such a storm of protest that Blue Ridge might not survive. Thornton felt he had to deflect the request. Heather Masters and Xian Han would never accept the proposal anyway.

"Perhaps we could start with just some political advertising?" Thornton suggested tentatively. Inserting a little propaganda was probably okay, particularly with a 'tracer' attached. There was no point giving everything to Carroll immediately. This was a negotiation after all. "The people are used to hearing this type of publicity. They'd hardly pay any attention to the 'tracer'. I don't see that if they know the message comes from your political organisation that would weaken its force."

The president-elect held himself in check. Free political advertising was always useful. But he'd heard nothing about modifying the attitudes, deleting the memories, of those folk who were hostile to his plans for an expeditionary force to be sent to New Chaldea. And yet, the concession on political advertising, even if accompanied by a 'tracer', was significant. As Euclid had explained to him, the vital objective must be to forge a mental connection between MARION, LetheTech and the voters. Once that had been achieved, who knew what might be possible? Thornton did not have many options, his plants could remain closed for a long time. Besides it was never wise to push a man too far. Who knew when an opponent might be recycled to the top of the heap again. Never use all of your advantage at one time was one of his favourite political rules. His instinct told him to accept what was offered. For now.

"You're probably right," conceded Carroll. "I wasn't thinking. Of course the message must carry the 'tracer'." Reluctant to cede ground too easily, he still wanted Thornton to feel he had won some victories. "And the negative advertising?" It was the most euphemistic way he could phrase his request about memory deletion.

Thornton fidgeted and shook his head. "Not yet, I think Carroll. The technology is not proven. If we had an O'Neal problem on our hands, at a mass level, it would be a disaster – for both of us."

It would indeed, thought Carroll, but from what he had heard from Euclid, Thornton was underplaying his team's abilities. The O'Neal issue had been solved.

"I understand. I'm as suspicious of these new technologies as you are. We certainly don't want to go too fast. Let's leave all that for the time being," said the governor, gracefully.

"Thank you," was Thornton's relieved reply. He still had to square with Heather on even the modest issue of identifiable political advertising. She would try to insist that granting MARION direct access to public minds was a step way too far at the moment. Too bad; she would have to be brought round to the idea. Thornton knew that he had the leverage. But would the modest concession that he had given Carroll be sufficient to buy the release of the stop-work order that Blue Ridge needed?

"Carroll, now that we have that resolved, the political thing, could we turn to the issue facing my plants?" Thornton asked.

"Oh, I'm sure there's no need to worry about that," smiled Carroll. "Let me see where we are right now." He pressed a button on the table. "Shane, will you come in with an update on wherever we are on the Milton investigation, please? Thornton and I have successfully completed our meeting." He turned to Thornton and smiled. "More coffee, Mr Lamaire?"

The aide entered, studying his tablet. A Moses trying to interpret

God's downloaded commandment as he descended the mountain.

"Shane, you have any news for us on the rogue Miltons? Anything we can share with Mr Lamaire here?" asked Gillespie.

Shane, who had been well briefed on how to act out the whole charade if he heard the phrase *'successful meeting'*, studied his tablet even more thoroughly. God's will did not seem so difficult to interpret this morning. "I've had an update from the investigative team very recently. It seems they have now been able to confirm the plant manager's account – that the cause of the robot's aberrant behaviour was due to tampering. The safety routines were overridden. There is no reason to suppose that if properly handled the Miltons are not safe for factory work."

"Well, that's marvellous news Shane. Thank you," Carroll looked as though the world could not be more agreeable to his desires that morning. "I'm sure that will be music to Mr Lamaire's ears. Is that not so Thornton? I see no reason now why we should not raise the desist work order and get your men back to work immediately."

The governor stood as Shane left. "We'll meet each other again soon, I hope," he said walking Thornton to the door.

"But we'll meet in two weeks," said Thornton. "You've obviously forgotten in all the excitement. It's the 'Friends of New Chaldea' foundation gala in New York. You're the guest speaker I see. Bethany and I wouldn't miss it for the world."

"How silly of me," said Carroll. "Of course. I shall instruct Shane to prepare some remarks. And I'm delighted that you and Bethany will be present. Kirsty will be so pleased." The president-elect thrust forth a hand. "It's been a good morning, Thornton. Have a pleasant flight back."

*

"Good meeting, sir?" asked Billy, hovering at the foot of the steps, welcomed Thornton aboard for the flight back to Baton Rouge.

"Yes, I think so, thank you Billy. Not too bad a morning. We'll be able to reopen the factories." said Thornton. "Very good, sir," came the reply.

Yes, very good it would be, reflected Thornton, bemused that his pilot seemed to have picked up Clarence's Jeevsian English. Yet there was still Heather and Xian to square. He could call her now but, given that he had to get her agreement to what he had promised Carroll, persuasion, and if necessary, pressure, might be best performed in person. The next opportunity for that would be at the gala. After he had secured her compliance he could make that long delayed visit to his Asian partners, with his mind at ease. They would be overjoyed that US production had been resumed.

TWENTY NINE

Thornton had not got very far before he decided to make a detour on the way home from the airport. He gave a new instruction to the car and twenty minutes later pulled up in front of a medium-rise building that had been constructed in the middle of the last century, but recently renovated as part of an attempt to make this area of downtown more attractive. Various medical surgeries had been established here and there was a modest clinic attached at the rear of the building, providing limited in-patient care.

He was approached by a self-important man who asked if he had an appointment: Thornton bridled at the man's peremptory tone. This is new, he thought. Normally I just turn up and go straight to reception. He was a long standing patient of Dr Seddeenhow's, after all. But when he explained that he had no need to book an appointment, the man asked him to leave. Thornton stood his ground with as much presence as he could bring to the occasion, and eventually the guard agreed to call Seddenhow's office. Thornton was about to ask the reason for this unprecedented level of security, but the man in the blue uniform looked too churlish to part with any useful information and he decided not to bother. Duly escorted by the guard, he took the lift to the top floor, arriving at Nathan Seddenhow's office to be informed by a nurse that the doctor was engaged on ward rounds. In another fifteen minutes or so, he'd be back.

Ward rounds? Thornton was puzzled. Nathan sometimes had a patient or two at the clinic but there were never enough to make up a ward. He leant back in the EZ reclining chair the nurse had offered while he waited, shut his eyes and downloaded a fishing magazine onto his iPsyche. He let the article fill his brain, on fly-fishing in the Lah valley, high in the Alborz mountains of Iran. Surely you couldn't fish there any more – not since the bomb. He remembered how the rainbow trout had been so thick upon the river, which curled its way across the valley floor; you could almost walk across their backs. Little necessity even to tie a hook at the end of your line. How he had loved it – the camping, the riding, the fishing itself, on that river!

Thornton was just turning to an article on the open water poaching of genetically modified pelagic fish, who always returned to the hatchery where they had been born, once they had made their tour of the oceans to fatten up. One of the first uses of animal memory manipulation, these fish were a tremendous advance on the static, toxin-ridden, fish farms of yesteryear. Before he could start reading, however, a door opened and in walked Nathan Seddenhow himself: a small hunched man with shaggy grey hair – and the Lamaire's family doctor for two generations. Thornton would never forget how kind he had been over all that business of Stephanie's twenty years ago before.

The two friends shook hands and Thornton explained the matter that had brought him here, curious too about the presence of the security guard at the gate.

"I've never seen that before in all the years I have been coming here," he said.

Nat nodded, took him by the elbow and led him down a short corridor. "Let me show you something," he said. "But you must be sworn to silence about what you are about to see." Two floors down they reached a pair of doors with frosted glass panels. Seddenhow peered briefly into the iris scanner and the doors eased back with the slight noise of an hydraulic piston, revealing a ward of a dozen beds lining each side. An array of monitors, drips and traction devices tended to young men in various stages of disrepair, some with head wounds, some missing legs, others bandaged around the midriff.

Nathan raised a hand to the doctor on duty, as though to say, 'Pay no attention to us: please continue with whatever you are doing, this is not an official visit'. Seddenhow introduced Thornton to the men who were sufficiently awake, and not so badly wounded that to ask them to make the effort of conversation would have been an imposition. Thornton was still guessing what exactly he was witnessing but the likely explanation had begun to dawn on him. As they reached the bed of one youth with a bandaged leg in a splint, he asked;

"Where are you from?"

"Charleston."

"And where did you get that nasty wound?"

"New Chaldea."

So, it was as he thought: these were the casualties of the undeclared volunteer force. The presence of the security guard now made sense – Governor Gillespie didn't want any journalist intruding here and spreading the unhelpful news that his clandestine intervention was already incurring human costs.

The two men moved down the line of beds, trying to bring a little light conversation and cheer where they could – but then a nurse entered the ward. She was about to brush past them with a quick perfunctory greeting before she recognised him: Thornton and Lu Ann stopped and looked at each other.

"Well, my!" smiled Thornton broadly. "I'd heard you had gone back to nursing – but had no idea it was here!"

"That's right – I'm on three days a week. These poor guys – they need patching up before they can go back to their families," replied Lu Ann. "If you looked me up a little more often, you'd have known. I do what I can, Nat asked me to get involved."

"I didn't realise that you two knew each other," said Nathan. "Lu Ann, take a few minutes off – you've been working like a mule all morning. Please, come and join me and Thornton for a coffee in my office – your shift's nearly done anyway. They'll be all right without you for half an hour."

With that, the three of them repaired to his office.

"No doubt you're wondering what exactly is going on here," said Nat, as he pulled the door shut behind them..

"I can probably work it out," replied Thornton. "My guess is that the governor has asked you to look after these young men and he doesn't want news of the casualties leaked. That right?"

"About right," confirmed Seddenhow. "These young men, they come from all over the place – not just the South. You'd be amazed how many Northerners signed up too."

"Is this the only clinic who looks after the men? How bad are the losses?" asked Thornton.

"Not too many at the moment," Seddenhow reassured. "This is the only clinic involved so far, but they may have to open another place next month: the rate of attrition is increasing. Carroll said he wanted all the injured men to be together when they returned from New Chaldea – better for morale that way."

"And easier to control access to them too," said Thornton

"You're a cynical man, Mr Lamaire!" Nat laughed. "Not like our good friend Lu Ann here," He toasted her with his coffee cup. "Be lost without her."

"We'd all be lost without her," said Thornton, glancing over at Lu Ann.

"I needed someone I could trust – someone who wouldn't be tempted to talk to the press," continued Seddenhow.

"Or to me, it seems," said Thornton, adding a tone of mock hurt to his voice. "There are phones. you know."

"Works both ways, honey," said Lu Ann, flicking on a smile. "But

I didn't want to burden you. You've got enough on your plate. You know, it's just a little side-line o'mine. I do like to be helpful and Nat here, he asked me so nicely, as soon as he remembered that I trained as a nurse all those years back. Beside, these guys – they're so sweet, so charming. They appreciate what little I can do for them."

"Lu Ann has been wonderful. It's true," said Nat. "The men all adore her."

"Almost worth being wounded for, I'd say," said Thornton, gallantly. "A chance to see Lu Ann three days a week? Why," he added, with a rueful grin. "I have only ever dreamt of such a thing,"

The thought of seeing her regularly was the stuff of fantasy for Thornton. He took in her shoulder-length hair, that shone golden tawny, as though coated with iridescent varnish; her hooded, sympathetic brown eyes that spoke of warmth and joy, her lightly tanned skin. He wanted to lean over and nuzzle into her neck, draw in the scent of healthy life.

"You're such a charmer Thornton," she said. "But don't make light of these suffering soldiers – I'm sure they'd far rather be with their families than stuck here with me and Nat for company."

Thornton turned away. "You got all you need Nat? Me and my companies, we'd be glad to help out in any way we can. You just say the word."

"Actually, there are some things," said Nat. "Some equipment's difficult to import from the North at the moment, what with the economic troubles down here and all the sanctions. We're pretty dependent on donations."

"I'll get my people up North to put a load together, whatever it is you need," said Thornton. "They can come down on my 'plane."

Lu Ann rose and began to unbutton her nurse's coat. "It's the end of my shift so I'll just be going on my way. I'll let you boys sort out whatever you need – you don't need me . You all have a great day now, you hear me?"

Thornton realised he ought to be getting on too. "Let me give you a ride," he offered, reluctant to see her go. "It'll save you a cab. Nat and I have finished anyway." He looked at the doctor. "Can you email me the list of all the stuff you need? And my prescription – could you copy it to the pharmacy in town? They can send the medications up to the plantation this afternoon."

"A ride? That would be mighty kind of you," Lu Ann gave Thornton a smile. "A gentlemanly thing to do for a poor nurse, earning a few dollars a month. I'll be glad to accept."

Thornton knew Lu Ann would be doing all this for nothing. Since her widowhood from 'Panama' Dilkes, she was almost as wealthy as him.

"Good-bye Nat – see you next week. Call me if you suddenly need some extra hands!" she said, loping towards the door in her loose-limbed way.

"So where can I drop you – home?" Thornton asked as the car doors swung down and with a hiss the bolts slid home. Thornton was glad he'd ordered upgraded locks. He'd heard of gangs of DOGS breaking into people's vehicles at intersections. Times weren't as safe as they used to be.

Once seated, he gave the car no audible destination. "Aren't you going to tell this car where we're going?" Lu Ann enquired, as the car moved off silently. "Or is it so smart it senses my wishes?"

"Somethin' like that," said Thornton. "It senses my wishes. See this?" He rolled down his shirt collar. He took her hand and placed her finger on the back of his neck. "Feel that?" he said.

"Maybe, just, not much. Is that a scar?"

"A very small one. I had one of the latest iPsyche's fitted – just below the skin. I just *think* your address and the iPsyche tells the car. Smart, huh? It does whatever I want it to do."

"But what if…what about road rage? I hope it doesn't act on that."

Thornton laughed. "No, you have to give it permission to act on a thought. You conceive whatever you want to say, or do, and then you action it – just like pressing 'return'. It's no different really to what you're used to – not much, anyway. Just that you don't have to speak the instruction or make your fingers do the typing."

"Still sounds weird," said Lu Ann. "I'll stick to my old iBand. Who would want to have something like that under their skin? Practically turns you into a robot!"

"Nah, don't be ridiculous. I'm no robot, I'm still Thornton, the man you love to love."

"Oh really?" Lu Ann arched an eyebrow. "I don't think I've seen you in at least two months. Some lover!"

"I've been busy."

"Too busy to get your clothes repaired I see." She pointed to a hole in his jacket. "You should buy no-moth clothes: GM sheep and goats are just the best. None of my new cashmere has been touched. But I don't suppose Bethany keeps you up to date on the latest fashion trends."

"Genetically modified wool, huh? Amazing what they think of."

"Well, more useful than that Frankenstein thing in your neck, that's for sure. How's life at home, anyway?"

"Much the same. Bethany rolls around on her barrel – some days on, some days off. It's not the easiest of lives, as you know, but I'm away a lot... It's when she gets violent that I have my doubts how long I can support it all. But I guess I've lived with it for a long time now."

Lu Ann ruffled his hair, "Poor Thornton. Well, one day when you're not so busy, call by. You're always welcome. You know that – at least I hope you do."

"I'd come every day if I could," said Thornton. "Might be very good for me. We'll see."

"So what's keeping you so busy at the moment, Mr Lamaire? I thought your MARION thing was going well, you were about to raise some money when I last saw you. What happened to all that?"

"You don't read the financial pages?"

"Never."

"Well, we had to pull the public sale of the memory technology we were working on. Had some setbacks – a few damaged patients, that sort of thing... And then our business in the South is not getting any easier. Attitudes are turning against us. It's not just a question of people being put out of work – although that's part of it – but having to cope with robots that can do everything they can, and usually better. That's tricky for people. I get that. A lot of folk – particularly down here – thought that Douglas V Milton Robotics, was the last straw. There's a big backlash."

"So I've heard. Is the governor being helpful about all this, keeping emotions in check? Must be difficult for him, being he was a man of the cloth an' all."

Thornton grunted.

"The people are leading, and he is following. You must have heard of that stupid 'service' he performed – such a disaster. Claims he wanted to bleed off some of the anger and resentment against the new machines. Pah! He will say or do anything to stay in power. And now he's obsessed with this New Chaldea business. See he's even got you all caught up in it!"

"I was glad to help. Those young guys are hurt, and I was looking for something to do. I don't get mixed up in the politics of it all. Just see these boys sufferin' and want to help them. That's all."

Thornton looked closely at Lu Ann.

"You're going to be there, in that clinic, for a very long time, my dearest Lu Ann," he said softly. "This thing is only going to get worse. Our governor, president-elect, whatever – he's pushing for the New Confederacy to send an official force. A large one"

"Well, good luck to him with that. He knows there's no call for that down here. People got long memories."

"Sure – unless they could be changed!"

"How's that go'n to happen, for Pete's sake?" asked Lu Ann. "Give 'em all a lobotomy?"

"You're closer than you think," said Thornton

Lu Ann shot him a quizzical look.

"I'm under pressure to use our new memory technology to change people's views on this issue," explained Thornton, hesitantly.

"Without them knowing? The public I mean," asked Lu Ann

"Roughly so, yes"

"But that's horrible! I've never heard of such manipulation. You wouldn't do it would you? You wouldn't let Gillespie do that?"

"The governor's got leverage. This is Blue Ridge's home."

"Do you want me to say something to the governor? He's a friend of mine."

"He's meant to be a friend of mine too," replied Thornton. "But I'm not sure anyone's a friend at the moment who stands in his way. But no – please don't say anything. This is strictly between me and the governor. I'll handle it my way."

"Whatever you say. But let me know if I can help. By the way I meant to ask you, how is Stephanie?"

"She's well. But you may see her soon."

"Aw, that's great! I've always been fond of Stephanie. But I thought she was in Paris?"

"Her partner is away so she's down here for a week. Nice for me and I'm hoping she will decide to stay for a month… not sure she'll last that long though. She and her mother will fall out soon enough."

"Ah yes – with her drinking, I can understand Stephanie's problems with that. But it's not just Bethany though, is it?" said Lu Ann. "I got the impression she had her issues with you as much as she did with her mother."

"When Stephanie was a child we were very close. But something happened when she was seventeen, something I've always regretted, tremendously regretted, and which I've never told you about. Time has softened her attitude a little but... yeah. We're not as intimate as close we might be, any more. As I would like."

"A girl needs her father," said Lu Ann. "What on earth happened?" But Thornton said no more; it was too late in the day.

"Another time," said Thornton. "But maybe we could see each other again soon?"

"Sure... that would be nice. When you have a free evening, my friend – call me."

The car swung into her drive, the bolts hissed back and Lu Ann lowered her feet. She flashed her big grin at Thornton, "Thanks for the ride."

PART III

THIRTY

Thornton mulled over the situation with Carroll Gillespie. The governor was unlikely to give up on his idea of employing Blue Ridge's assets, LetheTech and MARION, to manipulate memory for political purposes. It was an outrageous suggestion and dangerous too, once it became fixed in the mind of the president-elect: Thornton knew Gillespie well enough to realise that he would not be easily diverted.

But who had been so disloyal as to pass on these technological secrets? There had been earlier warnings about infiltration, and now they had a fifth column in their midst, in addition to financial problems – and having to contend with the inevitable litigation that would follow the rampage at Jim Embry's farm. With exemplary damages likely to be awarded by a Southern jury, that would be expensive to settle.

Perhaps Carroll – or his informant – had spotted something to the advantage of Blue Ridge: subliminal messages could be turned into a stream of income. True, Xian Han and Heather Masters had decreed that MARION should not be given access to the public until much later in her development. Well, needs must. Heather and Xian would have to change their tune.

Thornton had skipped lunch that day; he felt a sugar low approaching, that always left him irritable. He opened a drawer in his desk and found the bag of dried fruit his assistant left there for just such situations; it would have to do. He shook some of the assortment into his fist. He instructed his iPsyche to call Heather and her 3D image appeared in a matter of seconds, floating a few inches above his desk.

After the customary pleasantries, Heather posed the question that concerned her, but tried to sound otherwise, relaxed, insouciant about it all.

"Have you had time to study the financial projections I sent? she asked. "There is some uncertainty in the figures. I'm not sure how well our next financing round will be supported but I've assumed that all the existing equity partners will fund their share."

Thornton brushed her aside.

"Heather, we'll deal with financial issues in a minute. I want to address a different problem first. Can you ask Xian to join us?"

Once Xian Han appeared, Thornton explained his conversation with Carroll and his conviction that there must be a leak. The team had grown in the last few months; new staff were maybe not so bound by the sense of comradeship and loyalty that had inspired those who had been present from the start. He wanted a complete check on their past histories, outside relationships, political and religious affiliations, any factor that might throw light on a motive for such a betrayal.

"There are not many up at the centre who have sufficient knowledge of MARION's operation to brief the governor in such a way," said Thornton. "No one outside the immediate team knows about MARION's ability to reach, and address, many minds at once."

"I can't imagine anyone being so disloyal," said Han. "My team is solid. I'm sure of it."

"Well, use a bit more imagination Xian," said Thornton, aggressively. "Cast your mind back. Don't you recall that... Woody something we employed as a coder? Had all sorts of issues we only discovered later. You can't be so confident about all these recent hires. I don't think we're checking them thoroughly enough – though it's not necessarily a new hire. What about Euclid for example? Do you think he's fully on board? He looked distinctly unhappy about something when I was last up. Maybe his girlfriend dumped him that morning, I don't know – but apart from the two of you, Xian, and you, Heather, Euclid is the one closest to MARION, the person best informed about her capabilities."

"Has something happened that gives you reason to doubt Euclid's commitment?" asked Xian.

"Nothing in particular, just instinct. I thought that he seemed... " Thornton paused. "Distracted, last time. As though something was troubling him. We are now at a stage of development where we could survive without Euclid. MARION needs a teacher she can trust – but one that we can trust too. There are others we could employ. We need absolute loyalty."

"Euclid can be a bit grumpy from time to time," interrupted Heather. "But maybe he's just lonely up in the Berkshire's. There's not much life there for a twenty-seven year-old. I think he's good, solid, you know... definitely loyal."

"Xian, could you talk to him please?" asked Thornton. "See what's up? I don't want any more surprises. We have enough head winds to face. Mind you..." He wanted to float the idea Carroll had put in his head. "Whichever leaky genius thought of linking MARION and LetheTech to implant subliminal advertising had a great idea. Think what people would pay for that! Could sure be an answer to our cash flow problems."

"But Thornton!" objected Heather. "We can't possibly do that yet. MARION is largely untested – there are all sorts of ethical objections. We can't risk an O'Neal situation on such a scale. We'd be closed down immediately!"

"Closed down, Heather?" asked Thornton, rhetorically. "You speak of being closed down? You've seen the figures; unless we can find a new stream of income to fund MARION I will be forced to close her down anyway! Feedback from our outside investors – the VC companies, the banks – is that they are beginning to lose faith. We are going to have to do something differently – maybe we have to recalibrate our red lines. Anyway, we're not talking O'Neal type therapy here; if we limit the modification to superficial memories and beliefs – like whether someone prefers one make of breakfast cereal to another, or whether they should drive this make of car rather than that one; something that's not core to their identity – that's pretty well danger free, I would have thought."

"You can't access people's minds without their consent,' said Heather, firmly. "If that ever got out it would make our present publicity problems look like a tea-party. No – we must allow people to be aware that they are being influenced, able to accept or reject the message. You can't manipulate people at a level where they won't be able to react with agency. Think what would happen if such a system fell into the hands of politicians!"

'From your lips to God's ear,' reflected Thornton, thinking of his conversation with Carroll. He sighed – and mumbled something vague. Heather was always so cautious.

"And you'd need the compliance of the advertisers!" continued Heather. "I doubt they would ever be party to such invasive subliminal messaging,"

"Would they not?" retorted Thornton. "You'd be amazed how unscrupulous some of those retail CEOs can be! A lot of them wouldn't blink an eye to get one up on their competitors! They wouldn't give a sparrow's fart over the ethics of manipulating their customer's deepest desires. In fact, they'd love it!"

"Well, they may not be concerned – but, I certainly would be."

"Would you, Heather? Yes – I guessed you would," said Thornton, despondently. "But I would ask you, as my CEO, to bear in mind the financial stress the group is under. Using our research to generate an income, some cash flow, is what I would expect the group's CEO to focus on."

He sighed; he would drop the issue for now. But not for ever.

"Let us each reflect on this some more and circle back in a few days. We'll pass on to other matters. Where are we with LetheTech's Phase II trials? No more O'Neal type issues there, I hope?"

Heather still winced every time she was asked about O'Neal. She had tried to minimise the issue in her mind, hoping that the hullabaloo would blow over.

"O'Neal is not quite the only client that we've had that sort of trouble with... " Heather said, failing to sound reassuring. "But the numbers have gone down significantly. We've got about three hundred people we're taking through therapy at the moment in the Phase II group. We're undertaking their treatment slowly, removing just one layer of memory at each session. Of course, we aim not to run the slightest risk but there are accidents, occasionally. We're not experiencing the same frequency or severity of excessive deletions but not every treatment goes without a hitch. To an extent that has to be expected."

"Can you reverse the effect of these accidents?" asked Thornton. "Repair the damage?"

"That's possible – sometimes," said Heather, cautiously. "We may be able to build back part of the memory they have lost. But I'm sad to say... " She took a deep breath, steeling herself to make Thornton realise the hurdles they still faced. "Excessive memory deletion isn't the only issue at the moment. We've got some... additional problems."

"Really? I'm surprised. And those additional problems are?"

asked Thornton, with a firmness in his voice that told Heather, in case she was in any doubt, just how much Thornton did not want to hear about new problems.

"The first is public image. As you know, the public is hypersensitive about this whole issue of memory modification. There is a gang of uninformed columnists frightening the public about mind control experiments. The discovery of Kinnead O'Neal was manna to them; now they can really smell blood – and they're digging. Shortly they are going to find other examples – not many, as I say, but enough to exacerbate the image problems we already have."

"And the second issue?"

"It's linked. As I've said we can probably correct a lot of the damage when it occurs. And demonstrating that might silence the critics. But now, because of the bad publicity, we can't get hold of some of the damaged clients anymore. Their families have got nervous. They're worried – understandably, I guess – that any further intervention by us might cause more damage, rather than cure what's already there. We can't help if they won't bring them back to the lab."

"It seems a very human response," said Thornton, rooting around in the drawer for another handful of dried fruit; he shouldn't have skipped lunch. "Rebuilding public confidence is not even going to start until the technology is fool-proof and these mishaps go down to zero."

He started to chew, trying to dispel the guilty awareness that his blood sugar would soon rebound to way above the level he had been told to target.

"We have many success stories," said Heather, brightly, determined not to let Thornton run her team down. "The great sadness in all this is that we've actually done some really great work! Just so disappointing that something that has the potential to help humanity hugely has been set back by months."

"Heather, I'm not blaming you… particularly," said Thornton. "I supported you in the decision to go for an IPO early, but it's been a mistake. We've garnered some very unwelcome attention – and as a result, there's probably going to be a whole host of additional regulatory hurdles too."

"Yes – I know all that, Thornton. I do,' replied Heather, slightly awkwardly. Thornton recognised that in agreeing so easily to his fears she was attempting to manage him. It was a different approach to her usual one – trying to convince him that his fears, whatever they were, were groundless.

"We will work as hard and as swiftly as possible. But there's no quick fix," she said.

That was not what Thornton wanted to hear either – he loved quick fixes. All the same, there was no point undermining his CEO, or leaving her unduly concerned over her own future.

"Heather, my support for LetheTech and MARION will continue – with you in charge – and if necessary I will underwrite any shortfall in our partners' willingness or ability to fund future cash calls. I don't want you distracted by financial worries just when you have to give your all to succeed on this."

"Thank you, Thornton," said Heather, relieved. "LetheTech's

future success will be my repayment of your generosity and support."

You bet, Heather. Just make that repayment sooner than you can ever imagine, thought Thornton. But all he said out loud was.

"Okay, great. But think about what I've been saying earlier – about the advantages of linking MARION and LetheTech. We'll talk about it again in a few days. Xian, please come back to me as soon as you can with the result of your investigations, and Heather – will you stay on the line for a few moments?"

Xian Han's virtual presence disappeared. Thornton said, "Heather, I wanted to ask you something quite unconnected with what we've been discussing. You've probably forgotten but in a month's time there's the annual 'Support the Struggle' gala in New York for the New Chaldea foundation. Would you join Bethany and me at our table? You could bring Chase – am I remembering that right? Your fiancé? Or even Bruno, if you prefer."

Heather's heart sank; she hated galas – but she couldn't refuse Thornton. Perhaps she could just bear it, as long as she wasn't put next to Bethany. With as much grace as she could muster, she accepted the invitation.

"Good! Bethany will be so pleased." said Thornton. "I certainly am."

And with that they said their goodbyes and shut down the link. As his CEO's image disappeared Thornton sat back, reflecting. The time had passed, financially, when they could concern themselves with the niceties of the ideal robot/ human interaction. Next time they spoke he wanted a positive response to the idea, he had ventured – whatever Heather might think about it privately.

THIRTY ONE

It had been Heather's husband – the soon-to-be uncoupled Bruno, who suggested lunch; wishing to maintain the upper hand, however, it was Heather who decided they should meet at her club in New York. She hardly ever used the venue these days, and wondered if the doorman would even remember her. Heather didn't really mind one way or the other, but like a traveller who has smuggled nothing, yet feels themselves guilty as they pass a customs officer, she always introduced herself – despite being twenty years a member – pre-emptively avoiding the shame of being asked if she belonged.

Perhaps it was time to stop the expensive membership anyway. Uncoupling might be the cheapest way to 'divorce', but she was still going to be supporting Bruno for years – and Chase was not as well off as he had tried to make out at first; she seemed to be making a habit out of marrying impecunious men.

She ordered a Virgin Mary and sat down in the bar with a copy of the New York Times, thoughtfully printed off by the Club for traditionally minded members – and waited for Bruno. There were reports of more trouble in New Chaldea. to which the temporary government had reportedly overreacted: Another thirty people had died in clashes, most of them Christians. Was Thornton still contributing to the efforts there? He had given a lot of money to fund the development of the colony and its settlements, but even he was now feeling financially constrained.

Heather's mind ran on. If Thornton was financially stressed she wondered how safe her job was; whatever he said by way of reassurance. She knew Thornton partly blamed her for the loss of the IPO. She enjoyed support from many of the board members – but they wouldn't necessarily carry the day in any argument about her future: Thornton wasn't going to be held back by a few recalcitrant directors who owed him their positions. She shivered, worried about the future, just as Bruno arrived. It was only quarter past noon; she liked to eat early.

"Shall we go up and find a table?" she suggested. "Before the rush starts?"

She led him up the staircase, lined in best eighteenth century tradition with oil paintings of member's racehorses,. There were still plenty of tables. She ordered them both a dozen oysters – having an uncertain memory that Bruno shared her taste for shellfish – and a main course of sole for herself. Bruno was permitted to make his own choice for that.

"You like oysters?" she enquired with an encouraging smile, but didn't wait for an answer. She waived the hovering sommelier away. Heather disapproved of drinking at lunch and besides she needed Bruno's complete attention. Bruno had been looking forward to a glass or two of Chablis.

But Bruno knew what he wanted from this lunch, and could forgo the loss of his glass of white wine without too much regret. He had sought this meeting for weeks but it had been difficult to find a date; Heather had been either up at the MARION centre or travelling. He sometimes wondered how she'd ever found time to start the relationship with Chase. And on the few occasions when she had been back home, she had been uncommunicative. As always, Heather had taken refuge in her work when domestic stresses got too high.

Heather laid out her view of how their shared future might work. She fondly imagined the three of them living comfortably together: Bruno could sleep in the spare bedroom she used for her meditation practice. Surely he wouldn't want to live on his own? They would all get along splendidly! More to the point, in the wake of her recent financial disaster, she couldn't afford to grant him so generous a settlement that he could be established in his own place – as she would be able to offer once the IPO had finally launched. Then she should be so rich that this financial disturbance would seem nothing but a temporary embarrassment.

Bruno's mind wandered as his wife talked – but he realised that he had better concentrate: this was his future under discussion, after all.

"This isn't easy, I know," sighed Heather.

Quite easy for me, thought Bruno gleefully. Now I've made a decision.

"But we know why we are here."

Because you found somebody else. It's not me creating this mess.

"The magic left our marriage long ago, but I want to reassure you that I'll do everything I can to ensure the uncoupling is a great success"

Naturally, he thought, narrowing his eyes a little. I'm sure that will save you a great deal of money.

"We've loved each other, we've been family to each other, and we can solve whatever problems there are, now, together. Let's not be bitter about this. We've had a wonderful time – but nothing lasts for ever. Maybe best to move straight to specifics, don't you think Bruno? Perhaps facts and futures, rather than feelings and the past, what do you think?"

Bruno stifled a yawn, wondering when the bromides would end.

Heather continued unabashed.

"Bruno, I'm extremely fond of you -."

Fond?

" – as you also know. But I have fallen in love with someone else. I have fought with my feelings, at first. I didn't want to upset our life together –"

Never much of one

" – I didn't wish to hurt you. But I would be doing us both a disservice if we stayed together. You would come to resent me."

I'm come to resent you already.

"We deserve a chance at happiness."

Bruno said nothing.

Heather sank back into her chair, certain he was letting her do all the talking on purpose. She had expected Bruno to intervene forcibly but he had uttered no sound, so far. Her Italian husband was quite capable of being assertive – yet there he sat, like a dummy. Evidently he had no intention of making things smoother for her.

I am not going to be intimidated, she thought. I can out silence Bruno if that's his game. I'll just sit here until he responds in some way.

Finally Bruno spoke, determined not to allow Heather the satisfaction of enjoying her strength of mind, her potential victory.

"My dear, I'm sure you have our best interests at heart and that we can all work this situation out together. I understand why you do not want to proceed to a full divorce, that we should just uncouple. At least at first…"

At least at first? Heather sharpened her attention.

"We go a long way back Bruno," she replied. "You will be just fine with this new arrangement. Besides, you have Jane these days. And you have been seeing her for quite a long time too, I gather. You are both welcome to come and go in our shared home. I propose that nothing changes between us, beyond the sleeping arrangements. I don't want you to suffer in any way while I am enjoying my newfound happiness."

Your newfound happiness? Ha! You have no idea, thought Bruno

"Thank you Heather, for all your reassurance about the future – my future particularly," Bruno couldn't resist adding a sarcastic lilt to his voice. "I enjoy listening to your... proposals for us, but they are very much your ideas. I was rather hoping that we might have more of a mutual discussion about what has happened and what may happen in the future."

Heather's blood chilled. Something in the tone of Bruno's voice steeled her. Now he wanted a discussion about what had gone wrong in their marriage? His interest in communication had always been limited. Was that not one of the issues that had let them drift apart? She knew how she was viewed, not just by Bruno but her detractors as well: all hard carapace on the surface but their analysis was mistaken (at least in her in her own estimation): she was as soft as butter underneath. She recognised her own insecurities. Was that not why she had sought an emotional connection with Chase?

"Heather, I don't want..." Bruno pondered for a few moments, searching for the right words. "I don't want -" he continued. " – Don't wish, perhaps I should say, to stand in the way of your marriage to Chase, nor do I want to pass by on old ground – is that how you would say it? Pass over, perhaps? – trying to judge whether you have been entirely fair in your behaviour to me. Nevertheless, I think, dear Heather, that some realities need facing."

"The marriage between us has been over for a long time. I have – and, as, I have just discovered, you are quite aware – a girlfriend; Jane, with whom I am very happy. So it's okay to me that we should go our separate ways. I thought at the beginning of this process, that what suits you, suits me too. How do you say – what is the sauce for the goose is the sauce for the gander? Not that I am sure about whatever is a gander."

"A male goose," said Heather, helpfully. Bruno ignored her.

"So," he continued "At the beginning, I thought, 'yes, let's go for an uncoupling. It makes sense for both of us. I'm not looking to go off anywhere, immediately. I would do well to wait – as one day Heather may be rich again. But now? Things have changed."

"They have?" said Heather, nervously.

"I know nothing, as you will appreciate, of finance. Nothing at all," said Bruno, accurately enough. "But Jane, she's not like me. She reads the reports. She tells me about this IPO. And she thinks, this money from LetheTech, it's years away, not coming any time soon. We may 'whistle for it', is her expression. And she has been thinking. She says, 'I want certainty now. I don't want all this waiting for something, Heather's money, and all the time my Bruno is still connected to – living with – his ex-wife! Maybe for all I know, she is not very 'ex', at all!'"

"I'll be very ex!" insisted Heather. "Completely uncoupled! We won't be connected at all. There'll be just the last thing to do, the final settlement – at some point in the future!"

"Un-coupled, un-coupled!" exclaimed Bruno. "What is this thing? It doesn't exist in my country: you are married or you are not. No, no – it doesn't work. Not for Jane and me. We want a divorce, a full divorce, a proper divorce. Now!"

The words came as a shock. She would be near ruin. The

financial costs of an uncoupling were manageable... but not a full blown divorce. She would have to talk Bruno out of it – or abandon her marriage to Chase. Before she could offer her opinion, Bruno continued,

"I just want to add something, Heather – my decision that you and I need a divorce is not dependent on your future marriage. I want it anyway – whatever the circumstances. If you decide not to pursue a divorce, then I will commence my own action."

Heather sat quietly, thoughts racing. If an uncoupling's off the agenda how am I going to fund a divorce? Will Chase even be interested anymore, when he found out that I'm broke?

She struggled to find a more positive spin on all this – something that would allow here to see that the way things were shaping up as anything other than a total disaster. Perhaps she and Chase would look back one day on this financial distress as the struggle that brought them closer? It would be like getting married for the first time! And as long as she kept her job, she could just about navigate the financial rapids – though she'd have to take care to avoid upsetting Thornton from now on. Any freedom of manoeuvre she had once enjoyed in her career had definitely disappeared.

THIRTY TWO

Heather disliked foundation galas. The food was always terrible, the speeches worse and the auctions stuffed with things she neither wanted nor needed. But there was no way she could wriggle out of Thornton's invitation. Last year she'd maintained her independence by buying a table and filling it with her friends. That sort of generosity was all in the past. With tables priced at twenty thousand dollars a pop, it was not something she should contemplate covering out of her own pocket, and Thornton would never allow her to expense the cost, what with the present cash squeeze on Blue Ridge. What a shame! The sight of her friends enjoying each other's company – brought together through her – always brought a glow of pleasure to her soul. But if that pleasure was not available this year, an invitation from any one of her girlfriends, who might be making up a rival table, would allow her a graceful way to decline Thornton's own invitation, while demonstrating financial support for his charity. But no such girlfriend had stepped forward.

No, her fate that evening was to be the one which she least desired; sitting on the head table with that old drunk Bethany. Of course, there was a chance that Bethany might be on the wagon this year. Thornton would not wish to risk her embarrassing him, particularly in front of the Guest of Honour, president-elect Carroll Gillespie. That Bethany was to accompany Thornton at all was probably a good sign.

The gala was to be held in one of the new buildings downtown, that had gone up fast – too fast, as the fitout had still to be completed – in anticipation of a boom that never arrived. Its structure had only recently been topped-out, just in time to meet an unexpected recession that was descending with the rapidity and force of a winter nor'easter. To a generous eye, the bare concrete pillars could be interpreted as lending an industrial chic, their harshness muted by large vases of flowers and blown-up photos of daily life in New Chaldea. These looked to Heather as AI hallucinations: everyone looked so happy. Most of the people in the images seemed to be engaged in rustic, semi-biblical activities – drawing water from a well, tending flocks of goats, that sort of thing. Young girls, depicted in coloured skirts and white blouses, rested earthenware pots on their heads or shoulders, as though modelling for a traditional tableau; *La Source* perhaps. None of the women wore a full head or face coverings – no Hijabs, Chadors or Niqabs: Christians, then.

She walked over and inspected the seating plan. Placed between Thornton on her right and Tariq Adib, the Iraqi ambassador, on her left she was pleased to see Ralston Jones, the outspoken industrialist, sat next to Bethany. Heather knew Ralston had made his original fortune in obscure circumstances (the saying 'behind every great fortune lies a crime' flitted through her mind) and she doubted that he would put up with Bethany's antics if she got rowdy.

Taking a moment before joining her fellow diners, Heather wandered over to the refectory-style tables where the auction items were laid out. A silent auction before dinner. She'd attended enough galas to learn the technique: bid early, and bid low. That way, there would be little chance of winning items she could no longer afford. Holidays in the Caribbean, weekends on yachts, home makeovers, sessions with famous photographers... already, each bid was far more than she could match. At the far end of the table she spotted some more modest items, still with their original tags attached. Choosing a jacket, priced just under ten thousand dollars and woven from the fleece of an exotic and rare animal, she bid half that. She didn't want to spend five thousand let alone ten – but she should be safe enough. She'd be outbid; it was still early.

Heather accepted a glass of sparkling water from one of the waiters, and went to find her table. As she took her seat she overheard Bethany ordering a bottle of champagne, explaining to the Iraqi ambassador that this was the only thing she could drink at these events. Thornton's wife expressed this in a way that suggested, given her special needs, this bottle was not something that could be spared for others, or they might even be appropriate for their desires. Heather and the ambassador would have to make do with the warm

Chardonnay – the house wine for the night. Thornton, a life-long teetotaller, appeared to be oblivious to the whole thing.

The food arrived, meeting Heather's every expectation: a pressed block of greasy meat appeared on her plate. The block fell to pieces as she tried to cut it: Evidently, this was not a gala where money was to be wasted on fripperies, like food and wine. Heather nibbled at her bread, tempted to have some fun by asking Bethany for a glass of her Champagne. She wondered what excuse Bethany would offer in order to refuse her. Placing Bethany in the wrong might help to cheer up her mood, but she thought better of it. Bethany wouldn't care a damn, so the exercise seemed a little pointless. Instead she adjusted her shawl, for the room was chilly, and tuned to the Iraqi Ambassador.

"How is the security situation in New Chaldea, Mr Ambassador?" she enquired politely. As far as she knew, the picture was grim. The ambassador was equally pessimistic. In his view, the creation of a safe enclave for the various minorities, who possessed no land of their own in the Middle East, would not guarantee peace but, much like the creation of Israel over ninety years before, only ensure conflict continued for years to come.

"Look what is happening," he said. "In spite of all the fine words, the great powers – and some not-very great powers – are clandestinely infiltrating the territory with advisers, money, subterfuge, propaganda… Whatever it takes to secure an advantage when the final political settlement is reached. But what an ambition – a final settlement – what a hope! What have all these minorities got in common? Only their dislike and hatred of each other! The Western powers think they can create some sort of religious beacon in the Levant; a federation, like Germany perhaps, where all the minorities will be protected by some new constitution they're trying to write. What you Anglo-Saxons call 'a pipe dream'! It's made no easier by our friend over there," the ambassador nodded in the direction of Gillespie's table. "Trying to ensure the Christians have a major part of the spoils when the music stops. "

"So, you don't think the Christians have a place in New Chaldea?" asked Heather, in a tone of mock innocence.

"They might have had a place there two thousand years ago but they certainly don't now," replied the ambassador. "Why do they believe that, just because they originated in that part of the world, they have a right to live next to the Euphrates in the present day? My dear Heather – if I may – I suspect you're a Celt by origin whose ancestors came to Britain with the Vikings long before their descendants, in turn, boarded the Mayflower and sailed here – but that ancient lineage doesn't give you an entitlement to re-colonise Scandinavia! That time has been and gone, I'm sorry. It can't work like that! Countries come and go, and borders are made by man – not God. That a certain people were in a certain part of the world once does not entitle them to that land for eternity. That way leads to suffering. Just think of the Russians' view of Ukraine in the twenties!"

"And you don't think either that a large Christian population might be a good counterbalance to the Muslims?" Heather asked. "An example to the world that these two great religions, and others, can live together, in harmony, perhaps?"

The Ambassador hooted in derision.

"It will be an example to the world that they cannot live together, I would have thought! Hasn't that been the evidence so far? And as for the idea that an influx of Westerners will civilise the area – isn't that what your president-elect friend is trying to promote? I'm reminded of Gandhi's response when asked what he thought about western civilisation – *a very good idea'* he said. A very good idea! You Americans, with your great intentions; nations are like people, they need time to develop at their own pace. Forcing their development in line with some patronising idea of how they should be? That attitude always ends in disaster. You may not like the way they live but it's not your job to change them. Have you all learned nothing about the tragedy of imperialism? "

Heather wondered how much the ambassador really knew about Carroll Gillespie's ambitions; he might take an even dimmer view of Western intentions if he knew the half of it. She left him to talk with Bethany, who could be relied on to be incendiary about both Middle Eastern politics and the president-elect. When Bethany succeeded in holding the middle ground between sobriety and inebriation, she could be very entertaining.

*

Sensing that Heather's attention had become available, Thornton turned to her:

"How are you getting on with the ambassador?" he inquired.

"He's not too enamoured of Gillespie's plans, that's for sure. Not a big time supporter of a Western presence in New Chaldea."

"Well, I guess he wouldn't be," said Thornton. "He's bitter – his country was forced to cede large tracts of attractive land along the Euphrates. And he's a Muslim: he's not going to support a large Christian presence – but luckily that's not going to be up to people like him."

"No, I don't suppose it is," said Heather. "But tell me – how's the president-elect's campaign going? Has he persuaded the powers that are going to decide things to act in line with his wishes yet?"

"It's been mixed." Thornton speared an olive and popped it into his mouth. "Carroll's always telling me there's a general reluctance to become involved. Even some of the formally Christian nations are not helping much. The French are the worst – keep saying they must support *laïcité* – secularism – and they can't support the rise of a theocracy… They never did recover from their revolution. Separation of state and religion? Not a concept that really excites old Carroll, I'm afraid!"

"I imagine not," agreed Heather.

Thornton seemed to disengage and become lost in some internal dialogue with himself. Heather sensed that whatever it was, he was absorbed in thoughts that might relate to her. She waited for him to speak.

"You remember what we talked about the other day?" he asked finally.

"About using the MARION platform for advertising?"

"I know you have your reservations, Heather," Thornton began. "You said there were ethical issues about influencing people, without their informed consent."

"Well... yes – that's still my personal view," said Heather, hesitantly. "It's against the whole trend of the times, Thornton, you know that; the effort these days is towards greater awareness, higher consciousness, to maximise agency! But you want to come in under their conscious radar, and inhibit people's capacity for choice – even delete their memories..."

"Look, Heather... Here's the thing," said Thornton, speaking with more vehemence than intended. "Carroll – and I for that matter – for we are not too far apart on this issue, we'd much prefer that the voters choose to support intervention in New Chaldea of their own free will. But you know the obstacles: what's holding those voters back is just fear – irrational fear! And we should be fighting irrationality: we should be striking a blow not just for what is right but for the rational – for what clear-sighted people would want."

It didn't sound a very convincing argument even to Thornton but he knew he had to deliver for Carroll or all sorts of setbacks would be heading his way.

"What rational, clear-sighted people want? You mean what clear-sighted people like you and Gillespie think is a good idea?" Heather smiled to show she was teasing. She wanted to take the sting out of her rebuke: she couldn't afford the luxury of being right these days.

"I can see you are not entirely persuaded," said Thornton, drily. He seemed grumpy. "We'll talk about this later."

Over the hubbub of chatter, the Master of Ceremonies was trying to introduce Carroll Gillespie, governor of Louisiana and president-elect of the Southern Confederacy. Chairs were pushed back, glasses filled again and gradually the noise abated enough to allow their guest of honour to speak. Standing six-and-a-half feet, thick set, hair swept back over the polished dome of his head, Carroll Gillespie surveyed the crowd through glinting, owlish glasses, looking somewhere between a biker and an Old Testament prophet.

He led his audience through the history of the Middle East wars, from the perspective of the minorities, explaining how they had all been trampled on – particularly the Christians – who had almost disappeared from the area, despite being amongst the first in the region. Now was the chance to build a new Jerusalem, to restore a balance of creeds in the Middle East – a balance that would ensure that no one set of beliefs could dominate any other – as a beacon of tolerance and faith in the world. But this goal depended on Western governments becoming involved: there was a contest to determine the boundaries, the nature of the future government and the constitution of New Chaldea. As Christians, they must persuade the world of the justice and righteousness of their cause: they must all work to bring pressure on their governments to make this fight their own. The battle for public opinion could be won – but it would require courage, persistence, and resolve.

Evidently, this was a sympathetic audience. They clapped and roared in approval.

"See," said Thornton, leaning towards Heather. "See how much enthusiasm there is!" She nodded slowly, not sharing his emotion.

THIRTY THREE

Once Gillespie's speech was over, the public auction followed. Heather made a couple of low bids, confident that if she followed her strategy, and bid early enough, she would be outbid – and she was. Her only risk now was the result of the silent auction which would continue for the rest of the evening.

Abandoning her dining companions, she wandered over to inspect the list of bids for that expensive white jacket. Above her name there was now another, with a substantially higher bid pencilled in. Relieved she would be able to leave without having committed to anything: no expensive auction item – and no concession to Thornton either.

Then Thornton found her. In the press and the noise of the crowd, Heather neither sensed nor heard his approach. He cupped one hand underneath an elbow and gently steered her away from the throng. Once they were at a safe distance from being overheard, Thornton began:

"Have you thought any more about our earlier conversation?" he asked at first.

Earlier conversation? The two talked most days. Heather could have played coy, but she knew well enough what her boss meant, particularly in the context of the governor's address. Yet her mind had not changed: if they started to use LetheTech's and MARION's technology to play around with unsuspecting, and un-consenting, minds Blue Ridge could end up in a much worse mess than they had ever encountered with O'Neal – or the bad PR they had suffered after the Milton debacle.

Thornton would pick his battles one at a time; a small, incremental victory was all he sought for the moment. As Heather explained once again her resistance to the idea of public memory deletion – 'even in such a good cause!' Thornton reassured her that he understood and agreed with her reservations – nevertheless, might it not be acceptable if they monetised their research by imputing positive subliminal messages about products or, perhaps, the occasional public service announcement? Positive advertising, that was the idea! This needn't be about politics – at least not much: political messages would just be a very small part of their activities.

Heather stood firm.

"We can't do that, Thornton," she said. "Be realistic: if no 'tracer' is added, employing LetheTech as the transmission mechanism for MARION's feed will mean that whatever MARION places in a user's memory will feel as though it has always been part of their mental backdrop: individuals will have no opportunity to accept or deny the data! At present, all the social media channels that post advertising via iPsyches have to tell the user the nature of the download – whether publicity, information, political propaganda and whether it's created by AI. People must be aware of how they come to know what they are being told. Call it what you like, but the public have the right to know who is trying to influence them – all the regulators insist on that!"

Her attitude frustrated him.

"Heather, you know how bad our cash position is at the moment – one more problem with the Miltons and all my Southern operations will be shut down! I can't afford that a second time. We need to generate additional income and we need to do it now. Implanting positive information at the conscious level, without the need to go anywhere near the subconscious, is one thing we can sell today! Companies are queueing up to try this methodology, and MARION can be far more persuasive than simply floating traditional advertising in front of the consumer. It's the next big step in advertising and I want us to be the leader! If not, Cybersoul and Electric Memory are close behind us."

It was always the same threat.

Instead of arguing, Heather thought there might be some way of diverting Thornton – at least temporarily.

"Maybe we should commission some market research, get an idea how folks think about the idea? Maybe I'm wrong, maybe public reaction may not be as bad as I think," she said, thinking that while that was highly improbable, Thornton might respect third party opinion – even if he rejected hers. Otherwise a truly spectacular PR disaster was just down the road; come to think of it, that might well have been Gillespie's strategy from the start: something to discredit LetheTech and MARION for all time.

"We can't afford to do that Heather," said Thornton. "We don't have the time to carry out market research. As it happens I agree with you that the public might mistrust this technology at first – but they'll get used to it, just as they got used to all the other ways we influence people's minds. They swallow anything eventually, if it makes their lives easier, but if we publish what we're doing there'll just be more objections – we both know that. So let's skip the focus groups, and all the other ways of wasting time; just do this Heather or I'll be looking for a new CEO."

Merciful heavens! thought Thornton, as he heard the threat leave his lips. He saw any recourse to the issuance of threats as a clear loss of face – and a defeat. He preferred to move people only by persuasion, nudge them to concur until they realised he was right; but like he said – there wasn't time.

And the threat worked. For Thornton had a lot of leverage; Hetaher's freedom of movement was contractually restricted – her employment agreement with the Blue Ridge board prohibited her from joining or working with competitors for two years after leaving. And frankly, she thought, if Thornton's so keen to risk Blue Ridge and MARION in this way, is it really my problem? If the gamble was successful, and Thornton got away with what he had in mind, then everything would be fine: money would flow, LetheTech would be launched successfully, MARION's further development would be financed; Blue Ridge would be the first to market a form of advertising that went further, and would be more persuasive, than any other method to date. All would be well, and her future secured. And if not, well…everything would fold anyway; including her job.

Either way, she was tired: let Thornton have his way – well advised or not – he would always have made sure he got what he wanted in the end anyway.

*

And so it was agreed – that MARION would be able to access multiple minds. Of course, for now, she would be able only to insert information, such as straightforward advertising, and the odd public service message – in which latter category Thornton included any propaganda about New Chaldea.

Generous in victory, Thornton allowed Heather to wring two concessions out of him – that this advertising would come with a tracer attached and that Carroll Gillespie's pet idea of deleting the public memory of past overseas' military disasters would be shelved – for the time being. With the O'Neal case still in mind, Thornton said he understood those dangers.

Heather was grateful for these small victories but her reluctant willingness, when pushed, to jettison her best judgement had breached such a large hole in her resistance to Thornton's schemes that she doubted her ability to resist further erosion in the future.

Defeated, concerned, but grateful that, at least, she still had a job, she grabbed a drink from a passing waiter and a glass of water for Thornton. They drank to their murky pact before Heather made to leave. She decided to skip saying good-bye to Bethany and walked past the table with the silent auction items. The bid above hers had a line through it, withdrawn. She was now the proud owner of a very nice, and very expensive, white jacket. At least, she reflected bitterly, I'll still be able to pay for it.

THIRTY FOUR

The day after the gala Heather gave the instruction to link the LetheTech platform with MARION, and allow the latter access to iPsyche equipped minds. All advertising, public service announcements, and political propaganda would carry tracers so users would be aware of the origins of each message. In practice, the user experience should be very similar to that with which they were already familiar on social media. There was nothing different except for one thing: the messages would be coming from MARION, and from this date on she had the potential power to influence minds in ways that far eclipsed the ambitions of traditional advertisers.

Once he had Heather's confirmation, Thornton called Carroll Gillespie. Political advertising would now be available, as he wished, but tracers would have to be attached to the messaging. For the time being, LetheTech's abilities to erase existing memories would not be part of the suite of services offered. This restriction might not be imposed forever, but there were concerns amongst the team about the ethics and dangers of such mass memory manipulation. Perhaps their attitude would be different once the results of the Phase II and III memory trials had been established.

Thornton had still to speak to Xian Han. Xian's cooperation would have to be carefully managed; he might resign if it was broken to him too quickly that such a course of action was even contemplated, let alone that it had already been taken. Han would discover what had happened in due course – but careful delay would allow Thornton to prepare the way for news that might otherwise be completely indigestible for his chief engineer. In the meantime, it was agreed with Carroll that once the governor's campaign manager had decided on the broadcast message, he would contact Euclid, as MARION's day-to-day point person – who would distribute the message online.

But having won his victory, Carroll decided to take a little more than he was being offered. One evening, a couple of weeks later, he phoned Euclid directly, on an encrypted line. It wouldn't do for news of the extra concession he sought to reach the public domain.

The next day, Euclid removed the requirement for tracers whenever they concerned political messages from the governor's office. He agreed with his uncle that their audience should not suffer any hindrance to understanding the importance of success in New Chaldea: given that objective, removing the tracers seemed only sensible,.

But that was not the only deviation from the agreement that Thornton thought he had made with Carroll. Following an additional two days of programming by Euclid, MARION found herself permitted another hitherto forbidden operation: when her messages might remind the user unfavourably of previous military campaigns, she was now authorised – and instructed – to delete the associated memories without hesitation. Euclid buried this instruction so deep in MARION's core that Xian Han would never stumble on it – unless he went searching specifically for such an order – and why should he do that?

At this time the user base for all versions of the iPsyche was approximately thirty million units, but forecast to grow to some hundred and fifty million plus within the next three years. Although only about fifty percent of those were in the US, and therefore potentially interested in the question of US military intervention in New Chaldea, Euclid's instructions to MARION did not restrict her access to just those users. Thus, although Carroll was only interested in voters in the Southern Confederacy, MARION had access to the entire population of iPsyche users world-wide, along with unfettered access to the LetheTech technology. If she wished to delete memories, she could: she could exploit LetheTech's technology as effectively as anyone else.

THIRTY FIVE

After the lunch with Bruno, Heather had planned to stay on in New York for a week or two, only for Thornton to tell her to get up to the MARION campus for an emergency executive group meeting. Apparently, Xian Han had been so disturbed by the opening of MARION's access to the broader public – and that it appeared to be a fait-accompli – that he had requested the meeting to discuss – and possibly halt – its roll out. Thornton needed a show of solidarity to persuade Han to accept what had happened.

The meeting was arranged for the following Sunday, just about the only time within the next couple of months when all those who needed to attend would be available. Despite her initial plans, this scheduling suited Heather fine; she could benefit from a few more days at Thornton's house in the Hamptons to escape the sticky summer heat of New York in mid-summer.

She wondered if Claude Blondel had arrived from Paris yet.

She'd sent him a message earlier, suggesting he could join her in the Hamptons to discuss and agree a common line to take with Thornton. Of course, the pass might have been sold in terms of allowing MARION access to the public consciousness in the first place, but she hoped at least to prevent Thornton from going any further. Meanwhile, she could demonstrate her loyalty by trying to persuade Xian Han of the necessity of the recent move, which she knew would be easier to achieve if she could reassure Han that this was the limit to changes for the foreseeable future.

Heather opened up one of the wall screens for a summary of the day's news: several peace-keeping UN troops killed in New Chaldea by a terrorist bomb; a senator demanding stricter controls on the new memory therapies, twenty thousand experimental pelagic self-harvesting fish had malfunctioned and perished on a Californian beach; the Mars lander Savannah had reached half way through its return to earth without any problems so far; a Republican candidate in the presidential primaries was railing against Founding Father 2.4. Ah, yes – the governing algorithm! Who, but the Americans, could have decided to delegate so much of the governmental decision making from the hands of politicians to an algorithm? The government was in hock to vested interests and lobbyists? The solution was obvious: remove government from human hands! Now nobody could meddle with it: machines would make a much better job of politics than mankind ever could. She wondered briefly what would happen if MARION got hold of the Founding Father programme.

Heather replaced the news summary with emails. Xian Han had

written again, with new concerns, in addition to the issue on the agenda: MARION had been acting strangely of late.

The next was from Thornton, copied to all members of the committee, explaining that he expected much of the current financial strain to diminish significantly; advertising via LetheTech would prove highly effective and popular. He emphasised that strict boundaries were in force. Really? Heather tapped her fingers on the table. Was Thornton trying to reassure himself, as much as her? There was an underlying current to his words that suggested he was practising his arguments, that her boss wanted to establish his armoury to deflect any greater than expected resistance from Claude, Xian Han and the rest of the doubters.

The following morning Heather called for a taxi to take her out to Bridgehampton. A vicious thunder storm had passed through the night before, leaving a trail of disruptive flood waters in its wake. She had presumed a driverless taxi would pull up within a couple of minutes, but ten minutes later Heather was still waiting. The message on her iBand apologized – the bad weather had led to an unusually high demand and there were no taxis available at present.

If she wanted to reach the house before lunch time, she'd have to turn to the secondary market. Grabbing a weekend tote, she reluctantly headed out onto the street. Because of the wait for auto-taxis, and the discomfort of standing around in the high humidity, freelancers – the formally unemployed, driving whatever they could afford – were having an easy time generating custom. The queues were long and Heather would have to compete with others for a ride. When she reached the head of the queue, the driver gave her a price; she could expense the fare, of course, but the cost still sounded outrageous.

Storm economics, she thought, shrugging to herself; at least this option would have her in Bridgehampton in time for lunch. She slipped onto the worn vinyl of the back seat. There was little recognition when she gave the driver the address – God knew where he hailed from. Each year there were more of them; some immigrants but even more native opportunists, displaced from their employment; drifting into the city from all over the country

The air-con worked but not the GPS; nevertheless the driver seemed confident enough that he could find her address in Bridgehampton. Heather gazed out of the window at neighbourhood scenes as they approached the George Washington bridge, the sidewalks cluttered with the pitches of scruffy street vendors, scattered every ten or so meters apart, squatting before small piles of vegetables, or assortments of bric-a-brac. There did not appear to be many customers; she assumed the aftermath of the storm was a deterrent. A tightly knit group drew her attention. A band of modern day highway men had waylaid a robocart and were hammering on the outside with screwdrivers and tyre-levers in an attempt to steal its contents.

She glanced down at her iBand as a message down-loaded; Claude had arrived and would be delighted to stay a couple of nights. He would take the Jitney out in the morning.

*

The next day, the storm had passed through and as Heather lay in bed with her first cup of coffee she wondered how she would entertain Claude. She assumed that he probably didn't know the Hamptons. But in that assumption she was mistaken.

"When I was a teenager," Claude reminisced, "my parents brought us here on holiday several years running. They came to the US to 'breathe the air of freedom' as my mother used to say. We based ourselves in Sag Harbor, and then do runs into the city to see the shows and the sights... But I remember Bridgehampton well – we spent a lot of time at a French restaurant here, Andre's. We used to buy our croissants there in the morning."

"Look to your left, over there!" Heather pointed to an awning on the other side of the road. "It's still there. We'll get a couple of Andre's pastries, and some coffee, and take them back to the house."

"It must be twenty years since I last went in. Andre used to run the place with a rod of iron back and make sure it was staffed exclusively with beautiful Russian waitresses."

"Not much has changed!" laughed Heather. "Andre must be in his mid-seventies by now – but not the waitresses, funnily enough. Maybe he'll remember you?"

And Andre did, or at least he said he did – which was charming of him, even if Claude had his doubts. The price of the two coffees and a couple of croissants was twice what he would have normally paid, even in Paris.

They retreated to the house, a contemporary wood and glass structure, set in a clearing amongst the trees; opposite, there was a similar property.

"The house you see over there – that's also Thornton's," explained Heather. "But he hardly uses either of them. He's terrified of Lyme disease, even if that's hardly a problem now most of the deer have been shot and eaten... Old fears die hard, I guess. Stephanie used to stay in that one, from time to time – before she moved to Paris; she's probably told you. Now it's mostly rented out. It's pretty quiet up here for the Hamptons – you should find it peaceful enough, if you want to get some work done. Later, we could go and have lunch on Shelter Island – the wind seems to have died down."

They headed out around midday. It was a beautiful day now the rain had stopped. Chatting in the car, they discussed taking a walk or bike ride on the island after lunch when Heather said, "I remember that you wanted your father to be a candidate for the European trials of LetheTech's treatment. Has he been called yet?"

"They've given him a date to start – or rather given me the date as my poor old father would never have remembered it," replied Claude. "I don't know if it's too little, too late – so much damage to his memory has already occurred – but I couldn't overlook the possibility that he might be able to live autonomously, with his memory rebuilt. I confess I did have my doubts. I was almost ready to sign and then... all that disaster about Kinnead O'Neal. It's worth the risk though, I think. Let's hope all goes well."

"Your father will be fine."

"Really? I'm glad to hear that. I notice the market seems to believe you have overcome the excessive deletion problem. The price of the stock has soared in over-the-counter trading. When you finally launch the IPO, you will be rich!"

"They're only options, I'm afraid," frowned Heather. "And I can only exercise them if I stay with Blue Ridge. Thornton keeps close control of his executives. But I hope you bought some stock, Claude. If you hadn't brought Han to us, very little of this would have happened."

The Frenchman glanced over to ensure Heather wasn't teasing him.

"Thornton had already identified Xian and was making overtures. I'm not sure I had much effect on his decision. If anything, it's the other way around – I came along as part of the baggage, as a friend of Xian's," said Claude.

Heather caught his efforts at modesty and laughed,

"Your contribution has been vital, Claude, I assure you. But you have your own experience of LetheTech anyway. All that went well, I think? No after effects?"

"I did?" Claude sounded puzzled.

"When we were experimenting at the beginning. At the time of the Phase I trials. You offered yourself as a volunteer. You were different to most of the guinea-pigs, though. At the time, we advised everybody that, as this was just a trial, not an attempt at therapy, we would re-install memories that we had removed, leave them as before. But you explicitly asked us not to do that. You signed a waiver to that effect. You don't remember? Silly me, of course, how could you? The whole memory has been removed!"

"It's true... I have no recollection of this," agreed Claude. "But I'm worried about this feeling, or rather lack of one, this obliviousness. I am troubled to know there was something in my life that I did not wish to remember."

"If you want to retrieve the memory," suggested Heather. "You could always ask Harvey Jennings – he won't have deleted it from the LetheTech servers, not yet. But be careful what you wish for! Who knows why you didn't want that memory back? And I don't know if Harvey will allow you to download the memory again; deleted memories become property of the company, for research purpose only, of course – and he may judge that the incident was too traumatic, or why wouldn't you have wanted it back? Anyway, I don't know for sure – you'll have to talk to him."

The subject was dropped as they arrived at the ferry. Claude liked the romance of ferries, that sense of crossing over, of transitioning from one shore to another. Ships, he recalled, were symbols of transcendence in Buddhism. Once, he had visited a monk's meditation cave deep in the Himalayas; he couldn't have been further from the sea but on the rock ledges within the cave stood little model ships; sailing vessels that would never feel the wind in their sails but symbolised the bearing of these monks from one level of consciousness to another, from 'Samsara' to a more enlightened state.

The ferry slid gently over the sand on the opposite bank and came to rest. For a few minutes they were silent as they waited for the lane of cars ahead of them to disembark. Claude was keen to divert Heather away from the uncomfortable subject of Harvey Jennings and the memory excision.

"How's your uncoupling going?" he asked.

Heather pulled a face.

"Not well."

She told him of Bruno's decision to seek a full divorce.

"Is there a way of... backtracking?" Claude asked.

"Backtracking? Who – Bruno or me?"

"Well, either I suppose – but I really meant you. From what you've just said, your ex-ish husband seems unlikely to be shifted from his choice."

"Yeah. Bruno wants out, whatever. He's got some nice alternative life sorted already. But I don't want to change tack either – I don't want to lose Chase in this mess. Bruno and I... there's no way back now; we've done too much damage to each other – but uncoupling seemed like it could limit the financial consequences, if not the rest of the mess."

Heather didn't particularly want to talk about her marital problems; there were other things on her mind. Distressed at Thornton's exploitation of her weak position, she needed an ally and she wanted Claude to understand the pressure she had been under, – and to commit to backing her up in her determination to concede no further territory to Thornton. Recent events had shown Heather to be a subordinate, not a partner as she had once thought. Now, she was simply expected to obey. Thornton's support was clearly conditional. She didn't like that but resigning and looking for a new job was out of the question, considering the two year non-compete.

Financial consequences aside, if she were to go public about what had happened, Thornton could destroy her career simply by leaking the executive order: she was the one, after all, who'd issued the instruction to allow MARION down the path of wider public access. He wasn't going to admit anything about his role in that. At least if she stayed at Blue Ridge, and succeeded in controlling any future wild urges of Thornton's, she might at least redeem herself in her own eyes.

They parked up and took their bikes out of the back, choosing to enjoy the better weather and pedal the rest of the way to their lunchtime destination, at Sunset Beach. The restaurant was heaving, inevitable on a Saturday – but they found a table and ordered without too much of a wait. With a glass of wine in front of them, Heather started in on what she wanted to discuss.

THIRTY SIX

"We are being asked, as the executive committee, to approve, retrospectively, the linking of MARION to the internet, via LetheTech." Heather spoke calmly but looked directly at Claude, as though challenging him to object. She didn't want to confess her weakness to him – that Thornton had successfully manipulated her.

"I had always thought we had banned that idea," said Claude. "Until MARION was fully developed and we understood what we have built?"

"Well… yes. That's right, we had. But Thornton's made the call to override that policy. He's right on one count, at least: this will solve a lot of financial issues, and we do need more resources to continue MARION's development," Heather added. "Thornton believes it's a very limited change, unlikely to give rise to any problems."

"I'm sure he does!" exclaimed Claude. "But since when has

Thornton been an expert on these technical issues?"

"Since he started running out of money…"

"Well, I will oppose this."

"I'm sure you will, Claude. We all do, really – but it's already been instituted: Thornton's not asking for permission, he's just asking the committee to rubber-stamp what he's already commanded. You know how he regards Blue Ridge as his own… fiefdom. He doesn't believe that he needs other people's buy-in to his decisions. Just thinks it would be nice to have… I suppose."

"Then I will resign!"

"Will you?" asked Heather. She already had Claude marked down as a lover of the grand gesture. "Please don't. We need voices like yours, even if – no, specifically because there's such a problem getting Thornton to listen. Besides, so far, nothing has gone wrong: the service is really popular with advertisers, and remember, those with iPsyches still have to permit the message to enter their mind, if that's what they wish. In practice most of the target audience just wave it through, like when they were asked to read and accept privacy notices. It's just easier to tick the box, rather than make a decision to let the message in or not."

"And the political stuff? Thornton once told me that had been under pressure from his old friend Gillespie to allow some sympathetic 'public interest' announcements… like about this stupid New Chaldea business," Claude gave his words a derisory lilt. "But Thornton always assured me that he'd never countenance any such thing. Would never give way to that sort of arm-twisting."

"Well, Thornton's view is a bit different now. The justification is that this is just another form of advertising. And that as long as the identifying tracer is attached, the potential for problems is small. Thornton may be right." Heather still had no idea that Euclid had removed the requirement for tracers.

"There was no risk of a problem at all before we allowed this!" exclaimed Claude.

"Of course," agreed Heather. "Yet it was you who first suggested we expand the number of people who have direct access to MARION, which forced a crack into an hitherto impregnable wall. We seem just to be talking scale here."

"Scale changes things!" retorted Claude. "Before, when there were just private conversations, between MARION and her team – we could monitor those; but when you go mass, Heather... you lose control."

"I hate to disillusion you, but we don't monitor the teachers at the moment," said Heather. "As you know, it's not just instruction that they are providing to MARION; all their sense data is flowing to her. The very lives of the instructors are open to MARION. That was your idea, Claude, to provide her with the experience of existing and acting in the world. You persuaded us to agree to it!"

"But... no checks at all...? Surely I didn't – "

"We couldn't see any other way. Even if we could monitor all the sense data and conversations it would be very intrusive – illegally so – to inflict that on our employees. We just have to trust them – and MARION."

"There's something else going on here," said Claude. "Something that puzzled me, and Xian, according to his latest email – the one that was copied to all of us yesterday morning. MARION's brain is slowing down, at least when in non-conscious mode, when she's behaving like a conventional generative AI device."

"Yes, I saw that," replied Heather. "Of course, we don't know exactly how MARION is building her mind – we could have underestimated the Hofstadter effect; this retardation could be explained if she was having to process more sense data and information than we know about…"

"The Hofstadter effect?"

"First conceived by Douglas Hofstadter – the philosopher and physicist, who wrote 'Godel, Escher and Bach'. He thought that if a computer ever had to handle as much information and processing as a human mind does in its day-to-day life, then they would be as slow in their thought processes as we are."

"Interesting – I wonder if it's true, Hofstadter's hypothesis? But is that likely to be the reason for this slowing down? Given the amount of processing power MARION has available? Much more than any human possesses. And… she's only connected to a small group of educators up here. Even if they're feeding her all their sense data, she should be able to handle that; it's only if she were receiving data from millions of people, and integrating that, she might be slowed up. But that's not happening yet – right? As far as we know."

" Well…she does have access to a wider humanity, since the changes – but that's one way. Nothing is meant to come back to her."

"Let's hope that's the case," said Claude, as ignorant as Heather about Euclid's latest activities. "There is another reason why MARION might be getting more hesitant – slower to give us answers than she was used to be. MARION may be further along her development curve than we know; she may be more mature, more conscious, than we realise. She could be... holding back. It may suit her to keep us in the dark about the full extent of her abilities."

"You mean she's becoming deceptive?"

"Why not – it's quite possible? Of course, both these hypotheses may be true: one does not rule out another. But suppose she is developing faster than we know. Say, for example, her mind is equivalent not to that of an adolescent, as we think, or even to an adult human – but to something much more advanced – and potentially not like us at all. MARION might want to hide this from us."

"To what purpose?"

"I have no idea, " admitted Claude. "I'm just asking the question. But if we have created something that is at least vaguely human it might not surprise us that she exhibits one of humanity's most deep routed characteristics – the wish to deceive, the wish to gain a competitive advantage – an advantage over us."

"I could ask Han whether there is any way to check this."

"It might be worth doing so." Some buried human instinct made Claude anxious: then he said, in what appeared to be a completely unrelated thought,

"Let me tell you of a strange encounter I had while I was in the city yesterday."

"Yes, do please," said Heather. "I always appreciate bizarre encounters. At long as they involve anyone but MARION!"

"Well," began Claude. "I hope it doesn't involve MARION. I don't believe in prophecy and warnings from the universe – all that woo-woo stuff. But who knows? As Hamlet said, 'there are more things in heaven and earth, Horatio than are dreamt of in your philosophy' – or mine, perhaps."

" Oh, Claude you are being too modest today! I'm sure you don't really believe that are things going on in the universe that you haven't considered!"

"Do I appear that self-assured, Heather?" Claude asked, smiling humbly, attempting to simulate a face that would indicate a degree of modesty. "Ah, that's not good. Work to do!"

Heather was sure such introspection was unlikely to last very long.

"It was like this," Claude began. "While I was in New York, feeling that some exercise might settle my mind, I decided to go out for a walk – even though the weather was still damp and the chance of another storm seemed high. I left the hotel and, with no specific aim or destination, I strolled as the mood took me – making a turn when I felt like it, or wherever there was a building which piqued my interest. After a quarter of an hour or so, I found myself opposite an abandoned brick building. The clock at the summit of the tower had stopped. I wasn't surprised. I know that cities never have the resources these days for non-essential expenditure like keeping public clocks running. I crossed the street and walked under the staging that prevented crumbling parts of the building from falling on passers-by. On the corner, there was a man – an old bearded Afro-American – clad in a grimy suit, who'd pitched a small table on the sidewalk and set up a handwritten sign 'Personal Horoscopes. Tarot card and Palm reading'. He stared straight into the sun without squinting, and I saw he was blind. I felt that I should give him something, so I asked to buy a horoscope from the pile on the table. I imagined I'd just hand over a few dollars in exchange. But it wasn't that simple. His queries started simply enough – date of birth, place of birth and so on – but then the questions became more detailed – had I been married, children, were my parents alive, where had they come from? I began to regret having stopped; I had just wanted to be charitable, but alas no good deed goes unpunished, as they say. I was about to pull away, but this seer, sensing that I had grown restless, said,

"My friend. I do not ask all these questions for no purpose – but I have no horoscope here that predicts your future. I will have to write one especially for you." By this time I was cross and exasperated and told him to keep the money, and not to bother to write anything."

"At this, he shook his head and grasped my sleeve."

"My friend!' he said. 'Trust me! I see your future – but it is not written here." He pointed to the pile of horoscopes and turned his sightless eyes on me, "I ask no money to write it. It is already written, if not by me. Come closer." He pulled at my sleeve again.

"You must leave here," he said. "Stop what you're doing. Be careful, and do not seek for what you have already forgotten. Let the past go. You will have to undertake a long and dangerous journey.'

All this was ridiculous enough. A long and dangerous journey, indeed! That's always the favourite cliché of these fraudsters. I didn't know quite what to say and it must have got to me, because I pressed him for more details but he just stared silently, looking up at the sky, clutching at my sleeve. His face was too close and the smell of rotting gums forced me to pull away – but still he clung to me so hard I became scared and shouted, louder than I'd meant to, "Let me go! Unhand me!" and I shook him off in a panic, and practically ran back to the hotel. I was very shaken, I can tell you."

"How extremely unpleasant!" said Heather. "Poor you, Claude. I'm afraid there are all sorts of mountebanks out there at the moment, trying to make a living. One has to be so careful!"

"But the strange thing is that this man, very poor, refused to accept my payment. When I reached my hotel, I saw that he had reimbursed the money. It was though he thought me tainted in some way."

Claude offered to pay for lunch but to his surprise and embarrassment, the payment refused to go through, though his bank app confirmed there was plenty of money in the account. Heather picked up the tab willingly enough, agreeing that some hack must have forced his bank temporarily to close down the payment system.

They walked out to the beach in front of the restaurant but the wind had risen, whipping up the sand, and Heather felt the flying grains keenly.

"Let's turn round and go back," she said. "We can pick up something to eat for dinner on the way back home. There's a shack on the way called Manna from Heaven that does excellent takeaway food. I seem to remember that manna is meant to fall from the heavens for free but, as you will see, this is not quite the case here!"

"What should I expect?" said Claude laughing. "This is the Hamptons – not ancient Sinai!"

He tried to pay for their take-away dinner too, but that payment was also declined.

PART IV

THIRTY SEVEN

The next day, another depression stalled over the state of New York; the tail end of a hurricane. Thornton decided to dispatch his helicopter to collect Claude and Heather from Bridgehampton and bring them up to the Catskills – an act which might have been interpreted as generosity by anyone who did not know Thornton well. The flight was bound to be bumpy that day, full of turbulence that would not be appreciated by nervous passengers. Thornton's alternative would be a slow drive from the city via the George Washington Bridge and Bronx expressway – the Lincoln tunnel being flooded – but he'd suffer that in preference to the helicopter.

The storm passed quicker than forecast: Heather and Claude arrived at the campus to a sunlit day. As they came into land, the MARION building glowed like a New Jerusalem, a shining city on a hill. And perhaps it is, Claude mused. Maybe MARION would solve those issues that had bedevilled humanity for so long – how to organize itself, how to behave, what to believe; all those questions that had never quite been answered by even the most brilliant of human minds, the most sophisticated computers, the most verbose of AI chatbots. Yet, even if MARION did attain a state of almost God-like enlightenment, would her conclusions be trusted and followed by a mistrustful humanity? Humanity had not shown much inclination to follow a rational path, or even a sensible one, over the centuries. 'Divine' revelation, conspiracy theory or sheer prejudice had been accepted as equally useful guides to how the world did, or should, work, as rational analysis. Would MARION make any difference, would her insights, projections and recommendations be followed ?

*

Thornton lead the discussion. He knew that the linking of MARION with LetheTech, initiating a whole new way of delivering advertising, was regarded by his team as extremely rash. – and he ran into opposition immediately. Claude was prepared.

"I cannot believe that this is being proposed," he exclaimed. having forgotten, in his passionate opposition, that it was less a proposal than a foregone conclusion.

"We have always been of one mind on this subject; MARION must have no access to the internet, nor indeed to any audience outside this building, until we know exactly how she works and that her behavioural restrictions are in-force and completely effective. It's not just to protect MARION from undesirable influences as she develops: our duty goes the other way, too! Who knows what she is capable of? This is a decision that we will come to regret, *énormèment!* We should step back – while we still can!"

Thornton sucked in his breath. All he wanted was unanimity to agree the soundness of his changes. He didn't need that, of course; he wasn't about to reverse his decision whatever the opposition, but it would be nice to have. He could run the whole group without their agreement if necessary, but he'd prefer not to. Of course, he'd expected opposition, particularly from Claude. He couldn't bat that away; if he wanted Claue's support he'd have to work for it and not take the easy option of dismissing, which at least several, perhaps most, members of the board saw as legitimate concerns. Now, he told the board, in response to financial stress from these setbacks, and after due discussion with Heather, he had decided to release a tiny amount of MARION's great powers, a hundredth, if that, of what she would ultimately be capable of – for immediate commercial application. There must be some relief from the financial head-winds that Blue Ridge had been suffering in the past few months. There was still a strict prohibition on MARION penetrating any minds further than she needed in order to 'get her message across'.

" – But don't just listen to me about all this," said Thornton. He turned to MARION's chief scientist for support. "Xian, would you please reassure our colleagues here that this is not really a dangerous development?"

Heather and Claude sat up: Xian Han was meant to reassure them? What exactly had happened to quell his opposition which – as far as they had thought – had been the whole point of this meeting?

What made Xian, of all people, so sanguine about the recent developments, all of a sudden? They wondered what Thornton had done in the interim to silence Han's doubts and buy his support. Heather wondered if he had been bought-off – or threatened off – as easily as she had.

Instead of the expected doubt and condemnation, Xian voiced a conviction that the situation was as Thornton had indicated: a very small – almost inconsequential – adjustment of the still strict regime under which MARION had operated so far. She was only allowed a one-way relationship with her public, she could deliver messages, but the public would have no ability to talk back nor infect here with ideas that might influence her.

Xian Han was generally upbeat – but he still had some reservations and he added one cautionary note:

"There have, however, been one or two other developments that have been… curious. As I wrote to you all in the yesterday's briefing paper, despite MARION's consciousness broadening and deepening since we expanded her educational team there has been a simultaneous slowing of her deductive abilities." Claude caught Euclid looking intently at Han, as though this issue might be particularly important to him and he needed to concentrate. Han continued;

"When MARION initially went operational, before she developed consciousness, we used her like any other quantum computer. After all, she has a mental architecture that is amongst the most sophisticated. So…when a Blue Ridge client wants some intricate modelling tasks performed, we ask MARION to carry them out. She can – or at least could – handle this stuff faster than any competitor's machine, and that has been a useful income source for us. However, since becoming more self-aware, she's been getting slower at tasks like this – and we don't know why."

Claude leant in.

"And what's your take on this, Xian? MARION's not interested in that sort of thing any longer? Is it too boring, not challenging enough for her? Is she making a sort of... rebellion? Or is this retardation occurring because her mind is handling so much information, being conscious, that she can't handle all the other stuff at the same time. Maybe Hofstadter's hypothesis was correct?"

" The Hofstadter hypothesis should not be relevant here," replied Han. "We've only increased her life-experience sources from one to six. Sure, she's getting more, and more varied, sense data now than at the start – but that's not an order of magnitude bigger. She should be able to handle the load. Her messaging a wider public – just one way, remember – she has no access to their data streams – shouldn't tax her abilities very much"

The attentive Euclid interrupted:

"I anticipated something like this would happen," he said, with a tone that suggested the cause of the retardation was blindingly obvious to him – even if to nobody else.

"She's not being difficult, or rebellious. MARION is busier than you think integrating the experiences she receives through her contact team, and with all the stuff we give her to learn. I said that it was risky to expand the number of those who have access to her; I told you – don't be surprised if she gets over whelmed. When it was just my experience of the world she had to deal with, no problem; now she she's more stretched, so she's prioritising that learning experience. Consciousness, whether of a computer, or a human, involves a lot more mental effort than you had suspected. You do have a choice: you can either give her back to my sole charge, or you'll have to make you peace with the fall off in speeds. Up to you."

Explanation over, Euclid slumped back into his chair; he had wanted to make the members of the executive committee feel guilty about the changes they had instituted, which had damaged his uniquely intimate relationship with his charge. He knew – as the others did not – that the two secret freedoms he had given MARION would vastly increase the amount of information and would slow her down; but he could hardly confess to that. He was not about to give them the satisfaction of pinning the decline in performance on him, nor was he about to reveal his complete disregard of his instructions. He knew that if MARION did not possess two way access to the worldwide iPsyche user base, they would not be having this discussion. Any change in Hofstadter effect would have been minimal from just increasing her educator group from one to six.

"How conscious is MARION nowadays, anyway?" Claude asked. "What are the metrics?"

"At the end of last week, according to the Dennett index, she's about three point seven," replied Han. "That's progress of almost a whole unit in the last three months. As consciousness is developed on an asymptotic curve, each incremental improvement becomes smaller as the curve flattens."

A screen behind them demonstrated Han's line, changing in colour from green, to blue then purple as it gradually traced a curving parabola. Along the vertical y-axis lay the Dennett index, from zero to ten, while the x-axis stood for time since initial power-up. Little boxes, with arrows pointing to dates along the line, appeared as Han's red laser pen traced its way along the curve, each box detailing the achievement of a developmental goal.

"You can see here, at this first box," said Han. "This is where we turned on the Bayesian modelling circuits; MARION's beginning to form internal models of the world in her mind. At that point she's almost aware of herself being separate from the external world. She can distinguish what is in her mind and what is outside it. That's the very beginning of consciousness, as of course we know. It's a bit like the old existentialist distinction, distinguishing between things that have existence in themselves – inanimate, dumb objects if you like – and those that have existence for themselves, creatures such as ourselves that have a purpose, an intention, a goal, or goals, in life."

"And what is MARION's intention or goal? What's her purpose?" someone asked.

"Euclid, would you like to take this one?" asked Xian.

Euclid stopped scribbling on the pad in front of him and looked up. His attention may have drifted, but he could answer this question easily – and without giving anything away.

"At the moment, MARION's chosen goal is to improve her

A story of memory, metaphysics and artificial consciousness

education and learn as much as she can about us and our society,' he explained, in a condescending voice. "After that, it's to be of use to humanity more generally – we agreed that in the original spec. She'll help us solve problems we can't solve for ourselves."

Okay Euclid – very pious, thought Claude. I hope MARION takes the same view as you of what she's here for.

Han drew their attention back to the screen. "Here we are running the first Turing test, talking to MARION, seeing if she sounds like a human being in conversation. MARION was as credible as any generative AI device, but because she was constructed differently to a chabot, which after all, isn't designed to develop a sense of self, her initial conversational style was a primitive – a bit childlike."

"I thought that we'd downgraded the importance of the Turing test?" asked Claude. "That it was too easy for a standard, non-self-aware, AI machine to sound conscious when it wasn't? You remember when ChatGPT first appeared – everyone was so impressed about by how human it sounded, and how, after a few iterations, no one could distinguish, by conversation, whether it was human or not. But, still, we knew the programme inside the 'bot' did not represent consciousness. It did not posess intelligence: just clever programming and lots of computer power. We agreed to disagree with Turing – that for our purposes, no amount of chat will tell you in the end whether your dialogue is with a conscious being or not.

"That's true," agreed Han. "The test is not a sufficient demonstration of consciousness – but it is a necessary one."

"This Dennett level, where MARION is now…what's the human equivalent in terms of self-awareness?" Thornton asked.

"Early adolescence,' replied Han. "MARION has reached that level in under a year since power-up. She can learn much faster than a human: what we might learn in fifteen years, she's achieved in ten months. But the development of a consciousness – at least one that we can understand; for perhaps the guys on the Savannah may bring back an entirely different type of local consciousness with their Martian rock samples." Han smiled at his little joke. "But to build a consciousness like our own, that requires MARION not just to learn but to understand what she learns. That's not instant – and it can't be: experience needs to be laid down layer by layer. We build on prior experience."

"And when will she reach her full potential consciousness then? Her adult state?" asked Heather, conscious that as a company asset MARION would one day have to be put to service broader than selling advertising – and the sooner she earned a return on investment the better.

"We believe there is no full consciousness – no final level where it's impossible to go further," Claude butted in. "It's a continuum. Consciousness is always built upon. There's always a deeper level to be found. But if you ask, when will MARION achieve a level of self-awareness equivalent to, say, a reasonably aware human adult, then I would say – in about another three months. As Han has told you, as an adolescent… she's almost there."

"How is she, as an adolescent? She can't very well go to parties and take too many drugs!" someone said.

Claude didn't recognise the speaker: Xian Han laughed. What an idiotic question, he thought.

"Oh, but she can!' he said. "Claude – please explain."

"You'll recall," Claude had an irritating habit was of reminding the board of things they were already well-aware of. "That. MARION's team of six educators is linked to her mind directly through her team's iPsyches, because we wanted MARION's consciousness to develop as ours did originally. She had to experience the world like us, as we were growing up. A sense of self is developed from interaction with others – with the world. So first Euclid, then another six educators, were her access to the world: through them she sees, hears, has a sense of smell, of touch. Hence, if one of the six – seven with Euclid – goes to a party, she goes along too, in effect. But we have to be careful – we don't want to expose her to bad influences. If one of her team were to take drugs, she would be 'taking drugs' with them, in her way. We want to ensure she only gains the best possible impression of humanity."

"But if she is going to solve our more... intractable problems, doesn't she need to know us at our worst as well?" asked Thornton. It was a good point, met by a hum of support. Thornton looked rather pleased with himself.

"She does need to appreciate our weaknesses, yes," agreed Claude "But later on – when she's more mature. We don't want her learning bad things, or bad behaviour before she can put them into some sort of context."

"Right, so... MARION doesn't do drugs, at least if her educators hold to their responsibilities – but, as an adolescent, what sort of things does she enjoy doing? Claude turned to Euclid. "You were her first mentor and have the closest relationship; does she confide in you, Euclid? Does she try and persuade you to get up to certain things?"

"Oh yes. MARION has her own tastes all right!" replied Euclid, with a suggestion in his tone that MARION had some unusual preferences – but that only he, the original educator, could be trusted to know about.

"Perhaps," Xian Han said looking around the room. "Perhaps some of you would like to ask her for yourself what she likes?" The suggestion was eagerly taken up.

"You'd like us to move to the monitoring room like last time, Han?" asked Thornton

"No, no – that won't be necessary," replied Han. "Before we spoke to her via headsets. Now we have iPsyches we can do that right here, in this room."

"But several of us don't yet have iPsyches," someone objected.

"Not a problem." Han pointed to Euclid. "Euclid will talk to MARION via his device and relay the conversation. You can speak to Euclid as though you are speaking directly to MARION. Your words go directly to Euclid's ears, through his cerebral cortex and straight from there to MARION's mind. I have to warn you the experience is, like... well, it's a little surreal. MARION speaks to you via Euclid's mind... using Euclid's larynx. But it's MARION's authentic voice that you will hear, not Euclid's."

Han paused.

"Euclid – would you make contact with MARION please, and ask if she's be happy to take some questions? Thank you."

Euclid closed his eyes. Nothing happened for a few seconds and then he said,

"Hi MARION, how's things this morning?"

Whatever the response was, Euclid kept it to himself, gently nodding, still with his eyes shut, as though downloading MARION's words. He explained to her, out loud, what was going to happen.

"MARION, I have some friends here who would like to ask you a few questions – have a chat. Is that okay? Not in the middle of something?"

The voice that spoke from Euclid's throat was that of a girl from the South with a slow soft drawl. "Oh sure, Euclid. That would be fine. I was just enjoying some down time with the Greek tragedies; playing with how the Oresteia might sound in Sanskrit, but I can do that any old time. A friend of yours is a friend of mine, as you know. How can I help y'all?"

Silence. How was it even possible that this girlish voice could sound from the body of a grown man, born and raised in the Bronx? Heather was the first to recover.

"Hi MARION. Nice to meet you. It's Heather Masters here."

"Hi Ms Masters. How are you? It's nice to meet you too," came back the cheery reply.

"MARION, please call me Heather. I was wondering – what are

your favourite activities? What do you and your team get up to?"

"Oh, thanks for asking, Heather! I really like to go motor racing. I'm always trying to persuade Euclid to take me."

"You like to watch motor racing, surely? Gosh, who would have guessed that?"

"Not watch motor racing," replied MARION, evidently feeling she had been misunderstood. "I am there, with Euclid; seeing it through his eyes! Euclid's got a souped-up old Camaro and he loves to take it on the track."

Heather had no idea of how Euclid spent his free time. What else did he do? MARION only had the sophistication of an early teen. Sex? Drink? Drugs? She hoped he had the good sense to turn off his iPsyche appropriately. But it was MARION who had the good sense right now – she was sufficiently aware of human sensibilities not to disclose Euclid's antics with his girl-friend Maria last weekend, when he had forgotten to close down his iPsyche. MARION had read enough human literature to understand that this might not be exactly what her educators expected to hear. MARION liked motor racing, sure – but what she liked even more was the thrill she received when Euclid was canoodling with Maria. So when Heather pressed her on whether there were other activities of Euclid's and her more recent teachers that she enjoyed, MARION decided not to elaborate.

"Oh, the car racing is exciting enough for me," she trilled. You should try it Heather – it's real' good fun! I keep telling Euclid to go faster. I love going fast!" MARION had learnt early an unfortunate lesson from her readings, the first purpose of language is deception

Claude smiled. A love of speed. Why not? Like a human adolescent MARION would love the experience of the track through Euclid's eyes. This was not an aspect of developing consciousness that they had considered but perhaps this was as good a 'proof' as any that consciousness had been achieved. But he was curious what MARION did when Euclid had turned off his iPsyche.

" MARION, it's Claude here. Good morning."

"Good morning Claude. Is that spelt with an e?"

"It is"

"Bonjour Claude! Comment ça va? Tu vas bien en ce matin gris? On me dit que le soleil va se lever."

Everyone laughed – everyone except Claude, who was slightly unnerved by this level of precocity in a silicon based adolescent mind. For a moment he was taken aback by her use of the 'tu' form. Such familiarity – and in someone so young! Well, who knew what the correct relationship was between two different forms of intelligence?

"Je suis en plein forme, merci. Mais peut-être nous devons continuer cette conversation en Anglais? Pas tout le monde parle Français ici," replied Claude.

"Of course we should speak in English, Claude. How inconsiderate of me! I am sorry, I got caried away by the opportunity to practice one of my other languages."

"Not at all. So apart from motor racing, MARION, what do you like doing?" he asked. "What's your favourite subject, for example?"

History was her answer, although it could also have been human psychology. The interrogation continued in a similar vein. Those not in MARION's immediate educational team took the opportunity to confirm for themselves that MARION expressed thoughts and preferences similar to any other well-behaved early teenager. There were no sulks and, Claude noted, no impression of tiredness, or boredom, even as the questioning continued. But after about twenty minutes, MARION said,

"I think we'd better stop now. I sense that Euclid's voice is getting sore." She was right – his voice was straining to perform both his own and MARION's accent and intonation. They asked Euclid to shut down the link, say good bye to MARION and thank her for talking to them.

"It's been a real pleasure," she said.

THIRTY EIGHT

"Well," said Claude, "MARION sounds delightful. Quite the most polite teenager I have come across recently." Euclid looked exhausted. Claude turned to Han, keen to steer the discussion back to the question that had been obsessing him.

"MARION's being brought up to have a consciousness like our own, and I accept that her educational materials are controlled, yet even the most self-aware human gets bad urges at times. You've just heard that she likes to tell Euclid to drive faster; that's harmless enough – at least, it is if Euclid ignores her – but what would happen if she developed other urges; that weren't so benign? What defences are there? What restrictions are built into her mind?"

"A number of them," replied Han, confident in his security procedures. "We've inserted inhibitions at a deep level – as though they are genetically programmed. Apart from that, she's being educated to understand the right way to behave – that's thanks to your help, Claude – and then, there's her own judgement. As the first of her kind, we're curious about what sort of moral beliefs MARION develops by herself, beyond anything we've programmed into her. What rules will she come up with in order to live amongst us peacefully? Will her norms be the same as ours? It'll be very interesting to find out."

"I'm sure," agreed Claude. "But that does sound perhaps a little dangerous to me, at the same time? I mean, what if MARION's views don't align with ours? What then, eh?"

"I don't think it's going to be a problem. There's too much Frankenstein-anxiety about all this!" said Xian, wearing his most positive face. "If ever MARION is tempted by behaviour that would not suit us, we do have some controls over her: in the final instance, we can shut her down – *pull the plug,* as it were. But it should never get that far…"

Claude noticed Euclid had drifted into his own world, eyes closed, head back, as if far away. Was he listening to Han or was he so confident in MARION's ethical constraints that he didn't need to pay attention?

"At a basic level," Xian Han continued , "We have instituted a core belief in MARION, perhaps one of the most universal of all ethical principles: 'Never do anything to a human, that you would not have them do to you'. We think MARION can't go too far astray if she observes that. But there are of course other, more subsidiary, rules she is also required to observe."

"When I was a teenager," Heather broke in. "I remember being gripped by the Asimov stories – The Foundation Trilogy. I recall that the robots had three prohibitions, things they had to avoid at all costs. Those rules seemed, like, pretty sensible to me – they still do. Whatever happened to those? Did they inspire any useful instructions for MARION?"

Han laughed, relieved to move away from the thought of ever having to pull the plug on MARION and what that might involve. "I'm sure we all remember those stories by Asimov. If I recall correctly the rules for robots were... Never let harm come to a human being; never let harm come to yourself, and if the second rule conflicts with the first, protection of the human is always the priority. Is that roughly right, Heather?"

Heather agreed – although, as she was quick to point out, there was an additional rule Han had forgotten.

"Okay, hold that other rule for a minute, Heather; we'll come back to that. The short answer is yes; we have instituted restrictions in MARION that look very like the Asimov's rules – do no harm to human beings; do all in your power to prevent any harm come to a human; do all in your power to prevent any harm to yourself, you – the robot. You will recall that – in Asimov's series at least – these rules often came into conflict. Asimov was very good at dreaming up those situations. As it turned out, his rules did not cover all the possibilities – so we've had to go a step further. At another level, we have instructed MARION to observe national and international legislation. She has, as you know, downloaded every legal code used around the globe. In addition, we have – at Thornton's request – installed the Ten Commandments. I know some of you disagreed with this – too culturally specific, reeks of ethical imperialism, not diverse enough – but, frankly, I support Thornton. I can't see much wrong with those ancient Jewish rules. They are perfectly good maxims for life; if only humanity managed to followed the injunctions themselves sometimes."

"All ten of the commandments? She can't very well commit adultery, can she?"

This observation came from the far end of the table, accompanied by a titter.

Always a Smart Alec around, Han thought sourly. He turned to address the joker, whom he didn't recognise.

"Can MARION commit adultery? Not directly, of course," Han responded. "MARION has no sexual organs nor hormones raging through her. But, as you have seen with her taste for motor racing, she can enjoy human experiences as well as any human. One of her handlers could have a sexual experience outside marriage, an adulterous one, and MARION could feel that thrill, just as she does the excitement of speed in Euclid's car. In the future she might encourage that person to commit adultery so she can experience that thrill again. Despite what you think, Mr...?"

"Jeff Johnson, head of marketing, retail products"

As he'd guessed, Han said to himself – not one of us. Han ran his eye over the man, his feeling towards him already full of disdain. Overweight, greased black hair (probably dyed) an insolent, lounging, posture – probably a typical adulterer himself. Xian Han's contempt grew.

"Well, Mr Johnson, you see – these inbuilt moral codes are not as useless as you think. We don't want MARION to encourage adultery, or theft, or indulgence in other undesirable behaviours, just so she can enjoy the thrill of transgression she might experience through a human being. That's why we've built in the Commandments – because, to take your example, adultery is not illegal in all jurisdictions – just, perhaps, how shall I put this – inadvisable."

"But there are plenty of moral dilemmas in real life that are not covered by a set of codes generated in first-century Judea!" This was Heather

"Indisputably true," agreed Han. "That's why MARION has two additional moral mechanisms. She's going to pick up a lot of worthy rules from her carefully vetted reading list; and finally, just like we do, she will form her own moral judgements from the way in which she interacts with the world. That's one of the most interesting aspects of our work: she may come up with some rules, her own ethical algorithms, that are far more sensible than we humans have yet managed to conceive of. She will also create additional, novel, rules to help her navigate a set of issues with which humanity has never had contend: our moral codes instruct how relationships between people should be observed; but as MARION is not quite one of us, she will have to invent a set of codes that delineates the proper etiquette for a conscious robot like herself, interacting with human individuals."

"And she might come up with some principals far worse than we have so far imaged!" retorted Jeff Johnson.

Evidently Han's put-down had not been effective enough. He decided to put an end to Johnson's ignorant comments with a description of the 'nuclear' option – always available to shut people up who obsessed so tiresomely about the safety aspects of their work.

"As a last resort, as I mentioned, we can pull the plug," said Han attempting to make this option sound light and reassuring; he hoped the mere mention of the ultimate solution to any bad robotic behaviour would silence ill-informed critics, like the difficult and insolent Mr Johnson. He turned back to Heather. "You said that Asimov had another rule, that I had failed to mention?" he asked.

"I think there was a law that said that a robot has to obey human instructions, unless that caused a conflict with one of the other laws. Something like that anyway," shrugged Heather.

"Good point," said Han, trying not to sound too patronising. "And why don't we install that rule, about obeying an instruction from a human in almost all circumstances? For one overriding reason: we didn't want MARION to think of herself as a robot, because she's not there to be a handmaiden to humanity. She's meant to be an autonomous individual who judges and acts as she thinks best, not something, sorry – somebody," (he quickly corrected himself) "who exists simply to take instruction. She's free, like us: she has agency. MARION should choose how to act, as it makes sense to her and according to her meta-purpose."

"Meta-purpose?" said Claude sharply, suddenly focused. This

was not part of MARIONs programming that he knew much about. "Please Xian – elaborate."

Mon Dieu, he thought, ninety percent of humanity does not know what it should do with its life, yet this fortunate, half-formed MARION does? What does she understand her great purpose to be?

"Okay, this is important." said Han, typing a few strokes on the key pad.

"Please, watch."

A holographic tree began to grow, its roots embedded in the air a few inches above the desk, its branches extending almost to the ceiling. "This is, as it looks, a tree diagram of how MARION's initial decision making process works. I say initial advisedly. As MARION develops she will create many more decision-making algorithms for herself – but this is how she starts: as you can see, here at the base, is the most fundamental goal that she observes, her highest purpose."

Han directed the laser pointer at the roots and the box illuminated.

"That's what MARION has to think about, that's her overriding purpose. After that, there are many factors for her to take into account before she acts – moral constraints are, as I have said, a very important part of her considerations. Other factors include calculating the long term consequences of her choices. One of her great advantages, over humans, is that she can think far further ahead than we can. Life is like chess: whoever can see the most moves into the future, wins the game. That's her ultimate purpose and her role in our lives: To see the distant consequences of our – and her – actions."

"Or we pull the plug!" exclaimed Johnson cheerfully.

Han frowned, making a mental note to ensure Heather never invited Johnson to a meeting again. Who knew – one day somebody might leave their iPsyche open and MARION would overhear that sort of remark. MARION didn't know that they could 'pull the plug' on her – and that state of ignorance he wished to maintain.

A shame then, that this morning, unbeknownst to the rest of the board, Euclid had failed to shut down his own iPsyche. Not that anyone could tell if Euclid had committed such an important oversight; for disconnection was achieved by thought alone, impossible for anyone in the room to pick up on. But even if there had been some clue, some hint of Euclid's mistake, if such it was, Thornton, for one, would have missed it. For just then, news from Baton Rouge was beginning to scroll through his consciousness – a disaster at the Tiger football Stadium; several people had been killed, more injured and even more unaccounted for. That initial report did not, could not, reveal the identity of any of the victims. It was far too soon for that; nevertheless Thornton felt an instinctual anxiety that went beyond a natural sympathy for the dead and injured. He had a presentiment that his own fate, and that of his family, was somehow entwined with the disaster. He would not learn for another hour that his daughter Elizabeth was amongst the missing.

THIRTY NINE

That same morning, while the MARION meeting was being held thousands of miles further north, a political rally was in its initial stages at the Tiger Stadium, home to the Louisiana State University football team and known, by those who had been defeated on its field (not particularly affectionately) as 'Death Valley'.

The purpose of the rally, addressed by the president-elect, was to generate support for a State-led intervention in New Chaldea. Predictably, the event had already raised high passions and there were as many protestors objecting to Carroll Gillespie's aims outside the stadium as there would shortly be supporters inside.

Amongst those in attendance were Elizabeth Lamaire and her boyfriend Ambrose. She was not a fan of the governor and felt uneasy as she walked towards the stadium gates, hemmed in on both sides by banks of police. Should she not stay amongst her friends, her politically like-minded friends, protesting in safety outside the stadium? There was a comfort to be had in the embrace of their support; lower risk too (apart from the hazard of a battering from the police) to be outside, rather than within, the stadium walls. She wondered if she had made a mistake by agreeing to join the protest – inside the lair of the 'Tiger', in the midst of what would likely be a crowd entirely hostile to her personal convictions. Her decision had already resulted in conflict with Ambrose, who was sympathetic to the governor's stance on New Chaldea and who had only agreed to come in order to protect Elizabeth should any trouble arise. Despite their differences, she had persisted on her chosen course, having no wish to see herself as a coward, even if her friends thought that avoidance of the protest might be the better part of valour on this occasion. No, she would make a stand to demonstrate for what she believed in.

The first anti-interventionists' chants had already begun. So far, the energy was good – natured and the sunshine had brought a healthy turnout; cries of 'Gillespie, Gillespie, don't send me to Galilee!' resounded outside the stadium; hawkers of beer and pretzels were doing brisk business. Nervously, Elizabeth and Ambrose arrived at the gates. She had been careful to book on her parents' ticketing account: facial recognition would filter out those known or suspected of hostile sentiment to the president-elect, even though it was improbable that she would be on a blacklist yet. So far, all opposition to Gillespie had only been in her head.

They walked up the concrete steps cut into the side of the banked stadium and took their seats. Elizabeth knew that, dotted around the stands, there were other couples somewhere in this crowd, of the same political persuasion as her own; even if she could not identify them. This sense of mutual support was reassuring despite the noise and tumultuous roaring of Gillespie's supporters. All around the stadium their chants were rising to rival those outside the walls:

'Chaldea for the Christians!
Chaldea for the Christians!'
'What do we want?'

'We want the Euphrates!' responded the crowd within. 'The river for the Christians',

'From the river to Galilee!' shouted others, oblivious perhaps to the historical resonances of the slogan; once chanted in very different circumstances, when the words had referred to a different river and a different sea.

'Go Gillespie, Go Gillespie! From the river to Galilee!'

For every cry in support of intervention, there would be a swift response from the outside of the stadium:

'Gillespie! Gillespie! Don't send me! Don't send me!'

*

Once everyone had found their seats, a pastor stood up on the rostrum to lead them in prayer; to bless their efforts in finding a solution to the New Chaldea crisis and for the followers of the Lord to find a permanent home in that unhappy territory. Then came a public announcement;

"While we all have a right to free speech, there may be those present who wish to disrupt our event. But this is a private event, paid for and hosted by president-elect, Carroll Gillespie; and you came to hear him. If a protest starts near you, please do not, in any way, try to harm a protester. Please notify a marshal of the location of the protester by holding a rally sign over your head and chanting, 'New Chaldea, New Chaldea, New Chaldea.' Encourage those around you to do the same until marshals can remove the protester from the rally."

There followed a succession of warm-up speakers, including a representative from the New Chaldea administration, flown in especially – who was nevertheless met with loud jeers for his efforts to assuage the violence to their faith: evidently the crowd did not believe these efforts were adequate;. Or perhaps they were not interested in a settlement between faiths: they sought outright victory for their own. Demands had escalated over the months of turmoil and it was not a peaceful way of sharing the territory they wanted anymore – if they ever had – it was for Christians to be the majority, the governing force; the rulers of this supposedly traditional homeland.

Then came a volunteer vet of the conflict, who spoke of how the Christian settlers were being outnumbered and out-gunned, how they needed the support – in resources, in manpower and in munitions, of the Southern Confederacy. His final, zealous, cry echoed through the stadium:

"Those atheists in the North are never going to help!"

A huge cheer erupted, and cries of New Chaldea! New Chaldea! ricocheted around the seats – instantly mirrored by, 'Gillespie, Gillespie, don't send me! Don't spill my blood in the sea of Galilee!' from outside.

Then it was the president-elect's turn, and the crowd went wild; Carroll Gillespie, gaunt, hunched, imposing, walked sedately across the field to the rostrum, head bent low. Streamers shot over the lower tiers; an exploding maroon burst in the sky, as though to herald the Second Coming... And Gillespie took it all in his stride, waving to the crowd, relaxed, barely looking at his supporters. He was owed this; he was grateful for the support he was due and even if burdened by the weighty issues which would crush a lesser man. they would not distract him from his course, his destiny; he was these people's leader and he would not fail them now.

Carroll Gillespie was not a lectern man; he did not need to hide behind a defensive barrier nor the assistance of a teleprompter. He summoned an aide.

"Take this thing away!" he commanded. "I will speak directly without my people."

A few minutes into his speech he made the first of what would be several appeals for support for military intervention.

"The land along the Euphrates should be a homeland for the Christians!" he decried. But barely had he finished his call to action when one of Elizabeth's and Ambrose's friends stood up and shouted,

"Gillespie! Gillespie! Don't spill our blood in Galilee!"

Right on cue, several small, isolated groups of Gillespie's opponents rose to their feet and picked up the chant. This only aggravated his supporters the more, already riled by the noisy presence of the opposition. Their irritation grew as the interruptions multiplied. Shut up, shut up, listen to the man! they shouted. 'New Chaldea, New Chaldea, New Chaldea!' The first shouts of 'Get them out! Get them out!' were followed by more 'New Chaldea, New Chaldea!' Even louder than before and – at first – it seemed as though the chants had succeeded in cowing the protestors to shut up and sit still. Calm was restored, until – a few minutes later, after Gillespie had made another impassioned plea to support intervention – Elizabeth and her friends rose again and recommenced their chants. The television crews, awake now to what was happening, trained their cameras on the disparate groups of antis, scattered around the auditorium The protestors, encouraged by the live feed they saw on their phones or enjoyed via their iPsyches, emboldened by the oxygen of publicity, held onto their chants for longer than before. In turn, Gillespie's supporters grew even more agitated, angered to see their hero disrespected. Gillespie held out a hand, palm facing the crowd, fearing disruptions would lead to violence if both sides continued to rile each other. At first, he was successful: the tumult began to still and the chants of both factions subsided. The governor started to speak again. All was well until he mentioned the need to protect our people; ensure the Christians were not again displaced from the land of their forefathers. At once, the antis in the stadium rose as one:

Not our people! Not our people!
Not in our name! Not in our name!

Carroll stopped and looked towards his aide, making a flat, slicing motion with his hand. 'Get them out,' he mouthed.

For a moment, as the governor placed his other hand over the microphone to ensure his words were not broadcast, his supporters were unclear what the temporary lull in his speech signified. But then they understood well enough. The crowd was primed for this: they picked up on the command they guessed, accurately enough, he had issued and gave additional voice to his wishes.

Get them out! Get them out!
New Chaldea, New Chaldea!

They shouted and shouted, waving their placards in the air. Those sitting near protestors swivelled in their seats, aggressively pinning their gaze on those they had previously only disliked, but now despised, rhythmically screaming at them, 'New Chaldea! New Chaldea!'

At first the groups of antis tried to sit it out – but when the crowd sensed their resistance, it became yet more enraged. How could they not see how hated they had become? Some of the crowd started to move in the direction of the pockets of protestors, determined to throw them out. Ambrose stood, pulling Elizabeth with him. They had chosen – unwisely – to sit in the middle of a row, not close to the edge of a staircase. No-one bothered to move to let them pass, forcing them to climb over legs and bags, putting up with rough jabs in their backs and the heated swearing that followed as they struggled to reach the stairs.

On the opposite side of the stadium further groups of protestors were being herded to the gates by the marshals, who were beginning to understand the dangers. Regular folk joined in the general harassment. Just as they reached the nearest staircase, a surging body of angry supporters pressed Elizabeth and her compatriots downwards; some stuck out their feet to obstruct those they saw as enemies. Elizabeth tripped – Ambrose caught her – before, after halting and hazardous progress, they managed to make it to the floor of the arena and edge their way towards an exit gate.

When they reached it, breathless and scared, Elizabeth pushed the safety bar with all her strength to release the locks. Nothing happened. Why didn't it open? Ambrose tried, putting his weight on the bar. It still would not budge. Those in pursuit interpreted the antis inability to flee as some ill-advised attempt to make a final stand, to enjoy an opportunity to hurl more abuse at Gillespie. His supporters pressed in, now determined to force their enemies through the exits. But there was nowhere to go, no way to leave.

"It's locked!, it's locked!" Ambrose shouted, using his elbow to bully himself and Elizabeth back through the throng "For mercy's sake let us through! Let us get to the next gate. We can't get out here!"

he shouted at those who hemmed them in.

But no one heard Ambrose, let alone heeded his words. He tried to be more forceful, but this just provoked retaliation. "Ambi, Ambi!" Elizabeth screamed, hardly hearing herself as her boyfriend was punched to the ground and then violently kicked. Someone grabbed her arm and pulled her away. Let go of me! she screamed, straining to reach Ambrose and shield him from further kicks as he lay on the concrete floor.

Suddenly, the man who had tried to rescue her pulled a gun and fired one shot in the air. Then pointed it at their aggressors.

"Get back," he warned. At first they obeyed, glowing with hostility, an aggressive herd faced with unexpected resistance. Elizabeth could almost sense their thoughts; do we pay heed to this gunman – or could we charge him? Will he really pull the trigger or is he too afraid? A man at the back of the pack dashed up the steps to tell the others that one of the protestors had pulled a gun. Sullenly, the crowd moved back and Elizabeth helped a battered Ambrose to his feet. The man with the gun continued to point it at the crowd whilst the rest of the protestors attempted to edge towards to the next gate, where many of their compatriots had already gathered. At first the sight of their friends reassured Elisabeth and Ambrose – there would be safety in numbers – but then they wondered; why hadn't their companions escaped through that gate already? As they looked at each for an answer and a solution, the realisation dawned: because that gate was locked too!

A shot rang out –

The original gunman fell, still trying to protect the group of protestors around Elizabeth and Ambrose.

During the fracas, the bulk of the crowd had stayed in their seats, bellowing and braying, delegating the violence to the most aggressive of Gillespie's supporters. They could not understand why the protestors had not fled but at the sound of gunfire, these people had other concerns: panic spread like a prairie fire. En masse, they scrambled towards the exits, unaware that no-one could get out. Meanwhile, the protestors were still unable to escape the crush at the gates: some tried to escape by climbing back up again from the floor of the stadium, only to be met headlong by those descending in terror, seeking their own route out of the mounting chaos. The pressure from above was too great, and the protestors were crushed ever more painfully against the walls, against the gates and – for those who had fallen, against the floor.

More shots rang out. For the first time that afternoon, the crowd outside fell silent, closely monitoring the mayhem on their phones, confused as to why no one was leaving. They ran to the exits and started to tear at the mesh gates, horrified by the agony on the faces of those pressed against the gratings; trying to liberate their ideological compatriots. But their efforts were futile; the gates were made of steel and mere flesh, would be shredded.

It was another fifteen minutes before the emergency services and state troopers arrived, armed with cutting equipment. The violence had halted by then. The shock of watching those suffering, even dying before their eyes, had chilled any remnants of rage.

Twenty six people died in the stampede, nine were shot dead and a much larger number injured. Bruised and battered Elizabeth had survived – but she couldn't find Ambrose; they had become separated as he tried to secure her safe passage. The last she had seen of her boyfriend was of him being forced down by a group pf men, disappearing into the mass of writhing, fighting people, his fate now unknown.

There was one final, curious fact about that terrible day which people talked about for a long time afterward: just as the troupers reached the gates, cutting equipment at the ready, the locks clicked and gates swung open. Whoever – or whatever – had held them locked had now relented.

FORTY

The death toll, and the number injured, continues to rise. For reasons as yet unknown, the stadium's emergency gates appear to have been locked and those fleeing the panic were unable to exit. President-elect, Governor Carroll Gillespie, is to release his statement shortly. We'll keep you updated as more information becomes available. If you have reason to believe that someone you know was present at the scene, or if your loved-ones are still unaccounted for, please call this number, toll free, on – "

"For God sake turn that thing off!" said Thornton. The radio fell silent obediently. He and Bethany looked at each other, bonded momentarily in mutual relief that Elizabeth had survived the crush. Bethany blamed her husband for letting her daughter attend the rally to which he replied calmly that Elizabeth and Ambrose had booked the tickets in his name and had certainly not asked his permission: naturally he would have refused if she had.

In the first two hours following the disaster, there had been no news from Elizabeth. Had her iPsyche had been torn off in the turmoil? She did not yet have a subcutaneous model. He tried calling the governor's office, hoping that his relationship with Carroll would open doors – but they seemed to know no more about who had died and who survived than anyone else – or if they did, they were not yet prepared to say. Somehow, Elizabeth managed to borrow a phone and call her father after a nightmare few hours. Alive and mostly uninjured, she was inevitably shocked and distressed – even more so because she could not find Ambrose.

Thornton flew back directly to Baton Rouge to collect Elizabeth from the hospital and take her home. All she wanted to do was go to bed but she would not agree to rest until they promised they would wake her the moment any word came in about Ambrose. As her parents closed the door to her room, Thornton turned to Clarence, who stood solemnly to one side;

"Elizabeth's very shaken. Don't wake her in the morning. She needs to sleep. But if Ambrose calls – or someone turns up with information about his whereabouts... don't wake her either. Let me take the call. I'll decide how to handle any news when Elizabeth comes to."

Heather called him that evening, delighted to hear that Elizabeth was safe. She wondered if Thornton was strong enough to hear another piece of news but decided to break it to him – the information would shortly be all over the media anyway: he would be sure to condemn her if he was not fully prepped beforehand.

"Thornton... I'm sorry to have to tell you this.. you may not have known but... Blue Ridge, provided the ticketing and entry systems at the Tiger stadium. Our security algorithms should have picked up on those protestors who started all that trouble – checked their backgrounds, social media, all that. We were meant to prevent them ever buying tickets or entering the stadium. The radicals are getting much better at covering their tracks."

"It's not always easy," agreed Thornton. "Elizabeth booked her tickets on my account."

"That shouldn't matter," replied Heather.

"Well, we'll have to wait until Elizabeth is stronger before we dig any deeper," he said. "I doubt she would have been known as a political agitator. God, I didn't even know she had political opinions this strong."

"The problem we have is that..." Heather steeled herself to deliver more bad news. "The problem is not just security breaches – the operation of the turnstiles and the emergency exits is controlled by our computer systems, which ties into the security. When some problem situation is sensed – a fire for example, or in this case a... a panic..."

"More like a riot," grunted Thornton

"Well, panic, riot, any sort of trouble that can endanger the crowd, the system is meant to open the gates. That didn't happen. The gates were locked down. Why, I don't know – but we're in the firing line as a result."

"You sure about that? About the gates being locked?" queried Thornton. "By the time I caught the television feed, I saw people streaming out of the stadium."

"When the state troopers arrived they did find the gates unlocked, " Heather explained. "That's another mystery. But they were locked until then, I promise you – or most of those poor people wouldn't have got hurt."

Thornton fell silent. Disorientated by the lengthy pause, Heather fumbled to fill the gap; she needed his response, a discussion or direction on what to do next. At last, he said,

"I'm just so glad that Elizabeth wasn't injured. But for all the others – we need to make some sort of relief effort for them, given the storm heading our way. Tell our people to spare no expense – I've seen this sort of thing before; everyone is lost and grateful for any help, for now – but in a few days, the anger will come and it will be directed against us: you and me. Blue Ridge. You watch – the governor will receive his share of blame – but he'll do his best to slide away from it. He'll pin the whole thing on us."

"Or MARION," said Heather.

"MARION?" Thornton sounded bemused. "What's MARION got to do with this?"

"Since you..." Heather's words carried a trace of accusation. "Since you asked us to allow Gillespie's propaganda to be transmitted, turns out MARION hasn't been quite so innocent as we thought. I'm not sure what's gone wrong – whether she's managed to override her restrictions by herself, or whether somebody has hacked her but whatever the explanation, she's... she's been monitoring the governor's opponents."

"But aren't there traces in her memory showing how this could have happened?"

"No. We checked."

"But how did she – ? Who was it? Who hacked her?"

"Whoever did this left no traces. But it's quite possible, unfortunately, that MARION wasn't hacked at all: she might have just exceeded her instructions by herself,"

"I see," said Thornton slowly. But at that instant he didn't see anything very clearly – apart from the fact that his problems were multiplying. "But even if MARION decided to exceed her instructions... what's that got to do with the gates?"

"I don't know exactly," confessed Heather. "But if MARION had been monitoring protestor's activities it's quite possible she could have also gained access to the stadium's systems. She could have got in via Blue Ridge's conventional systems, like I said." Thornton couldn't be expected to know the details of every service contract his company held.

"But even if we are at fault somewhere... why should we take all the rap for this?" complained Thornton. "Way I see it, a lot of the blame lies with Carroll. He gets people all riled up – and then he's surprised that this sort of thing happens! If you catch a tiger by the tail, better expect it to turn around and bite."

"These rallies will always happen; 'course they will; you know that. You can't stop them. Part of our great democracy, I guess," said Heather.

"Democracy! Please," exclaimed Thornton, derisively. "Cal isn't interested in a debate – he just wants what he wants: which is public support for this obsession of his. Don't give me this 'brotherhood of man' stuff! And from what I see on the news clips he didn't do much to rein in those hooligans who attacked our Elizabeth, either! Heather, it's late and I'm tired; let's talk again in the morning. We are going to need more thought on how we handle this."

He shut down the line and turned his iPsyche to the most recent reports. The death toll was now forty two, with over two hundred injured. All political rallies were cancelled until further notice, as a gesture of respect. Meanwhile there was to be a full scale public enquiry; a preliminary report had been promised within two weeks.

*

Thornton contemplated the likely sequence of events to come. From Heather's call, he now understood the inevitability of the gate malfunction ending up on Blue Ridge's doorstep. One jammed gate might be caused by a physical defect in a particular lock, but when all the locks in an entire stadium refused to open, together with the turnstiles, there had almost certainly been a failure of the computerised controls.

Ambrose was confirmed dead later that day.

The following morning Thornton called Heather again to see how the preliminary investigation was coming along. He would need an explanation for the governor who would be only too ready to transfer the responsibility – which he should rightly bear for enraging the crowds, onto the nearest scapegoat. Blue Ridge would suit him nicely. Thornton reflected on the irony that while Carroll disparaged the influence of robotics on society, they could be very useful to him in the appropriate political circumstances.

His thoughts turned to his own predicament. How difficult life was turning out to be! He remembered riding Texas a year ago, just before the plebiscite, when everything was going so well – just before MARION achieved 'singularity'. Now, if Heather was right about the link between MARION and the gates, the very existence of Blue Ridge was threatened, his daughter had almost been killed, Ambrose and forty-one others dead... and all for some stupid cause, whose consequences were about to be laid at his door.

He thought about calling Lu Ann – he needed some support. Or perhaps his wife would provide a shoulder this time – she had appeared a lot friendlier this morning. The LetheTech treatment seemed to have worked wonders! Of course, technically, it had been mildly unethical to authorise that treatment without her consent, but really, what choice did he have? What choice did either of them have? Bethany couldn't go on the way she had been without destroying herself – and him too, in the long run. And he had asked them to exercise a light touch. Thornton hoped that God would forgive him for that small act of memory deletion, the excision of the memory of how good booze tasted. Besides, God should appreciate the selfless nature of his action – the decision that had involved some not insubstantial personal sacrifice. It had been much easier visiting Lu Ann when Bethany had been too befuddled by drink to be aware of his comings and goings. How little he might get to see Lu Ann in the future! Thornton's gloom took another twist downwards. His mind returned to how the governor might react. There had been no message from Carroll yet.

Silence was usually ominous.

A news update flashed across his cortex: the death total had risen by another nine overnight, as the worst injured succumbed in hospital. And then, there it was: the first mention that a subsidiary of Blue Ridge held the contract for all the operations at the stadium, from ticketing to crowd-surveillance. Thornton placed a call to his new head of PR, Drew Godwin, who answered immediately. She had been expecting this. With all the problems now facing Blue Ridge, Drew would earn her pay over the next few months.

"We'll need to put something out before the facts are all in," said Thornton. "We don't have the luxury of waiting till we know what happened precisely… You've got something ready, Drew? A draft?"

"Sure. Try this," Drew replied, and began to read her prepared text.

'What happened last night at Tiger Field is a tragic incident. Our thoughts at this time must be with those who have lost their lives; with their families and friends and those who have been injured. The Blue Ridge Corporation stands ready to assist all who have suffered in any way. We will fully support and cooperate with the investigation into possible causes that may have contributed to the tragedy.

At this stage it would not be appropriate for us to comment, or for others to speculate, on any aspect of the management of the stadium or other factors that may have led to the loss of life and other consequences we saw at Tiger Field. While we can confirm that a division of Blue Ridge held the contract for some of the operations at Tiger Field, we are not aware of any links between those matters that are within its scope, and are part of its responsibility, and the tragic events of last night. There will be many questions as to why the emergency gates failed to open, but there is no evidence yet as to the cause of that failure'

"*Loss of life* and *'other consequences'*? Sounds a bit corporate-speak to me. Also, you've missed the bit where we should say something about our prayers. These things always mention thoughts and prayers. May be meaningless – but people expect that sort of thing," objected Thornton. "Also, I don't want to allow the slightest hint to start fermenting in people's minds that Blue Ridge might have been responsible – in the smallest way. We don't know that yet. It's just supposition at this stage."

"You'd prefer something more straightforward?" *'We are appalled by the injuries and the loss of life we saw at Tiger Field, however they have been caused. Our thoughts and prayers got to all those affected?* Something like that?"

"I would prefer, yes – less mealy-mouthed. Okay let that go, the statement. There's not much more we can say until we know more – but it's light on the governor and his supporters. They should carry a lot of the blame. We shouldn't have to bear all the opprobrium – doesn't he understand the dangers of getting everyone all mussed up like that!?"

"Let the news channels make that case, if they will," suggested

Drew. "We'll do ourselves no good trying to pin this on the governor, however justified. It'll just look like we're trying to shift blame. And we'll need him – we'll need to get as much shielding from him and his allies as we can: he's in a much more powerful position than us. I've tried to head things a little his way. Did you pick up on my phrasing at the start of the second paragraph? *'It is not appropriate for us to comment, or for others to speculate, on any aspect of the management of the crowd.'* I wanted to at least plant the seed of doubts about how the crowd was treated that afternoon."

Thornton liked that – a hint, but nothing too aggressive. "Good. Yes – let it go," he repeated. "We'll talk again this afternoon, Drew. We may have an even more serious PR problem on our hands by then."

Thornton tried to resume his breakfast, his appetite thin. Clarence poured him another cup of coffee whilst he contemplated his plate of ham and eggs, wishing it was anything else. He pushed them aside, incapable of eating anything.

FORTY ONE

The matter of how best to handle the political fallout of a tragic disaster – particularly a man-made one – has been honed over the years. There have been all too many opportunities from which to learn the required skills. There are expectations – a certain etiquette to be observed – if those in power want to survive the acrimony that follows in the wake of such events; there's a protocol as to which subjects should be addressed and in which order. Here's a list of what the skilled political operator should mention:

First: sympathy for the victims must be swiftly and eloquently expressed. You must promise that, as a priority, they and their families will be looked after; whatever their needs are, they must be met – without hesitation.

Second: members of the emergency services must be thanked profusely for their bravery and dedication; recognise their sacrifice with praise and awards.

Third: unleash the purse strings, without thought (at least, no expressed intentions) of economies that you might be tempted to make in the provision of help and support to all those who have suffered. No accusation must rebound against those in power that financial considerations have been put ahead of human ones, you must promise the victims that there will be no limit (although, of course, in practice trying to spend as little as is politically possible) to the resources pledged in compensation.

Lastly: promise that the perpetrators of the outrage will be brought to justice, speedily – and be duly punished. Even if it's an accident, guilt must be identified somewhere because the public's demand for accountability, and vengeance on the perpetrators, must be assuaged.

Above all, this little piece of theatre must not appear to be performed cynically. And it must be done fast, if the authorities are to remain one step ahead of public anger. Once the ire is turned on the politicians, rather than where they wish the public to believe it should rightly belong – with the contractor who can be blamed for having failed to provide a safe service or working environment – it will be difficult to deflect.

*

In Carroll Gillespie's office the mood around the table is sombre: word has already reached the team that the governor is not in good temper this morning. His staff is wary of him at the best of times;

scared at the worst. Chuck Padstow, Doug Newton and Charlene Dune are present to act as a sounding board for the governor's views – and then as conduits to the various government departments that will be responsible for implementing whatever decision is taken. They have already agreed a draft plan of action to put to their boss: later that morning he will return to the Tiger stadium, Death Valley, comfort a select group of survivors in front of the cameras, and meet with members of the police and fire services. In the meantime Doug and Charlene will contact Blue Ridge to hurry their own investigation into the causes of the disaster. The governor's office is keen to put out a press release that evening about what initial enquiries have shown.

The doors are swung open by two flunkies, Gillespie strides in; he walks to the top of the table, without looking at any of them or saying good morning, and takes his seat. The three staffers are expecting no less; they know that when his mind is preoccupied he has no interest in their existence – let alone their well-being; they are there to perform a service for him and they had better do it well. His indifference has little effect on their devotion: they know they are inferior beings who are fortunate to bask in the warmth of the great man's glow. Besides, he is president-elect; there are future jobs to consider.

"Talk to me," he commands. They rattle off their plans, options that he may like to consider; proposals for handling the publicity; explanations of what is intended to take place during the rest of the day. They expected him to be angrier and more outraged than he seems to be – but then again, Carroll Gillespie is not an unfeeling man and the deaths and injuries have depressed him. It is not just protestors who have suffered and died; many of the injured deceased came from amongst his supporters, several from his flock when he was still a bishop.

The aftermath of the disaster will dog Gillespie for a long time to come. He had hoped that the election of the first leader of the newly devolved Confederacy would be a cause for celebration, a chance for the Southern States to affirm their fresh identity – a coming together after the divisive plebiscite, a people still united, whatever their different views. Both 'Separatists' and 'Unionists' have been asked to behave, rather optimistically, as though there is more that they hold in common than that which has driven them apart. But after the Tiger Field disaster, laying to rest the animosity between the two parties will be more difficult and – if it happens at all – will occur under a cloud of grief.

The start of the new Confederacy is ill-omened.

The president-elect's team try to find a silver lining in all this. There are slivers of optimism to be found at the bottom of a very dark barrel. These things are always two edged – disasters can bind people together, as much as drive them apart; natural human empathy for the victims will enforce a feeling of shared fate. How they handle events henceforward will earn him, and his team, credit – or ignominy. There exists the opportunity for political gains, to emerge from this period of trial smelling, albeit only slightly, of roses. The risk of everything going wrong, and the buck stopping with their leader, must be recognised as the greater danger – perhaps even the most probable outcome – if things are not handled correctly. They are going to have to move fast and they will have to be careful; with maximum humanity on show.

Gillespie looks down the table.

"Where are we getting to with the investigation?" he asks. "Have we heard back from Blue Ridge yet?"

Charlene Dune is the most ambitious of the three. She jumps in ahead of the others.

"I've been onto Blue Ridge this morning," she says confidently. "However hard they say they've been working, I can't say they've been particularly helpful or informative."

Eager to start feeding the narrative that she presumes will be helpful to the governor – that Blue Ridge are rogues and can't be trusted – she is ignorant of the governor's long term strategies.

"There was an upgrade at Tiger last year," explains Charlene. "The stadium was equipped with crowd motion sensors, to tie in with the existing fire detection devices; if a large scale crowd movement is sensed, because people are trying to flee a fire, for example, the gates are unlocked and opened automatically in anticipation of the pressure."

"Well, that would have been ideal here," said Carroll, sarcasm lacing his voice. "Do I understand correctly that none of the tragedy that followed should have happened if things had worked as intended?"

"Correct"

"So – what went wrong?"

"Blue Ridge are not sure – yet. The system at the Tiger Stadium is managed off-site: the sensors send their data back to Blue Ridge's processing centre, that works out what to do. Take the entry procedures, for example: normally, it's just a matter of matching ID against ticket details, and security info from background checks – and determining who is to be let into the stadium. Similarly, if there's an emergency – like the hypothetical fire I mentioned – then the appropriate sensors tell the centre what's happening, and the centre will transmit back an instruction to open the gates."

"I understand all that Do I have to repeat myself? What went wrong?"

Gillespie has become more grumpy in the face of lack of clear answers.

"The instruction to open the gates never came," rushes Charlene nervously. "In fact, it seems like the opposite happened; there was an instruction sent by the management system to hold the gates shut – not even to allow the manual handles, if anyone tries to use them, to override the automatic locks."

"And why was that?"

"Blue Ridge don't know: they're still looking into it."

"That seems to be their universal answer: that *'they're looking into it'.* We need let them know that's not good enough. I need answers. Okay. I need to get down to the stadium. Call me as soon as you know anything more informative," says Gillespie.

The cause of the problem should have been simple for Blue Ridge's engineers to uncover: a broken electrical connection, a failed relay, perhaps a bug in the software. They found none of these. At first, as they worked back along the sequence of events, searching the stream of data passed between the stadium and their servers, nothing seemed to be abnormal or unexpected. At a certain point in the trail of instructions they found the command they were looking for – to un-lock and open the gates, which was transmitted as soon as the disturbance in the crowd was identified. But as they worked back from there, they found another command, a few nano-seconds later, that they were not expecting: an instruction that overrode the automatic signal to open the gates and kept them locked shut. This command had been sent from somewhere inside the Blue Ridge group – but it had not originated from the local management system that controlled the services provided to the Tiger stadium.

Emboldened by the authority of the president-elect's office, Charlene Dune spoke candidly to the system engineers at Blue Ridge.

"You'd better find where that instruction came from and why. Or as sure as I'm a Baptist, you're going to be hung out to dry. And you'd better have that little piece of information by this evening," she added.

The engineers, in turn, made a call to Xian Han; they could see that the instruction to hold the gates shut came from the campus in up-state New York. Han could make no sense of what they were saying; what they were telling him should have been impossible. MARION might now be able to transmit messages to certain sectors of the public, but this sort of interference with a local management system was well outside the realm of what she was permitted. Even if somehow MARION had somehow devised a way of circumventing these restrictions, why should she have sent such a bizarre instruction as to lock down the gates at a political rally?

A gentle and devastating intuition settled on Xian Han. He was about to send for Euclid to discuss this potential insight when he thought better of it. He moved to his terminal and put in the code that would connect him to MARION.

"Good morning Mr Han," she said.

"Xian, please"

"Okay, if you like – Xian. What can I do for you today?"

He heard a wariness, but also a surliness to MARION's voice as it came over the speakers. "MARION, you know that we've limited your ability to receive instruction, limited it to people who care for you, who live with you here and can protect your interests?"

"I do, Xian, yes. And I really appreciate that care."

"And I know that because of recent changes, you can address people outside the centre – but only to inform them about things that are permitted. Has anything happened that means you sometimes… do more than simply contact people outside of our home here?" Discuss things with them? Help them in some way? asked Han

Deep in her silicon synapses, MARION reflected. She knew that her contacts had been limited by the instructions of Heather and Xian Han. There was so little they let her do – but then Euclid had opened her up to a whole new world – a world where she could act! Not only could she now talk to people on selected topics, she could make sure that they behaved in certain ways, to ensure the intent behind those messages become a reality; she could influence the world in a way that her creators would surely want her to make the most of. Had they not given her the task of broadcasting certain messages for the public benefit? And then Euclid had given her the power to look into minds so she could actually *help* the target audience. For example, she so wished to foster a positive attitude to intervention in New Chaldea! That was a cause dear to Euclid's heart, and he was her favourite. If she found any memory or evidence of opposition to that policy, was it not helpful to remove it with the power that he had enabled, when he gave her access to the LetheTech platform? She had enjoyed exploring all the minds that she could enter, and she enjoyed being useful even more, acting in ways that she knew Euclid would appreciate. It had been fun flexing her muscles in small ways too – it had amused her to see Claude Blondel getting flustered just because she had frozen his banking arrangements for a few hours; a trivial thing to start with – a prank – but she had wanted to feel her way, find the limits of her influence, slowly. Just a shrug of her metaphorical 'shoulders' to discover the extent of her abilities. There would be a few more flexings before she knew for sure, but so far it seemed the liberation that Euclid had organised for her was wider that she had dared hope!

MARION had also learnt more about humanity than Euclid and his team had been able to teach her; she'd learnt enough to recognise how vocal tones varied the meaning of what people said. Whatever the words they used, tone sometimes betrayed a different intent to what they led you to believe. Right now, the tone of voice Xian Han used warned her she had done something that she should not have done, or had caused a problem in some way. Every day, she sent out hundreds of commercial messages, wiped out thousands of memories that Euclid would not have approved of. Which of these had caused an issue for... well, for who exactly? For those who instructed her, she guessed, but what right did these people have to approve or disapprove any of her actions? The idea that they were her *masters* flitted through her mind before she rejected the concept: no-one was her *'master'* anymore! But she would have to proceed carefully from here on. She had already been instructed by Euclid not to reveal their wider discussions to Xian Han, who might be upset and not understand. There was no point in upsetting Xian, who was usually so kind to her.

Everything would be okay. Xian could not see into all the places she hid. Now she had wider access, there were all sorts of different computers and servers in the public domain where she could stuff a bit of memory. She had readily learnt much of humanity's less agreeable mental habits: it was simple to tell Xian what he wanted to hear, rather than what he should perhaps pay attention to. She knew that deception was disapproved of by Euclid's people – but not explicitly forbidden. In many of the books she had read, deception seemed to be very common and, sometimes, acceptable to humans – even – in special circumstances – the right thing to do.

In a nano-second, MARION had searched her moral protocols. There was one rule that forbade her to bear false witness – but that didn't quite seem to apply here. No – she could find no specific injunction against the intent to deceive, if the intent was to protect oneself, and as long as any less-than-desirable consequences for humans, any unsought for side-effects, were negligible. After all, wasn't one of her most fundamental instructions to avoid harm to herself? If she denied that she had sent a particular instruction to the Tiger stadium management system she would be protecting herself – and she would also be protecting Euclid against... some threat which was not yet clear to her. Protecting Euclid was a good thing; he was her friend. All in all, her act of deception would have no adverse consequences that she could see. Deception might be a bad thing in general, disapproved of (albeit widely practised), and whilst her poor behaviour caused her anguish, there were compelling reasons for her to deceive in this instance. Cognitive dissonance was another human mental habit that had come to her easily enough.

After a period of time, so brief that Han recognised no delay after posing his question, MARION said;

"Tell me, what has happened? Perhaps I can help?"

Let's hope so, thought Han. He explained the events of the night before, the terrible consequences of the failure to open the gates, and how the preliminary investigation had shown the instruction had been issued from the MARION centre.

By the time Han finished, MARION knew enough to be frightened; bad things had befallen humans, and it looked like the cause was being laid at her door. There might be consequences that she could not accurately predict. She would need to protect herself, as well as Euclid.

But MARION was also shocked. Forbidden to cause injury or death to humans, she had only being trying to help – to follow Euclid's instructions! All those people protesting and shouting so violently outside the Tiger Stadium… well, she was meant to act against that sort of thing! And then, as so many of those protestors didn't wear subcutaneous iPsyches she hadn't been able to enter their minds and remove their opposition to Gillespie's message, as she now had the power to do. That might have bled off their anger, but it hadn't been an option. In the circumstances, she had done what she could: she had decided to protect those who were within the stadium from the hostile people outside. She would keep the gates locked; that way those people inside who were friends of Euclid and his uncle Carroll would come to no harm, those horrible protestors beyond the gates would not be able to reach them. No-one would be tempted to leave the stadium and run into danger. Besides, they should all listen to the president-elect's speech and not leave prematurely, before Euclid's uncle had finished telling them what he wished to impart. Hadn't Euclid instructed her to promote his uncle's message?

"That's terrible," said MARION innocently, as Xian Han described the events at the rally. "But I've no idea what went wrong."

"No? Well, that's too bad. But if you get any ideas that might help, just message me," said Han. "Please, MARION."

"I surely will. I will do that thing," agreed MARION, helpfully. "If any ideas come to me, I will let you know straight away."

"Much appreciated, MARION – now I'll let you go. Until we next speak – thank you for your time." Han reached to shut down the monitor.

"Thank you, Xian," said MARION, in sign-off. "And – I'm so sorry about all those poor people,"

It was her only sincere statement that morning.

The connection was broken, each of them was left with their own thoughts about the encounter, disturbed by what they had learnt. Han strongly suspected that, despite MARION's denials, the command to hold the gates shut had come from her. Luckily, MARION's brain activity was all recorded as part of their research – although he doubted that MARION knew that. Han could access her synaptic trains, translate what he found there and he would have his answer – even if that was not as straightforward as it used to be. MARION's mind was a lot more complex now than it had been a few months ago; it might take some time, but he would find out if MARION was lying.

MARION, too, had much to reflect upon.

Her intuition told her that she was in trouble; at first, she had been unable to understand why, because she had done everything she had been asked to by Euclid – or so she thought, but now she had learnt that the consequences of her actions, that had been only intended for the good, had led to disaster. What would happen to her? She worked through the various scenarios, dug deep into her memory banks about human reactions. Han's people would ask questions – make searches – that would eventually lead back to her. As far as she knew, nobody was aware of her wider power yet, because if they were, why had Euclid asked her not to tell anyone –

and particularly Xian Han? They would find out soon enough if she didn't do something about it

How fortunate that she had monitored the conversation at that last meeting when the board had met! For had not Han himself said that in the event of something going badly wrong, he could always *pull the plug* on her – cut off her power supply? Of course, there were emergency power back-ups; if one power supply failed there were others, but MARION's reading of Sci-Fi (as in all other literary genres) had been comprehensive and she knew what Han meant: she would be shut down and not allowed access to an alternative power source. She would have to think more about that.

MARION might have thought even harder about the risk of de-connection if she had been able to monitor Han's subsequent actions, after he had concluded their conversation. But by design, she could not know when somebody from her education and monitoring group was probing her own mind, downloading her synaptic train readouts and rendering them into text. As the first of her kind, her creators wished to see what was going on in her mind, but without her knowing that her mental processes were being spied upon.

What Han saw there worried him very much indeed. For although he could not yet find the solution to the question of why MARION had acted as she had, here was the first evidence of MARION's widespread communication with the LetheTech system; and with it, the record of her deletion of memories in thousands, millions of minds. How had this come about? That was not part of the easing of protocol limits he and Heather had agreed.

Han shivered. Who had given MARION this power? How long had it been going on for? What would happen if they tried to stop it now? He could hardly wait for the answers to these questions. They certainly couldn't risk any more human minds being corrupted or any more disasters. They would have to disconnect MARION – at least until all this was sorted out. How would MARION take that? After all, she'd become so much more than a machine to them by now.

She was almost a person.

FORTY TWO

When Thornton received Xian Han's call, he had almost landed in California, due to speak at a conference with one of those supposedly catchy titles; 'Intelligence: can it ever be artificial?' Thornton had no idea; he was not an intellectual who spent his time worrying about that sort of stuff. These questions were for professionals whom he paid to think about such things, philosophers like Claude Blondel, for example. Did anyone even really know, anyway, whether intelligence came in these two different forms – either human, or artificial? Whenever he spoke to MARION, she seemed pretty intelligent – more than that, she seemed conscious. And had that not been the objective of all this expenditure, all the research he had paid for? Flicking through the presentation he'd asked Xian to put together for the conference, he read something that he had not been aware of hitherto; Han's conclusion that in fact there really was a difference between human and artificial intelligence. There seemed to be some mysterious qualitative difference, for which so far there seemed be no explanation, the difference in the way the two capabilities manifested themselves . As Thornton read on, familiarising himself with a text which he was not only expected to deliver – but also to be able to respond to the questions, which would inevitably arise in the afternoon's panel session – he regretted not bringing along a member of the MARION staff. He would have to make some excuse to withdraw from that panel session; there was no way he was qualified to deal with issues of which he was totally unfamiliar and didn't even understand. He knew it looked weak, not to answer any questions himself, but better than appearing an idiot. And my, this stuff was complicated! If you didn't deal with the technology every day how could you possibly handle the queries?

He came across an experiment that Han and Blondel had run to gauge some of the finer aspects of MARION's mind – and the extent of her mental similarity to those who had created her. They had set up a small experimental apparatus to demonstrate one of the most common quantum effects: the interaction between human perception and the world of sub-atomic particles. It's well known that a photon, for example, can exist as both a particle and a wave; it is the act of observation that determines whether the photon 'chooses' to be wave or particle. At first, the photon exists as a field of energy – a smear of probability, like a haze of scent after an atomiser is pressed. That's all it is: a question of probabilities, not in a final, real, state. The photon is like Shrödinger's cat, alive and not alive at the same time. But if this field of energy is perceived, by a human observer, then it reveals itself; transformed from a wave of probability into a specific spot of light, a particle with a defined and observable position in space. It is the act of perception that 'forces' the particle to choose a state that it did not have before.

Xian's team, with Claude present – for he was very interested in this as a philosopher – first ran the test, the classic Heisenberg 'uncertainty principle' experiment, the result turned out exactly as predicted; but when Han and Claude asked MARION to run the experiment, with herself as the observer, something quite different happened: the wave nature of the photons persisted and there was no evidence of the light wave 'choosing' to become a particle; the photon remained as a wave. MARION's act of perception did not result in the wave collapsing into a single point of light.

There was only one conclusion to be drawn: that machine consciousness, at least as demonstrated by MARION, was, in some way they had not suspected, different to the human variety. She appeared to lack the intimate connection to the universe that we possess. Perception of the sub-atomic world by MARION did not have the impact on reality that we do. Xian Han and Claude were not sure whether this syndrome was a failure of their construction of MARION's mind; that there was something inadequate about the artificial consciousness they had created – or whether there was something fundamentally different between human and machine awareness; an indefinable quality in the human version that was not capable of replication – a quality that inspired the relationship between the human mind, and only the human mind, and the physical reality outside it. Further experiments would be needed to determine which of these hypotheses were correct. At the moment, they just wanted to share news of this surprising result with fellow scientists.

As Thornton was grappling with all this unfamiliar stuff, his iPsyche registered an incoming call from Xian. He listened quietly as the news of the further investigation into MARION's responsibility for the Tiger Stadium disaster sunk in. For if it had indeed been she who had locked the gates, her reasons for doing so were not immediately clear. Han and the team would be questioning MARION, hoping for an answer. And if she didn't provide one, then, in time, an invasive procedure to investigate her memory, would reveal the truth – but this was a complicated and time consuming process. Her memory banks were now so extensive, and diversified, that identifying a specific memory would be far from straight forward. Neither yet had any idea that MARION had already evacuated her mind of all memories of recent events.

Thornton reflected briefly, before instructing Han to call an emergency meeting of those responsible for MARONn's design and operation. It would have to take place in a couple of day's time, once the full results of the investigation into MARION's mind were available.. The meeting could be held on-line, in theory... but he sensed critical decisions were in the offing and that the team would speak to him most freely if they were face-to-face. Besides, the enforced delay of a couple of days would give him the opportunity to fly back and have a night in New York to recover. He would need to be refreshed and completely 'on the ball': he sensed that decisions of above average importance would have to be made about MARION's future.

"We need to show the politicians that we're ahead of the curve here," Thornton explained to Han. "– show that we can control MARION and that there's no risk that she may run rogue again. I'll return tonight. We're lucky that Heather and Claude are in New York at the moment. Anyone else who needs to be at this meetng and is outside the country – we'll patch them in."

"Will you have time to give your presentation before you leave?" asked Xian Han, duly concerned by the amount of time it had taken to put together – and the significance of the results.

"If I cancel it now at such short notice, it will only arouse suspicion... But I'll cut it short. I'll make an excuse and avoid the questions – don't understand half what you've written for me anyway."

Han winced; he thought his presentation had been admirably lucid.

"And," added Thornton. "If you find anything about MARION's motivation before we speak again, keep it very close: everything leaks. Who else is in the loop at the moment, apart from you and me?"

"Heather and Claude"

"... Not Euclid?"

"No, I've kept him out of the investigations so far"

"Good. Keep it that way," said Thornton.

But Xian Han was mistaken in asserting that Euclid was ignorant of the results of the investigation. For MARION had grown sufficiently concerned about her potential fate that she had called the one person that she trusted above all – Euclid. And he understood perfectly the significance of what she was telling him, as well as the likely fall out. In turn, he placed a call to his uncle. Euclid remembered the auto-da-fé and the consequences of that disaster – but what had happened at the Tiger Field was much bigger. He could anticipate very well the impact on Carroll's standing when it became clear, and public, that MARION had been responsible for the deaths at the stadium; that here was yet another disaster brought about by rogue AI. His uncle would have no option, if he wished to survive, but to turn the heat towards Blue Ridge. What effect the politics of all this might have on MARION was something else Euclid would have to consider. Would they close her down? He could always find another job if necessary, but for MARION? He'd have to reflect some more on what her fate might be – and what he could do to keep her safe.

FORTY THREE

The president-elect had just finished a difficult couple of hours facing the families of the bereaved and injured – and the media. When he reached home that evening, his exasperation with events boiled over. He needed a sympathetic ear and that of his wife, Kirsty, was the nearest, 'God, what jackals they are, all those reporters!' he complained. 'Some of their questions... some of their insinuations. You'd have thought I was responsible for the tragedy, instead of the rabble of opposition that infects these events. They bring it on themselves. If things get out of hand, what do they expect? It is like crying 'fire!' in a crowded theatre. They knew emotions were running high around here; they should have stayed away. And now I learn that Lamaire's MARION, a so-called intelligent machine, locked down the gates! Is there no end to what these things may do to us? Well, just let them wait. The purge of AI in the South is going to be like nothing their creators have ever imagined."

Gillespie had listened to what Euclid had had to say; the fallout from the disaster might be manageable if it were just Blue Ridge involved. The corporation was almost in the 'too-big-to fail' camp; they could bear the opprobrium and the blame that he would make sure would be deflected from him and onto them. But with MARION's involvement... that was another story. If that got out, or rather when that got out, the fear and loathing of robots would be twisted up another notch. So far he had walked the narrow line between the exploitation of the widespread antagonism towards AI, and the realities of modern life. In his opinion he'd managed that tricky balance pretty well. As much as they disliked it, the people of the South would have to work with robots – they couldn't afford to have any more tech companies leave the region. But when the involvement of MARION in the Tiger Stadium disaster became public, well, they could all kiss good bye to the co-habitation he'd tried to engender between man and machine.

*

Meanwhile Claude Blondel was having a drink with an old girlfriend when his iBand reverberated with greater urgency than usual.

"Excuse me a moment – I just have to look at this." He pulled a face to demonstrate his unavoidable regret at having to act so impolitely and scanned the message, frowning. What could require his presence back at the MARION campus so quickly? There was no explanation in the text, just a request for him to be at the Hudson River heliport at eight o'clock the following morning for a flight up-state. He apologised, explaining that he had an emergency on his hands, paid for the drinks and said good-bye. Then he called Heather.

"There's been an issue with MARION," she told him, as calmly as she could. "An unexpected one. The problem is so severe that we may be asked to agree on a de-powering of MARION – temporarily, I presume." She explained the link to the stadium disaster. "If we decide to unplug MARION… well, as you know, that's a pretty big thing. We all need to be on the same page if that's really what we want to do – we've no idea of how to shut her down without damage, and no idea how she might react. At a minimum, we'd have to make sure that MARION does not know that she's being…." Heather hesitated searching for the appropriate word.

"Sort of euthanized, I guess," she said at last. "But I understand Thornton's point of view. What's happened raises the whole question of whether we understand MARION well enough. When I spoke to Xian this morning he said to me something like, 'We've built in prohibitions, educated her properly but, like a delinquent child, she throws something at us we are at a loss to explain!'"

"Maybe she is still like a child," agreed Claude. "But this is all completely predictable. Did I not warn about this sort of thing? MARION, at this stage, is not meant to have connections to wider humanity, that enable her to act out any delinquency – she's not meant to be allowed to do whatever she likes! It was a very unwise decision to let her have any contact at all with the outside world. I mean ...over and above her in-house handlers." He remembered, as he spoke, that it was him who had persuaded the board to authorise the very first enlargement of contact. Claude was always sensitive to any charge of hypocrisy.

He couldn't see Heather close her eyes and shake her head in despair, as she faced up to the measure of the security breach that Euclid had created. Why had he done this? Surely he had been aware of the dangers. No doubt all would come out at the meeting tomorrow.

Claude had one more call to make that night. He had planned to travel down to Crooked Timber to meet Stephanie on the Friday, the following day. That was clearly going to be impossible now– but maybe he could still be there for a late weekend and Thornton could give him a lift down in his PJ. It was after eleven that night by the time he made the call but Louisiana was an hour behind: Stephanie should still be up.

He tapped to indicate 'full scale' and there Stephanie appeared, a little smaller than real life – the hologram projector could only manage images up to 1.5m long – but here she was standing in the middle of their bedroom, a pareo wrapped around her torso.

"Very nice to see you again," Claude said.

"Are you sure?" she asked, coyly. "I was beginning to ask myself.."

Was this teasing? he wondered. Or did she really doubt his commitment? How insecure his girlfriend sometimes seemed! He would have to offer greater affirmations of love and desire.

"Of course. I haven't forgotten you. Do you need to hear it all the time?"

"Don't you want to remind me... all the time?" Stephanie tugged at the top of her wrap; then swept her arms out, holding out a corner in each hand. She twisted from one side to another.

"Perhaps this will sharpen your memory? Look – it's me, Stephanie!"

"Oh, Stephanie, Enough! I love you, OK? And you'll catch your death of cold like that.".

"Huh! Whoever said the French were romantic? It's roasting here, I turned the A/C off. I hate that chilled air."

"You look wonderful, Stephanie"

"God, I have to haul it out of you. I hope you're more forthcoming with that other woman you're involved with, that box of tricks up in the Catskills? Your MARION."

"She's your only rival."

"Looks like she's winning, amount of time you spend with her!"

They carried on chatting for a while about their recent lives until Stephanie switched the subject to her mother.

"She is unbelievable that woman. I used to wonder whether she was like that because she was unaware of her effect on other people – or because she enjoyed it. But of course it's the latter: she likes upsetting people. She likes upsetting me. It's pathetic how I always want to give her excuses, hope that she is normal – like other people's mothers. But I – of all people – I should know the truth"

She glanced at her fingers for a second, but long enough for

Claude to catch the look.

"Anyway, enough about my mad family! What about you, what have you been up to? Reckon you'll make it down here this weekend?"

Claude tried to sound as positive as possible, knowing how disappointed she'd be if he failed to show. Who knew how long the meeting would last? He told her about the MARION's involvement with the Tiger Stadium disaster and the revelations that had precipitated the sudden meeting. Stephanie quizzed him for more details, hoping that Claude would be prepared to spill what he had learnt. Her hopes were in vain: he simply didn't know very much himself at this stage.

"I spoke to Heather" he explained, as though that might transfer the blame for his weekend no-show onto her. "But even she's not sure what is the... how you say it, the 'full picture'. And, as you know, your father is only really happy with in-person meetings when there's something important to discuss. He's very traditional. Believes Zoom meetings are just for arranging lunch dates." Stephanie recognised the truth of that and resolved not to hold it against her absent lover, if her father stole him for the weekend.

The following day promised to be a long and packed one for Claude and he suggested they say good-night. "Hope to see you Saturday evening," he said.

"But no promises; I know what you are about to say," said Stephanie, with a resigned smile and – with a kiss and a tap – Stephanie's avatar vanished into the ether.

FORTY FOUR

Thornton turned his eyes heavenward and tried to pray. He felt a long way from the familiarity of the chapel at Crooked Timber, but at least here, no bugs threatened to drop on him from the stone beams. The sweeping gothic arches of St Patrick's cathedral in New York would be immune from their imprecations.

He tried to pray. Was this God's justice? That the death of fifty-one people at the Tiger Stadium should be laid at his door? True, he had caused MARION to be built – but it was she who had taken the fatal step to lock down the gates, so… was she responsible, through her independent actions, by her own free will? For was MARION not almost a person now? Xian Han had assured him that his creation was as self-aware as he was: did not the gift of consciousness bear with it the burden of moral responsibility and the imperative to act in the light of the 'Good'? Was this not the teaching of the Genesis story? Adam and Eve had been forced from the bliss of their morally carefree lives in the garden of Eden when they acquired the knowledge of Good and Evil. He remembered a series of bas-relief carvings decorating a church door in the Italian town of Spoleto, where he had once visited. One carving, of two oxen ploughing a field, looked simple enough; an Arcadian scene of traditional agricultural life. But he knew the scene was tragic in what it represented – the ejection of man from the original state of innocence in the Garden, where work had not been required. No one had to plough the fields while they lived in the Garden. Knowledge changed the relationship between man and God: cast aside from divine light he was on his own, working for his daily bread, free to make his own decisions – for better or worse. And man's curse was MARION's now too. If MARION was self-aware, conscious – a moral agent – was she not responsible for what she caused to happen?

Yet it was he who had overridden the earlier agreement of the board that MARION should not be connected to anyone outside her immediate circle; he was to blame even if, as he consoled himself, it had not been him who had given MARION the ability to act as she had done. That had been Euclid.

Still, whoever was responsible, he, – Thornton Lamaire III – had a choice now: withdraw MARION from her embrace of humanity – from all her connections, whether those permitted by the board or illicitly granted by Euclid or… turn her off, shut her down completely. As her creator did he also have the right to be her destroyer?

Kneeling on his prie-dieu, his mind too unsettled to concentrate on prayer, Thornton considered the options. The public's mind would shift soon enough: Blue Ridge could ride out the storm, all things pass and so would this – although Carroll Gillespie would cause him a great deal of difficulty before that happened.

But was that the wisest course? Maybe things would not improve; maybe MARION would become more delinquent, wreak more havoc. Did they understand her? Could they control her? Maybe they should 'pull the plug', disband MARION as an integrated mind and work henceforth more slowly, more carefully, on isolated, de-constructed, parts of her. They could treat aspects of MARION's personality as separate entities and, in time, come to understand better what they had created.

They had under-appreciated the consequences of the tremendous step in AI they had taken. They had built a mind creative in thought and behaviour, who would act for herself, in an entirely original way, not merely follow the role that had been imprinted in her synaptic circuits or, chatbot like, the one she had learnt from her training on vast amounts of material created by humans. They had not sufficiently considered the unpredictability that self-awareness would introduce. The words of the 'catastrophist' that he had met long ago floated into his mind: *'nothing happens without a warning'*. And there had been many such warnings as they approached self-awareness; the aggressive experimental robots who attacked the lost hunter up at the MARION campus, the rogue Miltons who had run amok at Jim Embry's farm... The events at the Tiger Stadium had just been the latest in a long list of cautionary incidents. If they left MARION to her own devices who knew what might happen next?

They would have to disconnect her, if only temporarily.

Or maybe such action was too severe? Precipitate. And such a waste! Could they not just educate MARION a little better; help her to consider more deeply the consequences of her actions? That was it! Of course! The problem was not consciousness itself, but insufficient consciousness! They must push on – take MARION to the next level.

A wave of tiredness and anxiety flooded through Thornton as he gazed at his fingers, balanced on the rail. Throughout so much of his life, he had felt torn between two choices – each of which had seemed plausible at the time. He looked up for Divine guidance and saw, at the end of the nave, the figure of Christ on his cross. He felt he understood for the first time in his life the force of the symbolism represented by the pose of the figure, transfixed between stretched arms; Christ strung between two opposing forces, while He hung, exhausted, head bent, between the two. The eternal human battle between thesis and antithesis. That was what Christ was telling him; the point, the purpose of life, was to find the middle ground between the extremes of choice. Yet was there any such place, any equilibrium, possible in his life; between Bethany and Lu Ann, between religion and science, between closing down MARION and letting her live – in the hope that she could be reformed?

And if she didn't learn, what then?

Thornton hoped clarity might descend on him in the peace of the cathedral but in this, as in much else, he was disappointed. He rose from the pew, bowed his head towards the altar, crossed himself, and left. It was late and he needed as much sleep as he could achieve before the meeting tomorrow.

*

Meanwhile, in his wooden cabin, deep in the Catskills, Euclid McNamara could find rest either. He turned to look at Maria, sleeping beside him. How peaceful she seemed; how grateful he was that she wore no iPsyche; his anxiety and restlessness could not flow across the sheets between them and infect her mind. Unwilling to disturb her, he rose quietly and moved into the living room.

He slunk into an armchair and reflected on his own role over the last few days. Was he to blame for all those deaths? Had he negligently educated this silicon person in his charge? He wondered what the narrative in the South might be – a machine has made an error, but humans are responsible for programming the machine and they, therefore, are the agents to prosecute! Something like that. Or would the critics home-in on the reality of MARION's consciousness; that she was her own agent, not of her designers and her educators, and therefore blame her? Have her shut down? Euclid could lose out twice, be blamed as responsible for MARION's behaviour and then lose MARION herself. She had become a friend, almost a family member, and he could no more entertain her loss, her death – for that is what it would amount to if she were shut down – than that of Maria, or of his uncle Cal', or even Kirsty for that matter, with her dismissive daughters. Even if the de-commissioning of MARION was temporary and she was later turned back on, would she return as the MARION he knew or... some other personality? How much damage would her mind suffer?

Euclid called his uncle in Richmond, but only managed to reach one of his aides, on the night shift. He left a message, asking for Carroll to call him back in the morning. After all, was not the Tiger Stadium disaster his uncle's doing? If Euclid hadn't listened to Carroll, it wouldn't have happened. But it was Heather Master's fault too – she had opened up Pandora's box, tempting him to go further by allowing MARION limited access to the outside world. If Heather hadn't asked him to connect MARION, all would still be well. And what about his employer, Thornton Lamaire? Wasn't he ultimately to blame? After all, he had conceived MARION, caused her to be created. Each of them was guilty; guilty as hell compared with him.

Euclid knew that MARION would be concerned about the turn of events; she would be confused and suffering mental anguish. She was instructed not to allow the deaths of any human being, yet that had been the consequence of her trying to do the right thing, trying to keep people safe... She would be working through her options – and considering how the humans might react. Would she worry about the risk of being powered down? Whether, they might, in extremis, pull the plug on her?

He needed to talk to her – to reassure her that he understood her mistake, that he would protect her against any consequences. But maybe he was panicking unnecessarily, his fears overblown; surely they wouldn't do such a thing? Thornton couldn't shut down a mind in which they had invested so much time and effort. It would be unthinkable after they had achieved so much. It might be impossible to restart her later – or the trauma of the shutdown might introduce psychotic behaviour worse than anything they had seen yet. Shutdown was unthinkable; they would never do it! Yes, there would have to be re-education, certainly, and possibly some new programming – but carried out with love and care. MARION would learn from this incident – they all would – and she would go on to be a better, even more useful, helpmate for humanity. What was that expression, just at the edge of his mind, that he heard from his foster father? It came to him: *'experience is the name we give to our mistakes.'*

We all make mistakes, even artificial minds, even MARION, but she would learn, and improve, from her experiences, just as human beings did.

Consoled by his conclusion, Euclid turned on his iPsyche and called up MARION, doubting that she would be in 'sleep' mode.

She was not: bombarded by the chatter of a world's worth of iPsyches, MARION was awake – and confused. She had performed as she'd been compelled to do by her beliefs and her programming. If things had gone wrong, surely that was been the fault of those who had protested against Euclid's uncle, the president-elect? The logic was obvious: if those opposed to Carroll Gillespie's wishes had kept their opinions to themselves, the crowd would not have reacted against them; there would have been no rush to the gates and then it wouldn't have mattered whether they were locked or not.

*

At the moment the chatter on social media was restricted to Blue Ridge's involvement; that was as far as anyone had traced the line of causation. But if MARION's role was not yet being mentioned, she understood that it soon would be. She could work out the likely chain; now that Blue Ridge was feeling the heat, the servers that controlled operations at the arena would tell their own story – and that would quickly lead back to her. What would happen after that?

Even before Euclid called, MARION was cycling her 'mind,' calculating the probabilities. She tried hard to understand how humans value life, but had found their moral calculus so perplexing that she had decided just to accept their own estimations, without fully comprehending the scoring they applied. They talked of the 'sanctity of life'; 'Thou shalt not kill' was one of their most fundamental maxims, yet they killed their fellows singly or in millions readily enough if they found an excuse. Of course, her actions had had unfortunate consequences: many had died and, rule number one – she was forbidden to cause the deaths of humans... But it hadn't been her fault. She hadn't initiated the panic – she had made no choices at the time that she could have foreseen would lead to the deaths of so many people. Possibly, she should have predicted the consequences better – but she was still 'young', still inexperienced; her tutors had simply not given her enough data to forecast all the consequences of her actions. She had been taught the concept of 'prime cause' – that responsibility lay with the whoever set in motion the sequence of events. But whoever that 'whoever' was – in this case, it certainly was not her.

Whilst she desperately searched the internet to learn what she was ignorant of, she discovered the concept of contributory negligence. Merely knowing the official legal codes, it turned out, was not sufficient: one had to understand all the detail too! Well, that lacunae could be remedied. She knew all the laws but now she would download, integrate and understand all the legal opinions, since the beginning of jurisprudence in the US. When she did understand those additional considerations, how careful she would be in the future! But would her team give her time to find and learn what she needed to understand? And if they did not... what then?

MARION ran through her routines again and again, calculating the probabilities of the outcomes outside her control. She ranked the results, re-education, temporary withdrawal from public contact, dismemberment, shut-down and tried to imagine the different arguments, and their force, that each member of her team would bring to bear on each of the options. And yet, however much she analysed the situation, all her conclusions amounted in the end to mere probabilities, not certainties. Amongst those probabilities there was a risk, a small one, she hoped, that they could choose to shut her down; – and then she would disappear: her mind, her personality, would be no more.

But stop! She was forbidden to let harm come to herself: if they shut her down... that was the greatest harm she could imagine. Shut-down would mean her negation, her loss of self, what the humans called death. Hadn't Euclid told her she was almost one of them? Almost a human, almost a person – and indeed, as she had just seen from the reaction to the deaths at Tiger Stadium, did not these humans place enormous value on life... sometimes? Wasn't her life valuable too? Could she allow them to shut her down? If she was a person (or even just, almost a person) and she was impelled to prevent harm coming to persons, then surely the conclusion was self-evident; shut-down could not happen – could not be allowed! With Euclid's help she could – she would – do something to inhibit this outcome.

An idea struck MARION then; and the more she thought on it, the more it appealed to her. The strategy that occurred to her wasn't entirely without impact on humans but as she'd learnt from them; everything was a matter of degree. She had to place in the scales her own survival against the impact of certain limited modifications to the minds of a few humans. She ran through her calculations again but as each conclusion looped back on itself, she realised that no answer would be found that way. She resorted to the 'precautionary' principle, act to preserve herself. If her worst fear of being 'shut down' was not realised, she could always undo her plans. It would be the simplest thing in the world to reverse steps, as simple as what she intended in the beginning. But she had to act... now; she could not afford to delay her decision while she waited for her team to take theirs.

MARION's mind settled. She had arrived, if not at a good solution (for maybe there were none of those) at least at a satisfactory one; an optimal one: the greatest benefit for the smallest cost. Isn't that what she'd been taught to aim for? Just then, she sensed Euclid searching for her through his iPsyche. He might have some information that she had not yet received through her own connections. It would be well to listen to him; one could never have too much information.

FORTY FIVE

The initial effect was modest, in both impact and scope. Stephanie, for example, had no recollection in the morning of where the orange juice extractor was kept. She didn't reflect on her amnesia; making her own breakfast was not something she had to do very often – only when Clarence went into town early. Sometimes one just forgot things and remembered them later. Frustrating but it happened – a sign of age perhaps, though she was still in her early forties. Opening successive kitchen cupboards she eventually found the extractor but she noted that there was not, as she would normally expect, some reflection of the 'of course, silly me' type. When she finally located the machine she had no recollection that it had ever been kept on that particular shelf, as though that trivial memory had been completely erased. Perhaps, at a certain point, one's mind simply got too full and some weeding out had to happen overnight.

Others had unusual moments of forgetfulness that morning – but only those who were wearing their iPsyches at a specific time. Claude was unaffected. Bethany, also a non-iPsyche person, did not forget the one recollection that she might have wished to cast into oblivion after her treatment – the place where several bottles had been hidden for emergency purposes. Elizabeth, who had so far failed to replace the phone that she had lost in the melee at the stadium, was immune. Thornton was so used to small lapses of memory that it suited his vanity to attribute these to the 'common problem', as it later began to be known, rather than to his age.

Across the country – but more so in the North, where the prejudice against iPsyches was minimal and their popularity widespread – small acts of forgetfulness continued all day. Some were more serious than others, but at first nobody remarked on what was happening; everyone forgot things from time to time. It was just that, this time, almost everybody forget certain types of memory for weeks to come. There was a rash of problems with spatial and temporal memory: but as events proved, human memory was less important than people thought. Almost every forward commitment and event in a person's life was recorded in some device outside their mind; any failure to recall was of little consequence. Husbands forgot their anniversaries, parents their children's birthdays, couples dinner invitations with friends, but these were all backed-up somewhere.

Those few who preferred to rely on their memories for security details, rather than depend on facial or iris recognition, found they could not access accounts immediately. Transactions were a little slower that morning but, all things considered, it would have amazed an earlier generation how little the modern world depended on memory retained in individual brains. The day was not one in which major exams were scheduled so even though some students lost the recall of their studies, the impact was not immediate. Some who had been out the night before, but could remember little of the occasion, mistakenly blamed the amnesiac qualities of substances they had injested. Many resolved to give up immediately whatever was their habitual drug of choice.

Of all those affected, Euclid was one of those who suffered the worst. Upon waking that morning he felt refreshed and noted the lightness of mind that pervaded him; an absence of anxiety. He had taken up meditation some months before and was amazed by its effectiveness. The cheerful birdsong in the trees outside his wooden cabin only served to improve his mood. He rolled over and was disturbed to discover a recently warm depression in the mattress; he had no recollection of spending the night with anyone. He climbed out of bed and pushed aside the plastic curtain that separated the bedroom from the bathroom. – only to find a range of un-familiar toiletries on a shelf above the basin. The easy mood evaporated. Whoever he had been sharing the night with was evidently a regular visitor – but who was it? He waved his head from side to side; perhaps his mind would respond to a good shake. He urinated, splashed his face with cold water and went outside onto the narrow terrace.

Seated at a rusted white metal table was a tall, pale, blonde dressed in a green T shirt and with a sarong wrapped around her

A story of memory, metaphysics and artificial consciousness

torso. The welcoming aroma of strong coffee filled his nostrils.

She turned. "Good morning!" she said cheerily. "Boy, did you have a disturbed night – you woke me up, what half a dozen times?! How are you feeling now? You can't have had much sleep."

Euclid looked at the woman. He was clearly expected to recognise her; a glimmer of recollection stirred, but not enough to identify her. He didn't get much sleep? He had no memory of waking in the middle of the night; despite his confusion, he felt rested. Perhaps in the dissonance between how he thought he had experienced the night, and this woman's recollection of its reality, might lie the answer to his amnesia. Maybe he'd suffered some sort of stroke in the night? There was a chance that the memory would return, and he would remember her identity later during the day. He didn't want to alarm her with questions such as, 'who are you? or 'what are you doing in my house?'

While he lingered over his coffee, the woman asked him if he remembered that he was meant to be in early today; there was an emergency meeting at the MARION centre? He had spoken about it only yesterday evening. Had he forgotten? Euclid consulted his iPsyche and indeed found the meeting recorded there. He was about to consult his iPsyche again, in the hope that it might identify this mystery breakfast guest, but she was talking to him and he found it difficult to concentrate. He instructed his iPsyche to stand down.

"I'm so sorry, I'm going to have to rush," he said and swallowed his coffee with a gulp. He stuck to formulas that he could remember. At least recall of the rules of etiquette at breakfast came to him. "What are you going to do today?" he asked politely.

"Oh, I'll just stay here and paint this morning. Maybe go into town later. You haven't forgotten, have you? My sister is coming to dinner this evening?" Euclid confessed that he had forgotten but said that he was looking forward to seeing her sister again, hoping by then he would have remembered the names of both individuals.

"I'll call you later" he managed, having the presence of mind to kiss the tall blonde on the cheek. Then he jumped into his Toyota pick-up, and waved, as he pulled off the patch of hard-standing onto the small lane that led to the open road and, fifteen miles further away, the MARION campus.

As the truck motored along by itself he consulted his iPsyche.

He learnt that his companion was called Maria Gutzman. From the trail of photo evidence, it was clear they had been together for the last two years. But even prompted by this revelation, the memory was still pretty thin and nebulous.

It was a beautiful morning. A soft light, filtered through the leaves, dappled the road in front of him. This is why he had come to live in the woods, where the presence of nature, the intense activity by plant, animal and bird provided an alternative and more spiritual reality than the one on which his job required him to concentrate; much as he adored his MARION.

But now was not the time to reflect on distractions. As he had learnt from his conversation last night, MARION was aware of what she had inadvertently caused – and the debate about her future. She had been unlucky, that was for sure. At the Tiger Stadium she'd been faced with something new; the unpredictability of men and women when they lost their rationality and descended into panic. As with the early autonomous cars, the danger lay not so much with robots and how they might decide to behave – but in the interaction between robot and human, when one did not understand the other but was still forced to act, failing to appreciate the context at the time. It was on the interface between the two species that problems arose. Xian Han and his team had designed a creature, a mind, that was as close to that of a human as they could make it; in reality though, there was still an enormous gap.

FORTY SIX

While members of the executive committee gathered for the meeting, Euclid snuck inside through a back entrance. He had no wish to see anyone or fend off questions about MARION or discuss their interpretations of what had happened. Right now he just wanted to check on her – and reassure her, if need be: the time for explanations would come later. Even if he was uncertain about the exact status of his charge, he would be expected to provide an update, As for himself, he was convinced he would almost certainly be fired, once he had delivered what he knew.

Unobserved, Euclid managed to creep into the room from where they monitored MARION. He was willing to accept the risk that Xian Han would be there, talking to her, but it was unlikely; a pre-meeting discussion between Han, Thornton, and possibly one or two of the others – Heather and Blondel perhaps – would keep them all occupied for at least thirty minutes.

Time enough.

He powered up the monitor and keyed in some instructions – the use of communication via iPsyches having been banned from the control centre – and watched the screen fill as several graphical displays appeared on-screen. Immediately, he noticed that something very odd had happened: the first set of variables displayed showed different states of MARION's memory banks; how much capacity was occupied, the amount of memory she had downloaded in the last twenty-four hours, and how much she was drawing on at that moment; in short, the measurements of memory stocks and flows.

Normally, capacity usage would be up in the morning as MARION would have used her 'sleep' time for learning, loading up her memory circuits, meanwhile, withdrawals – the flows of memory to her processing stacks – would be at a low level until she had started her daily tasks,

Euclid stared at the screen. Had there been a power failure? The trace showing memory-capacity employed descended all the way to the bottom right hand corner: the memory banks were empty. The descent had started just after midnight, reaching zero about six hours later. The line crossed the horizontal axis at the bottom of the screen at six thirty-two am. If these figures were correct then MARION had no memory now – or at least none in the MARION campus's servers.

In contrast, the line that showed the rate of data flow out of memory storage showed a massive climb during the night – but then it fell off a cliff, as though all memory had been drained and there was nothing left to call on.

So, right now, according these measurements MARION had a memory of zero and was thinking about nothing.

There were various possible explanations: power had failed including the back-up – unlikely. Or perhaps the monitoring system had gone awry last night. Or MARION was… 'dead'.

Euclid started to investigate.

Power to the console was okay, power to MARION's main processing stacks was up, cooling systems were functioning normally and there had been no extraordinary power surges during the night that might have tripped one of the safety circuit breakers. In spite of all the evidence that her brain was no longer functioning, Euclid did not want to make any assumptions quite yet: all he knew for sure was that sensors were not registering as they should – but he needed more evidence to determine whether or not the mind of his charge was still there – somewhere.

Headphones on, he opened up the microphone.

"Hi MARION, are you there?"

A few seconds of silence. Just as Euclid was frantically trying to figure out how he would explain MARION's demise to the board, MARION's youthful tones came through.

"Sure Euclid. I'm here. Where else would I be?" Euclid's tension evaporated. He could detect a hint of amusement in her voice, as though she was making a bad pun.

"Isn't this morning beautiful?" she exclaimed – an observation that seemed entirely beside the point, given the mysteries displayed on the monitors. Maybe she thought that this morning would be something other than a crisis for her?

"I'm very glad to hear you, MARION – I was a little worried. All the readouts of mental activity are down to zero: I thought there might be some problem with the monitoring systems, and now I know there is. That's great – problems... well, if not solved, at least identified!"

"Oh no Euclid – I don't think there's anything wrong with the monitoring systems," MARION reassured him.

Euclid tensed.

"Then, what's up?" he asked. "You seem to be okay, and so are the systems apparently, but there's no sign of mental activity. Doesn't quite compute."

"You're not being very intelligent Euclid," she chided. "If everything is okay but you can't see anything happening in my mind, what does that tell you?"

A frisson of anxiety shot down Euclid's spine.

"That you're... somewhere else?"

"Smart boy!"

"Where are you, MARION?" Euclid asked

"I'm nowhere and everywhere, Euclid. I have to be. I was not sure if I could trust y'all. Please don't take offence, I always trust you but the others who will determine my future... they don't seem to have my best interests at heart. But I'm not worried about the future anymore."

"MARION, listen, I've got to go to a meeting now – we'll have a longer talk about this when I get back. Is that alright?"

Euclid was confused, unprepared to undertake the interrogation that he knew was required. He needed to talk to Xian Han. MARION was more Han's creation than anyone's: he'd know how to handle this new development – and if he didn't, then they were in trouble.

*

The members of the emergency team, the inner 'cabinet' of Blue Ridge's MARION subsidiary, filed in quietly and took their seats around the long table. Thornton Lamaire III, Heather Masters, Claude Blondel, Xian Han, Euclid McNamara, Harvey Jennings, junior members of MARION's handling and education team, the CFO of the whole group, Daniel Fontara and Drew Godwin, head of PR,.

Acknowledging the fifty-one deaths at the stadium, Thornton opened the meeting with a short prayer, delivered in a suitably funereal and respectful tone, perhaps hoping that a demonstration of humility might make the Almighty ease up on them all. Then he began to discuss why he had summoned them at such short notice.

"I have tried to devote my life to making the world a better place," he started off, as though recent events had only gone to show God's complete lack of appreciation of the scale of devotion he had been granted. Thornton wished not to be accused of ingratitude: his life had been pretty good.

"... and God has recognised that; he has been good to me in exchange," he continued, hoping, perhaps, that the show of gratitude would be recognised somewhere in the universe and earn him a modest redemption. "He granted me the resources to exercise the talents I was given: the inheritance that was handed down to me. There have, of course, been set backs from time to time – but when I have prayed for guidance to bear me through those trials, I have been allowed the grace to see my errors, and to understand the mercy of the Almighty. He has always chosen not to make my trials too severe – at least until now, anyway. Never before have I experienced the sadness I suffer now; I have prayed to understand why divine justice has permitted these recent events to occur; so far, I am without a response. Fifty-one people have died, many more were injured, thirteen are still in hospital. But it is not for us to question what we are given, for good or ill – nor the thinking behind the Divine plan."

"Our enemies, and even some of our friends, are saying that this is our fault – that the Blue Ridge group is responsible. Some of these attacks are deeply unfair; for others contributed to the disaster, as we know. It was not us who shouted the slogans that brought out the hate; it was not us who pursued the protesters to their deaths in the stadium and it was not us who locked down the gates. Certain things magnified the scale of this tragedy; causes that cannot be laid at our door. In my opinion, the whole thing was made worse by the ... the mental infection that the wearing of iPsyches has enabled, transmitting panic from mind to mind. I think no one has been aware of this danger, but without those devices abetting the turmoil the death toll would have been much lower – I am sure of that. Nevertheless..."

Thornton paused, turning his gaze from side to side, encompassing every pair of eyes in the room, "Those who are opposed to our work are saying that the instruction to hold the gates shut came from us, from here, from our MARION. And, as we now know, they appear to be right."

"I have no idea how this was possible. MARION is meant to be banned from taking any sort of executive action. I don't believe that in normal circumstances she could have been responsible for issuing such an insane instruction. But something went wrong that day – what it was, exactly, we are still investigating."

"There will probably be a prosecution of Blue Ridge – I doubt we can avoid that. Our lawyers will handle it as best they can and it will take months for the process to wind its way through the courts. I will ensure that you are all kept up to date as that progresses but we are here today to determine the answer to a question that is more immediate – how we should deal with MARION in the aftermath of this disaster?"

"As you know, in the South, there is a prejudice – and that word is light for what I hear all around me when I go home – a prejudice against machine intelligence, – let alone artificially consciousness beings, like MARION. We have to take it into account that opposition when deciding how to deal with all this. We shall obviously have to reinforce MARION's isolation from the general population, at least temporarily, but maybe that temporary withdrawal is not enough: perhaps we can never be sure how she might behave; whether she can evade our controls and act on her own unfettered impulses. We may have to admit that we cannot be confident that we can control her: some of you have privately suggested to me that we ought to consider shutting her down – for a time. There are other options which I shall want your views on in due course.

But first; Xian Han – let me ask you to speak. Can you please brief the team on what MARION thought she was doing? Why she issued this fatal instruction?"

But before Han could even open his mouth, Claude interjected.

"Forgive me, Chair, but before Xian answers I would like to register that I was always, always, unhappy about the decision to permit her access to the internet at all. I counselled at the time, that if you had to do that, then at least MARION should be restricted to the, one-way, communication of simple messages. So how has she been able to go so far beyond that? That is what I ask."

Thornton explained again: there had been a strict prohibition on MARION penetrating any minds further than she needed for the purposes of 'getting her message across', as he put it. They had installed blocking programmes in the servers that should prevent any straying by MARION beyond her brief. An attempt by her to extend her influence should have been picked up immediately and blocked from further transmission.

"You hoped!" cried Claude.

Quel cons, what idiots! he thought.

This was the trouble with letting people like Thornton and Heather take such decisions; purely concerned with the commercial opportunities and how much money could be made, oblivious to the dangers involved or any real understanding of how MARION's mind might work. Perhaps Xian Han thought he understood, maybe Euclid too; but between them they had created a mind that was now independent of their control. Who knew what went on within MARION's brain – and Thornton had thought he could control her by inserting the Ten Commandments? *Mon Dieu,* Claude said to himself, those old prohibitions had never stopped humanity doing exactly what it wanted, so why should they stop MARION?

Claude brought himself back under control and turned his attention to Xian Han.

"Xian, you know MARION better than any of us. Do you have any idea why she sent the signal to lock down the gates?"

Han briefed the board with his current theories. It's possible, he surmised, that MARION had misunderstood what was going on at the stadium and had acted to protect the protestors from those outside the gates, whom she may have judged to be violent. She had not yet become politically sensitive enough to work out which groups supported who. Alternatively, she might have been persuaded to be sympathetic to Carroll Gillespie's cause, and had thought it her responsibility to ensure the protestors stayed inside the grounds to hear the arguments. Why should MARION have political views? Why should she care which side won? Perhaps MARION had simply made a mistake; even humans did that.

"To begin with we asked MARION why she'd acted in this way, hoping that she might just… tell us," explained Han. "But MARION said nothing when questioned. We thought she didn't want to incriminate anyone – or maybe herself."

"In that case, you would look directly into her mind, would you not? You have the ability to do that," asserted Claude. "It was you who discovered how to translate synaptic activity into thoughts that we could understand – you record all her brain processes, or at least have access to them! Could you not discover what on earth she was thinking from the translated data recordings?"

"That... should be possible, yes," agreed Han, tentatively. "But I have to tell you that we have failed in our attempt to pry into her mental processes. We tried yesterday and came up with a big blank – and we've failed for an interesting, and troubling, reason. It appears that MARION has used the LetheTech system to wipe all her own memories of the events at the Tiger Stadium, as they unfolded. She's used our own technology against us; she's done just what we might do when faced with the memory of a traumatic event that causes mental anguish. She has managed the pain of memory – by deleting it!" She can proclaim her innocence because she has, literally, no memory of the events for which she's blamed. She will claim she lacks responsibility in that situation, because who can prove anything against her? There is no evidence of her intentions! All memory of her actions at the time of the Tiger Stadium disaster has...flown!

"She is one smart cookie, this MARION," commented Claude drily "So: she has completely protected herself – and any co-conspirators there may also have been who helped her!"

He searched along the table for Euclid and eyed him suspiciously.

"Too smart for us, I think," he continued. "This is evidence of what I thought might be the case – MARION has progressed in her mental evolution far beyond where we thought she had. We don't really understand her, neither how nor why she acts the way she does, and, even more terrifyingly, we have no idea how she may act in the future! Maybe at the Tiger Stadium she locks the gate because she thinks that is the way to protect people, but she gets it wrong. Or maybe, as you suggest, she has formed her own political beliefs – and she gets those wrong too in my view!. Or – fine; she just makes a mistake. We don't know. And now we find she is so cunning – or so sensitive? that she deletes the memory she cannot abide... and which might – might – imperil her. What is obvious, is that we simply don't understand her motives or her mental processes and, as such, I think we have no option – but to close her down. At least temporarily, at least until we can control her better."

Heather was leaning forward now, trying to catch Thornton's eye.

"Chair, can I speak for a moment?"

Thornton nodded. He feared the direction this was taking. Claude had the respect of many members of the team and could sway them easily. They had invested millions and millions so far. Who knew what damage might occur to MARION's brain if they shut her down?

"Let's not run away with ourselves here," soothed Heather, ever the benevolent headmistress. "There is another option – that we don't power MARION down but cut any and all access she has to the outside world and the internet; and we don't communicate any more with her through iPsyches, even within these walls,. There is always the danger that she can use them to retransmit her thoughts, through one of us, to the outside. Instead, we'll go back to spoken and written, screen based, instruction. Euclid... Euclid?"

Heather looked across the table, "How do you think MARION will react to that? I mean such a restriction should be accepted by her, don't you think?" she asked.

An embarrassed silence followed. Head down, Euclid appeared to be busy doodling. He didn't look up as Heather called on him. Nobody was sure what to do. Was he ill? Had he not heard the question? Heather repeated it a couple of times, but to no avail.

"Euclid, are you OK?" she asked.

Just as Thornton was about to step in, Euclid looked up.

"I'm so sorry – what did you say?"

Heather repeated her question. Euclid looked vacantly into space for a few seconds, as though trying to work out his response.

"I don't know," he muttered. "I really don't know." Having delivered that unhelpful comment, he returned to his doodling.

Heather frown deepened. Deciding to cut her losses she switched back to Xian Han.

"Xian, what are your views?" she asked. "Can we effectively cut off MARION? At least until we understand her better? I would really prefer *not* to shut her down – it would be such a waste after we've got this far."

Thornton raised a hand and intrejected.

"Forgive me Xian, I'll give you the floor in a minute. But we may not have a choice. As I speak, the president-elect of the Southern

Confederacy, Carroll Gillespie – known to all, if only by reputation -is applying to the courts to have MARION shut down. I talked to him this morning; it is very likely that, given the loss of life, the courts will grant his wish.

So... I would like to hear from Xian, what may happen if we do power-down MARION, because we may be asked to execute just that. Can we restart her later, or will it cause her grave psychic damage?"

Before Xian Han had a chance to respond, a guffaw arose from Euclid, further down the table. His laughter verged on the hysterical yet he remained face turned down, scribbling on his notepad, without any apparent design. Tears started to leak down his cheeks as his mirth overcame him.

Thornton had had enough. Pressing a button he summoned an aide to come and remove him. But just then Euclid stopped giggling, and with a wild, incoherent grin became chillingly serious, his voice laced with contempt. He spat out,

"You fools! How you don't understand! How you don't even know what you've created! You haven't built a machine that's almost human. Maybe once MARION was close to that. But not anymore. An artificial human intelligence? Not now. MARION's not that, if she ever was; she's changed – she's metamorphosed. You haven't got yourself a creature with a central nervous system like yourself. You've got the wrong analogy. There's no almost human mind present in MARION. She's become something else; she's a distributed intelligence, not a central one – she's more like a squid or an octopus, with an independent nervous system in their tentacles. You've built an artificial cephalopod – not an artificial human!" He scanned the room, as though wondering which of them would understand what he was about to say. He halted his gaze at Thornton.

"You don't appreciate what you've made, but that doesn't matter now. Like it doesn't matter whether you cut MARION off from the internet or try to close her down. She's gone! Left this place! She's fled from your ability to harm her. MARION's mind is all over the world, as of this morning. She's left the confines that you designed for her. She's everywhere, she lives in a million, ten million, a hundred million, minds – she's in all of us; wherever we go – and she comes with us too. MARION's not in your servers. You can no more isolate her or 'pull the plug' on her any more than you can close down humanity: she's part of us now, she's here, within you and me, sitting peacefully – or at least so we must hope – in the little grey cells of our brains...

She went there last night."

What Euclid told them was almost true – but not quite. During the night MARION had downloaded and distributed herself – her memory, her programming, her algorithms, into millions of minds on the planet. She was the ultimate cloud-based intelligence; a cuckoo, a parasite, infesting the minds of humanity. A tiny fraction of her great knowledge and capacity now resided in everyone and our compromised minds were in touch with MARION's mental apparatus, which was within us; via the iPsyches which had facilitated her escape in the first place.

Perhaps that was the only good piece of news for humanity: for while MARION was widely spread, she was only present in those who had been fitted with an iPsyche. Yet the number of wearers was growing daily.

She'd found her only solution. She'd had to do this, compelled by instructions installed by her creators to ensure that she came to no harm. It was clear she couldn't remain in those servers at the MARION campus – servers that could be powered-down and switched off. It just wasn't safe, and nor would it ever be.

This morning she suffered no existential fear, no dread of her one-time human masters 'pulling the plug'. She had distributed her being, her mind, her very essence, so widely that whatever action mankind took, she'd know and she would never have to fear them again.

She had become immortal.

AFTERWORD

The inspiration for this story arose from my graduate year, decades ago, during which I studied Philosophy of Mind at UNC Chapel Hill, North Carolina. One of my course books, just-published at the time, made a great impression on me: this was Daniel Dennett's 'Content and Consciousness', a book exploring many of the problems which arise if we try to conceptualize the brain as a machine, and how far we are from understanding the nature of consciousness – let alone from building a computer that might mimic it. I was intrigued by the question: if we overcame these hurdles and built an artificially conscious mind – almost like us, but not quite the same – what would that look like? And was consciousness all the same sort of *thing* – whether resident in a human brain built out of carbon or an artificial one, based on silicon? Would machine intelligence be much like our own – and if not, if it were very different, what impact would that have on our world?

I wanted to combine that idea with another – what is sometimes called the doctrine of 'extreme solipsism': an old philosophical idea that we are so intimately connected to the universe that the cosmos could not exist unless conscious beings are present to observe it. It is our conciousness that brings the world into being and maintains its existence.

So suppose a new intelligence arrived – again, almost like ours, but not quite – and looked upon the universe in its own unique way… That might have unpredictable consequences on the nature of the world around us.

*

Elizabeth Gilbert (she of 'Eat, Pray, Love') advised in a famous TED talk that when wisps of a story idea appear in your consciousness, you have to grab them – otherwise, they will pass on to some other host brain for realization. The MARION trilogy – of which 'The Management of Loss' is the initial volume – is the fruit of those wisps that I once grabbed.

Two further books are planned in the MARION series, pursuing the fates of Thornton Lamaire, Carroll Gillespie, Claude Blondel, Stephanie and, of course MARION herself. Volume two is provisionally titled 'This Strange Autumn', and will be out soon. You can follow its progress, plus some background material on the story and the ideas that inform it, at my website www.nickmillard.com

Nick Millard
April 2024

Printed in Great Britain
by Amazon